BREATH less

USA TODAY BESTSELLING AUTHOR
EMMANUELLE SNOW

Smart Lily
Publishing

Breathless
Emmanuelle Snow

First edition - November 2022 (V_1)

ISBN eBook: 978-1-990429-38-5

ISBN paperback: 978-1-990429-71-2

Previously published in 2022 as Wild and Country

Editors: Shalini G.

Cover: SMART Lily publishing inc.

Published by SMART Lily Publishing inc.

———

Emmanuelle Snow
www.emmanuellesnow.com

CARTER HILLS BAND UNIVERSE
(SUGGESTED READING ORDER)

Carter Hills Band series
False Promises

HEART SONG DUET
BlindSided
ForeverMore

Whiskey Melody series
Sweet Agony

SECOND TEAR DUET
Cruel Destiny
Beautiful Salvation

BREATHLESS DUET
Wild Encounter
Brittle Scars

Upon A Star series
Last Hope

Midnight Sparks

Love Song For Two series
<u>LONESOME STAR DUET</u>
Fallen Legend
Rising Star

All titles available at
emmanuellesnow.com/books

*For the best experience, read in the order as shown above

AUTHOR'S NOTE

This book was previously published as **Wild and Country**.

Still part of the Carter Hills Band universe, it's now in a series of its own.

Same amazing emotionally-charged and realistic love story between Tucker and Addison, just with a new title.

For a better experience, read after **Sweet Agony**, **Cruel Destiny**, and **Beautiful Salvation** in the Whiskey Melody series.

Happy reading!

Emmanuelle

WHAT THE REVIEWS SAY

- "I've been a HUGE fan of Emmanuelle Snow since I got my hands on her first book, so it should come as no surprise that I absolutely loved this book. This is without a doubt Emmanuelle's best work yet!" **(Tanja, OMGreads)**

- "There are a lot of subgenres in romance, but Ms. Snow is a genre of her own. Because she writes about life and what we all live through. Love is not just words for her, but the actions her characters show, the way they are committed to each other. Every single day. That is what makes this book so special." **(Book Reviews by Shalini)**

- "I wasn't prepared for their story. It was beautiful and heartbreaking. Full of hope and love too. Now I can't decide which one of Emmanuelle Snow's books is my favorite. They're all special in their own way. " **(Goodreads)**

- "I couldn't put this book down as it was a real page turner and had you on the edge of your seat while turning the pages wondering what would happen next and it was so addictive with great characters and a storyline that pulled you in and just wouldn't let you go and kept your attention throughout the whole book." (**Goodreads**)

- "Emmanuelle Snow always delivers a fun, spicy and heartwarming read." (**Goodreads**)

TRIGGER WARNINGS

Disclaimer

My books are realistic and emotional romance reads.

I'm an advocate for mental health, and some topics could be sensitive for certain readers since they are portrayed as close to real life as possible.

I've listed the potential trigger warnings for each title on my website.

Be advised that those trigger warnings could potentially be spoiler alerts for the storylines.

Those sensitive topics have been written with the utmost care and respect. Please reach out if you have questions or comments.

All books contain sexuality, mature content, and language not intended for people under 18 years of age.
For other readers' sake, please avoid spoilers in your reviews.

Thank you and have a wonderful day!

Emmanuelle

emmanuellesnow.com/trigger-warnings

Lou, I believe in you. I'll always believe in you.
It's you and me against the world, remember?
Fight for what you want.
You'll do great things because you're a special kind of someone and
there's only one like you.
You may be small today,
but you'll be the bigger man one day.

I love you
Mommy xx

BECOME A VIP

TO NEVER MISS A THING

Snow's VIP

Join **Emmanuelle Snow's VIP newsletter** for all the cool stuff, promos, new releases, giveaways, and gifts.

emmanuellesnow.com/subscribe

Snow's Soulmates

Join Emmanuelle Snow's Facebook VIP group, **Snow's Soulmates**, to chat with her and other readers, get updates, and more bonus content.

facebook.com/groups/snowvip

A GIRL LIKE YOU

THE SONG

Girl, I noticed you for the first time
    last night
Looking pretty with your hair down
    and flushed cheeks
My heart sizzled when you
    walked in
But drowned as you stood too
    far away
Because all I wanted was to call
    your name
All I wanted was to claim you
    as mine

[CHORUS]

Girl, I wish you could see yourself
    the way I do
'Cause your smile is bright enough
    to light up my days

The sadness in your eyes should be
    stolen away
And replaced by a million dancing
    sparks
Girl, I wanna be the man who adds
    colors to your life
'Cause I would cherish your heart
    and never let you go

A girl like you can change the world
    with only a smile
A girl like you can jolt my heart with
    only a glance
You looked my way, and my pulse
    ran wild
My body buzzed to life, and your
    pink lips I wished I could kiss
The sea of your eyes drew me in,
    sapphires beckoning me into the
    night

[CHORUS]
A girl like you should stay wild in
    her dreams
A girl like you should take the world
    by storm
Let me be the guy who anchors your
    life and holds your hand
And when you need a rest, I'll lend
    you my shoulder
And when you need a hug, my arms
    will hold you tight

[CHORUS]

A girl like you belongs with a guy
    like me
And a guy like me loves a girl
    like you

Music and lyrics by Carter Hills

1

ADDISON

I slumped down on the couch of the posh hotel we were staying all weekend and huffed, a wine bottle hanging from my fingers by its neck. Glasses were overrated, anyway. "That's it. I'm over men. I'm done." My childhood best friend snickered. "I'm serious, Dah. This time I mean it. You know I do."

I scanned the space around me. Large windows with a direct view of Nashville's busy streets below, high wooden beam ceilings, dark flooring, and handcrafted wood furniture. Chic and tasteful, with an unmistakable country vibe.

"Yeah, right. I'm sure you won't last a week. Two at the most," Dahlia teased.

My friend, and the bride-to-be, inched closer, and I zipped her up. Her cut-out mermaid gown was a gray-lavender hue and looked both sexy and demure, showing just enough skin without being indecent. Perfectly Dahlia Ellis.

Before I could return to my lazy position on the couch, she beckoned me with a finger to follow her. Sitting on the edge of the bathtub, I glugged the wine straight from the bottle and watched her apply mascara.

"Addi, there are good men out there who would appreciate your light. Don't punish all of them because you dated a few who were total dickheads." She grinned at her reflection. But it was meant for me. And it warmed my heart as she continued, "I'm confident you won't last in your quest to ignore them all when they turn on the charm."

"Laugh all you want, girlfriend. You'll see. Be prepared to be shocked. This time, I'm not backing down. Anyway, remember Felicia from college? She messaged me last week. It's destiny."

"The one you 'experimented' with?" my friend asked, curving her fingers into elaborate air quotes, her gaze fixed on her eyelashes in the mirror, not sparing me a look.

Another sip. "The same. We could have been in love and lived happily ever after. The timing was just not right."

"Huh, you said the same thing about Carter once. Besides, I thought women weren't your thing," Dahlia added with a quirked brow.

"It's not the same. And perhaps I changed my mind. Who knows? I might be into women more than men after all. Think about it, we should have been a couple, you and I. Everything would have been much simpler."

"You think?"

I shrugged. "We get along fine. And we're friends, so our relationship would have had a solid foundation. Look at you and Nick. Friends, then lovers. I believe that's the secret to long-lasting love. Back to business..." I sighed. "Felicia and I experienced some pretty memorable moments together. It's just Shawn happened to cross my path, and I couldn't resist him. Stupid me. Stupid men. I'm telling you their species is old news. You're lucky you found two awesome ones in your lifetime. What are the odds? God knows I've tried. I usually don't back down easily, but hey, maybe it's time I try something else. That I understand once and for all what life has been trying to tell me all these years—"

Dahlia shook her head, focusing her attention on me for the first time since I started the conversation about my disastrous love life. "Addi, you know how much I love it when you're not being overdramatic."

I poked my tongue out, and we both burst out laughing. Peace washed over me. Dahlia Ellis had that effect on me. Her presence was enough to ease my doubts. And bring a curve to my lips even when I didn't feel like expressing joy. "That's why you love me. I'm entertaining. Despite myself. Anyway, where are the bridal shower festivities taking place? I can't wait to party the entire weekend. The distraction will do me good."

Dahlia reached over and landed a kiss on my cheek, her eyes searching mine. Worry shimmered in them. "You okay?"

I nodded.

"You'd tell me if it wasn't the case, right?" I sensed the apprehension in her question.

"Always. You're the only one I willingly confide in."

With a warm smile that promised everything would turn out just fine, she went back to applying her makeup. "All over town. Tonight, we're having dinner with only the people closest to us. And tomorrow, a get-together with some of my good friends and the guys on a yacht before splitting up and maybe meeting them again later."

"Rewind for a sec. We're having your bridal shower with your future husband and his friends?"

"Yep. His best friend. Guys from work. That's the idea."

"Yeah, I should've been the one organizing the whole thing." Dahlia raised a hand, ready to argue, but I kept going. "For what it's worth, I'm sorry I let you down. I was really looking forward to throwing you the bachelorette party of the century."

A new weight grew heavy on my shoulders. In the fog of my latest relationship blowing up, I had lost focus on what really mattered. This time, my tears had knocked me out more than ever. But I was back now. And no way was I failing the girl I considered a sister again.

Dahlia pulled me into a hug. "It's okay. Don't chastise yourself. It'll still be fun. And you did plan most of the wedding already. You deserve a night off. To enjoy yourself. You, me, booze, music. And the man I love and his friends."

I leaned back, studying her for a moment. Dahlia had no ounce of evilness in her. She really meant everything she'd just said.

"What is it?" she asked, a frown marring her forehead.

"Real sweet, Dah. After I told you I was done with men, you're going to make me spend hours with a bunch of Nick's buddies. And alcohol. If I didn't know your heart, I'd think this was a test. To check my newfound determination." One more sip of the wine. *Be strong, Addi,* I repeated in my head. I flicked my hand and pasted a smile on my lips. "Know what? Doesn't matter. I won't back down. I'm done with men, and I'll prove it to you. Tonight. I won't flirt, and I won't kiss. Nope. Nada. D.O.N.E. Just watch and learn, girlfriend."

I held out my hand, and we shook on it.

2

TUCKER

"I was really hoping we'd go to a strip club or fly to Vegas or do something crazy and fun. When you said bachelor party, I never thought in a million years it would happen in Nashville." I sighed because it was a real bummer. "I should've known better, man. You're a stupid fool when you're in love, a sucker for all things romantic. Remind me to buy you a pair of brand-new shiny steel balls as a wedding present. You might need those sooner than you think."

Nick rolled his eyes, handing me a beer.

"Tuck, you're just jealous. Always have been. If I remember correctly, you're the one who stated, and I quote: 'Settling down isn't for me. I love diversity. And to be able to sample everything on the buffet.' I can still hear and see you when you announced it."

With a frown, I threw my beer cap at him.

"Yeah. When you say it like that, I sound like a fucking ass."

"Man, it sounded the same when you said the words as

a teen. Lucky for you, Nashville is full of hot women. One rule, though." My best friend, and the future groom, lifted a finger. "Stay away from Dahlia's best friend, Addi. She's been through a rough break-up, and she doesn't need you to complicate things more. Okay? She's family, and her heart is hurting. Women get attached to you easily. Even if you're not interested in a relationship. No games this time. She's out of reach."

"Is this a warning?"

He breathed out. "It should be."

Nick waited for me to say something, his bottle hovering in mid-air in front of his lips.

"Is she hot?"

Something bitter twisted in my stomach, but I spoke the words he expected. The ones everyone thought I had the insensitivity to say.

"Tuck. Come on. You think all women are hot. You never look at their faces, only their tits and asses. Stay. Away. I'm not kidding this time. We're getting married in six weeks. Don't do anything to make things awkward. Don't get on Dahlia's bad side before the wedding."

I threw up my hands in the air between us. "Impossible. Your future wife is a fan of mine."

"Yeah, she is. But don't give her a reason to change her mind."

"Fine. The maid of honor is out of reach. What about the bridesmaids? Are they also forbidden?"

Nick shook his head with a crooked smile. "Did you even hear a word I said when we spoke about the wedding before? It will be small. No bridesmaids. Just us four at the altar. Means you better behave."

I jumped up to stand and adjusted the cufflinks of my crisp white shirt, a contrast to my dark skin, and continued,

"Change of plans then. I need a date for tonight. Where can I find some pretty creature in a short amount of time?"

Nick rose to his feet and clapped my shoulder. "No date needed. It's only dinner with friends and family. You, me, Dahlia, Addison, and Carter. A few other people. And Dahlia's parents. Fuck, you really registered nothing."

"I did. Me, groomsman. You, groom. Women in dresses. Booze. Music. Everything that's important. Anyway—wait. Your sister isn't coming?"

"No, Jessica is attending some surfing competition in Hawaii. It's fine. Good news. Your bestie Jack will make an appearance, but he'll be with a babysitter so we can enjoy some grown-up time. He's spending a few days with Dahlia's parents afterward."

"Pause for a sec." My brain had just processed what Nick said a minute ago. "Carter Hills will be there?"

"He's Dahlia's best friend. What did you expect?"

"How's your relationship with him? Still strained?"

Nick huffed. "Better. I guess. We're not quite friends, but I still have high hopes one day we will be."

"All good for me then. Do you think he'll sign something for me?" I teased with the biggest smile spread over my face. "Autograph my pec or my shirt? Do you think he keeps posters in his trunk?"

"Okay, you gotta see a doctor, man." He shook his head, reeling in his smirk. "Since when did you become a groupie? Last fall, you faked having too much work to avoid coming to his show with me. Tickets you bought, remember? And now you want him to sign your man boobs?" He sent me a knowing gaze, with barely contained amusement and despair at my idiocy. Yeah, Nick Peterson could call my bullshit from miles away. My lips parted, but he kept talking. "Never mind. You do you."

I shrugged, baring an all-teeth smile.

"Do you think black ink would look good on my skin tone? Or should I get one of those golden markers?"

"If I were you, I'd opt to transform the autograph into a permanent thing. I know a guy who can ink you for cheap."

I tapped my chin with a finger, pondering it over for his sake. "Would you add a guitar or a heart next to it? Or maybe a music note?"

"Tuck, you're incorrigible. Geez, it's been too long since we hung out."

"Hey, I said nothing."

"No need." He shook his head. "Just in case a part of you is serious in some ways, we must set some ground rules until the wedding. Tell me. Why didn't I pick Jace as my best man?"

My smirk widened, and I winked. "Because he's married to your ex-fuck girl, who owns his balls and who happens to think you're a pathetic loser because you refused to date her when she decided your little arrangement didn't suit her anymore. And let's be honest. I'm the best choice." I scanned the suite. "Why isn't he here this weekend, though? I thought he said he was flying in this afternoon."

Hurt flashed in Nick's eyes.

Jace was our other best friend. We all grew up together.

If I had known Jace would be a no-show this weekend, I would've carried him here myself. No matter what his evil wife used as an argument.

She had a record of perfectly timed excuses to keep our friend away from us.

The devil, or Pamela White according to her driving license, had organized a fishing expedition, something she knew Jace would never miss, somewhere in the Atlantic Ocean the same weekend Nick was getting married. Such a low blow.

The guy chose to marry a mean control-freak. Nobody forced him.

But he had said he wouldn't miss this weekend. He swore he'd be here.

Nick was like a brother to me, always there, and Jace, the pesky cousin who was flitting around. The three of us had been inseparable growing up, and we got into trouble more than once. Jace distanced himself after he eloped with the devil.

"What's the reason this time?" I asked. "Let's not kid ourselves. We both know Pam is behind Jace's whereabouts."

"Her birthday. Her sister is in town one week before-hand to celebrate with her. He said he felt bad about leaving her in Chicago since she refused to tag along," Nick said as he took a sip and shrugged. "It sucks. We've been friends forever, the three of us. I still don't get why she hates me so much. I don't think I ever will. She's the one who slept with one of my two best friends—"

His stare moved to a spot on the carpet as he peeled the label from the bottle, lost in his thoughts.

Feeling a bit like a jerk for bringing that bitch up, I asked, "What are the rules? You're never not organized, so you already must have a list ready for me. Just in case I was planning on going rogue."

"Tuck, don't be a jerk."

"It's me, man. You can trust me. I promise to follow them the best I can. But only for the weekend."

"Six weeks, Tuck. Not just this weekend." He exhaled, and flecks of annoyance tinted his words.

In our relationship, I was the unpredictable one, the wild friend always in pursuit of good times and short-term fun. Nick was more thoughtful, aiming for long-term commitments and a conservative way of living.

"But—"

"No buts," my friend cut in. "You sure you wanna do this?"

"Yep. Give it to me."

"Okay. First. No getting too close to Addison. Second. No fangirling over Carter. For whatever reason, if that's really the angle you wanna play. The guy is now able to tolerate me for more than a couple of hours. Don't give him a new excuse to hate me."

I chugged the rest of my beer. "Man, the guy can't hate you. You're the kindest and the most harmless person I know. You're almost boring with your lovey-dovey ways. Don't forget you were nicknamed *Chicago Lamb*."

"No. I wasn't."

I shook my head. "You should have been," I muttered. "No kidding. You're too soft. Give Carter Hills a run for his money. I can help you. I don't care if he's mega-rich or the president of Nunavut."

"Focus, Tuck. For once. It's important to me. And to my future wife." Nick pinched the bridge of his nose. "And by the way, Nunavut isn't a country. No president there."

I smirked. The guy was so predictable. At least, he was to me. Most of the time. And bantering with him prevented me from thinking about all that was bothering me these days.

"Smart ass, I know where Nunavut is. I was just testing your geography skills." *And doing my best to make you forget the fact that Jace isn't here.* "About Carter Hills hating you, I'm sorry. But you can't blame him. You're the guy in the middle. And that woman of yours is quite a catch. I'd be possessive too if I were him. Just sayin'."

Nick exhaled a noisy breath. "Let's just say he's over-protective of Dahlia and Jack and sees me as a threat. Or he used to. Now we're surfing a calm wave. We're getting along. And I wanna keep it that way."

"The guy is a douche."

"I wish. But he's not. You should have come to that concert. You would've seen for yourself instead of taking my word for it. What he did for Derek... I'm still speechless when I think about it. Truth be told, he's amazing to Dahlia and Jack. Their friendship is truly special. Getting into their close-knit circle—or rather duo—can be chal-lenging. After everything they've been through, it's under-standable. One last thing. Don't tease me in front of him for entertainment purposes. Please. That would be shitty. Even coming from you."

"Never. After all, I'm the reason you and Dahlia found each other. If I hadn't sent you to Green Mountain in the first place, you'd still be alone and miserable. I'm glad my cupid ways worked. You still owe me for that one. I'll cash in on my dues soon. Once I figure out what to demand in exchange."

Nick tilted his head back and let out a heartfelt laugh. "Keep sending yourself flowers. You know you're delu-sional, right? Nobody owes anybody anything. If we'd kept tabs down all those years, you'd be the one in debt. For every single time I saved your ass." My friend pointed to the scar across his eyebrow. The one he got after he jumped into a fight because I kissed a football player's girl-friend and the entire team decided to get revenge. "Tuck, about those rules—are we good?"

"Yup. I'll stick to those two. For the rest, I intend to make this weekend one to remember." I uncapped two more beers, and after I handed one to Nick, I raised mine to click with his. "To you, man."

———

"Are you ready, pussy-whipped-man? Your woman can't wait to see your sorry ass. I bet the girls are curling each other's hair in the room next door. Or maybe they're rubbing each other's bodies with oil. Geez, I'm getting hard just thinking about it." I shook my legs to remove the tension tightening my crotch. "While I'm here, do you want me to gel your hair or shave your butt? That's as far as I'm willing to go for your bachelor party weekend. Just say the word and I'll give you a beauty makeover."

"She said that?"

Did my best friend hear a word of what I'd just said or only process the part where I told him Dahlia was getting ready next door? "Her friend arrived one hour ago. They'll meet us in about thirty minutes at the venue. Your fiancée dumped all this info plus sent a dirty text while you were in the shower."

"Tuck, don't read my stuff. Already told you that. Like ten thousand times in the last twenty years. Gimme my phone."

Nick rolled his eyes, and I laughed, unable to take my friend seriously when he was acting like a baby over a text message. It wasn't even *that* dirty, anyway.

Dahlia and Nick had rented half the top floor of City Garden, Nashville's finest hotel, for the weekend. It helped that the future bride had founded the Carter Hills Band with her best friend when they were kids. A few years ago, before Dahlia retired from the music scene, the band was the biggest country music sensation in the world.

Dahlia and Nick were two of the most incredible and

generous human beings I had ever met. Their hearts were in the right place. And they never did anything half-assed. Both successful small-business owners, I bet they spared no expenses for this weekend. And from what I'd noticed so far, renting half a hotel floor for a couple of days to celebrate their upcoming nuptials didn't seem like a big deal.

"We're ready to leave, I think," Nick said as he exited the bathroom. "I can't believe this is happening."

"Man, are you getting cold feet?"

"Never. I love her, Tuck. She's the one. I knew it the first time I laid eyes on her."

I clapped him between the shoulder blades. "I know, man. Seeing you with Dahlia is almost enough to make me believe in love. Almost." I winced, but his honest smile shattered my train of thought. "You guys just fit. I don't know how to explain it, but she's the one for you. No questions asked. I'm happy you two found each other. And that I put you on her radar, if we're being honest."

Nick's grin widened. "Thanks, man. It means a lot. Not the radar thing, though. Whatever."

I adjusted his shirt's collar and the lapel of his jacket.

"There. Better. You missed the Tucker touch."

I winked, and he pulled me into a hug.

"Thank you. For always having my back. And for being here this weekend and everything."

I tsk-tsked. "Don't go all emotional on me, man."

He straightened his back and regained his composure. "Not a chance."

Three inches shorter and less muscular than me, Nick and I looked like complete opposites. With his blond hair and amber eyes, he had the serenity of a guy who'd experienced the ups and downs of life reflecting in his eyes. More comfortable wearing a pair of jeans and a T-shirt than a suit, he preferred nights in with his family to the loud music of any bar or nightclub.

I, on the other end, was built like a pro football player, with dark skin, wide shoulders, crew cut, always dressed to impress. I had expensive and diversified tastes. Amazing food, grandiose apartment, designer clothes. And women.

And yet, our friendship had lasted over two decades. Even in our differences, we were similar. And had each other's backs. No matter what.

"Now let's go. I can't wait to meet the two people I'm not allowed to get too close to," I teased with a wink.

We made it to the top of the building, two doors down the street. For the entire night, we had the rooftop to ourselves. A green fake-grass rug lined the concrete floor. A bar in a little shack made of recycled barnwood was on our right, next to a makeshift dance floor with fairy lights hanging from beams above. A long white table decorated with golden plates and green foliage was set in the middle. Tall vases filled with pink dahlias and baby's breath gave a country-chic vibe to the decor. From here, we had a perfect view of the Nashville skyline from every angle. No doubt why my friend and his fiancée chose this place for tonight. It was magical.

Even my untenable heart felt giddy as a server passed pink champagne in crystal flutes around.

"Let me introduce you to everybody," Nick said, tugging at my elbow. Before we could move, Dahlia came to us, with a tall girl in tow. Blonde hair and the most vibrant blue eyes I'd ever seen overpowered my senses.

"Hey Tucker. So glad you could make it." Dahlia leaned forward and kissed both my cheeks before stepping back. "This is my best friend, Addison." She motioned to the girl, now deep in a conversation with Nick, before moving closer. "I hope Nick has already warned you to not mess with my friend. The two of you together are sure to create wildfires. And she's been through enough already. If you tango with her, I'll break your neck myself."

"Are you joking?"

"Try me and find out," she said in a deadpan tone, a mixture of humor and something fierce like protectiveness dancing in her moss-green irises.

"Jesus, Dah. You and Nick have become a pair of cutthroats."

She tipped one eyebrow as if to say, "Did I make myself clear?"

I lifted both hands between us. "No maid of honor for me. Understood."

Who knew Dahlia Ellis, the girl with the voice of an angel and the sweetest person I'd ever met, could serve threats the Chicago way? Guess the Southern ways weren't too different from ours after all. She leaned back and offered me a warm smile, all traces of her harsh words gone, her voice smooth as honey. "I'm so happy to see you. You don't visit us often enough. Enjoy yourself tonight, and let's catch up later."

Nick wrapped an arm around her waist and pulled her to him, kissing her temple and whispering something in her ear that made her giggle.

"Addi, this is Tucker, Nick's best friend," she said, introducing us in record time, making sure we couldn't exchange more than a "hi" or a "hey." She tugged at her friend's hand. "Come on, Carter is here. Let's have a drink, the three of us. It will be like high school all over again."

Addison stared at me, giving me a slow once-over, a gleam in her eyes. The girl was *trouble*. I could already tell. I hoped the future bride and groom had served her the same warning they gave me.

Just a thought.

Her lips parted, and she mouthed something I didn't quite catch, her eyes still trained on me.

I offered her my most dirty look, zooming in on her rack and making sure she noticed it.

Dahlia led her friend away, offering one last silent "hands-off" warning when her eyes met mine over her shoulders.

"Whoa, what did you do to piss off my future wife, man? I thought you two were best friends. Your words, not mine. You usually have a blast together." Nick scratched the side of his head, his gaze following the girls traipsing away.

I sipped my champagne, offering him my most unaffected expression. "Oh, we're good, man. More than good, actually." A smug grin stretched my lips. "She just threatened to break my neck, but hey, we're all right. Don't worry."

"Damn, she's hot. Every time she holds her ground with you, I love her more." They grinned at each other from a distance. Love was like newborns or puppies; it turned people into weirdos. "Don't meddle with a Southern woman. Whatever you do, don't ever say I didn't forewarn you."

Carter Hills came to introduce himself next.

"How is it going, man? Heard a lot about you," I told him as we shook hands.

"Great things, I hope." His eyes darted to Nick for half a second.

"Always."

Something—or someone—caught Carter's attention behind us. A wide smile curled up his lips, and he excused himself. I turned around to see a middle-aged couple, whom I assumed to be Dahlia's parents, holding their grandson Jack's hand as they exited the elevator.

Carter hurried across, and after he greeted them—now I was sure they were Mr. and Mrs. Ellis—he swept the boy off his feet, his broodiness now forgotten. Carter's face lit up as if he'd just won something priceless. From his well-over-six-foot height, he resembled a giant next to the little boy.

"Okay... From up-close, the resemblance is even more striking. Fuck. Right now, I could've bet my savings they were father and son."

"Yeah." Nick downed the rest of his champagne. "I'm pretty sure his brother and he could pass for twins."

Dahlia neared them, and Carter enveloped her in his arms and kissed her forehead. They exchanged smiles and seemed to understand each other without speaking a word.

"Now a lot of things you said before make sense. Don't you feel like kicking his ass or something? I know I wouldn't like my girl being all cuddled up in another man's arms if she were mine."

Nick blew out a long breath. "See, I've learned to accept it. That's the way they are. Dahlia could've dated Carter in all these years, but she didn't, so why should I be jealous? That would just make me miserable. They are family, as they say. Nothing more. I trust her. I really do. Now I am just happy to be a part of her life. And Jack's."

"Carter too?"

"He will have to be the acquired taste."

A burst of laughter escaped my lips at his drawl.

"For sure. Anyway, she's head over heels in love with you. That much is evident." I studied them for a few more seconds. "You're right, man. She doesn't look at him the same way she looks at you." I raised my hands in surrender. "I won't meddle in your relationship. You guys can have threesomes, if you desire, none of my business. Unless you want me to join in... But I'm telling you, I'm not doing you, man. Tried it once. A man, I mean. Not my thing. Never doing it again."

"Shut up," Nick said. "Too much info, Tuck. Your sex life is your thing. No need to gimme the four-one-one. I already know more than I should. Way too much. Stop putting these images in my head. They never fade away afterward."

I let out a loud laugh and ordered two whiskeys from the server as he neared us.

An hour later, we all sat at the table. Riley, Dahlia's former manager, rose to his feet to make a toast.

"Let's see. I've known Dahlia for a long time. We used to travel the world together. Without a doubt, she's one of the most amazing and caring women I know. Dah, I've seen you at your highs and your lows. And I can honestly say—today, you shine. No, you sparkle. It was about time you got your groove back on. I've met Nick a few times already, and I can predict you two will go the distance. You're made for each other. And come on, when was I ever wrong?" Carter threw a balled napkin at him. "See? Carter agrees. He knows I'm speaking the truth. He's the living proof." Everybody laughed. "Anyway, I wish you guys many years of happiness. You're what we should all aim for. Unconditional love. To Dahlia and Nick. And to soulmates."

We all cheered.

"Nick, welcome to the family. You're now officially one of us," he said, lifting his glass one last time before sitting back down.

A few more people said words before we dug into our five-course meal.

The blue of the sky transformed into multiple shades of pink, and someone turned on the fairy lights over the dance floor, giving the rooftop a warm glow.

We ate like royalties. The food was insanely delicious, our wine glasses and tumblers always full.

Addison stared at me from across the table, the blue of her eyes hypnotic. I'd felt the heat of her gaze on me from the moment we sat down. For the last hour, I'd been averting mine, doing my best to avoid locking eyes with her, no matter how tempted I was. Somewhere between the third and fourth course, she rubbed my shin with her foot under the table. I pulled my leg back. No, I wouldn't go there. Not a chance. I was strong. I gave my word to my best friend. Addison was out of reach. And I loved my life way too much to risk Dahlia putting me into an early grave. Way before my time.

With one mission in mind, veering as far as possible from the troublesome maid of honor, I went to the restrooms, needing time to cool down. And give my overzealous teammate a stern talking-to. I usually never backed down from a challenge. Even less, a lady's challenge. I loved women. Always had. A little too much, according to my friends. And I could never stay away if they gave me the *come-hither* looks. But I didn't do relationships. Never. And I never saw more than one woman at a time. Those were my rules. And to wear a rubber. All the fucking time.

I was freakish about catching some disease or shit. Heard they made your junk red and itchy. *No thanks, I'll pass.*

In front of the mirror, I adjusted the collar and rolled the sleeves of my Esteban Fu button-up shirt, my everyday go-to clothes and my designer of choice, my jacket already discarded. Yeah, I looked elegant. And fucking hot. I smirked at the image the glass reflected.

Too bad I couldn't use my charm on anybody tonight.

I would enjoy a good chase. Get my blood boiling and more. But no, not tonight.

When I exited the men's room, the blonde temptress cornered me, drawing a hand over my chest, her long pink fingernails toying with the buttons of my dress shirt. I held my breath, curious about this encounter. Wearing a steel-blue gown that tied at her nape and ended mid-thigh along with strappy high heels, she looked gorgeous. Even with those extra inches, I towered over her as I watched the goddess in front of me. A star amongst a sea of dark dresses, her blonde hair fell over her shoulders like a radiant aura around her. She sported an intoxicating smile, and her heavy-coated lashes made her irises appear bluer than before. More alluring.

"Tucker, right?"

"Yep," I said. A server walked by and offered me my drink of choice. I accepted and brought the tumbler to my lips, studying her features and the fire in her eyes. "At least it was the last time I checked."

"Oh, a sense of humor. I like that." She laughed and lost her balance on her four-inch heels. I clamped my fingers on her waist to steady her. Something coiled inside me, warming my core where our bodies connected.

"Ooooopsy. So sooorry," she slurred, revealing how drunk she was.

Addison pushed her hair over her shoulder, her smile devilish and enticing.

"Stop looking at me like this, Tuck. I can call you Tuck, right?"

"Guess so," I shrugged, keeping my back straight and doing my best to look unaffected by her antics. I had made a promise to my best friend. And my words counted for something. But Jesus, this woman.

"Anyway, *Tuuuck*," she said, her voice sultry and sinful,

putting emphasis on my name, "just so you know, I'm over men."

Every molecule in me woke up, reacting to the intimacy of her touch. To her tone. And the luring energy emanating from her.

The heat circulating in me reached a searing point.

My grip tightened around the glass in my hand.

"You are?" I asked, my voice a loud growl, my interest in her growing with every passing second.

"Yes," she said with a firm slant of her head. "Men break hearts. No matter how much you love them or how many times you suck their dicks in a week, they always end up breaking your heart." She waved her fingers over me. "This means you too break hearts. I can tell. You have this thing that makes women crave you." She leaned closer and sniffed me. *Yes, she fucking sniffed me.* I blinked, wondering if Addison was for real or if she was playing a game. "Oh, and you smell too," she added, her voice a whisper against my skin.

With a step back, I lifted my arm blatantly and took a whiff of my armpit, scared I really did smell, then dropped it back down.

"You're crazy, sweetheart. I don't smell."

She scrunched up her nose and sighed, then waggled a finger at my face. "Nooo...not like that. You smell like sex. You probably have a big dick and are very capable with your tongue. Am I right?"

Who was this girl, and where had she come from? No wonder Nick warned me off her. I was wrong when I thought she was trouble. She wasn't. She was pure evil. Sent on this earth to be the end of me. I realized I had to be careful. All this time, I thought I was a player. But here she was—pure dynamite. And could play the game too. Damn it.

Speechless for one of the first times in my life, I stared at her. Amusement danced in her eyes, and I was pretty sure it did in mine too.

My body pulsed to her symphony. I rolled my lips over my teeth to avoid saying something I wouldn't be able to take back or doing the unfeasible. Like getting the explosive tension out of the way by locking us in the restroom and ramming into her until I fucked the *sassiness* out of her. Addison was drunk. And I had promised to stay away. Two major turnoffs.

I breathed out, barely in control, many scenarios enacting in my head. All of them involved us getting naked and panting, while her small hand lowered down my abdomen.

My stomach muscles clenched.

"Are those abs you are hiding underneath that shirt? Six-packs are a real turn-on. Do you agree?" Her sensual voice twined around my control, cracking the tough shield I had over myself.

"You tell me, sweetheart. I'm not usually patting a man's stomach the first time we meet."

She fought a roll of her eyes, never breaking the contact. "Women possess them too. Don't discriminate. Like I said, I'm over your species. God should've named you T-R-O-U-B-L-E. I should re-baptize all of ya. It's a good thing I love women now. Not being picky."

I chuckled. "And yet, you're the one feeling me up right now. Are you enjoying it? Never would have guessed you're into women."

Her fingers traced lower, and a shiver traversed through me. Addison's eyes turned to slits, and she cocked her head to the side.

"Nobody told you to never make assumptions?" she asked.

"Nobody told you to never send mixed signals?" I countered.

Her gaze ate me up, and I could almost palpate the electricity ricocheting in the space between us.

The fire that had been simmering low inside me for a while now rekindled. My senses heightened. My heart did what I'd define as a complete revolution. Whatever this woman did, it worked. I felt alive facing her. Like I hadn't in quite some time.

We fixated our gazes on each other. Her throat rippled. Her breathing accelerated.

My cock pushed against the zipper of my trousers, bewitched by the blonde tornado ripping through my control.

I downed the rest of my drink, wishing it was cold water and that it would kill my arousal.

Addison gave me a doe-eyed look, not backing down from inspecting me as if I were her next meal.

Two words: excruciating torture. A test of my resistance. All I could imagine now was that sinful mouth around me.

Back down, I ordered my dick. *Don't expect anything from this woman. Not happening.* I whizzed a quick breath out, urging my common sense to make an appearance.

As if she could hear my train of thoughts, Addison blinked away whatever spell had taken her hostage, shutting down the desire that had been simmering between us. "Back to business. The thing is, I know I'm right. I know my men. You are all the same. Except for Nick. Nick is fine. He passed the test. Anyway, he doesn't have that alpha-vibe pouring out of him like you do. You're dangerous, Tuck. Very dangerous." She got lost in her own head for a moment. "Now that I'm choosing to only love anyone but hot-blooded men for the rest of my life, guys like you can't hurt me anymore. I'm done being played. Women don't have dicks, so they're safe. And they aren't heartless. Men are. Women are more compassionate. I had a girl lover once, and she used her tongue much better than all of you Neanderthal specimens combined. She could give you lessons. Do you want lessons, Tuck?"

"Oh, believe me. I need no lessons, sweetheart."

She tsk-tsked. "Don't go cocky on me, *Tuuuck*. Every man requires a woman's help. Adam, Eve. Barrack, Michelle. Harry, Meghan. Anyway, you get the point." She swept her bottom lip with the tip of her tongue, and it was one of the most erotic displays I'd ever seen.

I blinked and perused the space around us for another drink, desperate to cool off the arousal sprouting in my dick and slowly climbing its way up my being.

Something was going on, right? Was I being pranked?

Where were the cameras? And the crew? Was Nick on it? Was the entire sexy-meet a set-up? A test? Not that it was his style, but still, a guy had to ask.

I took a split-second decision to keep playing along.

"My tongue is made of gold, sweetheart. Don't judge a product you've never sampled before."

I sucked a deep breath in, trying to keep my composure intact.

"Too bad my vagina isn't interested. Guess we'll never know." She offered me a one-shoulder shrug. "See ya around, *Tuuuck*."

As if she couldn't convince herself to walk away, Addison studied me a little longer, her finger tracing the length of her mouth, her eyes devouring me in the process, unaware of the battle consuming me.

The one I could lose any second now.

She parted her lips to add something, and like a fool,

all my attention was diverted to those juicy temptations, waiting.

A heat wave crashed over me, flooding my body with sensations I'd never experienced before. Well, I had. To some extent. But never close to the intensity searing inside me right now. I memorized the line of her neck and the freckle below her left earlobe.

The womanizer in me had been poked, and all he yearned for was a little fun of his own and to have his way with her. Rip her clothes and make her come until she passed out from too many pleasure-induced-by-me orgasms. The kind of things she'd remember forever. That would brand my name on her.

We watched each other, my pulse throbbing in my temples. Addison closed her teeth around her forefinger. Was she even conscious of how sexy and diabolical she acted? My blood boiled hotter.

With a wink, she traipsed away, and I fought the desire to call her back, to settle this thing between us. To get the upper hand and lead my team to victory.

Armed with a loaded weapon in my trousers, I watched her retreat instead, once more urging my on-alert cock to stand down. Recede. Play dead.

A couple of deep breaths later, it finally listened, going from a strained full-on to a half-mast second-line team player.

My gaze scanned the rooftop. From the dance floor, Dahlia and Nick looked in my direction. My friend offered me a subtle shake of his head, pinching his lips like he was about to burst out laughing.

Dahlia made a cut-throat gesture with her finger and mouthed, "Don't even think about it. Out of reach."

They were in on it. All along, they knew Addison was a risk to my sanity. To my dick.

From afar, Addison looked all sweet and harmless, but she was a vixen wearing colorful clothes and hypnotizing smiles. One I was now dying to taste. I could read every strategy in her playbook. Because we shared a similar one.

I stood there, bothered and mesmerized.

Fuck.

Why did I promise to keep my distance?

3

ADDISON

I pushed Tucker away with one hand, ignoring the slackened jaw and *what-the-fuck-just-happened* expression in his eyes, and resumed my walk toward the pre-wedding party now filling the dance floor. When I touched him, his shallow breaths and pounding heartbeat vibrated under my open palm. I chose to disregard it. Because the zing traveling through me and the warmth pooling down my belly meant nothing. Instead, I focused on my steps. The ones taking me away from the temptation dressed like some Adonis. The more space I put between us, the more the thoughts of my encounter with him faded, making me relish the boozy bliss my head was swimming in. Even if my life depended on it right now, I wouldn't have been able to walk a straight line. But hey, who cared, right? I felt happy. And relaxed.

Alone in a chair, sipping a clear cocktail that I knew to be water—because Carter Hills didn't drink anything else since his brother died—my favorite country singer watched our friends dancing and laughing, a somber look pasted on his face. Back then, when his brother passed away, he chose to clean up his act and be there for Dahlia and Jack.

"You're not joining them?" he asked, pointing to the dance floor with his chin.

"I'm a litttttle bit"—I squinted and pressed my thumb and forefinger together—"drunk. That wine was deli-ciooous."

Carter straightened his back and leaned forward, his elbows resting on his knees, his stare intense and scruti-nizing my face. "Why are you so sad, Addi?"

I flicked my wrist as if it was nothing. Inside, an earth-quake shook my foundations. Up to now, I'd been doing a great job, or so I believed, at keeping my feelings bottled up. But something in the way Carter looked at me threat-ened to fracture my facade. "C'mon, girl. We've known each other for a long time. I can read you, you know? And right now, you're hurting."

"It's nothing," I said, averting my gaze. I used my fingertip to wipe the moisture building in the corners of my eyes.

"If you say so, but that sadness in your eyes is kind of a giveaway. All night, you've been acting like everything is good, but I know better." He shrugged. "If you want to talk, I'm here. How's Phen? I haven't heard from him in ages."

Phoenix was my twin brother and one of Carter's closest friends growing up. He moved to England to attend college, got married, and never came back home.

"Still on the other side of the Atlantic Ocean. Has twins of his own now."

Carter's eyes flared. "Wow, he didn't lose time to settle down. I'm glad he's doing okay."

"I miss him, you know. We used to do everything together. Now I'm lost without the one guy who never played me." Hot tears prickled the back of my eyes, and I blinked them away. The conversation had somehow sobered me up. "How are you holding up? I know it must be hard for you to be here tonight. This whole month and a half will be."

Carter scratched his forehead. "I love her so damn much, Addi, but I'm learning to let go of her. Getting better at it," he said, staring in Dahlia's direction as Nick spun her around on the dance floor, both so fucking bliss-fully happy it was sickening. "She always chooses the other guy. It's fucked up. I can't do this anymore. My love is always one-sided. Nick is fine. I'm not upset with him. He makes her happy. Jack loves him too. I'm mad at myself for not being enough. For not being what she wants...or needs. And for not having been able to get over her sooner like she asked. I hope she doesn't get married a third time. I'm not sure I'll survive watching the girl I've forever been in love with get hitched another time. Two is more than enough for this lifetime."

I pulled my chair forward and hugged Carter.

The guy had the biggest heart on Earth. Both times Dahlia fell in love, I'd witnessed his heart getting crushed.

"It would have been easier if you'd agreed to date me in high school. We'd have had each other to be miserable with," I added in a teasing tone. "Or maybe we'd have been happily married by now. Who knew what would have happened if you hadn't pushed me away when I kissed you —" I wiggled my brows, and Carter snickered.

"I'm sorry, Addi. I never apologized, but I acted like a jerk that time. You took me by surprise, and I panicked. I should have been flattered and not run away and given you the silent treatment afterward like I did."

I rested my head against his muscular shoulder. "It's okay. We weren't meant to be. We'll be fine. Both of us.

We just need time to heal. Or find whatever we're looking for."

"You think so?"

"I know so. One day."

"What's eating you up? Right now, what are you thinking about?" he asked.

I shrugged, doing my best to come up with words that would make some sense. "In a way, I guess it feels like my life isn't the way I'd imagined it'd be." Carter said nothing. Perhaps what I said resonated with him too, so I continued. "I have dreams and expectations. For myself. But I have no idea how to make them happen. When I try too hard, when I push ahead, it always backfires instead of going the way I expect it to."

Carter spoke in a low voice, "Then don't. Don't push it. Be yourself. Let them come to ya, Addi. You've always been the happy-bubbly person we all aspire to be. Things will work out. When they are meant to. You just gotta be patient."

I snorted. "Can I serve you the same advice?"

He shook his head, his protracted silence speaking volumes.

Feeling a tad better, I rose to my feet and held out my hand. "Wanna dance? For old times' sake. And for what could have been."

"Addison Wilde, you know I don't dance."

"I'm sure you can make an exception for me, Country Boy. The last time when Dahlia got married, you were a drunken mess. For the rest of this night, let's stick with each other."

Carter nodded and knitted his fingers through mine. "One dance. I can't believe you're making me do this," he said, shaking his head. "Only you, girl."

"Oh Cart, I'm full of surprises. Never underestimate me. You should be aware of it by now."

"That sounds more like the Addison I know. Welcome back."

He wrapped his strong arms around me, and I felt so delicate in his embrace, Carter towering over me by almost a foot. "Thank you for being my friend," I said as I sank into his chest and forgot about the things I had no control over.

———

"I'm calling it a night," Dahlia said as she hugged me hours later.

"Already?" I asked. "Is it even midnight yet? The night is still young."

"Almost. If I stay out too late two nights in a row, my face will be all puffy. I'm not used to partying this much. You should get some sleep soon. We're having a full day tomorrow. I've planned some great stuff for us."

I shrugged. "Don't worry about me. I'll head to that bar we like for an hour or two. Blow out some steam. You've always been too level-headed, girlfriend."

"By yourself? You sure?"

I nodded. "Yeah. I still have friends in town. I might give them a call. Or I'll make new ones. Don't worry about me. Now go and make love to your man while you're still a free woman."

I winked as Dahlia's smile stretched.

"Addi, you'll find your man too. He's somewhere out there. Don't be a pessimist. You'll get your happy ending. I promise."

I brushed her hair with my hand. "I love how you have

faith in me, Dah. But did you forget I'm not into men anymore?"

She let out a loud laugh. "My bad. For a second, I forgot."

"You'll see. I'll impress you. My next lover will be worthy of my love. I won't offer my heart to anyone not reaching the highest standards anymore. The next one will be marriage material. No, correct that. The next ones, with an *s*, will be rebounds. Hot and sexy. Tempting and forbidden. Then I'll find *the one*."

Dahlia hugged me again. "You deserve the best. I'm glad you got your smile back. Even if it's just for tonight. Even if it's slightly pretend. I love ya. Don't get into trouble. And if you do, call me. Night."

She kissed my cheek and joined Nick, who was standing near the elevator, his palm outstretched, waiting for her to slide hers in it. That. The simple gesture. This defined true love.

Not ready to let the thought bother me, I yelled at everybody and nobody, "I'm hitting the bars. Those who want to extend the fun, follow me." I downed the wine in my hand. And another one, just because I felt like it, and headed for the exit.

Before the elevator doors closed, a large hand glided between them. When they opened again, Tucker entered the car, looking fierce. The flutters in my stomach returned. Fast. And invasive. No one said I couldn't enjoy a great sight when presented with one.

Taking his place beside me, he stole all the vital air in the car, and I sucked in a jagged breath in response. His proximity made me feel lightheaded. Or was it the huge amount of alcohol I had drunk all night?

"Where are we going? I don't know the city, and I need a guide. I think you might be up for the job. Anyway, I'm pretty sure it's in my best man's job description to look out for the maid of honor."

Oh, he wanted me to play tour guide. Nothing else.

I could deal with it. This would keep me and my weak heart safe.

The low baritone of his voice as he let out a deep laugh shook my core.

Girl, get a grip on yourself. Yes, in my intoxicated state, my willpower had no solid ground.

If I couldn't find a sure way to stay away, this night would end badly. I could already tell.

All my radars were attuned to the man standing feet away from me. About six-foot-two, built like an athlete, with broad shoulders and a lean waist. His dark skin gave the impression he'd been molded in the most exquisite chocolate, with even darker, enigmatic irises and a smile showing perfectly aligned white teeth.

Tucker was everything I had a weakness for.

Smart. With a touch of sarcasm.

Even if I denied it, no way would I ever be indifferent to how he made me feel. Not me. Scratch that. My body. To how he made my body feel.

I got drunk on his cologne. The scent of a sea breeze enveloping me.

I clenched my thighs, refusing to let my imagination run wild.

I was over men. Over. Men. T-R-O-U-B-L-E.

I had to come up with an exit plan. An excuse to remove myself from his gravitational pull. My drunken brain made it almost impossible for me to map out an evacuation plan.

"You're not chaperoning me all night," I warned him with a finger. "I'm on a mission. To get laid."

Tucker moved his jaw back and forth and arched one

eyebrow. Its sharpness alone could tear my new resolution to shreds.

"And I can't help you with that because? Other than the fact I promised your best friend I wouldn't seduce you."

"Wait. What? You did what?"

He shook his head, shoving his hands into his pockets. "It's no big deal. Dahlia might have threatened my life if I fucked with you."

"Ohmygod. She's the best." I snickered. "I love her so much right now. Anyway, she's not my mother, and I'm free to do whatever I want. But to... Sorry, my head is all over the place right now. Too much wine—what was I saying?"

"That I wasn't on the list of potential fucks tonight, and I was asking you why."

"Ahh, yeah. That. I remember now. Well, first, you're Nick's friend. That would be weird, right? Second, you're —*you*." I drew circles in the air inches from his face.

"Me? What's wrong with me? What does that even mean? The last time I looked, it wasn't such a bad thing."

"God, do you need me to spell it out for ya? 'Cause I will. You're a man, Tuck. T-R-O-U-B-L-E. You lose all your points right there. I'm over your species. I already told ya. Not that I don't appreciate your gender. In fact, I do. A little too much. Like a pricey wine. In both cases, they come with promises of a great night but with the risk of a major hangover the next day. Tonight, I'm looking for a woman. Someone sweet who can think with her brain and not her dick, for a change. Someone who knows how to use her tongue expertly. And her fingers. You can't compete with that."

"Oh, sure. Right. Got it. You think women make better lovers." He rubbed the skin of his nape. "See, I agree."

"Your mother taught you right," I said.

He flinched at that. His face hardened. "Keep my mother out of it."

"Don't get all worked up, big guy. I was just complimenting how she raised you." I paused. The grimace on his face unsettled me. What did I say that put him on edge? With a hand, I stroked his forearm.

Tucker relaxed under my touch. The hard lines around his eyes receded.

He blinked, and a devious grin spread on his face, his harsh reaction to my compliment forgotten. Or pushed aside for now.

"If I understood you right, tonight, we're both playing the same field?"

I nodded, pride filling me.

"I'm willing to prove to you I'm much more qualified than you to entertain the ladies."

"In that case, let's make things interesting," I said. "Let's see who brings someone to their hotel room first. What do you say? Deal?"

Tucker seemed to ponder the idea in his head. "Oh, so you're not only a tease, but also a player."

I mustered up the widest smirk my lips could stretch into. "Tell me, Tuck. What will I get once I win this challenge? The stakes have to be high. To keep them entertaining."

He stared at me, his gaze so dark that my feet melted into the floor as he pinned me to the spot. "A weekend in Vegas, all expenses paid. If I win, you pay. If you win, which I'm pretty sure will never happen, then the bill is on me."

I extended my arm. Now I'd found someone to play with. "Deal. A three-day stay with a view of the Strip. Not some shitty motel in a clandestine corner of the city. The real thing. Classy and unforgettable."

"Good luck," he said with a wink. But under his confidence swam something I couldn't define. It must've been my imagination. Or the alcohol I'd drunk. Everything about Tucker screamed cocksureness and nights of limitless pleasure.

In Dahlia's and my favorite bar, we parked our asses for the night. It was one of my preferred nightlife spots in the city. I'd been living in Atlanta for the last few years, but every time I was around to visit my parents, I ended up here. Dahlia knew the owner; they'd toured together. So, he usually set us up with VIP rooms and the best champagne. Not tonight, though. Tonight, I was on the prowl. To forget all about my last relationship. And men in general. No special treatment needed.

Tucker ordered shots, and we each chugged three as we hung by the bar.

"If we fraternize, we'll look like a couple. No one will make a move on us," I said, wiping my lips with the back of my hand.

"Sweetheart, I can melt panties from yards away. See how it's done and pick up a trick or two. That's why I'll win this little beginner's challenge tonight. Hands down."

"Tuck, I can play dirty. You've never seen me in action. Get ready to have your mind blown."

I tsk-tsked and walked away, swaying my hips, knowing the effect it would have on him. And because I could. "I'll win," I whispered to myself as I watched him over my shoulder, his jaw slack and his eyes glued to my backside.

In a corner, I spotted a group of women, all wearing short dresses, showing off their legs and too much cleavage, looking drunk and ready to party.

"Hey ladies," I greeted, sliding between them. "I'll come straight to the point. I'm looking for a girl to rock my night. You see that guy over there? The one with the dress shirt?" They all eyed Tuck, giggling like schoolgirls. "Well, we've made a bet, and he thinks I won't go through with it. If he nears you tonight, please ignore him. He's cocky as hell. If one of you wants to make out, just say the word. I'm your woman. He thinks I'm bluffing, and he's wrong."

A girl with long black hair, ruby lips, and a sleeve tattoo inched closer. She looked like a model in her tiny leather skirt and high heels, her infinite legs tanned and skinny.

"Honey, you wanna give him something to talk about?"

I nodded. Nervous excitement coursed through me as she gave me a slow once-over, observing me through her thick, curled lashes. She cupped my cheeks, and without breaking eye contact, dipped her tongue into my mouth, moaning as she did. After a few seconds, I relaxed and lost myself in one of the most sensual kisses I'd had in a long time.

Everything inside me soared.

I was breathless and longed for more.

The girl, whose name I ignored, kneaded one of my breasts, and I dissolved into her touch.

When we broke apart, I was panting, lacking viable oxygen to my brain.

Yeah, I had forgotten how amazing being kissed by a woman was.

My cheeks warmed up. I cocked my head and noticed Tucker watching us, his mouth agape. My gaze traveled down to the bulge in his pants.

Our little bet got even more interesting.

Now he didn't stand a chance. At this rate, I'd get him so hot and bothered that he'd forfeit, and I'd win.

"Shots?" I asked my new group of friends. They all cheered, and I signaled the bartender to take our order.

———

The pounding on the door brought me out of my slumber. I tried to open my eyes but couldn't. My head hurt. No, my brain hurt. The pain was anchored deep inside my pulsing skull. I darted my tongue out to moisten my lips, but it was so pasty it made my stomach churn. My body felt heavy as if someone had wedged me in fresh concrete. Where was I? I patted the bed around me, but it was hard. Was I sleeping on the floor? Acid filled my mouth. This was bad. I had no memory of the previous night. The last thing I remembered was yelling at Tucker because he flirted with the girl I had been working hard to bring back to the hotel. She said we were bantering like children and we should get our shit together and left us.

Tucker?

Where was he?

Did we even make it back to the hotel? My entire body hurt, something beneath me too hard. My face felt as if it had been scraped with sandpaper. A buzzing sound reverberated against the walls of my skull.

The banging on the door resumed. Someone—a man —was angry. My brain was too numb to understand a word. Or to make out whose voice it was. But by his tone, I could tell he was pissed.

Sensations returned to my hands, my arms. Slowly, it made its way down to my toes.

Something happened last night. The flesh of my inner thighs was tender. I wriggled a hand down my front. No panties. Okay, I was butt naked. I could deal with that. I moved my hand back up and slid it between my breasts and the hard surface to cup it. I had no clothes on.

What did I get myself into this time? I begged my brain to give me a clue. Nothing. Zip. Blank state.

With a push of my hand, I lifted my upper body and opened my eyes. The room was trashed. Junk food wrappers and sample alcohol bottles scattered everywhere. I was sleeping on my front on the carpet of the hotel room. Not my best moment. How could my amazing night have turned into this? I missed the comfort of a fluffy mattress.

The banging on the door intensified. Oh yeah, that guy was upset.

"Come on, open up. We'll be late. You were supposed to meet me an hour ago."

Oh God, did I make some woman cheat on her husband? This was a nightmare. How would I get out of this one? Of all the people I chose to fuck last night, I had to pick a married one. And I didn't miss the irony of it.

I let out a shaky breath and closed my eyes, trying to stop my head from spinning and my stomach from churning.

A warm hand slapped my ass cheek, and I gasped.

"Hey sweetheart, you awake?"

The blood froze in my veins.

This was bad. So bad. Kill me now.

What did I do last night?

4

TUCKER

I stretched my arms and pried my eyes open, the thumping on the door about to crack my skull in two. I didn't remember the last time I got so wasted. The little challenge between Addison and me last night had turned into a full-blown competition. The girl could play. She deserved a medal just for her efforts.

Minutes after we arrived, she kissed a woman, full-tongue, straight in my face, offering me the most perfect jerk-off vision I'd ever seen.

The girl was a devil dressed like an angel.

She was bad. So bad. About to kill me with every flick of her tongue.

And truth be told, I had a weakness for bad women. All of them. No exception. Even the ones I promised to stay away from.

My dick had been hard for hours, watching Addison make out with strangers, caressing their tits, gripping their asses. Staring at them with intense lust.

Just thinking about it got my dick stiff. Again.

The soft breathing of the woman next to me brought a

smirk to my lips. At least I got laid last night. *Yeah, congrats, Dick. I knew you still had it in you.*

If only I could high-five my wingman...

Guess I won after all.

The more I drank, the blurrier the events of last night got in my mind. I remembered my conversation with Addison up on the roof, then she'd danced with Carter Hills. The sight of them had sent a wave of misplaced jealousy through me. They laughed together, looking intimate. How well did they know each other? He clearly didn't get the same warning I did. To avoid making a scene because I somehow felt as if looking after her was my dutiful job, I asked Mrs. Ellis, Dahlia's mom, if she would like to dance. She ended up being quite a dancer, and I spent hours twirling her around.

Then I followed the maid of honor to the bar. Because I had no idea how to flee her magnetism. And because my dick was a selfish prick and enjoyed her attention.

We drank shots.

She got me hard by kissing a woman.

A surge of envy roused in me. One that I could barely contain.

Desperate to be the one her lips were molded to, I drank more shots to forget about her.

My memory faded from that point onward.

I only had flashbacks of our night from there.

I flipped to my side and looked around. Why was I lying here?

With my fingertips, I rubbed my throbbing temples. Nothing two painkillers couldn't help.

My hand connected with the round ass a foot away from me.

The porcelain flesh was a great contrast to my darker skin.

My dick twitched. Perhaps we could go at it another time before breaking apart. Just to get all the lust out and secure it away for the rest of my stay.

"Hey sweetheart, you awake?"

The woman turned her head, and my words died in my throat.

"Wilde? What the fuck." I stretched my arm to grab a piece of fabric and used the discarded shirt to hide my junk. "Why are you here?" She blinked, watching me as if I'd grown horns. "Fuck, did we—? Nick is gonna kill me." I ran a hand over my face. "No. Dahlia will strangle me. And then she'll throw the pieces of me to sharks, so there won't be anything left." Will I burn in hell for this?

I closed my eyes, praying my hangover brain had conjured the entire scene, and shook my head.

When I peeled my lids open, everything looked the same. "I *will* burn in hell for this," I mumbled, mostly to myself.

The door of my hotel room burst open, startling me. Nick stood in the doorway, along with a concierge, his arms folded across his chest, an annoyed expression replacing the short-lived relief in his eyes. I grimaced. *Addison.* I raised my arm to fake scratch my nape, looking sideways to where she lay seconds ago, but she had disappeared. Did I dream of her in my room? I shut my eyes, trying to make sense of the scene unfolding before me. My best friend tipped the guy after assuring him of my well-being.

The door shut behind him, and Nick stalked forward, stopping a foot away from my sprawled self.

"What the hell, man. I've been knocking for over twenty minutes. I thought you were dead or had passed out in your puke. I really got scared for a moment." His eyes took me in. "Why are you sleeping on the floor? You're aware your room has a king-sized bed, right? Geez, Tuck. Are you all right? Should I worry?"

I stood up, dropping the shirt and forgetting all about my naked state. "Everything is fine, man. Just overslept. Somehow, it got wild last night." Perfect choice of word.

A whistle parted his lips. "C'mon, Tuck. Cover up. Your dick doesn't have any effect on me. Anyway, you were supposed to meet me for breakfast. I got worried. Addison is missing too. Have you seen her when you went out last night?"

I shook my head. "No. Addison who?"

His eyes surveyed the suite. "Never mind. What did you do to your room? It's trashed. Did you have a party in here?"

"Yeah, got a few people over." *Did I?* I snorted. I'd bet my best man title the chaos was Addison's and mine only. We drank, we partied, we fucked. Seemed about right. Didn't I say already we shared the same playbook? "They stayed late. I'll sort it out. Don't worry, okay? It's your weekend. I'm a big boy. Won't get in trouble further."

Bemusement flashed in Nick's eyes. "You do remember you are my best man and my only immediate family this weekend, right?"

Yeah, Jace would miss his wedding. And his bachelor party. He only had me to count on. How could I forget? Right now, I looked like an egotistical jerk.

I cast my eyes down. "I'm sorry, man. I mean it."

"Whatever. I'll be in my room when you're ready. You have fifteen minutes. It's almost noon. If you're not there, we're leaving without you. I'm really looking forward to spending time together. I've missed you since I moved to Green Mountain. And if you hear from Addison, please ask her to call Dah. She's worried sick."

I nodded, my head hanging low. Because what else could I do?

I locked the door behind my friend, and after putting last night's pants on, I reached for the bedroom. Addison was there, all dressed up, sitting on the bed, her hands locked between her thighs. "Listen, Tuck, about last night, I—I don't know what to say because I don't recall a thing."

I stood in the doorway, raking a hand through my hair.

"Huh, I don't either. Are you sure we—?"

"I'm sore. No doubt we did it. But I'm not sure we used protection, though."

"How do you—? Sorry, stupid question." I paused to regroup my thoughts. "Huh, okay. I want you to know I'm clean. Got tested last month, and I've been on a dry spell since."

"Well, I'll take the morning-after pill when I get home. No big deal. Can't take birth control pills; they give me migraines. And I'm clean too." She breathed out. "Now at least."

My eyes flared as I stalked closer. "What do you mean, you're clean *now*?"

Fury scorched deep down in me. This was no joke. I didn't mind sleeping around but catching some fucking disease. Not happening.

Her head dropped low, and her shoulders slouched forward.

"You know my vow about staying away from men. My ex...he cheated on me. Rather, he led me on. They all did at some point. Anyway, the guy I'd been dating for two months...it turned out he had multiple girlfriends." Her eyes dimmed with hurt. "One in many states. I only learned about it because he caught something and thought he gave it to me. Felt it was his duty to come clean about his dick's whereabouts. Like he was the savior in the story.

Anyway, I'm fine. Don't stare at me like this. I didn't screw around. He did."

Tears clouded her blue eyes.

Now I felt like an idiot for assuming the worst about her.

I sat on the bed next to Addison and held her hand in mine. It seemed like the most sensible thing to do after I fucked her without a condom and had no memory of any of it. Her touch quieted my racing thoughts. I breathed easier as we shared a moment. We both stayed silent, the reality of what happened hitting us.

After a long minute that seemed like an hour, I tried to ease the tension in the room. "Guess we both won the challenge then."

"Or we both lost," Addison deadpanned, avoiding my gaze. "I should get going. I'm supposed to go shopping with Dahlia, and I'm like almost two hours late. She must be running crazy."

"Huh, do you want to talk about it? Later? We could—"

She jumped to her feet. Her somber voice, lacking last night's confidence, pinched my heart. "Nah, it's okay. We shouldn't. What's done is done. Let's just forget about it. Bye, Tuck," she said, hurrying out of the room without another glance.

Twenty minutes later, showered and dressed in a clean Jaxon Arison button-up shirt and black trousers, I looked refreshed and felt better than I did earlier. With my headache almost gone and my hangover forgotten, I sauntered toward Nick's suite with a swagger in my steps.

"Any news of Addison?" I asked, acting as casual as possible, after he let me in.

"Yes, she's fine. She overslept too. Said she turned off her phone because she had a headache. Anyway, she's coming over soon. We just made a reservation for lunch at the restaurant Addi and I adore in East Nashville for the four of us," Dahlia said with a twinkle in her eyes, meeting my best friend's enamored stare.

Their love was nauseating.

"I thought you girls had plans?" I asked. The idea of spending more time with Addison turned my spine into an ice pick. Nothing good could come out of this after what we did last night.

"Change of plans. I know my bestie. What she needs is a meal with friends, nothing too fancy, and an afternoon nap to be in top shape tonight. Shopping can wait."

A knock on the door sent my pulse into overdrive, and pearls of sweat gathered at the back of my neck.

"Hey Addi, are you feeling better?" Nick asked as he greeted her and dropped a kiss on both her cheeks. She muttered something I didn't catch, my blood rushing so loud that it blocked all other sounds around me.

"Hey Tuck," she said as our eyes met when she walked past me toward Dahlia.

"Hey," I echoed, my voice rough, at a loss for more words.

Dahlia clasped her hands before her. "Ready? I'm so excited we're doing this. I haven't spent this much time with grown-ups in years. And somehow, sharing this day with you guys is really important to me."

She beamed, and I felt stupid for racking my brain to find a dumb excuse to bail out on all of them.

In the small eatery with black leather booths and dark iron chandeliers hanging from the ceiling, Dahlia and Nick sat next to each other, and I took a seat beside Addison. The narrow booth was a tad small for my stature, so our limbs brushed against each other the entire time, and her heat shot through me where our bodies connected.

The scent of her shampoo made me dizzy. It was too intoxicating. Too fruity. Too Addison Wilde. I loosened the collar of my shirt and rubbed my throat, trying to open my airways. I was suffocating. At this pace, I'd be dead due to asphyxiation before lunch hour was over.

"You two ready for your maid of honor and best man's pre-wedding speech tonight?" Dahlia asked, the sparks in her eyes still shining. She could light up the entire town with those.

"Yeah," I said.

Beside me, Addison coughed. "Sure. Super ready. Yeah," she said, pumping her fist. I studied her from the corner of my eye. Gaze down. Dropped shoulders. Curved back. Flushed cheeks. The girl was the worst liar I'd ever met. Was her best friend blind or so overwhelmed by the wedding that she missed the signs?

Under the table, I patted her hand, but she yanked it away as if my touch burned her. Before Dahlia could push the topic some more, I changed the subject. "When is the honeymoon?"

Nick intertwined his fingers with his fiancée's. They exchanged a ridiculous grin that only people in love flaunted.

"Carter has a month off later this summer. We'll leave then. Jack will stay with him, so we'll have a full four weeks to ourselves. Two in Fiji and two at home."

They kissed, and I averted my eyes.

"You okay?" I asked Addison under my breath.

"Sure. Never better," she answered, not meeting my gaze.

Back in my hotel room two hours later, I debated between lying down for a much-needed power nap or doing the thing that the voices in my head were nagging me to not do.

After deciding a nap could wait, I gathered my phone, a sheaf of papers, and some stuff I filled my pockets with, and bolted through the door. Not knowing which room to go to, I gave Nick a call.

"Hey man. Looking for Addison's room. I grabbed her key by mistake. Can you gimme the room number so I can take it back to her?"

"Sure. Thirty-five-eleven."

"Thanks," I said, cutting the line before he struck up a conversation.

Seconds later, I knocked on the door, stuffing my free hand in my pocket and trying to look relaxed. Addison answered after a minute. Fuck, did I wake her up? She had changed into dark gray sweat shorts and a see-through white tank top.

She folded her arms over her chest, guarding her room, wearing a disapproving frown. "What do you want, Tucker?"

The sight of her brought a smile to my lips, and without waiting for an invitation, I ruffled her hair and pushed inside, not intimidated by her little act. Yeah, Addison Wilde was as scary as a kitten while trying to look disgruntled.

With a loud thud, she closed the door behind me, breathing heavily through her nose. The wrinkle across her forehead hadn't receded as she swiveled to watch me when I sat on a chair next to the bed. This little mask of fury looked adorable on her.

I took a second and perused the room. Open-floor suite —same as mine—set up as a loft. It had panoramic windows offering a great view of Nashville, high beam ceilings, and a southern touch with its wooden accents.

"I'm here to help you out, sweetheart. You haven't written your speech for tonight."

"I have," she lied.

Still not convincing.

I waggled a finger. "Didn't you learn lying is bad? Stop already. I could tell earlier. And I'm here because I wanna help you save face tonight. We should get to work. I'm sure Dahlia expects great things from you. And you wouldn't want to deceive your best friend, no?"

Addison neared me and huffed, the most irritated look I'd seen on someone now painting her face, her fists resting on her hips.

My gaze swept over her. I couldn't believe not recalling her naked and under me last night. The crests of her hips. The swelling of her ass. The fullness of her breasts or the taste of her pussy. I shook my head, annoyed at myself. It had never happened before. Having sex and retaining no memory of it the next day.

"Why? Why would you want to help me? It makes no sense. You wrote yours? Congrats, you're the perfect best man. Now leave. I can do this on my own."

"Nope, you're stuck with me until it's done."

She glared at me. I hated that last night's misadventure had created tension between us and that she would have to deal with the repercussion on her own to avoid any unplanned surprise taking over our lives nine months from now. Even though I was as responsible for our crazy night as she was, I could do nothing but hold her hand and support her. Whatever happened, I refused to be just another man who failed her, one who would just abandon her in such a situation. I guessed if I were her, I'd be annoyed and pissed at myself too.

With a groan directed at me, she continued with her accusation, unaware of my thoughts. "You could shine as the perfect best man tonight, making me look unprepared.

Why don't you, Tucker? Tell me. Unless you have an ulterior motive. So, what is it? I'm all ears."

This woman. Even her anger couldn't deter me from my objective of helping her out.

I let out a warm laugh. "Call it team spirit, sweetheart. We fucked up last night. And fucked. If I had to guess, we went at it a lot. Anyway, I consider us friends now, and I wanna help you out. Don't overthink it. I don't usually offer my help that easily. And freely."

"Still not believing you. What do you want in return? Men always want something. They all do."

I sprang to my feet. "Whoa. I'm not that kind of guy, Wilde. I'm not being nice to get my dick sucked, if that's what you're referring to."

A dark blush covered her face.

"Fine. What do you have in mind?"

I emptied my pockets on the nightstand. Her ocean-on-a-sunny-day blue eyes rounded.

"Sweetheart, the best way to get over a hangover is by having another drink. It's drinking 101. Make yourself comfortable. We'll be here for a long time, you and I."

Six mini liquor bottles and around thirty balls of paper strewn all over the room later—we tried our luck at basketball using the trash can but failed—we came up with a draft that pleased us both.

"See, it wasn't hard," I said once I finished reading it out loud. "I kinda like it."

"Why are you helping me, Tucker?" Addison asked, her voice throaty. "You never answered the question."

I shrugged. "No idea. It seemed like you'd had a bad week. Or a bad month. Or whatever. I thought you could use a friend and some ass-kicking to get your speech over with. Have you written your wedding day speech yet?"

"Yeah. I wrote it months ago. I'd forgotten about the one for tonight. Let's say I've got a lot on my mind."

We clinked our bottles and knocked back the vodka in one gulp.

"Do you have any idea what went down last night?" Addison asked, her glazed eyes full of hope.

I shook my head. "If I had to guess, I'm sure I went down. On ya."

She offered me a death stare.

"The truth? No idea. It's a shame I can't even remember the taste of you. Or how good we were together. Guess it'll fuel my fantasies for a while." She threw a pillow at me. "Don't think too much of it, sweetheart. You should be the one crying because you can't remember how being fucked by a real man felt like." With our backs resting against the headboard, we stayed silent for a while.

"Thanks for helping me today, Tuck."

Okay, so we were back to Tuck instead of my full name. Progress.

"All my pleasure," I said as she rested her head on my shoulder. "I think we make a great team."

"Yes."

Soon Addison's breathing evened, and I beseeched my own eyelids to stay open. We both dozed off before either of us could make out what was happening.

———

The sound of sirens reverberated inside my head. They bounced across the walls of my skull. Were they real or a figment of my imagination? Right now, I couldn't tell. My eyelids weighed so heavy that it'd take an entire crew to force them to open. The sirens turned into a deafening alarm. My head spun, heavy and confused. Still sleep-deprived, I couldn't remember where I landed my ass last.

Something fastened around my waist shifted, and as if I'd been tased, I woke up. I scanned the room. Images of the last few hours flashed through my head.

I patted the bed, looking for my discarded phone. Instead, I found Addison's. At least now I knew where the alarm had come from. I turned the annoying sound off and stared at the screen, my brain taking longer than usual to make out the time.

I shut my eyes.

Opened them.

Blinked a few times.

Better. It brought the focus back.

"Wilde," I said, shaking her. "Wake up. We have to get ready." She mumbled something and sank her face deeper into my chest. "Earth calling Addison. Wakey wakey. Show me those blue irises. Get up right now, Wilde." I pushed her hair away from her face. Having her nestled against my body felt oddly domestic. And even if I didn't do love, this time somehow, having a woman in my arms just for the pleasure of it didn't freak me out as much as I thought it would.

She pushed my hands away as my fingers tickled her ribcage.

"Stop. Leave me alone. I'm exhausted. I need sleep. Let's just stay here and skip the festivities. No one will realize we're missing."

I chuckled. "You're right. Neither the best man nor the maid of honor shows up, and nobody will notice. Very clever." I squirmed from under her, disappeared into the bathroom, turned the cold shower on, then returned to the bed to lift her slumped body over my shoulder.

"Tuck, put me down," she pleaded. "Gimme another ten minutes."

"Remember, I'm doing this for you. Don't hate me. It's for your own good."

I lowered her to her feet under the stream. A high-pitched cry escaped as the cold water ran over her. With my shoulders, I blocked her exit, my feet rooted to the tiled floor by the shower opening. Addison reached for me, pulling at my shirt, and scratching me like an angry kitten, trying to escape the glass box. I held her in place with one hand. "Here," I said, switching the shower to hot as I fumbled with the knob with my free hand. "See, better?"

The minute I let go of her, she charged at me, jumping into my arms and twining her legs around my waist.

I risked a step back, but she didn't let go. "Come on, Wilde. This is how you thank me for caring for you?"

Her upper body molded to mine, drenching my shirt. "All my clothes are wet because of you. It's only fair yours are too."

I shook my head as she jumped to her feet, satisfaction brightening her face.

"You know this isn't actually my room and that I gotta return to mine in order to change. Real nice, Wilde." I unbuttoned my shirt to twist it and squeeze out as much water as possible. Addison stood there, speechless, staring at my naked torso, her lips parted.

I flexed my biceps and my abdominal muscles to give her something to fawn over.

"When you're done drooling, you may want to undress and shower. We gotta be ready in less than an hour. I'll pick you up in fifty minutes. And by the way, I can see everything through that shirt of yours."

She yelped. I winked and spun on my heels, leaving a mute Addison behind.

My feet landed on the hallway carpet at the same moment Nick was about to knock on the door.

He scanned me from head to toe, his throat working, question marks dancing in his eyes.

"Is everything all right? What are you doing here? Why are you shirtless? Two rules, man. Two."

I raised my hands in surrender, not hiding the trademark smirk I wore. "Easy, tiger. It's not what you think. Addison had a shower problem, and I helped her to fix it. Just got soaked in the process. What are you doing here, anyway?"

My friend studied me for a few seconds, then shook his head, not impressed by my excuses after over twenty years of friendship. "Just—just don't do anything stupid, okay? Addi asked Dahlia to check up on her in case she slept through her alarm."

"No need. She's getting ready. Give her some slack. She's a grown woman, not a toddler you two need to watch over."

"It's not like that. Told you she's had a bad breakup. She's been off lately. Dahlia is protective of her right now. Anyway, once you're all set and decent, meet up with us. We're having drinks in our suite."

"Yeah, see you in a bit." I walked away before my best friend could read through me and figure out I'd been lying to his face. Sorta. Did it count as a lie if I had no cognizance of breaking the rule?

Forty minutes later, I was about to go get the maid of honor when she appeared at the threshold of my room. Dressed in a floral tube dress and high heels, with her blonde hair tied into a sleek ponytail, she looked beautiful and dangerous. For all *man*kind. Men of our kind.

My gaze fixed on her eyes after giving her a slow, appreciative once-over.

"Wow, you clean up nice. I knew that a cold shower would do you good. You can thank me now."

Addison didn't return my smirk. Instead, I noticed panic flashing in her eyes.

"What's wrong?" I asked, stepping closer, my fingers trailing down her forearm. As if touching her had become my obsession. Something I had to do.

"Okay, well, here's the thing—I ordered something for tonight. A present for Dahlia and Nick. It was supposed to be here by now, but it's not. And I totally forgot to check the delivery time earlier today. I called the store, and they told me the package was on its way. But if I wait for its arrival, I'll never make it to the boat on time." She sighed and rushed with the explanations, almost tripping over her words. "Do you think you could stay back with me for another hour? I'd wait on my own, but I came here on the train. I don't have a car, and I don't like cabs and stuff. They gross me out. You got a rental, right?"

I nodded. "Cabs disgust you? Everybody takes them all the time, sweetheart. God, you're weird. You know what? Somehow, it suits you. Lucky you're not a New Yorker, or you'd go nuts." I checked the time on my phone. "Fine. I'll wait with you. I'll text Nick so he doesn't go ballistic on us for being late. Again."

In the lobby, Addison sat on a plush sofa while I rested in a sable brown oiled leather armchair, both of us sipping cocktails I got from the hotel bar. Dark wallpaper with a silver pattern adorned the walls. A stone fireplace with a wooden beam used as a mantle stood in the middle of the room. Wrought-iron chandeliers hung from the ceiling. The space looked like the foyer of a chalet-type resort in a decor magazine.

Addison kept checking the time, her leg bouncing in her three-inch nude pump. From behind my tumbler, I studied her. The girl looked amazing in her strapless dress, giving a hint of the swell of her breasts. I still couldn't believe I had those luscious globes all to myself last night and couldn't remember any second of it. Such a waste. Her blonde ponytail bounced over her shoulders every time she turned her head, and she had put on enough makeup to hide the dark circles under her eyes and make the blue of her irises pop. Addison Wilde was a gorgeous woman. The jerk who hurt her was just that, a jerk. No way would I ever be able to make a woman like her cry. Or hate me.

"Enlighten me. Is the Cumberland River big enough for a fancy boat?" I asked, trying to dissipate her anxiety.

"Yep. You should see the big-ass ships you can spot when you're in Riverfront park. There's even a showboat offering tours, dinner cruises, and live shows. Tourists love it. It's nothing compared to the yacht Dahlia and Nick chartered, though. Wait until you see it. I saw pictures. It's huge." She whistled. "I wonder why the owner would keep it here, in a river in Tennessee, instead of at a marina in some ocean front where most yachts would be anchored."

"That impressive, huh?"

She bobbed her head.

A man dressed in a delivery company uniform passed through the door, and she jumped to her feet to greet him, forgetting all about our conversation. They exchanged a few words, and she signed something before sauntering in my direction, a bright smile now lighting up her face, oblivious to the man's lingering gaze over every enticing inch of her. She waved the package at me, triumph in her eyes.

"Got it. We can go now."

"Follow me then," I said, pushing her forward, my hand molded to her lower back. As if it had been made to rest there.

Two blocks away from the hotel, the lane merging onto the highway was blocked, a truck lying on its side. "Damn it," I said, hitting the steering wheel with an open palm. "We'll never make it on time. Wilde, get the GPS on your phone to find another route. Else, the yacht will leave without us."

"No need, big guy. I grew up around here and know just the perfect shortcut."

I sighed, made a U-turn, and followed her directions.

"Next traffic lights, on your right, then turn left at the stop sign."

I maneuvered through the streets.

My gaze darted to the time on the dashboard, and I drummed my fingers on the steering wheel. We only had nineteen minutes left to get to our destination. And I loathed being late.

"Right here," she blurted without any notice, her finger pointing to our left. I hit the brakes, the sudden motion propelling our bodies forward before we collapsed into our seats, the car behind us almost rear-ending us. Instinctively, I stretched my right arm in front of her, the gesture meant to protect her. Or prevent her from any impact.

"Jesus, Wilde. A little advance notice next time would be appreciated." I flicked the flasher, and once my pulse settled, I followed her guidance.

Addison pointed to a supermarket and said, "Turn here."

Agitation simmered inside me. The tapping of my fingers danced to a faster beat, frustration making my body tauter. My eyes took in the time. Beads of fury danced in my stomach. "Are you kidding me right now? The time is ticking and you wanna make a pit stop?" I dragged a hand over my face and rubbed my freshly shaved jaw.

She puffed and cocked her head toward me. "What?

No. There's an alley just behind. It's a shortcut. We'll get there faster."

"Faster? I feel like we've been driving in circles for the last ten minutes." I grabbed my phone from the center console, turning the GPS app on.

Addison stole the device from my hand and held it as far away as possible from my reach.

"Gimme that," I begged, humor absent from my tone.

She shook her head. "Not a chance. I'm the one giving directions. We already agreed. I'll take you to the boat, big guy. Trust me."

I put the SUV in park. "Not now. We'll be late, and I'm not playing this game with you. Give my phone back."

"Nope. I'm telling you. There's an alley behind, and it will lead you to where we're going faster," she argued.

She played on my last nerves.

"Thirteen minutes left," she said with a large grin that drove me nuts.

Deciding to give her the benefit of the doubt and not wasting more time, I followed her instructions.

Once we exited the alley, we drove through a residential neighborhood, then turned right on another alley behind some sort of tattoo parlor, only to land on a deserted road parallel to the railway. Somewhere that appeared far from civilization but was actually two streets away from a residential neighborhood.

"Wilde, for the last time, you sure you know your way?"

She folded her arms over her chest, pushing those luscious tits up, and I glanced at her sideways, entranced.

Eyes on her face, man, I told myself.

"No shame in admitting you're lost. Or asking for directions," I said, my aggravation dropping a notch.

"Are you serious?"

Oh-oh, now she sounded half-offended and half-amused as if about to scold me.

Not willing to participate in a battle of wills, I gave her a stiff nod and spoke before she could add anything else. "Dead serious. Now gimme my phone."

Addison angled her body until her back rested against the passenger door. She studied me for a beat, shook her head, despair tracing her features.

"Tuck, Tuck, Tuck. Listen, you gotta learn to trust women. This is a bad habit of yours."

My insides clenched at her words, and I forced an innocent expression onto my face.

"Who said—? What are you talking about?"

"Sorry to ask, but do you have trust issues? With women? Because from what I've seen, it is evident." She wiggled her eyebrows. "Don't you agree?"

"Enlighten me, sweetheart."

She cleared her throat and raised one finger, a challenge burning in her eyes. "First, I mentioned your mother and wanted to compliment you. But you flinched." She raised another finger. "Second, when I said we had sex this morning, you asked if I was sure. Come on. How could I have put your cum there myself?" She lifted a third finger. "Then you insinuated I hadn't written my speech." She sighed and shook her head. "That time, though, I'm giving it to you. You were right." With a smug expression pasted on her face, she raised a fourth digit. "And now you thought I gave you bullshit directions to the yacht. The devil is in the details. Your behavior individually seems like nothing, but when put together, it's incriminating. And you gave yourself away just now with the stiffening of your upper back when I asked if you have trust issues with women."

I blinked. Something resembling fury mixed with

uneasiness seared inside me. I cracked my neck to the side, rolled my shoulders, trying to dissipate the thorny vice around my muscles before it lodged there longer than necessary.

"No, I don't. Since when are you a shrink?" I tried to hide the wrath lacing my words, but failed. My clipped words sounded harsher than I intended.

Addison studied me, not impressed by my weak comeback, her gaze drilling holes into my skull as if she could read what was going on in my mind. "But hey, you don't have to be defensive with me. It's okay. I recognize the signs. Because I don't trust men. Most of them."

She shrugged, furrowed her brows, then changed the subject as if she just hadn't uncovered my innermost fears and spread them out in the open for everyone to see. The ones I thought I had done a good job of burying deep when I was a twelve-year-old boy.

"Dahlia picked this part of the Cumberland River because we used to come here a lot when we were teens."

The knots around my stomach released their deadly grip, and I forced a deep breath in.

"Fine. I'll do whatever you say. And for your information, none of this has anything to do with trust. In women. You are wrong." I glanced at her sideways, but her face stayed neutral.

Without a word, she motioned to the deserted road with her chin.

"Show me the way," I said.

I relaxed my stance, happy the conversation had been forgotten. Or put aside for now.

"There." She pointed at an old warehouse on our right that had been turned into a gym. "Turn here. We'll save a lot of time. The parking lots are all interconnected."

We raced from one empty lot to another, the SUV

bumping on the uneven pavement. In the distance, I saw the yacht. It was huge and immaculate.

Tingles lined my spine. The excitement set in, replacing every tendril of tension in my back. Tonight would be fun. I could already tell.

"Nooo," Addison screamed, snapping me out of my reverie. "The gate. Look. It's locked." She slouched in her seat and brought her hands to her face. We were at the end of the lot, where vegetation grew through the cracks of the pavement, the building on our right clearly abandoned. I parked the car and angled my upper body to face her.

"Wilde, what the fuck. I thought you knew the place. You said so. Now we're screwed."

"Yeah, it will take forever by road to get there unless—" An idea flashed through her mind because her eyes flared, and a smirk twisted her gorgeous pink-painted lips. "How do you feel about a challenge?"

I snickered. "Sweetheart, I never say no to some fun. And I love a little risk. You should be aware of it by now. What do you have in mind?"

"Trespassing. Climb over the fence, jump to the other side, reach the boat. I know it's all rusty and shit, but who cares, right?"

My eyes traveled the length of her, appreciating every curve of her body. "You're telling me you'll climb a rusted fence in that dress?" I arched a brow and waited for her answer.

"I'm a lot tougher than you think, Mister I-Refuse-To-Get-My-Hands-Dirty. I'm a Southern girl, Tuck. Nothing scares me. Stop doubting everything and follow me." She grabbed her purse and package from the backseat and exited the car with her chin high and back firmed. "Turn around. I'll go first," she said, throwing her stuff over the fence before waggling a finger. "And don't sneak a peek up my dress."

"For your information, I saw more than your panties last night. And you're barely hiding anything with that piece of fabric."

Addison let out a long breath while removing her heels, then throwing them to the other side, one after the other. "It doesn't count if you don't remember. And my dress is perfectly fine, so stop complaining."

A wolf-whistle made its way through my lips. "Not complaining, Wilde. Never. The view is enjoyable from here. You're free to parade in front of me anytime. Clothes optional."

"Shut up. And turn around."

I faced the car for a few seconds but glanced over my shoulder once she started climbing.

"Need a hand?"

"I'm all good on my own, big guy."

I pressed my lips together as my eyes admired the woman. I could stare at her toned legs all night. The girl could climb. I had to give her that. She swung a long limb over the top of the fence as if she'd done it millions of times dressed in that tiny piece of clothing, and I got a peek of her red lace panties. I-want-to-get-fucked panties. My throat went dry, and I swallowed hard, turning my head back around to focus on the hood of my rental. The last thing I needed was to get caught and be on the receiving end of her ire. Even though I doubted Addison Wilde would get mad if she caught me staring. She had to be aware of her hotness.

Still, my brain formed images of her. Of *us*. Naked, entangled. Taking her from behind. She moaning my name. Pleasuring her, my face between her thighs.

A wave of heat crashed on me.

I blew out a breath, my mind drifting to Pamela White to kill the excitement bulging down below. Yep, Jace's wife had that effect on me. Erection murderer.

"Your turn," Addison announced, quashing my racy thoughts.

Her feet hit the ground, and I rolled my sleeves, ready to join her. Something about her made me want to be close to her. For a moment, I swore under my breath, wondering how I found myself trespassing on this abandoned lot instead of already sipping drinks with my friends. I was way too old for this game. Why did I agree to go with this plan of hers? I knew it was stupid. And yet, I rolled with it like a champ. Damn it. I swept one leg over the fence, careful to not tear my pants. Grinning with satisfaction, I planted my hands on the rail, ready to swing my other leg over when I lost my footing. Instead of climbing down as I had planned to, my shirt caught on the rusty grid, and it tore open at the front on the left side. From my nipple to my waist.

Addison gasped.

I froze.

Was I topless?

5

TUCKER

"**F**ucking stupid idea," I grumbled, jumping to my feet and rubbing my hands together to remove any dirt residue. With a grimace, I pinched the ripped fabric as irritation boiled my blood. "Look at me now. I'll spend the rest of the night half-naked. Great. What a wonderful idea you had there, Wilde. Come on, if you'd wanted another glimpse of me, all you had to do was ask. I would've even given you a run for your money."

Addison ate the distance between us and burst out laughing, her laughter so warm and contagious that some of my anger dissolved, and I joined in. Yeah, I appeared ridiculous, no doubt.

"Tuck, I gotta say, you *do* look stupid. Not sure your pricey shirt can carry off this new design. Lucky you, you have pretty nipples. You could pretend you got hurdled by a flock of needy women on your way here. And they ripped your clothes off with their long fingernails. Or their teeth. People would get engrossed in such a story. Super believable. They'd all talk about it, and you'd be a hero."

I blinked. And I blinked again. She nodded, seeming

convinced by her retelling of events that had never happened. Addison Wilde was... *Jesus*... For once, I had no idea how to describe her. Some of her last words replayed in my head.

"Pretty nipples?" I had fucked my share of women and never had any of them tell me my nipples were pretty.

Addison grinned. What was wrong with her? Couldn't she share my anger instead of complimenting my freaking tits? Pecs. Geez, she was toying with my mind now. Every parcel of it.

"Wilde, keep your compliments to yourself. Because none of it changes the fact that I'm about to board a multi-million yacht looking like a cheap stripper." My hands clenched at my sides. "In case you haven't noticed, I'm particular about my clothes. I love expensive designer shit. This," I gestured to my chest, "doesn't cut it. Not at all. I'm freaking mad right now. And it's all your fault."

She moved closer, pushing her blonde ponytail over her shoulders, and grabbed my upper arms.

"How is it my fault that you miss a step? Stop blaming me for your incompetence."

I took a step toward her. "Care to repeat that?"

My chest brushed against her body, her stiffened nipples rattling the chains of my self-control. Her breaths mingled with mine. The air between us heated up. Her lips pursed. Fuck. That mouth, it did nothing to tame my hunger. My dick sprang to life. Her soft breasts pressed against my torso. The contact drove me insane. Our heart-beats synced. The glare she sent my way turned me on instead of appeasing the throbbing in my lower body. All I wished for was to claim her as mine. Here and now. Finish what we started last night. Relive the episode I couldn't recall. The one urging me in such a compulsive way I had a hard time containing it in that instant.

My heart mistook my annoyance for excitement. Yearning. Lust.

No, it wasn't desire kindling inside me. Just a primal need to get her out of my system. To kill the ache.

I pursed my lips and drew a calming breath to unknot the tension rising in my core. Her presence invaded my senses, inverting the North and South of my internal compass.

Addison, looking all feisty and alluring, sighed and rolled her eyes. I forced my desire down, clenching my fists. I had no right to feel whatever sizzled in me. I stepped back, desperate to evade her gravitational field. To avoid touching her. To prevent myself from kissing those pouty lips.

Her exasperated tone cooled my ardor. "Don't be a baby, big guy. It was an accident. And it wasn't my fault. Now, if you'd listen to me for more than ten seconds, I have a solution. Not sure you'll like it, but it's worth trying."

I frowned. So far, all her bright ideas had turned out badly. For me. Okay, for her too. Maybe. It didn't matter that she looked all adorable and innocent. Addison Wilde had a devil's side I wasn't sure I liked that much. But couldn't seem to escape. Did I really want to? My hesitation spoke volumes. I was so screwed.

She was having another one of her light bulb moments. Yeah, right. What would it be this time? She opened her sinful mouth, and I braced myself for the volley of her words. Instead of speaking, she seemed to think better of it because, without saying anything, she lifted her mysterious package from the ground and tore the plastic wrap open.

I stared at her. Waiting. My chest rose and fell quickly, my anger barely contained now. Mixed with anticipation.

The sight of her, a grin on her lips and sparkles in her eyes, acted like a balm, easing my temper.

Until she unfolded the piece of fabric she fished from the bag.

My heart stopped beating. Yes, I was pretty sure I died right there. If that was her brilliant idea, what did her shitty ones look like? Oh yeah, I already had a taste of them. My throat worked for a few seconds, air barely flowing through because I had no clue if I should burst out laughing or crying or just run for my life. I opened my mouth to say something—anything—when the most cock-sure and adorable smile spread on her face as she watched my reaction. My gag reflex engaged. It fucking did. This was a joke. I was being pranked. Again. This scrap of fabric shouldn't be allowed to be called a T-shirt. It was an insult to all the T-shirts in the world. I blinked. Once. Twice. No, it wasn't a dream. This nightmare was real.

I was right last night. Addison Wilde was a minx. She would ruin me.

Dear God. Please help me, I prayed, casting a quick glance at the sky.

I owned pink dress shirts, but that thing bore the ugliest shade of...of... I lacked the pertinent adjectives to characterize its uniqueness. Addison flicked a switch hidden in its seam, and a battery-powered sign at the back spelling "GROOM" lit up.

She. Was. Messing. With. Me.

No way could this be real.

Dirty salmon-pink, size extra-small—sure looked like it —and blinking lights.

Fuck, I'd be the butt of all jokes throughout the night.

I closed my eyes and drew a long breath, the anger inside me increasing. My blood turned to lava. Could she see the steam coming out of my ears and nostrils? Two more seconds and I'd turn into a dragon. Goddamn it.

My molars would fuse together if I didn't relax my jaw.

Taking a deep breath in, I unclenched my fists, forcing my rage to stay down. Deep inside me. Far, far away from here. No, I wouldn't explode. Now wasn't the time to unleash every swear word in my vocabulary.

"That's the package we couldn't leave without? Are you fucking with me on purpose? It's terrible. Promise me you'll never throw a bachelor party for me. Not that I'll ever get married, but still. A man can't be too prepared for something that awful. I'm crossing your name off the guest list right now. See? All done. You're uninvited to an event that won't ever occur. Ugh, that's how bad this looks."

"Tuck, Tuck, Tuck. Why are you being a brat about it? You need a shirt. I happen to hold a brand new one in my hands. Try it," she argued, not affected by the words I just spoke.

"No. There's no way I'll ever wear—this. Whatever this is," I barked, pointing to the piece of pink fluff I refused to call clothing. "I hope bare chests are allowed on the boat, sweetheart. Fuck, I'll really be looking like a stripper."

I bowed my head, inhaling and exhaling, as a new wave of ire singed my insides.

Addison folded her arms over her chest and sighed. A mix of amusement and—was that annoyance?—danced in her deep blue eyes. She shook her head and pushed the awful atrocity against my chest with more strength than necessary. My gaze lingered on her pushed-up tits for a fraction of a second before returning to her face.

The corners of her lips were pinched together, and she had a don't-bullshit-your-way-out-of-this look plastered on her gorgeous face. Damn, even her upset face did something to me. My dick stirred in my pants. *Stay put, man.*

We're not playing that field, remember? Knowing Addison was out of reach made her even more attractive. A forbidden fruit. A banned temptation.

Her irritation brought my focus back to her. And I snapped out of my perusal. Oh yeah, the stupid groom T-shirt.

Her voice, as mellow as honey, dissolved more of my anger. How could she master this trick?

"Tuck, don't be prissy about it. Just wear the damn shirt already."

I folded my arms across my chest. "Not a chance. And did you pick a toddler's size? It's so tiny. No way will I ever fit in this. My head is bigger than this dishrag."

A grin transformed Addison's face, chasing away her aggravation. "What choice do you have?" She grabbed the phone from her purse and watched the screen. "The yacht is leaving in five minutes. Either you wear this fantastic T-shirt I designed for our friends or you spend the night in torn clothes. Not that I'll complain. Told ya, your nipples look nice. Your choice. Hurry up, the clock is ticking. Tick-tock. Tick-tock. Tick-tock."

Oh, this girl. If only I had the time to fight with her right now. Get that smug grin off her face.

My dick twitched again at the thought.

I don't have the time for you, I told him in my head. *Stay out of it. Last warning. The girl isn't ours to play with. Boundaries, man.*

Addison knew she had me. I was weak around her.

My body firmed.

The tension between us soared.

We faced each other, neither of us breaking our stance.

Her tempting lips parted, and right now, damn the consequences. I would have kissed the shit out of her, bent her over the hood of my rental, and fucked her till morning. Until I could fulfill and then erase all the naughty images swimming in my head.

Addison Wilde had a way of getting under my skin.

To make me want to pull my own hair—if only I could get a grip on it.

Those ridiculously blue eyes were trained on my semi-bared chest. If they swept down, they'd be aware of how bad I had it for her right now. And how the challenge she brought into my life excited me.

I lowered my gaze to my wrecked shirt. Nothing I could do would fix it.

"Let me tell you something. You owe me big time, sweetheart. You better open a tab because, at this pace, you'll be broke by the end of the night. And I mean it. You're responsible. For all of this."

Addison tipped her chin up, never breaking eye-contact.

"Oh, already told ya, big guy. I don't scare easily. Southern girl here. Born and raised. Your big-city threat doesn't impress me much. Sorry. You'll need to do better than that to unnerve me." She glanced at her phone. "Tick. Tock. Tick-tock. What will it be, *Tuuucker*?"

The way she said my name. Slow and with a hint of arrogance. Even that made me want to bend her over. Damn Nick's rules. The guy knew what he was doing when he made me swear to keep my distance. He knew I would have a hard time resisting the temptress. That I would sell my soul for just a taste of her.

"Tick. Tock. Tick-tock."

A loud growl crossed my lips as I said, "Fine. Gimme the thing you're bold enough to call a T-shirt." I snatched it from her hands, held the sides of my torn shirt, and ripped it off me just to gauge her reaction, then slid the pink monstrosity over my head, gritting my teeth. Her cheeks flushed as she nibbled on her lower lip while pretending to be unaffected. She blinked and took a harsh breath. Once. Twice. Was she as unsettled as I was at this instant?

And I myself couldn't breathe, my attraction the root of it, but also this tasteless T-shirt I wore. It was so tight that the seams stretched as I tugged it lower.

"Happy now?"

Addison hid her victorious smirk behind her hand. "Oh Tuck, you look amazing. It was made for you. I should have got one for you in the first place. Maybe you'll let me throw you a bachelor party after all. See, I can read your mind, and my name has been put back on your guest list. Thank you for trusting me with the task of dressing you for your special day." Ignoring the glower I fired at her for the presumptuous tone, she cupped her heart with both hands. "It will be my honor. I promise to make you proud. Can't wait." She paused. "Would you mind playing model for a few hours? I'd like official shots of you sporting one of my creations. I helped ya; you help me out in return. Only fair."

She took her phone out and pointed it at me, her finger pressing the shutter button.

"Oh yes. Show me that scowl. The ladies love a handsome grump. You're hired."

A groan tumbled out of my mouth. Guttural and animalistic. Addison was playing with fire and enjoying every second of it. And the more she teased, the more I enjoyed her presence. It was a sickness. Something that poured fire into my blood. Killing my brain cells. Fucking with my existence. Addison Wilde had annihilated me. And she was having a blast doing so. "If you wanted to make sure I wouldn't get laid tonight, well, you succeeded. Congrats, sweetheart. You could've just said so. I know I'm a pretty memorable fuck. The best you'll ever get. No need to go all possessive on me now that you've had your way with me. It's sad you can't recall it, I agree. Somehow, you'll always wonder what it felt like. My dick inside you. Your screams as I pounded into you. The sound of flesh on flesh. Your rapid breathing. Toes curling. The best lay you ever had."

She gasped. And did nothing to hide the fire dancing in her eyes.

She blinked, flustered, her eyes big and her breasts swollen. *Yeah, enjoy the self-denial, woman.*

I pivoted on my heels and stalked forward. "Let's go before our friends kill us for being late. Again."

We walked in silence through the high weeds.

Addison's stare burned into my skin. I could feel it on my back the entire time.

I cocked my head to watch her, and she offered me a lopsided smile. Pride. Recognition. Longing. Emotions danced across her face. I'd never be able to stay indifferent to her charms. Agitated, I locked my ache for her. If only the pre-wedding festivities were over by now and I could book the next flight home.

For a second, I felt bad for Addison. She'd miss giving Dahlia and Nick the gift she had made for them to help me out. Selflessness filled her heart. What else could explain her actions? I mirrored the tilt of her lips, unable to cast her out.

So far, this weekend was nothing like I'd imagined. I regretted not fighting to be in charge. After all, planning a bachelor party was supposed to be the best man's job. Dahlia and Nick had insisted on organizing everything themselves. Deep down, I bet a part of them knew I would've gone overboard with it. Yeah, I couldn't blame them for opting to keep some control.

I refocused my attention before me, the yacht in full view.

Addison's glee bounced on my back, and I halted, waiting for her to get in step with me, and reached for her hand. Her fingers intertwined with mine as if we had rehearsed the small gesture many times before. Her hand fit perfectly in mine. In silence, we moved forward. Together.

"Thank you. For trusting me," she said after a beat.

How could I stay mad at her? Addison possessed a strong yet vulnerable persona. I saw the two sides of her. And the mix of both was a deadly combination. I could imagine people turning their entire world upside down to catch a glint of happiness in her features. To follow her anywhere. To bask in her contagious energy. Because a part of me felt this way.

What was her ex thinking when he slept around and broke her heart? This woman, no matter how bad I tried to portray her, was kindness personified. Sure, she was crazy, and her ideas were atrocious—she really believed they were awesome even when they made absolutely no sense—but still, she had an endearing personality and a challenging spirit. That I could tell. Because, despite myself and my best friend's warning, she had sucked me into the vibrant vortex that defined her.

"Tell me, you really designed this?" I asked, still flabbergasted that I agreed to wear the T-shirt, but trying to go back to the friendly relationship we'd shared earlier.

She shrugged. "Yeah. I design the T-shirts I sell online. For fun. I'm a graphic designer. I usually do dealership banners and ads. But designing fun logos and stuff has always been a passion of mine. I've been doing Carter's merch for years now. Anyway, I lied to you. I should have ordered the T-shirts weeks ago, but with everything going on, I kinda forgot and ordered them yesterday as a rush shipment. Sorry it's boring."

I stopped in my tracks. "Are you fucking with me again?"

Addison released my hand and kept walking. I circled her wrist with my fingers to force her to stop. She spun to face me. "No. Why would I?" Even her irises were shitty liars. A flashback of the vulnerability I saw on her face this morning came back to me. When she confided about her ex and how he screwed with her heart.

It was my turn to shrug. "It's cool. The T-shirt isn't that bad. The color is enough to give me acne, and the size hasn't been thought through to fit an adult male, but other than that, I think it's pretty original. You're talented. I can tell. I had no idea you were behind Carter Hills's logo and merch. That's incredible."

Addison tipped her head forward. Was that a flush on her cheeks? "Thanks," she muttered. Was I making her shy? I thought shyness wasn't in her vocabulary.

The easy conversation and confidences we shared warmed a layer of my icy heart.

Hand in hand and feeling somehow closer to her, we resumed our walk.

She offered me a squeeze of her hand and a tight-lipped smile, her gaze filled with a hint of empathy. Or tenderness. A sign she was there with me and would have my back. Those details were not lost on me.

She put her heels back on just when we approached the yacht.

A fresh burst of energy jolted her, and she hurried forward, tugging my hand.

From up close, the motor yacht was magnificent. About sixty feet long, it had an open deck above the hull and single level living quarters below, giving a panoramic view of the river from all sides. We stepped inside the salon, and I was taken aback by the luxury it projected, with white walls and wooden trims and flooring and ornate decor. A table big enough to seat over twenty people had been set up in the middle of the salon, which led to the galley on the left and a navigation station on the right.

After a crew member welcomed us aboard, he motioned us toward the staircase leading to the upper deck. My hand rested on Addison's lower back the entire time as I climbed after her. Open-air, the deck was lined with dark plank wooden floors and white leather seats. The warm breeze swept our faces as we reached the last step. People mingled, holding their glasses, dressed to the nines.

All conversations stopped the moment our feet landed on the deck.

Eyeballs rolled in our direction.

Laughter replaced the chatter.

"Oohs" and "Ahhs" blasted into my ears.

I dragged a hand over my face. Great. Now I'd be the topic of stupid jokes all night.

The temporary peace that had settled between Addison and me vanished when I caught the twinkle in her eyes. Now we were back to each man—or woman—to themselves. And our banter would resume. Gone was the compassion from her features. She looked highly amused at the commotion our entrance created.

I breathed in, trying to keep the new batch of irritation swirling inside me under wraps.

Yearning and frustration blended together. With my eyes throwing daggers at the woman who had dressed me like a blind toddler, I steeled my back and upped my chin. "Showtime, I guess," I muttered under my breath.

"Ohmygod, Tucker. What happened to ya? You know Nick is the groom, right? Are you trying to tell us something?" Dahlia teased, her eyes glinting and mouth twisting with repressed mirth. "In case you didn't get the memo, I'm not marrying you. Sorry. Anyway, you look... Well, you look charming."

Dahlia was as much a bad liar as her best friend. I resisted the urge to poke my tongue out at her and strangle Addison at the same time. Perhaps that sounded a bit excessive.

Inside, I cringed. *Charming.* What the actual fuck! Nothing about the way I dressed was charming. I looked stupid. More than stupid. Ludicrous.

I forced a smile to my lips and met Dahlia's entertained demeanor.

"Great. I'm glad you think it's a good look on me because guess what? You get to wear one too. We'll match tonight, you and I." The humor vanished from her eyes. "That's right. Wilde got them for you and Nick. But since I ripped my shirt and didn't have time to change, I was the lucky SOB who got to wear the groom's. You're the bride-to-be, so do the math in your head, sunshine. We'll rock the town together later."

Nick joined us, sparks in his eyes, barely able to contain his laughter. *Fucker.* He clapped my shoulder, and I groaned, jerking away from his touch. "Sorry, man. No way you're playing bride and groom with my future wife. She isn't wearing hers." He focused his attention on the maid of honor, still standing tall beside me. "Did you make those?" She nodded, a large smile showing her pearly whites, pride undulating from her. "I knew you'd make something. They look amazing. I'm super impressed. Sorry it ended up on this loser."

Addison sighed and waved her hand. "Yeah. The worst part is that he can't even appreciate the art and creativity behind it."

"I agreed they were originals," I protested, none of them paying an ounce of attention to me.

Nick continued as if I'd said nothing, "That's a shame. I'd wear mine with pride, girl." Why did he have to be so non-embarrassed about everything? My best friend had become the biggest no-spine doormat since he fell in love. His expression almost had me convinced he regretted not being the one wearing the stupid shirt.

And now I had the certitude he wouldn't help me save face or find a solution to my wardrobe malfunction. The only person who could have had my back tonight had turned on me. Unapologetic.

I rubbed the back of my neck, trying to come up with a smart idea to fix my dressing problem on my own. Surrounded by people who acted as if I couldn't hear them mocking my look shamelessly, I massaged my temples and pondered my options.

"Come on, guys, be serious. I can't be the only one wearing this," I said, motioning to my chest with a hand, a sad expression taking over my face. Would they fall for it? I tried to pinch the cotton, but it was so tight I couldn't even get a grip. "I look ridiculous. This is supposed to be a couple outfit, not a lonely-groom kinda thing."

Carter sauntered our way, laughing so loud that he had to use his fist to wipe the teary corners of his eyes. Great. Another witness to my humiliation.

Amongst all the people present, he was the only one I could trade clothes with. He had about an inch over me, but my shoulders were broader.

"I must say, Addi, you surpassed yourself this time. When you told me you had a little special something for tonight, never would I have imagined it to be so damn spectacular." They high-fived, and smoke came out of my nose. Again "And I'm pretty sure it looks even better on

Tucker here." He faced me. "Man, you look like you're dressed in a ten-year-old's T-shirt. Kudos to you for agreeing to wear it." He extended his fist to bump mine, but I ignored it.

"At least on the real groom-to-be, it wouldn't have been so stretched. You wouldn't have a spare shirt in your truck by accident? One I could borrow for the night?"

"Sorry. All I have are smelly gym clothes." He offered me a rueful smile and brought his glass to his lips. Fucking great. This night was anything but fine. And it had just begun.

Dahlia and Addison moved to either side of me. "Babe, can you take a picture?" the bride-to-be asked my best friend. "I want to immortalize this moment forever. C'mon, Addi, get closer. It will go in our wedding album. Tuck, if hedge-fund banking doesn't work for you anymore one day, modeling should be at the top of your list while applying for a new job."

I fake-grinned as Nick snapped a picture, his lips still stretched to his ears.

Anger seethed stronger in my bloodstream.

"Okay, stop. All of you. I need a bride. ASAP. Anyone. Find me a woman. Someone single. No way am I going to a bar later dressed like this on my own. It's supposed to be a bachelor party. Not a make-fun-of-Tucker night. I can embrace this T-shirt while we're here and give you some-thing to talk about, but later I want an out. Think, people. Fast. Find me a fake bride, so I don't look like a stood-up groom who lost a bet."

Addison scrunched up her face and said, "Fine. I'll wear the other one. Are you happy now, Tucker baby? Geez. Where's your sense of humor?" She pushed the top of her dress down, not a care in the world that people could see her in a strapless, lacy red bra. The lace offered me a perfect view of her pink nipples, while she bunched her outfit around her waist. Fuck me already. My body reacted, recalling the events I couldn't. My skin over-heated. My dick swelled. Eye-fucking me, she slid her arms into the matching T-shirt and adjusted it over her mesmer-izing tits. Now that I got a glance, I'd never be able to unsee them. My mouth watered at the image of her round globes. Jesus, even that shirt looked bewitching on her. Her little act achieved what she wanted. She'd baited and hooked me, acting all innocent. Nick elbowed me in the ribs, offering me a drink, and it broke the spell I was under. The alcohol lined my throat and returned some moisture to my dry throat. My reaction to Addison undressing here was nothing short of fierce. The sting of jealousy surprised me. All these people had a front-row seat to the show and had peeked at what wasn't theirs to admire. Not that I had more right. Still. Somehow, it felt like I did.

"Stop ogling her like she's a piece of meat. Care to tell me what happened to your shirt?" Nick teased.

I sighed, downed the rest of my drink, and explained everything. Leaving out the parts where I'd daydreamed about ravaging her pussy while bending her over the hood of my rental.

From across the room, Addison watched me, sipping on a martini, eating olives from a pick, another vision hardening my dick. Was she playing with my sanity on purpose? Was she toying with me, knowing she was out of reach? Why did I fuck the devil last night? Now I was attuned to everything about her. Her smile. Her lips. Her rack. Her hips. Her legs. Fuck Nick. Why did I agree to stay away? I needed to bang that girl out of my system—and remember it. Once and for all.

Rule number one sucked. Big time. I couldn't wait for this wedding to be over to get my hands on the maid of honor. Then the rules would be outdated. Just a little over one month to go. I could live with that. At the pace she was infuriating me, sex with Addison Wilde wouldn't be soft. It would be animalistic. Yeah, I'd make up for all the times she got me tangled. I would ascertain the memory of my tongue between her legs haunted her forever. In the most excruciating flashbacks.

I'd bury myself so deep she'd never be able to not remember how good I felt between her legs.

Staking my claim, I stared back, my irises swallowing her whole. A chill ran through her. Even from the distance separating us, I saw it ripple the length of her. Her pulse ricocheted at the base of her throat. The games had just upped. And the reward would be so well-deserved and satisfying. I trembled at the thought. My lower-self hardened at the picture I painted in my mind.

"By week six, you'll beg me to end you, sweetheart," I mouthed behind my hand as I brought the tumbler to my lips.

And for the first time in months, I felt like my old self again. Alive and ready for the chase.

6

ADDISON

No matter what I did, I couldn't detach my eyes from Tucker's perfect torso. The shirt left nothing to the imagination. My mouth watered at all the things I wished I could do to him with only my tongue. *Stop, Addi. Get some control back. No men. You don't love them anymore. You. Are. Over. Them.*

Ignoring the heat in his stare, I resumed my conversation with a group of women. We talked about plans for tonight once the yacht brought us back to the shore. No matter how much I refused to give him any attention, I couldn't help the way my body reacted to him. It was aware of his presence. It felt him everywhere. Even from a distance. That had never happened before. With a palm splayed over my breastbone, I urged my pulse to hush. To stay indifferent and in control.

Mid-dinner, I cornered Tucker as he went to the restroom. It seemed like it had become a new thing between us. Me following him to the men's room. Right now, I was a bit tipsy on wine and cocktails, ready for the party to start later. Dinner was great, but I couldn't wait to hit the town.

"How is it going, *Groom*?" I asked, giving him my most flirty smile, batting my lashes as fast as I could. Booze helped me forget about my new no-men resolution.

"Wilde, you gotta stay away from me. Every time you're around, I get into trouble."

I dragged a fingernail across his chest and felt the shivers running through him. His nipples hardened. And so did his dick. His clothes did nothing to hide the effect I had on him. And I relished every second of it.

"Go, find yourself a woman, and I'll do the same. Not playing with you tonight. I promised I wouldn't. And I'm a man of my word. Bait someone else."

"Tsk-tsk. Don't be so boring, Tuck. We're bride and groom tonight, remember? And I'm sure Nick and Dahlia's rules don't apply in this case. We're gonna pretend we're madly in love. Isn't this what it's all about? You asked for a fiancée. Don't make me regret playing the part. A little fun never hurt anybody. Did you already forget what we did last night?" His throat worked. I had him exactly where I wanted. Men were the weak species. All of them. Nothing equaled the thrill coursing through my veins when they surrendered their power to the simple promise of a good time between the sheets. Tucker stepped back, putting some distance between us, his eyes luring me in even though his words told me otherwise.

"Anyway, I'm just here to tell you it's speech time and after that, we're splitting up. I'll miss my groom. Will you miss your bride?" I asked with puppy dog eyes.

He flinched but recovered quickly.

Shaking his head, he adjusted the crotch of his pants, not even being subtle about it.

"You're playing with fire, sweetheart. Soon you'll get

burned. Never say I didn't warn you." He released his junk and pushed past me, going back to where our friends were, still seated at the table. I breathed out. No idea why I did that. Something about Tucker made me want to be bad or brave. To test his limits. And see if I could break him. Now that all my doubts had vanished, I knew I had as much effect on him as he had on me. This pre-wedding weekend was pure torture. Men were my addiction. Always had been. I had to learn to live without one around. To be on my own. To break the heartbreak circle once and for all. Tucker was out of reach. And lethal. My best friend was right when she had served him a warning. He owned enough power to hurt me if he got too close. The zing we shared couldn't be faked. If we yielded to the temptation of our sizzling attraction, reality would haunt me once the sheets turned cold. One-nighters weren't my thing, but Tucker made me want to get out of my comfort zone and seize new opportunities.

Two hours later, some of us were cramped up in a limousine. Half the party had left to go to an underground bar owned by a friend of Carter, while the other half drove around town, bubbly pink drinks in hand, our bodies half out the panoramic sunroof of the vehicle.

Dahlia snaked her arm through mine, her head resting on my shoulder. "Because I was pregnant and everything went down so fast, I didn't have all this the first time," she said, gesturing around her. "Thanks for doing this with me. It means the world. I love ya, girlfriend."

I caressed her hair and caught the lone tear tracing her cheek. "I love you too. Are you okay?"

She slurred a little, but her level of intoxication was far less than mine. She huffed and smiled, the glossiness in her eyes quickly switching to happier memories.

"I am. For a while, I never thought I'd be smiling again.

Nick makes me happy, and my knees weaken whenever he's around. He's mine. I love him so much. We're two halves of the same heart. Even rain is exhilarating when he's there. He's my person. My soulmate. I want that for you too. You deserve this. Love. Butterflies. The whole package."

I pressed my head against hers. "Dah, I want it too. But I just never meet the right one. I'm tired of being used by my lovers. Starting to feel like I'm replaceable, like I don't mean as much to them as they mean to me. To trust them with my whole heart when they couldn't care less about protecting or cherishing it. They always deceive me in the end."

"Were you serious when you told me you were done with them, though?" Dahlia cocked her head to look at me.

I shrugged. "Yes. No. I don't know. I'm just scared to put my heart out there again. Guess we'll see."

"What did you do last night?"

I could read the worry in her gaze. My best friend really cared. And I loved her so much for always having my back and never judging my actions.

I avoided her eyes for a second, then shook my head.

"Do you think I could've inherited my father's gene… you know…the one?"

"Do you see any similarities?" she asked.

"Not really. Every time I'm down, it crosses my mind. My last relationship wasn't marriage material. I know it now. But it really shattered me when it ended. Made me doubt myself. And that propelled me into this spiral of anger and sadness. The idea of love—never mind, it's stupid."

"Addi, it's not. It's normal to wonder. I would too. Wanna talk about it?" she asked.

"Nah. Tonight is your night." I breathed in, ready to

change the subject. "What about that karaoke bar we used to go to? I haven't been there in ages. Do you feel like owning the stage for a few hours?"

Dahlia's contagious energy returned as if I'd just shot her with a dose of adrenaline. Drunk Dahlia was easy to convince and was always ready for some fun. Any other time, I would have helped to plan tonight's events, or I would've even organized the entire thing myself. I always reveled in coordinating events for my friends. But she was right when she said my latest breakup had affected me. For the last three weeks, I hadn't been feeling like myself. Sure, I was bummed about being single once again. But more than that, I was hurt. Hurt that someone I believed I loved not only cheated on me, but also gambled with my trust. Now I knew our relationship was not meant to survive the test of time, but still, I had respected him once. We were friends. Or I thought we were. Until it all blew up in my face.

"Addi, I looooove that bar," Dahlia singsonged the words, breaking my train of depressing thoughts, and squeezed my arm tighter. "I wanna sing something with you. Like we used to. Let's ask the rest of the party to meet us there. It'll be fun."

I dropped down and reached for the phone in my purse and messaged Tucker. He was the groomsman, so I figured he had to be the one making the calls. Sorta.

Me: Hey groom of mine.

He answered almost instantly.

Tucker: Wilde. What's up? Miss me already?

Me: Karaoke. You. Us. Ask Cart, he knows where. Thirty minutes. You in?

Tucker: With ya? Not sure. It sounds dangerous. For me.

Me: Always. But you love how much more fun your life gets when I'm in it.

He didn't answer for a whole minute. I was about to message him again when his reply came through. One simple word.

Tucker: Okay.

Me: Don't be late.

"All set," I said to my best friend, returning to my position next to her. "They'll meet us in half an hour. Let's go."

————

The song ended, and the two women who had taken the stage climbed down and disappeared into the crowd. The dive bar was just how I remembered it. Dark, not so clean, and filled with people only there to have the best time. No one here took themselves seriously. And I liked that about our little local hangout spot.

"Listen, all y'all. We have a bride and groom here with us tonight," some guy announced through a microphone. People cheered and applauded. "Let's give a warm welcome to the future newlyweds. Please come up on stage. We have something for ya." Damn it. The last thing we needed was to grab people's attention.

As if her thoughts mirrored mine, Dahlia's fingernails dug into my forearm as her voice became strained with tension. "Addi, I'm not going. How did they know we were here? There's a difference between singing something with you while people are busy chatting and drinking and being up there for everyone to stare at. What if people recognize me? Not that it matters, but I don't want them to recognize Cart, or he'll feel obligated to sing and might leave so that we can enjoy the night without being bothered. You gotta go, Addi. You and Tuck. Pretend you're us. Please. You're wearing the bride and groom T-shirts. No one will suspect you're faking it."

Next to her, Nick nodded. "She's right. I know people in Nashville usually let famous people be and stuff, but are we willing to take the risk and have them come here just because Carter is hanging out with us tonight? And hassle him for autographs and pictures?"

Dahlia and I both shook our heads.

"We all agree," he said. "What's the plan?"

"Sorry, babe," Dahlia said to him as she wrapped her arms around his torso.

He pushed a strand of her hair, gently smiling. "It's okay. I know the drill. That's what happens when I'm about to marry a superstar. I love you. Don't worry."

He kissed her, and I averted my eyes as Tucker grumbled on my left.

Carter moved closer. "Guys, it's fine. I'll sit in a dark corner if it gets too much. I'll just—"

"No, Cart, you're allowed to enjoy the night too. Dahlia and Nick are right. Tuck and I will go up there. I'm sure it's just a silly game they want us to play or a how-well-do-you-know-your-spouse kinda stuff. Nothing we can't survive."

A deep frown carved my *groom's* forehead as he heard

the plan. "Fuck no. Not becoming your circus monkey again, Wilde. Forget it. Been humiliated enough for the rest of my life tonight. I must have been asked to smile for two hundred pictures by now. My face will be all over social media. If it isn't already. Find other people to play a happy couple with." He folded his arms across his broad chest, every single muscle of his defined arms bulging. That T-shirt would be ripped sooner than later. Yeah, Tucker Philips was tall and well-built, and it still didn't add up in my head he was a hedge-fund banker. My fingers itched to trace the planes of his abs, my mouth longing to kiss his pouty lips and to feel his hard body wrapped all around me. I didn't have any leftover recollections of our time together to hold on to. And now my mind felt obligated to compensate. To make up dirty scenarios. Each time, I wondered if they were fantasies or repressed memories.

"Why do you always have to be such a baby about everything? I thought you liked challenges?" I asked, locking my eyes with his. Something passed between us. I had no idea how to describe it. Electricity buzzed on my skin. And I got drunk on his smoldering stare. My stomach tightened. My knees wobbled. No, even though he symbolized all my weaknesses in one man, I wouldn't get all hot and bothered for Tucker 'Player' Philips. I'd resist his charm. I'd resist *him*. I was a strong and confident woman. And men were so twentieth century.

"C'mon up, people. Don't be shy," the guy on the microphone said. "Ladies and gentlemen, please give a round of applause for the bride and groom."

Beside us, a man pushed Tucker and me forward. "Don't be pussies." He pointed at us over my head because, well, Tucker was too tall, and yelled, "They're here." No way could we hide wearing T-shirts with lights flashing on our backs. Nobody would ever believe we weren't the future Mr. and Mrs. Whatever.

"Wilde, you'll pay for this. Count my words," Tucker threatened me with gritted teeth, his jaw flexing. He firmed his back and followed me to the front of the bar. Ire radiated from him. And in some crazy ways, it turned me on even more. Genetic or not, I had a sickness in me. Or I was more fucked-up than I thought.

People wolf-whistled as we took the stage. Tucker's eyes were like machine guns, ready to shoot me dead. A rush of excitement swirled through me at the heat he cast on me. One I refused to escape.

"Nice shirt," a man yelled from the crowd. My *groom's* eyes narrowed to slits. He puffed his chest, ready to attack, stretching the taut fabric over his torso. I crossed my fingers, hoping it wouldn't tear apart. Carter was right. Tucker looked like he'd dressed in the kids' section of a store.

I touched his forearm, silently begging him to let it go. He relaxed under my palm, the tension in him evaporating.

Our hands linked together, and I hoped I could infuse him with some courage for standing here in front of all these patrons. With me.

The guy with the mike neared us, and my *groom* tensed again. "We have something special for the happy couple tonight. First, let's ask the future Mrs. Bride to sit," he said, pulling a wooden chair in the middle of the stage. I avoided looking at Tucker, knowing how upset he would be right now. Once seated, I forced the biggest smile over my lips and crossed my legs at the ankles and linked my hands together on my lap. Very prim and proper. Things were about to get interesting. I could feel every molecule of excitement in the air surrounding us.

"Now, Mr. Groom, you gotta pick a song for your future wife. Let's see your options." A list of songs appeared on the screen behind the stage. Tucker clenched his hands at his sides, his knuckles turning white. Even pissed and out of his comfort zone, he looked adorable. His eyes narrowed. He scanned the room as if trying to come up with an out. I bet he was.

My *groom* was cocky and sure of himself to a fault, but I doubted he ever volunteered to humiliate himself in front of a cheering crowd. Always dressed to impress, no doubt tonight was making him very uncomfortable. Naked and vulnerable. And I was the one to blame for every decision. My heart wrenched at his predicament and admired his fortitude to stand by me. From the moment we met, he had followed me in all my crazy ideas, and here we were. Tucker walking beside me on the stage. Ready to make a fool of himself. For me.

Standing close to me on my left, he swallowed and raked a hand through his short hair. I could almost see the sweat blooming on his nape from my spot, his skin glistening under the golden lights like tiny diamonds. He cracked his neck, and our eyes met. My smile vanished. He stole all the air from my lungs. A series of knots tightened my stomach as his uneasiness washed through me. Why were we so in sync all the time?

Studying my face a little longer, he picked a song, and the man announced, "You'll sing for her, man. With all your heart. You'll have the lyrics on that screen, just in case. C'mon, show us how much you love your woman. Give it your all. Show her how much you adore her. This is your chance. Rock her world." The man clapped Tucker's shoulder and handed him the mike. My *groom* turned to face me in the slowest slow-motion movement I'd ever witnessed, all colors draining from his face now. He shook his head and murdered me on the spot with his heavy, threatening gaze. I yelped but forced myself to look unaffected. Inside, my blood sizzled, and flutters partied around.

"Not doing this, Wilde. I'm dressed for Halloween, and I can't sing for shit. No way am I doing this in front of all these crazy folks. Forget it. I'm outta here," he said, just loud enough so only I could hear him.

I stretched my arm to graze his fingers. "Hey, look at me. We're doing this. Together. It's only me. We're alone. It's all pretend. Nobody is listening. We're just fooling around. Another little challenge between us. I'm right here, okay? We've got this."

He exhaled, his face twisting as if in pain.

"I'll owe you one later. Do this for Nick and Dahlia, okay? I'm with you. I'm not going away."

The music started playing, and a cheer resonated through the room as the crowd went silent. No doubt it was my best friend, worrying about us up here. I could feel her eyes on us. *We can do this,* I repeated in my head.

"You okay?" I asked.

He nodded. His Adam's apple bounced in his throat.

Once again, he would go through a situation he disliked. For me. With me. And it meant a lot. Because he trusted me.

He rolled his lips over his teeth, staring at me with something I didn't recognize.

"Take one for the team, big guy." A wave of fierceness had my body shaking with need.

Tucker shut his eyes for a few seconds, forced his shoulders back, and brought the microphone to his mouth, his jaw so tight that I feared he'd grind his teeth to dust.

His eyes snapped open as the first words left his lips. He had chosen a Carter Hills original. How ironic. The crowd started singing along with him. Everybody knew this country song. It was one of Carter's biggest hits as a solo artist. No doubt my friends were the ones behind the chorus. Their voices buried Tucker's. But still, all I could hear was him. Everything I could see began and ended with him. His eyes were transfixed on me. Kindling my body with awareness.

He relaxed his stance. The tension in his back left. He had played his role. Now there were devilish sparks shining in his irises. He kneeled before me, grabbed my hand, and sang as if we were alone in the crowded bar.

My breath caught in my lungs. Every cell in me danced to his voice. Heat pooled between my thighs. My nipples tingled under the intensity of his smoldering stare as he undressed me with his gaze.

For a moment, I forgot this was all fake.

It looked so real. Felt so real. Enough to turn me into a blazing inferno.

The way Tucker intertwined his fingers through mine. The way he ate me up with his stare as if I were his. The way he held my gaze hostage as my heart jackhammered in my chest.

I had never been on the receiving end of so much ardor. And my heart frizzled behind my ribs. How could any of this be fake?

> **...And when you need a hug,**
> **my arms will hold you**
> **tight**
> **A girl like you belongs with a**
> **guy like me...**

The song ended, and people applauded. We stood still. As if time had stopped. And everyone around us had vanished. Air rushed in and out of my lungs. Why was I panting?

A crooked smile slowly appeared on Tucker's face.

The beating of my heart hastened.

The uplift of his lips reflected mine.

My *groom* used the back of his hand to wipe his forehead and sighed. "Wilde, how did I do? Tell me I didn't make a fool of myself. Tell me you believed it?"

I tightened my grip on the fingers still laced through mine. *Believed it?* A part of me still had a hard time grasping it wasn't real.

"Are you kidding? You were perfect." Adrenaline pumped inside me, the rush addictive.

"Kiss him already," someone yelled from behind us.

"Kiss him. Kiss him. Kiss him," the crowd chanted.

We'd go to hell for this.

I didn't care.

Right here and now, all I craved was kissing the man who'd just sung to me the most romantic song ever. Because my head, and my heart, still hadn't comprehended it was fake. That I didn't mean any of this to him.

Without wasting a single second, I wrapped my arms around Tucker's neck and pulled him close. We fixated our gazes on each other, my breathing shallow and my heart thumping. So fast I was certain he could feel it. "Just kiss me," I pleaded.

Without holding back, his mouth crashed on mine, robbing me of all the oxygen molecules. Goosebumps bloomed on my nape. Lightning ignited my being. And my soul. And together, we caught fire.

Tucker devoured my lips as if we were still alone here. Tongues dancing. Hands grabbing. Hips grinding. Nothing chaste or meant to be witnessed by others. A bruising kiss that had my toes curling and me panting, aroused.

In that instant, I belonged to him.

He sucked my tongue deeper in his mouth while his hands grabbed a handful of my ass. I purred at the friction of his swollen sex between my legs, begging to be acknowledged. Every swipe of his tongue branded my body. Each cell thrummed with the force of the desire he aroused in me. Tucker was staking his claim.

My fingernails dug into his biceps, requiring his solidity to stay grounded in this world.

"Fuck, Wilde, you taste good."

Unquenchable thirst brimmed in his gaze as he plunged forward and lifted me into his arms, my legs winding around his midriff. He kept a hand over my backside to prevent me from flashing my panties to the patrons.

I held on to him, hypnotized by the pull he had on me. We stared into each other's depths, and like a beacon drawing me in, I slipped my tongue back between his hungry lips, attacking his mouth.

He groaned, meeting me thrust for thrust, tasting every corner of my mouth.

He fisted my hair and arched my head, deepening our connection. I lost the ability to breathe on my own, Tucker being the only source of air I required to survive.

Spellbound in our own world, in the frenzied beating of our hearts and the intimate moment we shared, I relished his tongue against mine and the heat of his erection nestling where it ignited my core.

A symphony began in my chest, and Tucker became the maestro playing with the strings of my desire.

The dark clouds hovering over me for weeks parted. Life didn't feel so flavorless anymore.

I felt more alive in his embrace than I did with any other man before.

Tucker's strong hand curled around my nape, holding

me in place as he kissed me some more. His lips, shaped to mine, injected me with something potent and dizzying. I felt wanted and important. Understood and desired.

Last night must have been incredible.

Shivers spread all over my skin at the thought of the events I couldn't even remember.

Our bodies spoke the same language like a well-rehearsed choreography. If right now was any indication of how well we danced together, Tucker and I were a force to be reckoned with. Something great and powerful.

My heart pinched at the realization that I'd never experience the first time with him ever again. That I would never have a chance to know how wonderful it must have been to be loved by him for a night. To be the center of his universe. Even for just a couple of hours.

When Tucker lowered me back to my feet, we were both breathless, intoxicated, watching each other with barely contained lust. My face felt flushed, my lips sensitive and raw, my breasts plumper. Little knots lingered in my stomach. A sirocco swirled inside me.

The man who called us onstage guided us toward the stairs leading down.

More applauses and wolf-whistles.

How long had we lost track of time? My finger traced my lips, reminiscing about the kiss that tipped my world off its axis. It made me believe I could be loved. And cherished. One day. That I could feel the same pull with someone else in the future.

My *groom* tugged at my hand and led me offstage.

I breathed easier now that all eyes weren't on us anymore.

People clapped our shoulders as we walked past them. Others congratulated us. Still surfing a cloud of bliss, I had a hard time differentiating reality from fiction. I offered them nods and smiles, sure I had the latter engraved on my face forever.

"Oh my god, this was amazing. You guys killed it up there. Here," Dahlia pushed a shot glass into our hands as soon as we joined them, "drink this." We chugged them before she offered us another one. "Thank you for filling in for us. You were incredible. No way could anyone have suspected you weren't getting married. It looked so real. Even I believed it for a moment. I felt like a voyeur watching a love story unfold before my eyes. It was epic."

The server came to us with a bottle of tequila. "On the house. For the future Mr. and Mrs. You guys rocked. Enjoy."

My friend pointed two fingers toward her eyes and then twisted them in Tucker's direction as if to say, "I'm watching you."

I yanked her hand down. "Stop, Dah. This is silly. We were just pretending. Give the guy a break."

Tucker's chuckle at my friend's not-so-subtle threat warmed my insides.

"She asked for it," he said with a wide smirk, showing off his pearly whites. And not one ounce of shame. "I serviced her like she begged me to. Dah, you should thank me for taking care of her needs. Happy to oblige."

I shrugged. "How could I not? It was hot." I fanned myself to amplify my words.

Tucker winked at me. "Anytime, sweetheart."

"Ohmygod, your ego, big guy," I said.

He leaned forward and pressed a kiss to my cheek.

My body still hadn't comprehended none of this was real because a fresh wave of flutters took over my stomach. My fingers itched to intertwine with his. To anchor myself to him.

"You guys. I swear this is a déjà vu. I have dreamed of

this scenario. You two teaming together and creating chaos," Nick chimed in, nearing us, unable to hide his amusement. He spun to face Tucker. "Like you would ever listen to my warnings. I should've known better." He shook his head, his smile reaching both ears. "I thought you would swallow her up there. Are you—" The surrounding noises drowned out his words, and I missed the rest of their conversation.

Dahlia took me to the side. "Addi, you didn't have to put on that much of a show. I'm sorry you felt like you had to. But, wow, we could feel the heat even from here."

I shrugged, hoping my flushed face wouldn't betray me. "No worries. Tucker spoke the truth. I asked for it. How could I not want him to? Have you seen him up there? Even if it was all fake, butterflies danced in my belly."

"Girlfriend, you'd tell me if it meant something more, right?"

I nodded.

"Are you okay?" she inquired.

"Yes. I am. The guy is handsome, and he sang to me. It was a onetime deal. Anyway, let me say this: Tucker Philips can kiss."

"That good?" She wiggled her brows.

"Yep. How about some tequila?" I asked, trying to change the subject. Fast. Before I exposed my inner thoughts.

"Come on," Dahlia said, her arm snaking through mine. "Let's drink to your performance. Or rather, Tuck's performance. And then we'll sing something together. Just like old times."

It was four in the morning when we came back to the hotel, all looking like we'd been up for days. Dahlia's hair was a tangled jumble; no doubt mine was too. She had mascara stains under her eyes. The last time I checked, I did too. Our lipstick had been gone for hours. And our heels hung from our fingers as we shuffled to our rooms.

My best friend leaned in and kissed my cheek. "Night, Addi. Thanks for everything. You are amazing. I'll remember tonight forever. I love ya."

I squeezed her arm. "I love you too. See ya later."

Nick kissed my cheek and hugged Tucker before leading his woman away.

In the hallway, I watched them exchange tired smiles, in love with each other.

My heart bled in my chest. Why couldn't I be the one stupidly in love for once?

Dahlia deserved her happiness. She'd been through so much. But somewhere deep inside me, I prayed for the same thing. To feel something close to how I felt on that stage earlier. Someone's most precious person.

I nodded before returning my gaze to the lovers moving to their suite.

Melancholy filled me and I sealed my lids, refraining from crying, too tired to sort things out in my head.

"Wilde, are you sleeping on your feet?" Tucker asked from beside me. "If you are, it's kinda disturbing. Just a thought."

I opened my eyes and poked my tongue out, offering him an excuse I hoped he wouldn't challenge. "I forgot you were still here. Got lost in my head. I'm so tired. I'm sure I could sleep upright if I had to. You did great tonight. And you can keep the shirt; it suits you. My best man gift to ya. Good night."

Tucker eyed me with an expression I couldn't decipher for a second but added nothing. I melted from the heat in his stare. My heart lurched in my throat. His brows furrowed as he gave me a once-over before shaking his head and sauntering away, his shoulders dropping and hands tucked in his pockets. The white lights blinking at the back of his T-shirt was the last sight of him as he turned the corner, and I found myself alone in the hotel hallway.

Forcing my gaze away from the direction he left, I resumed my breathing and fumbled with the keycard.

Once in the safety of my room, I backed against the closed door. Exhaustion and alcohol made it harder for me to order my thoughts. And my feelings.

The kiss Tucker and I shared had been replaying in my head since the moment we broke apart on that stage. And hours later, I still believed it was as real and breathtaking as it could get. Letting the attraction we both couldn't seem to escape affect my judgment wasn't an option. Or I'd be in trouble.

Resolved to move past tonight's episode, I shut my thoughts, ready to crash into bed and for the weekend to be over.

The sound of a soft knock behind me rebooted my lethargic brain. I spun on my heels, and using the wall as a support, I cracked the door open.

My heart leaped in my chest when I spotted Tucker standing on the other side of the ajar door.

His hand rubbed his nape, and he looked unsteady on his feet as he said, "Wilde, lost my card. It was in my shirt. I think. The one that got ripped apart." He paused and rubbed his eyelids with the heels of his hands. "Can I sleep in your room? Please help a guy out. I'll take the sofa. Let me lie down. Before I crumple."

My eyes found his exhausted ones. He was a breath away from collapsing.

"Yeah. Sure. Okay."

I let him in, and his hand connected with my lower back as he kissed my cheek, shooting warmth through me. "Thanks."

He walked past me, and I followed him with my eyes, missing his comforting touch.

Without even taking the time to undress, Tucker crossed the room and fell face-first on the cushioned piece of furniture.

To remove what used to be makeup off my face, I took a quick shower and padded back into the room, dressed in a nightshirt. No way would I sleep naked with Tucker around.

Ready to escape into my dreams, I slid under the pillowy comforter of my bed. But sleep evaded, even when it tempted me. I tossed. Then I turned. And counted sheep. I drilled my fingers into my ears, trying to tune everything out. Nah. Not happening. No matter how tired I was, this didn't do the trick. Tucker's snoring was all I could hear. It sounded like an old truck's muffler. I cursed under my breath as I left the cocoon of the bed and neared him. With my finger, I nudged his arm.

"Wake up, big guy. You snore. Real bad. Turn around or something. I gotta sleep too. Please."

He groaned but didn't budge.

I balled my hands.

Why did I agree to let him sleep here? Such a bad idea. Whichever way I spun it around in my head, it didn't sound better.

"C'mon, Tuck. Move," I said, shaking him with both hands now. He tilted his head, already gone so far away from here, his eyelids heavy with sleep. He almost fell off as he flipped to his side, watching me with a confused frown.

A few swear words left my mouth, and I hated myself for an instant. "I'll regret this tomorrow," I said, mostly to myself, before pulling at his hand. "Let's get you in bed; you'll be more comfortable. The couch is way too small for ya."

Tucker muttered something in his sleepy state but soon moved to his feet as I helped him up.

"You gotta brush your teeth first. My room, my rules."

He growled something I didn't catch.

In the bathroom, he removed his Groom T-shirt and dropped his pants on the tiled floor in one move, leaving him in only white boxer briefs. Damn it. Why did he have to look so good? All ripped chest and muscled thighs. I had him all to myself last night. This was unfair. I should be able to remember our night together. Everything he did to please my body. His expert hands and very capable mouth.

A heat wave washed through me.

With a sigh, I pushed the disturbing thoughts away before they could affect my imminent sleep and slid back under the covers.

Once Tucker finished brushing his teeth, he circled the bed to climb onto the king-sized mattress from the other side. The warmth from his body enveloped me even from a few feet away, and this time, with nothing to disrupt my sleep, I dozed off in seconds.

7

ADDISON

hen I woke up the next morning—was it noon already?—a cart filled with food waited for me by the side of the bed. A large smile spread across my face. With half-lidded eyes, I scanned the room. No trace of Tucker anywhere. Did I dream of his presence? Or did he leave already? My heart hiccupped, as Dahlia would say. Dozens of knots coiled around my insides. I breathed out. For a silly reason I couldn't explain, I wished he were here. Snuggled up against me.

I turned to my side, whiffed the pillow next to me, his ocean-breeze scent filling my nostrils. Yes, Tucker slept here. So, why did he leave?

With no answer to my question forthcoming, I went to freshen up and get rid of the aftereffects of my alcohol binge. My hair was a web of knots, and I gathered it in a messy updo at the top of my head, not in the mood to comb it. I splashed cold water over my face, trying to wake myself up a little more. I looked like hell, but after the fun we had last night, it was a small price to pay. I glanced one last time at my reflection, fixed my nightshirt, only to find

Tucker sitting on the mattress as I made it back to bed. In designer washed-out denims and a dress shirt, he appeared refreshed and ready to get on with his day. Did Tucker know what regular clothes were?

And what happened to his hangover? Right now, I doubted he was even a mere mortal.

I rubbed my heavy lids with the heels of my hands and plastered a smile on my face.

"Good morning, sweetheart. Hope you're hungry. Didn't know what you liked, so got you a little of everything. And black coffee. Just the way you like it."

His dark eyes brightened the room.

"You noticed?" I asked, my voice still croaky from all the singing and cheering of last night.

Tucker nodded, his gaze fixated on mine.

I died right there.

I was wrong all along. I possessed no control. Tucker was the one having power over me. Always had been. More than I'd ever care to admit.

"Got a few hours on my hands before my flight back home. Thought we could spend this time together. Nick and Dahlia are with Jack at her parents' place. They already left. They asked me to tell you they'd be back in the morning to pick you up. But for now, it's just the two of us, Wilde. What do you wanna do? You're the Nashville expert here."

His grin, warm and mesmerizing, tipped something inside me.

I blinked. Once. Twice. Dozens of times.

Why couldn't I get out of his magnetic field? Why was I so perceptive to everything about him? His smell, his heat, his heartbeat.

All traces of my hangover disappeared.

I closed my eyes, trying to ease the drumming of my

heart and to block Tucker out. Not working. He was all over me. He didn't have to touch me for me to feel him everywhere. I clenched my thighs together. The twirl of scorching desire pooling in my belly meant nothing.

It means nothing. It means nothing. It means nothing.

How many times did I have to repeat the words to believe them?

Tucker shot me a panty-melting grin.

Last night replayed like a loop in my head, no matter how bad I tried to lock it somewhere I'd have no access. My body vibrated with need.

He eyed me with a frown, and I stayed rooted to the spot, taking him in, the idea of playing tour guide for the day not enticing me at all right now.

I had better use of our time together.

Heat circulated from the top of my head to my toes. Tucker quirked a dark brow up, his gaze heavy, and I lost it.

Without second-guessing myself, I fisted the hem of my nightshirt and lifted it over my head before discarding it. His eyes rounded. His Adam's apple bobbed. The piece of croissant he held in his hand fell from his grip.

We stared at each other, neither of us saying anything.

His gaze set my flesh on fire. He studied me, unable to hide his approval. His pupils dilated. He traced the seam of his lips with his tongue. One hand enveloped his junk, and I followed the movement, the swell in his jeans unconcealed.

My mouth watered at the sight of him, aroused and not shying from it.

In that instant, I craved Tucker Philips, like I'd never craved anyone else before.

With confidence in my steps, I strode forward, pushed

his firm chest with both hands, and straddled him, thrusting my naked breasts into his face.

His chocolate irises traveled the length of my upper body, leaving a trail of fire in their wake.

My pulse throbbed in my temples.

Lust dripped from Tucker's gaze, coiling around me.

I could bask in it. I wanted to soak it all up.

Nothing he said or did could stop me from achieving what I desired. This little game between us needed to go up in flames, burning us in its heat.

He leaned forward, admiring my breasts, and his warm breath tickled my skin, turning my nipples into stiff peaks. His hand moved to rest on my naked thighs, his fingers featherlight on my skin but enough to melt me into a puddle of need. Every cell in my body pulsed at the soft touch. My vagina was on high alert, dripping wet. I tilted my head back, moaning when his thumb pressed into my flesh and moved up, dangerously close to where I yearned for him the most.

His tongue toyed with one diamond tip, robbing me of any rational thinking. My body begged to be at his mercy.

Tucker molded one breast to his other palm. I trembled against him.

His finger pushed past the crotch of my soaked panties, spreading my arousal, and I thought I'd faint from his touch only.

"Fuck, Wilde," he said with a husky voice. "You're wet. Jesus, we can't do this. I promised—"

I returned his fiery gaze, bewitched by the intensity I noted there. The guy wore his desire like a second skin.

Before he could think it over, my tongue dived into his mouth, famished, craving the taste of him. Unapologetic. Our lust spread like a conflagration, and we were its willing hostages. It swallowed us whole, my body ravenous for his. And his hungry for mine.

Tucker's hands cupped my cheeks, and after hesitating for a beat, he deepened the kiss, battling my tongue and sucking on my lips.

Shivers worked through me. The air surrounding us thickened.

Tucker yelped when I bit his tongue and left indents on his bottom lip, but never pulled away.

My hands traveled over his clothed body, memorizing the ridges and planes, desperate to touch every inch of the skin I'd admired the night before.

His palms returned to my breasts, shaping them to his touch.

Tucker leaned back, breathless, his muscular hands on my shoulders keeping me at a safe distance.

"Stop. Wilde, we can't do this. I told our friends I'd stay away from you. My words are important to me. They mean something. Why are you always trying to get me into trouble? This is really a bad habit of yours."

I held his hands in mine, knitted my fingers through his, and brought them to my bare chest. I shuddered when his rough skin scraped my sensitive flesh. My back arched when his tongue teased one nipple and his teeth closed around it, tugging and twisting the hard tip. Pleasure and pain mixed together.

I writhed in his embrace, purring like a kitten in heat, hooked to the man kneading my breasts.

His dick hardened underneath me, and I rubbed my aching center over the bulge, raring to feel its fullness in my fist.

The rolling of my hips increased, and with one hand around me, Tucker erased any space between us, pressing me harder against his erection, his groans permeating the air.

"You kept your word," I cried out, about to come just from the overpowering friction. "They didn't ask anything from me." A loud cry passed the rim of my lips. Desire engulfed me. I had to focus just to hold a conversation. "I'm the one who initiated this. I'm not some delicate flower who requires protection. I'm my own woman. And I know what I want. Right now, it's you. Oh god, it's all of you." A painful gasp escaped my lips when the pad of his thumb pressed against my clit. Tucker drew circles over my bundle of electrified nerves, and I covered his hand with mine to increase the pressure. "Harder," I begged. My thoughts jumbled in my head, and my voice quivered. "See? It's all me. Oh yes. Don't stop." I swallowed, about to come undone but not ready to let go just yet. "Like that. Yes. You were right. I'm the one perverting you. Every single time. Faster. Fuck me. With your finger, your tongue, your dick. I don't care. Just do it."

"Jesus, sweetheart, you're burning me alive. A wildfire."

He shut his eyes, struggling to steady his shallow breathing.

My entire being pulsed, and I dug my fingernails into his shoulders to anchor myself to this world.

"Stop fighting this. I want you." I licked the corner of his lips. My voice dropped to a plea. "Show me how good you feel." I bit his earlobe, and his eyes sprang open, his mouth returning to mine and devouring my lips. My hand descended to his crotch, and I massaged him, enjoying how his dick throbbed against my palm. I rubbed him faster, eliciting another groan from him. Deeper. One that vibrated through me. "And you can't deny you want me too." His dick twitched in my fist. "See?"

Tucker leaned back, his pupils now fully dilated, his

gaze dark and menacing. Gone was the amusement from his features. His tongue wet his lip, and I crashed my mouth on his, frantic with need.

We kissed like our lives depended on it. We blended together. Oil and flames.

With a strangled grip around his length, I robbed him of his common sense.

His hips jerked up. I increased my fondling.

I squeezed him tighter, relishing every growl and one-syllable word he uttered and every jolt of his sex in my grip.

With my hair whorled around his hand, Tucker pulled my head back, his teeth marking the skin of my throat and nibbling on the flesh of my collarbones.

I screamed my pleasure, the sensations he provided my feverish body exhilarating.

"Wilde, I'll go to hell for this."

"Then I'll go with ya. We'll rock that place. Together. In the meantime, show me what I missed the other night." His tongue followed the column of my throat. "Come on, big guy, stop stalling and fuck me. I have all these scenarios filling my head. But only the real thing can help me determine which are fiction and which are reality. I can't live without knowing any longer."

He unbuttoned the top of his shirt, and craving to feel the heat of his skin on mine, I took control and peeled it off him. Outlining the ridges of his abs with my fingertips, my hungry tongue followed each caress. Every piece of him seemed as if it had been carved in stone. High cheekbones. Square jaw. Firm chest. Sculpted abs. The intensity of the desire coursing through me reached new heights. With the tip of my tongue, I tasted every inch of his exposed flesh.

"Stroke me bare, Wilde," he ordered through clenched teeth. "Fucking do it."

With not-so-steady fingers, I unbuckled his belt and unfastened his jeans.

"Hurry up. I'm about to explode if you don't release some tension."

This bossy side of Tucker Philips revved me up.

His body tensed as I slipped my hand into his boxer briefs, fisting the heated part of him. I drooled at the sight as I freed him from the restraint of his clothes.

We both breathed out in sync. Lust sharpened his features. His face tautened as a new surge of need grew in him.

His shaft pulsated as I worked it from base to leaking tip.

"Faster," he urged me. "Jerk me off. Don't end me, though."

"So big," I exclaimed, working him, relishing the steel rod underneath the velvet skin as my hand moved up and down his shaft.

"You've seen nothing yet. Wait until I'm buried inside you, pounding you hard. We'll see how deep you feel me. Then I'll fuck that dirty mouth of yours. And show you who's the boss now."

I bent forward to take him into my mouth when he wrenched me away from the taste of him. His glistening cock saluted me when I released it.

"Not yet, Wilde. I'm not done with you yet."

I batted my eyelashes. "Tuck. Please."

"You begged for it. Now stand."

One of his hands grabbed a handful of my ass when I stood before him while the other ventured back between my thighs.

Demanding fingers pushed the crotch of my panties to

the side in a rough flick that tore the seam. I gasped when a thick digit slid without hesitation between the folds drenched with my arousal.

I dissolved under his attentive caresses.

"What took you so long? Fuck me," I said. Still seated, Tucker hastened the pace, pushing two fingers inside my moist channel. He leaned forward, his teeth grazing my clit. "Yes. Yes." My hips rolled over his hand. I held his head in place, about to come from his coarse stubble rubbing over my bundle of nerves every time his mouth played me.

"This is what you want, sweetheart? Dirty? You want me to rub you raw with my finger and my dick, pound you hard until you can't walk a straight line?"

A tingling sensation rose all over my skin at the sound of his low tone and filthy words. I nodded, wondering how I'd resisted the pull between us until now.

Ruthless, Tucker moved to his feet, holding me against him, the addictive movements of his fingers never faltering. With two steps forward, he pushed me onto my back. Fire in his eyes, face gripped with need, desire sculpting all his features. He was no longer the man I knew. I held my breath as a thrill rose inside me.

"Think you can keep up?" he asked, challenge coating his words.

I nodded again. Faster this time. "Will you fuck me already, or are you waiting for me to do all the work?" I asked. "Come on, don't tease."

"That dirty mouth again. I can't wait to fill it up. Jesus, I wanted to bend you over my rental yesterday and ram into you to shut you up. Because you drove me nuts."

"You should have. I prayed you'd bang me in that empty field. Because fighting with you over directions was hot."

His eyes darted to mine. He breathed out. The muscles of his jaw flexed. "You're something else. I can't wait to have my way with you. Now spread those legs wider; I need my fix."

I lost the use of my voice at the sight of the promises shadowing his eyes. My throat clogged with anticipation.

A scorching fervor ignited all over my bare skin when he kneeled on the mattress between my legs and ravaged my center with his tongue. Tremors started at the tip of my spine and crawled along each vertebra.

With measured movements, I rolled and pinched my hard nipples between my thumbs and forefingers, increasing the desire throbbing in me.

"God, you're hot," he said, panting. He stared at me, and seeing him between my thighs, his lower face glossy with my imminent release, broke me apart, then revived me.

Tucker's digits pressed deeper inside me, gliding back and forth and turning me into a blaze. Waves of unleashed pleasure built in my core.

A million unknown sensations rushed through my body.

Loud cries filled the suite when his mouth joined in and he sucked on my clit. He worked me until he transformed my body into a pile of molten lava. My insides seared. He wouldn't stop until I combusted to ashes.

My pelvis levitated from the bed, Tucker's intoxicating strokes the only thing keeping me grounded.

His tongue played my center, giving me no time to catch my breath.

My walls clenched around his fingers. I would detonate in no time.

Flames licked my insides. My hips thrust up to take more of his fingers in me.

His movements quickened, and stars appeared in my vision.

Tucker was right. We'd go to hell for this. Because right now, I knew it down to my bones that this wouldn't be the last time. It couldn't be. We were just starting, and already I knew I'd never stop longing for Tucker's fire.

8

TUCKER

y tongue slid inside Addison's warmth as my hands moved down to grab her hipbones. Scorching heat filled my balls. Not being buried inside her became almost unbearable. She shuddered violently in my arms as I slid my tongue deeper into her moist heat, hitting the right spot, while the pad of my thumb played with her engorged clit. Every moan exiting her mouth increased the inferno burning in me. "Wilde, you taste like forbidden, and I want more. I crave more," I said after I caught my breath and plunged right back in, circling her throbbing mound with the tip of my tongue and nipping it with my teeth.

Cries of pleasure left her mouth. Her moans made my cock grow harder until it was painful and I was ready to burst. This girl would shatter me. And I didn't care. Her fingertips pressed into my skull while she thrust her hips and sought her climax. Her pelvis buckled from the mattress. I assaulted her pussy with faster strokes from my tongue.

With her desire coating my fingers, I inserted my pinky

into her tight hole. A high-pitched whimper left her mouth. Opening her legs wider, she relaxed, granting me access. The erotic view triggered a new surge of arousal in me, and I pushed my digit further in, relishing the tightness surrounding it.

Accelerating the pace, I thrust my fingers into her pussy back and forth. Every mewling she let out brought me closer to my own release. Moving to sit on my ankles, my hand still working her, I gripped my cock with my free hand, pumping myself. Even if I tried, I couldn't avert my eyes from the perfection of Addison's body undulating before me. I leaned back between her legs and sucked on her clitoris. Her walls clenched around my fingers. She was close. I could feel the orgasm building, about to crash through her.

I caught her eyes, half-masted, and I balanced myself over her to kiss her lips.

"More," she muttered, pulling away, her head arching into the pillow.

Her tongue licked the seam of her reddened lips, before she chewed on them, her teeth bound to leave permanent marks when she went rigid underneath me. My own body tensed, about to rupture to shreds. It took every-thing I had to not explode. My hand returned to my dick, pumping it with zeal and chasing additional relief. In vain. Addison Wilde, spread on her back, naked and at my mercy, only multiplied my hunger for her. Sweat glistened in the valley between her breasts. Her back arced, offering herself to me. Utterly and completely.

"You really like it dirty, sweetheart?" I asked as I tilted my head back, desperate to breathe some fresh air while I watched her abandon herself to my fondling.

The bliss painting her face filled me with pride and revived me. She was a beautiful woman, but right now, she was drop-dead gorgeous with her flushed cheeks and gleaming eyes when she locked them on mine.

Something passed between us. The air charged with a million volts.

She trembled, and with my mouth back to licking her, I savored every drop of her release when she convulsed against my tongue.

The sounds emanating from her were a melody I could never get enough of.

My dick twitched. I couldn't ignore him anymore.

"Condom?" I asked through gritted teeth.

Addison pushed herself up on her elbows until our faces leveled. "I think we're way past that, Tuck. Now get this monster dick of yours where it belongs."

"You asked for it."

Removing my hand from between her legs, I moved on top of her until my knees rested on each side of her chest. Lifting her into a semi-seated position, I fisted her hair and pulled on it, forcing her neck to arc. I pushed my cock into her mouth in one violent move. My hand held her head in place while my hips jerked back and forth, my body unable to stay ignored for another second.

Surprise lit up her eyes, morphing into elation. And lust.

A gurgling sound escaped her mouth as I filled her deeper, and soon her hands splayed on my ass cheeks, increasing the rhythm of my thrusts and pushing me further down her throat.

Her moans of pleasure mixing with the suckling sounds of her mouth were all I could hear.

"Oh, you like it naughty too, sweetheart?"

She bobbed her head. Fast. All my restraints deserted me. "Don't worry. Soon you'll feel me everywhere. I swear."

Her cheeks hollowed, and I cursed at the ceiling.

Not ready to shoot my load just yet, I inched back, forcing her to release me.

"But—" she tried to argue. Before she could complain, I jumped to my feet and discarded every piece of clothing left on me.

Positioned between her legs back on the bed, the tip of my cock teased her entrance. Addison stopped me with one hand before I could enter her. "Put your finger back in my ass, Tuck. I love it when I'm full." Damn. This woman. It was as if she knew how to break me with just her words.

I leaned over her and smashed my mouth on hers, relishing the taste of her on my tongue, unable to resist those pouty lips any longer. Our tongues fought, hungry and desperate, before finding their pace. My hands caressed every curve and dip, memorizing them feverishly. I couldn't seem to get enough. Still propped on her elbows, Addison curled a hand around the back of my head, keeping me in place while she licked a trail from my lips to below my earlobe, then across my jaw. My fingers returned inside her, to their rightful position, enjoying how she writhed underneath me. Insatiable.

"Tuck, yeah, like this. Oh God—yes, please. Keep going. No. Stop. I need your dick. Now. Oh yes."

Her words made me hard for everything that she was. Leaning forward until I could feast on her slender neck, I continued my exploration, biting her flesh. Collarbones. Crook of her shoulder. I left fresh marks with my teeth. Swell of her breast. Curve of her neck. I devoured every-thing and missed nothing. I licked her, easing the sting I left behind. My tongue laved one rosy nipple, sucking the areola deep into my mouth. Her hips jerked up from the bed as a sigh left her lips. I combusted. I opened my mouth wider, savoring her flesh. Returning my focus to her pebbled nipple, I twisted the tip between my lips, tugged at it, cherished it.

"Wilde, you taste so fucking sweet."

Her eyes glazed over, lost in her own pleasure.

My fingers increased their tempo, spreading her arousal all over her folds, readying her to welcome my eager length.

My lips closed around the second peak, and the mix of her pale skin and my dark one was intoxicating as I kneaded her round flesh with my palm. With one hand still around the back of my head, the vixen underneath me pulled me closer to her. She searched for my mouth, needy. The pad of my thumb circled her clit, pressing and rubbing. She mumbled something against my mouth that sounded a lot like "Fuck me," and I couldn't wait any longer. I longed to be inside her, buried so deep I could anchor myself there for days.

My dick pulsed, standing tall and proud, squeezed between our bodies and begging to join in too.

As if she could sense its despair, Addison's small hand grabbed it with a firm touch and gave him some unyielding attention. A loud groan parted my lips. The one I couldn't hold inside anymore. She placed me at her entrance, and in one push, I filled her.

Giving her some time to stretch her body around mine, I stayed still, watching the expressions playing on her face.

Surprise. Elation. Desire. Pleasure.

I clenched my teeth while she shifted to accommodate my girth, my restraint liquifying with every second of being still, to give her time to set the pace.

Leaning forward and balancing on one arm, my mouth claimed hers with slow strokes of our tongues. I took my time, soothing the urge until she was ready. "You okay?" I asked.

"Yes. It fills good. Feels good. Whichever pleases you." On her back, she sucked in a breath. "Gimme a sec," she said, her lips a dark shade of pink and her eyes pleading for me to give her my all. "You're pretty big." She rocked her hips slowly, adjusting herself furthermore. "Okay, Tuck. Give it to me. And don't stop. I want it all. The good, the bad, the dirty. Just fuck me like you mean it. Like you should have last night after you sang to me. It was fucking hot."

My balls firmed at the request leaving her mouth. The tip of my spine tingled. I could come right now, but it would never be enough to satiate myself. Sealing my lids and inhaling through my mouth, I braced myself, not ready for it to end before it even began.

My dick pulsated inside Addison, and removing my finger from her rosebud, I leaned back and used both hands to spread her wider, so I could lodge myself even deeper. With her folded legs on each side, I lifted her hips from the mattress as I rammed into her, nearly touching her cervix, wanting to lose myself in her. I pistoned my hips, her body clenching around mine, making it even harder to prolong the pleasure with the rawness of our bodies connecting, the sound of flesh on flesh compelling me to move faster. Her hands fisted the sheets on each side of her. Her lips pursed, begging for more. Her eyes rolled back in her head as her own control evaporated.

The phantasmic vision sent discharges of scorching heat through me.

My body trembled, and my heart palpitated. A brand-new, thrilling sensation, I was experiencing for the first time.

Addison pushed her chest forward, and a pleasing gasp resounded through the room. Followed by a dozen more.

My cock quaked, addicted to every one of her whimpers. To every movement of her voluptuous body.

"Sweetheart, look at me," I begged, breathless, resolved to not miss a second, a look, or an emotion taking over her face as I brought her over the edge. My jaw flexed. "In or out?"

"Don't care. Just mark me, Tuck. Make me forget the idea all men should burn in hell. Make me believe this could all be real. You and me. Just for a day."

I blinked. Addison Wilde was everything I had an obsession for. Fearless, gorgeous, and crazy in her own way. I never slept with the same woman more than a handful of times before, but right here, I knew I could never follow my rules with her. I had a feeling she was like an addictive drug, making me dependent on her brand of loving.

Leaning in, I licked the pearls of sweat adorning her flesh, trying to etch to my memory the feel of her.

She breathed in, and when our eyes connected again, I knew something had shifted in me. An experience impossible to define with words. I felt it down to the marrow of my bones. To the boundaries of my soul.

"Wilde—"

"I know."

Two words. It was all it took to anchor me back to the moment.

Balancing on my hands, I pounded into her. With purpose and abandon.

I smacked her flesh with mine, drawing whimpers from her.

Every sound escaping her luscious lips brought me closer to a release.

Her hips buckled, and her fingertips pressed into my thighs, strong enough to leave bruises. We moved in sync.

I looked at her, really looked at her. The sight of her

blonde hair like a halo of light and her face suffused with pleasure fucked with the rules I had set in my head over a decade ago. It did. Now I knew for sure.

All my life, I had concluded that sex was just an exchange of pleasure between two people. Nothing else. Nothing more. That's what I'd always believed. Until now. I closed my eyes. It had to stay that way. For my sake. For both our sakes. Because no, I'd ever get attached to another human being more than I should. I loved challenges but would never put my heart at risk.

Declining to be entranced by Addison's angel face any longer, I withdrew my dick and flipped her around on her all-fours. With her back to my front, I was safe from her long dark eyelashes and the bottomless blue ocean of her eyes.

The view of her backside delectable, my palm gripped a handful of her plump butt. My tongue followed the curve of her spine, from her tailbone to between her shoulder blades.

"Bend down," I ordered.

Her head descended onto a pillow, her ass pointing upward in my direction.

With a jerk of her hips, she pushed her ass closer to my crotch, and I buried into her up to the hilt in one rough stroke.

My hands held her hipbones, guiding her movements.

Molding my torso to her back, I leaned forward, my hands searching for her breasts, shaping them to my palms.

She cried my name each time I hammered into her.

Addison turned her head and captured my gaze. The look she gave me fused every bit of me back together.

Cast under her spell, one I refused to be bewitched by, I averted my eyes.

"*Tuuuck*."

The word died on the tip of her tongue. But I heard it. And my name, pronounced in the breathless way she did, unlocked something in me.

I fought hard to stay detached.

My breathing eased once I felt I was regaining some sense of control.

Whatever I did, I couldn't prevent myself from touching her. Everything Addison was transcribed into two words: addictive and forbidden. Tasting her seemed like my birthright and connecting with her my prerogative.

Our bodies moved in a choreographed dance.

I gave Addison everything. And she took it all, meeting me thrust for thrust.

My hand smacked the bare flesh of her ass, and she let out an aphrodisiac moan. My cock hardened even more.

Still on her knees, pushing on her hands to lift her body up, she returned to an all-fours position. Leaning back, I leveled us into a variation of the reverse-cowgirl position, my legs folded and Addison's front leaning against them. With my hands anchored to her, I rammed into her from under, her ass bouncing up and down my thighs, her arousal coating my testicles.

With both hands, I lifted Addison and withdrew from her until I could slide down the mattress. Once her center aligned with my face, I lowered her over my mouth. I played her bundle of nerves with my tongue, pressing and sucking, nibbling and teasing.

She tried to bend forward, her hand reaching for my length, but I clamped her thighs, preventing her from changing position.

I continued my assault on her clit, inserting two fingers, then a third one into her channel and crooking them to hit the spot that would get her to come undone.

Resolved to not miss the look on her face as she came, I

detached my mouth from her flesh and flipped us around until I set myself between her legs while she lay on her back. Her ankles locked around my waist. Her arms looped around my neck, keeping me close, and her mouth devoured mine, shooting me with promises I didn't deserve. I felt precious in her embrace. Special. With my eyes shut, because I refused to see the depth of hers and be taken hostage against my will, I kissed her back. Her tongue enticed mine as my hand wound around the back of her neck of its own volition.

Her small hand cradled my cheek, and when I re-opened my lids, she brought my focus back to her. To us. As if she sensed I could get lost in her. That she had to bring me back to the present as my thoughts swirled fast in my head. "Tuck, I'm right here."

We stared at each other for a beat, frozen. Each intake of air burned the lining of my lungs.

Addison kissed me with ardent abandon.

I detached our mouths to ram into her.

Panting, we kept moving together, new waves of plea-sure building between us, more potent. More galvanic. The air around us tensed, ready to blow up.

"Still thinking you should take charge, sweetheart?"

I flashed her a wide smirk.

"Nah, I kinda love it when you boss me and flip me around."

My hands rested on her folded knees, and for a minute, we both got engrossed in the movement of my dick plunging into her.

I grunted and jerked my hips faster.

"Now. Let go," I ordered through gritted teeth, squeezing my jaw tight, about to detonate inside her. Her long legs wrapped tighter around me and secured the phys-ical bond we shared. Addison's hips undulated, and she cried out her orgasm, her head tilting back. I lifted my eyes just in time to see the bliss taking over every one of her features. There. The sight of her cracked an iron layer of my heart. Her inner walls milked my dick, but I got it out just in time to ejaculate all over her full porcelain breasts as I jerked myself once. Twice.

Her gasps, loud and primal, acted like a thousand volts dashing through me.

Her hand wrapped around my manhood, and she finished me to the last drop, my cum branding her in a possessive manner. Something I never did before.

The sight of it pleased the bestial side of me.

Once we both came down from the rush, we stared at each other, our chests reeling fast with every breath we drove in.

Without breaking eye contact, I watched her as she took in the white display I painted on her body.

Her eyes, darker than usual and glued to mine, validated how this little marking session turned her on.

Challenge filled her gaze as she traced a line through my semen.

A smile broke free on her face.

Did she even have any idea how hot she looked right now, covered in my seed?

With a mischievous glare, she brought a coated finger to my lips, urging me to suck on it.

Just when I thought I saw it all.

I blinked, flabbergasted, unsure if I'd landed back from the orgasm that tore through me seconds ago. With a swirl of my tongue, I cleaned her digit.

"Lick me, Tucker." She glanced at me with expectant eyes. With anybody else, I would've refused, but Addison possessed a pull on me that very few people had before. Without questioning her request, my tongue found her hard nipple, drawing circles around it, tasting the saltiness of her sweat and my cum mixed together. It was as intoxicating as the woman it now belonged to.

My fingers pinched her puckered tips, and I moved upward until our mouths collided.

There was no going back.

I caught fire, and now I craved her heat.

With one hand, I pushed her damp hair away from her forehead, searching her eyes.

"I'll push my flight back. I need a do-over. Or a thousand. Fuck, you're the most amazing woman I've ever met, Wilde. I can easily get hooked onto your brand of crazy. Can't wait for more."

"You can't leave me like this," she murmured. "I'm still not fully satiated."

"I'll remedy this. I'd never leave you not fully satisfied."

She nodded, and I kissed her some more. With my arms secured around her, her closeness the only thing I wished for at the moment, we rolled to our sides. I pulled her naked, still covered in my semen, body closer, my heart beating to her rhythm.

———

Addison bent forward in the large white-tiled shower, and I entered her from behind, her pussy tight around my wooden cock. We'd been going at it for a long while, and until now, I had resisted the urge to come. We stopped counting her orgasms after five.

None of this made sense. Never in my life did I have that much stamina. Addison had woken up something in me, and I feared my dick would fall once we broke apart. It wasn't normal to be jacked up for this long.

With one arm around me, she dug her fingernails into

my ass as I speared into her. Her cries reverberated between the glass walls.

"Wilde, if this fuck marathon is a dream, then let me die a satisfied man and never wake up from the euphoria."

My arm circled her waist, and I pushed into her with a purpose, feeling her body vibrating underneath mine. My pulse raced. Addison rose to her tiptoes and wiggled that sexy ass of hers. If I let her, I knew she could end me. Here and now.

I was dying to kiss her nape, to trail my teeth over the softness of her flesh. To make her mine. Here. Now. Forever. But that wasn't a game I was interested in. Our eyes locked over her shoulder, and something shifted in the air. A curve embraced the corner of her lips. My heart jumped in my chest cavity. Aware of her. Painfully so. No matter what, my heart would never enter the equation. It had to be kept safe. From feeling too much. A handful of times in my life, I'd almost failed my own rules. But sanity always reached my brain just in time, preventing me from going into a territory I refused to visit. Love. It wasn't in the plan. Not now. Not ever. And so far, I had succeeded in keeping my emotions separated from sex.

But Jesus, the ravishment on Addison's face sent mixed signals to my head. And to my heart.

"Wilde, I'll come soon," I warned, catching my breath, as I rammed into her, using her hips to balance myself, my legs wobbly.

She pushed away from me and turned around. When she dropped to her knees and engulfed my dick in her warm mouth, I cursed under my breath. Her eyes flared as they met mine. Giving me the most torrid show, she pushed her head back and twirled her tongue around the tip, licking and sucking me as if I had gifted her with the tastiest treat. An overload of sensations filled me. Something in the depths of me tore open. My body was anchored here, but I was floating around.

Unable to stay still, I pressed both arms against the shower walls. No way would I miss any second of this. The vision of this girl sent high voltage to my balls.

"What are—wait—fuck." All the words lodged in my throat. Addison gripped my ass cheeks and pushed my length further down her mouth until I hit the back of her throat.

She raked her nails over my ass, and I came before I could even comprehend what was happening. How did she do this? How did she control my body as if it belonged to her?

I tilted my head back, letting the pleasure race through me.

I was doomed. From now on, every woman I fucked would be compared to Addison Wilde. Whoever named her chose wisely.

My entire self got drunk on her, and I caressed her hair when I unloaded inside her mouth.

She spat my cream on the shower floor. "Not swallowing," she said, meeting my eyes.

"I'll never ask you to."

She returned to her feet, and with my arms around her, my chin pressed to the top of her head as we surfed the aftershock together.

"The next few weeks will be hell without you," I said as I got dressed, ready to leave, an hour later. My midnight flight was leaving in less than two hours, and it was not like me to be running so late. "Breaking the rules had never felt so good. Maybe my dick needs a rest after all. I'm pretty sure it'll be raw for the next few days." I held onto the woman who'd rocked my world so many times I lost count in the last ten hours. With a finger, I tipped her chin up and kissed her. I branded her lips with a promise of more. I'd be back. For round two. Or six. I had no idea anymore. This couldn't be the end.

Addison and I had become two parts of a whole. Yin and yang. I had no idea how to explain it, but I sensed it. In every cell of mine. There was a force, stronger than our combined wills, pulling us together. As if we were supposed to be united. The word attraction didn't cut it. What I felt could only be described as an addiction. It resembled nothing I'd ever experienced in my life.

She dissolved in my mouth. Her hand drew a line across my torso, sending shivers along my spine, from my skull to my toes.

"No strings attached, Tuck. It was clear from the start."

I shrugged, grinning against her pinched lips. "I know. I don't do relationships, remember? And I never implied for more, sweetheart. Still, we'll see each other again at the wedding. Who said we weren't allowed to have some festivities of our own?"

She pushed back, and her smile stole my breath away. "I'm not sleeping with anyone else until we meet again. I like you bare inside me."

"Oh Wilde. No way will I be able to think about anyone else, knowing I'll see you again soon. I still have to tap this pussy of yours. Over and over again."

"So gentlemanly."

I burst out laughing. "Sorry. You like it dirty, woman. I'll give you dirty. Until you beg me to hold you because your legs are too weak."

"You're not a cuddler, big guy."

"Nah, but I could make an exception. With you. For an hour or two."

"I'll take your word for it." She kissed me one last time and led me to the door as I shouldered my bag. "Dream of me, Tuck. 'Cause I know I'll dream of you every time I touch myself."

I pivoted to face her. "Don't say things like this, or I'll never make it to the airport in time."

I leaned in to kiss her, but instead, she licked my cheek from my jaw to my temple. Then she nibbled on my earlobe as she whispered, "Until next time, big guy. I bet you'll come running before those six weeks are over."

"I can resist you."

"Impress me then."

She pushed me out of her suite, grinning. Before I could speak a word, she slammed the door in my face.

Realization hit me. Hard. Like a train at full speed. Straight in the chest.

Nick would be disappointed in me. No. Dahlia would murder me. My dick softened in my pants. Our friends' warning was a ruse. To keep us apart. To prevent us from imploding and leaving destruction in our wake. They must have known who I'd be dealing with. They had to know Addison was a vixen.

I sighed.

Maybe they only tried to avoid wedding hurdles. The maid of honor and best man screwing could complicate things. A disaster bound to happen.

As long as neither of us developed feelings, it shouldn't spoil anything, right?

9

TUCKER

With a tumbler of whiskey in hand, I sat in the bar across from my office, studying Sabrina, the girl I had a date with tonight. She'd been talking about something for the last fifteen minutes, but kill me now. I had no idea what it was about. Not. A. Fucking. Clue. We'd agreed to this date before I left for Nashville, and now I was stuck somewhere I had no reason, and no interest, to be.

Since I'd been back from Tennessee almost a week ago, and no matter how much I tried to forget about that weekend, my thoughts always drifted back to Addison Wilde. All the time. As if she'd imprinted herself on my brain, and on my body, and had control over it even from a thousand miles away.

Two days after I landed back here, I was even tempted to call her. Yeah, so unlike me. Tucker Philips didn't reach out to women, except for booty calls. My self-preservation made an appearance just in time, thwarting me from giving in to my own unbreakable rules. No commitment.

No relationship. No love. Those were the three adages I'd been living by for as long as I could remember.

My friends called me Chicago's number one player. By my own definition, I wasn't a player. I was only preserving this heart of mine from being hurt like my old man. He'd sacrificed his heart a long time ago. I was the witness to his descent to hell. No, I wouldn't suffer through the same ride he did. I was smarter. And a whole lot stronger.

Sabrina caressed my arm, and usually, I would already have brought her home, spread her on my bed, and devoured her in a dozen different ways. But not tonight.

I wouldn't admit it to a living soul, but my game had been off lately. For the last couple of months, I'd found myself not attracted to most women crossing my path. Addison being the only one my radar picked up. I blamed Nick for all of it. He had made her a forbidden fruit I couldn't taste, and my ego decided she was worth the chase. And the risk.

I took a sip of my drink and managed to nod, pretending to be interested in what my date was chatting about.

What a snooze fest.

The morning after we first hooked up, when I told Addison I'd been on a dry spell, I wasn't kidding. And if anybody had asked me about it, I would have denied it, even under torture. After all, I had a reputation to preserve. It was like I had lost interest in the fuck game I'd been playing for a decade. All women I met looked the same, smelled the same, were the same. Only their names told them apart. In the last six months, I'd slept with three different women named Vanessa. Even if they didn't look alike, they still had too much in common. Big tits. Fake laughter. And too willing to open their legs at the first meeting.

Been there. Done that.

Nothing challenged me anymore.

Addison had been the first person to add a little zest to my life. To get under my skin. To play with my sanity and entice me all at once.

The idea I'd lost my touch, my magical seduction power, concerned me.

I'd never been off my game. Not a damn day in my life.

With a series of nods and what could pass as smiles, feigning interest, I brought my glass to my lips and took a long sip.

Sabrina—was that even her name? For an instant, I couldn't be sure anymore. Yeah, something was off. I never mixed women's names. Ever. I was a womanizer, but not a heartless jerk. I had manners. And values. Whatever people around me claimed.

Maybe I should go to the doctor. Get a health check. Blood work. A CAT scan. Anything.

I had met my physician two weeks ago. And he'd said nothing was wrong with me. Perhaps he missed something, some super rare condition, and I should get a second opinion.

I sighed, burying my face in my hands, my elbows propped on the table.

"Are you okay?" the woman—now I refused to call her Sabrina in case it wasn't her name—asked.

I shrugged. "Yeah. Sure. Tired. And a lot on my mind." *A siren who lives in Georgia. And some of the most amazing sex of my life.*

She moved to her feet, adjusting the straps of her white dress, offering me a full view of her indecent cleavage. Nope. Even that didn't do the trick. My old Tucker ways were dead. Something resembling panic swirled through me, tying my stomach in knots.

The woman bent at the waist, her breath caressing my earlobe. "Oh, I know the remedy to that. I'll freshen up and be right back." She winked and flashed me a grin before turning the corner toward the restrooms, batting her fake—I would bet on it—eyelashes my way.

As soon as she disappeared from my sight, I exhaled in relief. I dragged a hand over my face, trying to comprehend what it all meant.

With my other hand, I cupped my junk. No. Nothing there either. My dick had forfeited the game too. Was this how grief felt? Like you had no more interest in what impassioned you before?

I swallowed the emotions that raged inside me.

If this woman believed I would follow her, she'd have to wait for me forever.

Before I could think about it twice, I fished a bill from my wallet, placed it on the table after chugging down the rest of my drink, and got the hell out of there.

Yeah, jerking off to relax and get rid of my angst felt like a better idea than having this girl's lips all around my dick tonight.

Addison's last words before we parted ways replayed in my head. *I'm not sleeping with anyone else until we meet again. I like you raw inside me. Dream of me, Tuck. 'Cause I know I'll dream of you every time I touch myself.*

I had to admit, maybe her words carried more wisdom than I first thought. Right now, they sounded like a solid plan. One I decided to live by too.

———

Dragging my feet, I sauntered back home in no hurry to spend my Friday night all alone. Since my best friend left town a little over a year ago, I'd been compensating for his absence with women. More than usual. Not that I complained at first, but soon it became old news, and I missed male bonding. To make things more pathetic, my other best friend, Jace, the most pussy-whipped guy to walk the face of the Earth, was almost never available to hang out. Even our weekly Wednesday poker nights hadn't survived Nick's departure. Whenever they were in town, I spent more time with the Busters players than with my own friends. Sure, Barry Hamilton was a decent guy and a good friend of Jace and mine, but it wasn't the same as hanging out with the two guys I'd grown up with.

The high-rise building by Lake Michigan appeared in my peripheral vision. The best place money could buy Yes, I'd done pretty well in my career so far. I got recruited in college because I was gifted with anything related to numbers, and I'd secured a six-figure salary within two years of graduation. I worked crazy hours and never took vacations, but hey, I was at the top of my professional game at twenty-five. People had it worse than I did.

"Good evening, Mr. Philips," the doorman greeted me.

"Hey Leo. How is it going?"

"Great. Have a nice night, Mr. Philips."

"You too, Leo." I nodded to him as I entered the elevator car. The box felt smaller than usual, suffocating me. Trying to ease my breathing, I loosened my tie and released the first two buttons.

I slumped against the wall, leaning my head back and emptying my lungs, the weight of my thoughts unnaturally heavy.

How had my amazing life turned so depressing? I couldn't pinpoint exactly when it started being a bummer.

But this playboy existence didn't have the same appeal it used to. Now that my friends were all about to be happily married and had drifted away from our bachelor lifestyle, I could feel the weight of loneliness on my shoulders. They had moved on. From this. From me. And I got stuck here. Alone. As if the world had spun double time around me, the seasons changing and time ticking, while I stood here, immobile, frozen in the evolution of my own life. A heavy stone I couldn't see but could feel in every bone of my body. A scream rising from somewhere deep within me begged to be freed. To compel me to move on. But I had no idea how to and what the implications of letting go would be. Or how far the restraints I'd imposed on myself a decade ago reached.

With the intention to chase my grumpiness away, I changed into my workout gear and reached the second floor. A session on treadmills and a few rounds of weightlifting relieved the crippling sensation inside me. It usually did the trick to kick me out of my funky state.

An hour later, energized and with a more restful mind, I jogged up the stairs to the twenty-third floor, then took the elevator to the forty-sixth level.

My heels dug into the Brazilian walnut wooden floor the moment the door clicked behind me. My condo had an open-space design, so I could see the entire place from the entryway. The living and dining rooms were on the left side with floor-to-ceiling windows offering the best view of Lake Michigan and the buzzing city. The kitchen stood in front of me and consisted of a broad island and stainless-steel appliances. On one side was a door to the master bedroom and en-suite bathroom. And on the other side were doors leading to the two guest rooms, a bathroom, and a library I used as a home office. With high concrete ceilings and exposed brick walls, it had the old factory look people raved about while being less than five years old.

"Hey man. What are you doing here?" I asked, taking in the man sitting on my modular Italian leather couch, his feet stretched on the matching ottoman, a tumbler of whiskey in one hand. Not a care in the world about squatting in my place during my absence.

He smirked and I unfroze, walking in his direction. A matching grin stretched my lips as I pulled him into a hug once he got to his feet.

"I had some things to deal with in town. Thought I would crash here for a night or two. If I remember correctly, the day I left Chicago, you said I could come here anytime since I was now homeless, according to your standards."

He winked as I shook my head.

My hug around Nick tightened. "You serious?"

My friend stepped back and brought his drink to his lips and nodded. "I still have to deal with my stuff in the storage unit. I found some place to give most of it away. For a good cause."

"You'll be in town for two nights?"

Because, out of everything my friend said, that was all what mattered to me at the moment.

"Yep. You heard me right. So, what's the plan? Hitting the bar? Poker night?" He scanned the room. "Wait? No ladies hidden anywhere or waiting for ya in the shower, right?"

I shook my head. "Not tonight. A guy needs to recharge his batteries once in a while." I offered him my best cocksure smile, refusing to let him see the truth beneath the mask I'd created when I was still a teen. Hiding my fear of love under the pretense of fucking around to keep my heart safe from heartbreak. It was crazy, the shit you could get away with when you hid it under boundless confidence. Even from the people closest to you.

"What do you have in mind?" Nick asked. "For tonight."

He moved to the bar in the corner of the room and poured me a drink.

"Since I had no idea you'd be in town, I have no plan."

"Think we can bribe Jace for a poker night? I've missed those."

I snickered. "Help yourself. Since you left, Pam has tightened her grip on his balls. Last I heard, she wanted to get pregnant. Imagine the hell she's putting him through."

Yeah, Pamela White was possessive of her man. Years later, I still couldn't comprehend why both my friends had fallen for her. They were genuinely intelligent guys. So, it made no sense they fell for her charade. Nope.

"Let me call him. We'll see how it goes," Nick suggested. He clapped my shoulder. "Glad to be in town, man." And without telling him in words, I returned the feeling, hugging him close to me.

———

Slouched on the sofa, waiting for Jace to get his ass here, I ordered food through an app on my phone. "Wings or pizza?" I asked.

"Wings. Dahlia isn't the biggest meat eater. Buffalo would be great. Or the one with the hot sauce they added on the menu before I left."

"Hell's Heat, they named it. I'll take a bit of everything. Tonight calls for a celebration. You back in town is a rare event nowadays." Once I was done, I brought my attention back to my friend. "You came by yourself?"

"Yep. Something felt off the other weekend. Thought you might wanna talk about it. Or need a shoulder to cry on." He winked.

I shrugged.

"I'm listening if that's the case," he added sincerely.

I sipped my drink, hoping he wouldn't be able to read through my bullshit.

"Seriously, you were there for me when my life blew apart. You helped to put me back together when I was broken after Derek, when I thought I'd never be able to rise from the ashes I'd crumbled into. If you hadn't believed in me back then... I don't know. Green Mountain was your idea."

Each word he spoke filled me with the memories of the tragedy I hadn't visited in over a year.

"All I'm saying is, I'm thankful. I wanna pay it forward. Whatever is going on with you, tell me, and I'm here, okay? No matter the time or distance, I'll be on the first flight, sitting on your posh couch, wiping your tears or kicking your ass. I'll always be there for you."

Everything he said hit me in the chest. Where it meant something.

I averted my gaze for a moment, ordering my thoughts. "It's nothing," I finally said. "Nothing a vacation can't fix." No matter how hard I tried, I wasn't ready to open up to him. To tell him how lost I felt. How it hurt to see everyone around me moving on with their lives. First, I had to figure out if I was worried for nothing and if it was just a phase. A hiccup in my journey. And it would go back to normal soon enough.

"You sure? You'd tell me if it was serious, right?"

I nodded. "Yeah." I sipped my drink. "Just tired, I guess. Got that new account at work. It's big, man. And I've put a lot of night shifts in it. I'll be all right."

Nick leaned forward, his back straight, and his elbows resting on his knees. He watched me for an instant. "Got an idea. Why don't you come to Green Mountain for a few weeks? Stay on after the wedding. Could be fun to have you around, and the change of scenery could lift your spirits too."

"Wouldn't you guys be on your honeymoon?"

"Not right away. We're waiting for Carter to be off tour so Jack can stay with him. I know there aren't lines of barely dressed women waiting at the town bar or super exciting nightlife, but... I don't know. Dahlia's old house hasn't hit the market yet since we just moved into the farmhouse officially two weeks ago. And Carter was thinking of buying it for the new rental business he's got going on. It's yours if you want it. For as long as you want it. Think about it."

The Tucker Philips I'd always been would have refused the offer outright. Living in a small town, hard pass. But this version of me, off his game and lonely, thought spending some time close to his friends could do him good. Even in the middle of Crack-Nowhere, Tennessee. And that version won the mind battle.

"Sure, could be nice. Let me think about it." No, I wasn't about to blow my cover and let him worry about me. If I agreed too quickly, he'd suspect something. Nick already had enough on his plate. My uncle Mike's construction business he just bought, moving into a new house, the wedding.

I swallowed, hoping I was convincing enough while he gave me a pointed look.

"Let me check if I can clear my schedule, okay?"

His face lit up. "Sure. The invite won't go anywhere."

The concierge rang my phone, announcing someone was downstairs, cutting our discussion short, and I thanked the delivery guy in my head for his perfect timing.

————

Nick retreated to the guest room around midnight, an hour after Jace left. Boys' night had been everything I'd wished it to be. And more. Fueled by friendship, whiskey, poker, beer, and laughter. It made me forget all my problems for a night.

Incoming text messages filling my phone screen caught my attention as I exited the shower, a towel around my waist. I dried myself quickly and slid under the covers, my device in hand, curious about who would write to me at this time of the night. I prayed it wasn't some drunk chick searching for a quick fuck since I was on a self-proclaimed sabbatical.

A grin stretched my lips at the name appearing on the screen and the five messages waiting for a reply.

Addison: Hey *Tuuuck*, miss me already?

Addison: Just kidding. Maybe not. Do you, though?

Addison: Have you forgotten?

Forgotten? Forgotten what? I scratched the side of my head, raking my brain, trying to remember if I had agreed to something and it had escaped my mind.

Addison: We don't have much time left. I'd like to be done with it by the end of next week. Can you make it happen? Counting on you here.

Addison: Don't ignore me. I thought we had a
deal. And you haven't delivered yet. I'm still
waiting.

What deal?

Just when I was about to ask what it was that I'd
somehow forgotten, another message came in.

Fuck. Jesus. Damn it.

My entire body stiffened. And for the first time since I
left Nashville, even my dick had a reaction. A very hard
and a very thick reaction.

I swallowed, taking in the picture on my screen.

Addison. I knew it was her, even though I couldn't make
out her face, in lacy lingerie, offering me a view of her
upper body. I recognized the chameleon tattoo under her
left breast.

"I love the idea we all can change colors and adapt to a
new environment when we have to," she had said when I
had asked her about its meaning.

Another message chimed in.

Addison: Do I have your attention now?

My thumbs typed fast.

Me: Hey Addison. What's up?

Addison: Finally. Thought I had the wrong
number for a moment. Some other dude would
have had a great surprise.

My lips curled into a crooked smile, and I decided
to mess with her.

Me: What surprise? Did you send me a package or something?

Addison: ...

Addison: No. I checked. Was delivered to your number. Unless you're telling me you're not Tuck.

Me: How would you know? I could be anyone right now.

Addison: Are you?

Me: Maybe.

Addison: Stop playing dumb. We texted in Nashville. Remember, *Groom*?

Me: But it might not be me typing right now.

Addison: I'm pretty sure you don't have female company over. Dah told me Nick was with ya. Unless it's him I just sent that picture to. And if it was, he would have called me on it by now. Sorry, man. I'm not some dumb bimbo you usually date whom you can fool.

Me: I thought that's what we did the other day. Fool around. And if I remember correctly, you were pretty good at it. Just saying.

Addison: Gotcha. I knew it was you. Loved the pic, *Tuuuck?*

Just the mention of it sent waves of heat through me.

Me: I might.

I fucking did. It's like you have a special power that appeals to me, Wilde. And the key to my usually impressive libido.
My hand returned to my junk, loving how my body responded to hers, even from miles apart.

Addison: Wanna play a game with me?

I swallowed. Hard.
How did she do that? Have me wrapped around her finger?

Me: Depends. What are the rules?

More warmth traveled through me. I loved that she always succeeded in challenging me when I didn't expect it. To get a reaction out of me.

Addison: No rules.

Me: That sounds like something I'll regret then.

Addison: Did you regret fucking me, *Tuuuck*?

Me: Never.

Addison: Then you'll like this game.

The girl was a walking aphrodisiac, even if I couldn't see her.
I pumped myself a few times under the sheets, enjoying

the effect her words had on me. She was good. I had to give her that.

Me: Try me.

Addison: Call me.

I pressed the video chat button instead, but she refused the call. What now?

Addison: No video. We're not allowed to see each other playing this game.

Me: I thought there were no rules.

Addison: I changed my mind. Call me now.

Why did the words *call me now* sounded like *fuck me now*?

I adjusted myself under the covers, never releasing the grip on my dick, and pressed the dial button.

She answered after the second ring, her voice gravelly and full of lust.

Shit. This was bad. For me.

"Hey Tuck, so I guess you wanna play my game?"

I swallowed and swept my bottom lip with my tongue. "I love games, remember? But yours are dangerous. For me at least."

"Oh, I recall a lot of things. And you're a great player. Don't sell yourself short."

Okay, kill me now. I could come to the sound of her sultry voice only.

She continued before I could muster a reply. "I was lonely tonight. Wanted to get laid. But then I thought about you, raw inside me, and the promise I made before you left. So, I decided since you created this problem, you should be the one fixing it."

"Tell me more," I said, my cock swelling with every word she spoke.

"Fuck me, Tuck. I need to come. And I don't wanna do it alone. So, you'll do it for me."

"Woman, you're evil. This is torture."

"You're only allowed to use your voice," she said.

I cleared my throat. "That's another rule."

"I make the rules. Always," Addison said. "Now get to work. Tell me what to do. Tell me how to fuck myself, thinking it's you."

I moved the pillows around and lay on my back, pushing the sheets away, combusting underneath them, and placed the phone on my chest. I angled one arm under my head, never letting go of my pulsing erection.

My heartbeat pounded through my skull.

Addison's words kept me anchored to the present. "I'm soaked."

At this pace, I'd come undone before she even started.

"Touch yourself, Wilde. Push two fingers inside that tight channel of yours. And moan. I wanna hear you pleasure yourself. Don't hold anything in." I repositioned my hand below. "Put your other fingers in your mouth. And lick them."

Whimpers and sucking sounds resonated on the other end of the line.

"Now roll those pink nipples of yours between your digits. Hard. Until they're so sensitive they ignite every nerve end and your back arches at the intensity."

"Oh Tuck, it feels so good. Keep going."

"Wilde, are you aroused for me? Are you dripping wet? Are your fingers coated with your pleasure?"

She hmmed.

"Good girl. Press on your clit with the pad of your thumb."

"Like this?"

Oh. Little vixen. She was doing it on purpose.

"Harder. Like I'd do if I were here. Now rub over it, fast and slow. Let me hear you."

"Oh god. Tuck. Yes. Like this. Oh yes. Don't stop talking. I'll do anything you ask me to. A-ny-thing." Her pleasure dissolved her voice.

A surge of scorching fire licked my spine.

"Move those fingers in and out of you at the same time."

The tip of my spine tingled, and before I exploded all over my abdomen, I released the grip on myself for a moment, catching my own breath. And lengthening the pleasure.

"Tuck…I…oh…"

"Let go, sweetheart. I'm right here."

A symphony of purrs resonated from her end, and I resumed the movement of my fist around my steeled length.

"Do I feel good buried in you?"

She cursed her reply.

"Faster, sweetheart. Push those fingers deeper."

She moaned louder.

I increased the pace of my own pleasuring.

My pants mixed with hers.

We were about to convulse together.

A high-pitched sound filled the silence of my room, and as if my body had been waiting for it, I came in powerful jolts all over my abdomen.

I couldn't think of any other time I'd come for so long in my life. As if I had infinite sperm reserves.

"Now suck on those fingers, Wilde," I said once my

breathing returned to normal. "Suck on them like I'm the one doing the honors. Like I'm hungry for you. Because right now, I'm dying to taste you."

I heard a pop sound through the phone, and a lazy and satisfied smile lifted the corners of my lips.

We both caught our breaths. My pulse resumed at a more normal pace.

"How do you feel, sweetheart?"

"Better." I heard the contentment in her one-word answer.

"Good," I said, lifting myself on my elbow to grab a box of tissues from my nightstand.

"Thanks, Tuck." Her voice sounded relaxed. It had lost the previous lustful tone.

"Can I see you now?" I asked, spread on my back, spent.

"Nah, it would ruin the fantasy. Night."

I blinked. This woman. She was unbelievable.

"Wait. What were your texts about? Me forgetting something. About a deal between us."

Addison yawned, and I echoed right after. "Oh that. The video I'm making to go with Carter's song. For the wedding. You agreed to send me baby and childhood pictures of Nick. So I can make a montage for the wedding night. I'll add clips from the ceremony and reception to it later. I'm swamped at work, so I'd like to get it done sooner than later. This new client of mine is a jerk."

The gears of my brain worked, trying to remember the conversation. In vain.

"You forgot, right?"

I breathed out. "Yeah. Sorry. I have some and Jace does too. I'll call Mrs. Peterson tomorrow and see if she can send some over and try to forward them to you in a few days. Would it work?"

Enthusiasm returned to Addison's tone. "Yes. It would be perfect. I'll call you in five days or so to make sure you don't forget. Thank you."

"Wait." Her previous words came back. "Anything I can do to scare that client of yours?"

Addison snickered. "I don't need saving, Tuck. I'm a big girl."

Yeah, I know you are, sweetheart. But, for some reason, the idea she had to deal with a dickhead bothered me. I emptied my lungs to flush out my annoyance.

"If you change your mind, gimme a call. I'll kick his ass to another state. Night."

"Night, Tuck. Sweet dreams."

We hung up, and after I cleaned myself, I returned to my previous position, my eyes trained on the ceiling, wondering what was going on with me for the umpteenth time in the last week.

In Nashville, Addison Wilde woke up something in me. I had no idea how to describe it. But I knew it was real.

My phone chimed with an incoming text message.

Addison: For the records, I took that pill.

Me: Are you okay?

What else was I supposed to ask in this situation? It felt selfish to let her deal with our fuck-up all by herself.

Addison: Yeah. Fell sick for a day. All good now.

Addison: Good night.

Tucker: Night.

I put my device away, uneasy at the idea she got sick because of me. That our night of pleasure had undesired consequences.

My lids grew heavy, and sleep claimed me, my dreams filled with images of the girl I wasn't allowed to fantasize about.

The one I'd promised to never touch. And failed.

Big time.

10

ADDISON

"No, this isn't working. We've been over this thrice already. I can't use the pictures from the opening night for the new ad campaign. They're blurry. Nothing I can do to fix it." I paused and rolled my eyes. At least the people on the other end of the conference call couldn't see me. I breathed in to calm myself. Soon, I'd strangle them through the phone if I had to.

"You sure none of them are salvageable?" the client asked. Again.

Okay, what didn't he understand? My eyeballs almost bulged out of their sockets. Pressing my lips together, I adjusted the sleeves of my cream ruffle blouse, then took a deep breath. And let it out. Nope. Didn't work. I pushed my palms together under my chin, calling my inner strength to make its appearance to ease my temper. Yeah, better than using the same hands to murder this guy who, by now I was sure, was deaf. Or dead if he kept arguing with me over a damn picture of his not-so-handsome face. He and his team were just a bunch of morons.

Breathe in. One. Two. Three. Breathe out. Three. Two. One.

"As I informed your assistant, your director, and yourself multiple times already, no, we can't. You'll have to provide us with high-definition shots, or we can organize a photoshoot at your convenience."

"Stop," the jackass said, his twangy voice irritating me. "You don't understand. I want those pictures. I love how I look in them."

How could he be so obsessed with his own face?

Anger radiated from me. Yeah, the client was asking for my wrath. I usually possessed a more leveled mood at work, but we'd been arguing about this issue for far too long.

I cleared my throat, trying once more. "I understand, but it's not possible."

"But—"

"Let me finish," I cut him. "Next time, hire a professional photographer instead of a kid with a cheap phone if you wish to use those pictures for advertising or anything digital. Or if you are under some delusion of wanting your face plastered on billboards in the future. There are other ways to cut costs," I said, not bothering to hide my arrogance under pretty words, and moved to my feet, adjusting my neon-blue pencil skirt with my fingers.

The walls of the conference room closed around me as my blood boiled with annoyance. I'd had enough. Enough of that jerk. Enough of this circus.

The pictures weren't good. That was it. I was a graphic designer, not a freaking illusionist.

"Give us a second, Mr. Reinart," my boss Joseph said, pressing the mute button on the device set between us on the table. "Addison, where do you think you're going?" he asked, his attention now fully on me.

"My office. I'm done dealing with this guy. If he thinks he's that good-looking, he should go to a model agency, not own a used car dealership. I have work to do, and I've been wasting my precious time with this dickhead all week. Not anymore."

"Addison—" he warned in a stern tone.

I flipped a hand in front of me. "You know what, Joseph? I'm going home. I've been feeling like shit all day." I gathered my messenger bag, the file containing the client's notes and stupid photos, my mug of tea, and left the room. Only the clicking sound of my heels broke the tense silence as men in silk ties and pressed suits watched me leave.

Joseph must have switched off the mute button because soon I heard his annoyed voice resuming the conversation.

Rebecca, my best friend in town and assistant to the creative director of another campaign we were working on together, hurried after me.

"Addi, what's wrong? Are you okay?"

I continued toward my office, not slowing down. "Fine. Don't worry."

"Joseph will be mad you left him in there to deal with the egoistic loony by himself."

I harrumphed. "He's not alone. Seth and Callum are there. He'll get over it. You know Joseph barks but never bites. He needs me on the team. I'm the only one qualified here since Marjory quit, so I'm not scared about losing my job if that's what you're referring to."

She took a loud gulp of air in and got in step with me. Her small hand gripped my elbow, forcing a halt to my escape.

"Talk to me," she insisted.

I yanked my arm free. "Nothing to talk about. I woke up in the middle of the night twice every day this week.

And then it took me forever to fall back to sleep. And during the day I'm exhausted. It just affects my temper. Nothing an afternoon nap and a hot bath won't fix."

My friend pressed her palm against my forehead. "No fever. Go home. I'll hold the fort for ya. Turn off your phone, and go to bed. I'll bring soup when I get home later, okay?"

I nodded. "Thanks, Becca."

"Anytime. And call me if you need anything."

I pulled her into a hug, feeling a bit emotional. If I was being honest with myself, I was so exhausted—and either pissed or teary, if not both at the same time—a half-day off sounded amazing right about now. "There are leftovers from Cece's in the fridge under my name. Help yourself. I'm pretty sure you only packed a PB&J sandwich for lunch, anyway. You wouldn't want their famous pesto pasta to go to waste, would ya?"

A huge smile brightened my roommate's face. "Thanks. You're the best."

I shrugged. "I know. Can't help it."

———

Back in my apartment, I barely had time to remove my heels before falling face first on the mattress. I never went to bed without removing my makeup, but today I had to make an exception to my usually disciplined bed routine. Too lazy to slip under the covers, I grabbed the blanket at the foot of the bed, tucked it around me, and dozed off in a matter of seconds.

"Feeling better?" Becca asked, sitting on the edge of my mattress, her hand caressing my hair hours later.

The sound of her voice brought me back to this world. I peeled my heavy eyelids open one at a time. For a second, the room spun around me, and I tried to remember where I was and what time it was. Through the window, the sun hung low in the sky, so I'd bet early evening.

"Addi, you look like I've woken you up from a grave," my friend said, her voice soft and comforting. "How are you holding up? You have the groggy appearance you wear so well." A warm laugh followed her words.

I sat cross-legged before her and ran a hand over my face to chase away any trace of sleep. "I feel groggy too. And dizzy. My body weighs tons."

Becca's palm met my forehead once again. "Still no fever. Hungry?"

"Nah." I scrunched up my face. "My stomach wouldn't accept it."

"Rest some more then. I brought soup if you change your mind later."

"Thanks." I lay down on my back, bringing the blanket along. Flipping to my side, I curled into a ball, and sleep claimed me in no time.

The next morning, I sat at the small kitchen table, wearing a teal plush robe, one foot propped on the chair, my arm around my knee while I drank my morning tea.

"Hey, you're up," Becca said as she joined me, filling her travel mug with hot caffeine. "Glad to see you're doing better. Coming to work?"

I gave her a one-shoulder shrug. "I still feel under the weather. For the first time ever, I called in sick. All I can think about is my bed. I just got up because I had to pee. And shower because I had mascara smudges around my eyes. I looked terrible."

My friend tugged at my low ponytail. "Sure, you looked terrible, Addi. You always do." She snickered, and I joined in. She took a seat before me and studied me with a frown.

"What?"

"Do you think it could be…you know…?"

"Heredity kicking in?" I asked.

"Or something like it? I don't know. You haven't been yourself in weeks. The only time you've been wearing a smile was after you came back from Nashville a week ago. Other than that, since you learned dickhead cheated on you and might have given you chlamydia, you've been off. I worry about ya."

I sucked in a breath. My friend knew me too well. "Funny thing. I asked Dahlia if she thought this could be it. Me reliving my family history. But she didn't think so." I paused and fought the thoughts that scared me. "Truth? I can't tell for sure. And I thought I was doing better. I really did. This insomnia is new. Maybe it's a phase. I'm over my relationship. Been for a while. Even when we were together, in the end, I knew he was never meant to be the love of my life. What I miss the most is the idea of love. Sharing a bed. Not the guy. What if I can't find it anywhere else? What if I'm destined to become a cat lady or something? I love being in love. I'm not sure I'm ready to just forfeit the whole idea."

"Still thinking about meeting with Felicia? To try to renew what you girls had for an instant?"

"No. Maybe. I could. But I like men the most. It's stupid. I should really be over them by now. Forget they exist. Felicia is nice. We had some great times together…"

"But—"

"Yeah, there's a but. I won't commit to her. I just can't. She's not the one. That I can tell."

Becca watched me, sipping her hot beverage. "Addi, you'll find the one. One day. Not all men are cheaters-losers-liars. Dahlia got a great one. You can't stop gushing about him. And I have a good guy too."

"Ben is quite a catch. You're lucky."

"Addison Wilde, you're destined for greatness."

I extended my arm over the table and squeezed her hand, loving her warmth.

"Thanks. I hope you're right. Now go or you'll be late."

"You gonna be okay on your own?"

"I promise. I'll call you if I'm not."

Becca screwed the cap on her mug, grabbed her purse, and left after kissing my cheek.

After a morning nap, I sat on the couch by the large window to bask in the sunlight entering the living room with my laptop perched on my folded legs. Our apartment was small, but the location was everything. A ten-minute walk from one of the busiest commercial streets in Atlanta. A fifteen-minute walk from our job. I could be everywhere easily, and I even sold my car after my junior year in college since I never used it.

The place was modestly furnished, but we lacked for nothing. Two bedrooms with walk-in closets—those were considered rare gems in this city—an open floor plan consisting of two rooms coming together. Dining room slash kitchen and living room. Wide windows letting lots of sunlight in, tiled flooring, white walls, and bright blue accent in the form of pillows, picture frames, and other decor items.

I double-clicked on the file holding my latest T-shirt designs and got to work. I loved my job, but this, right here, was something that made me proud. The little business I'd started from scratch. In addition to designing shirts, I had proven myself pretty good at organizing events. Over the years, I had planned weddings, album launches, business inaugurations, and baby showers, among other occasions, including Dahlia's bridal store opening and her upcoming nuptials. If I could find a way to make my two passions coexist together, I'd be a fulfilled gal. Be my own boss and not take shit from people like Pierce Reinart ever again.

Hours passed, and I didn't notice the time flying when a chime on my phone startled me. I finished applying the glittery purple filter and pressed *save* before picking up my device.

The biggest smile I could summon bisected my face as I took in the picture.

Tucker: Now you can't deny I've always been the best-looking one between both of us.

I cupped my heart with a hand as I studied the two little boys—probably about six or seven years old—wearing shorts, sitting on the hood of a car, eating ice cream cones with matching grins.

"This is adorable," I said out loud before realizing nobody could hear me.

With a shake of my head, I texted my *groom*.

Me: Got to say, you two are pretty cute.

I could imagine Tucker's smirk lighting up his cocky face and snickered as the image formed in my head.

Tucker: I knew it. You find me irresistible.

Oh god, his ego.

Me: Don't let it go to your head. I never said you were still good-looking, though.

Tucker: Wilde. Wilde. Wilde. No need to say it. I

saw it in your eyes the day we spent locked up in your suite.

Tucker: I got my confirmation from the multiple orgasms I gave you out of my selflessness.

I tilted my head back, laughing, and dropped my laptop on the couch beside me. I made myself comfortable and typed with both thumbs.

Me: Sorry. Truth be told. I was faking it. Was scared to hurt your lack of modesty.

My face hurt, my lips stretched to their maximum. My heart cartwheeled in my chest, and laughter rumbled out of me. Yes, it felt good to be happy.

Tucker: Want me to take the next flight and prove you wrong?

I pushed my hair back, my laughter resuming.

Me: You wouldn't?

Tucker: Wanna bet on it?

Tucker: If I leave in an hour, I'd land by dinner time. Any plans tonight?

Me: Stop screwing with me.

Me: Truth?

Tucker: Always.

Me: Been having a few off days. Home today. My sleep is disturbed so left in the middle of a meeting with a client yesterday. The guy was being a douche.

Tucker: Whoa. You did that? Same guy you told me about?

Me: Yes.

Tucker: Truth?

Me: Always.

Tucker: You should have let me kick his ass. I'm a pretty good ass-kicker. Also, you need the Tucker magic touch. No wonder you can't sleep. You miss me, sweetheart.

Me: I do not.

Tucker: Wanna bet?

I poked my tongue out and took a selfie and sent it to him.

Tucker: Yeah, I remember that tongue. And the wonders it could deliver.

I pinched my shirt, fanning myself. For some reason I still couldn't explain, Tucker Philips had a way to shoot heat through me. In every possible way.

Tucker: Gotta go. I'll be there at five-thirty. Wear

a dress. And your hair down. I love it wrapped around my fist when I'm inside you.

I chuckled. And exhaled. Fervor zinged through me. Somehow, our little conversation had lightened my mood. And I felt better.

Me: Yeah, right. See you at the wedding, big guy.

Tucker never replied. I waited for at least ten minutes but nothing. My smile dissolved, and I got up to warm up some of the soup Becca brought home last night.

Lying on the couch with the remote in my hand, I tried to watch some TV, but nothing captured my attention for more than a few minutes. I huffed and surfed the net, then decided a nap would do me good.

The pounding on my door brought me out of my slumber.

"Coming," I mumbled, trying to return to the land of the living and escape the lethargic state I was in. "Becca, have you lost your keys again?" I couldn't believe it. The girl lost them at least once a week. Along with her phone. And once her purse. I tell ya, the girl would lose her head if it weren't attached to her shoulders.

I unlocked the door and swung it open, only to stare, moving my mouth like a fish out of water, blinking.

"Hey sweetheart. Are you gonna let me in or not?" Tucker asked, pushing past me and ruffling my hair as if I were a kid. "Where's your dress? Why aren't you ready? Are you still sick? You sounded fine earlier. Do you want me to make you soup or something?" He leaned in to kiss my cheek. "By the way, you look beautiful."

My feet stayed glued to the entryway. No matter how hard I tried, I couldn't move, frozen in time.

"Wilde? Are you sure you're okay? Having a hard time closing your mouth?"

I bobbed my head in the slowest motion. Tucker walked back to me, closed the door, and with his fingers intertwined through mine, pulled me out of my stupor.

He looked absolutely divine in his gray suit, dark purple button-up shirt, and black tie. Yes, I had to admit, purple looked amazing on him.

I snapped back to the present. "What—what are you doing here?"

He sighed with a shake of his head. "Told ya I'd be here at five-thirty. Wait... You didn't expect me?"

"Nah. Thought you were joking."

He pivoted to face me. "Sweetheart, I never joke about taking a woman out on a date. Now get ready. Our reservation at Cosmos is in an hour."

I blinked some more. "Cosmos? I'm sure this is all a dream. None of it is true," I said, gesturing around us. "Please pinch me. Nobody can get a reservation at Cosmos on short notice. This place is booked months in advance. Even on a Thursday night."

"Well, everyone is not me. Now go. I'll make myself at home while you change." He removed his jacket, hung it on the back of a chair, rolled his sleeves, and slapped my ass in an intimate way when I retreated from the room.

In the mirror by my bed, I took in my appearance. Oh gosh, I looked disheveled. My hair was all over the place, dark shadows circled my eyes, and my clothes were rumpled from spending the day on a couch.

Beautiful? Tucker Philips forgot his prescription glasses. Clearly.

Adrenaline shot through me as I heard him humming something from the living room. *Cosmos.* The guy really went all in for this—date? What should I call it when the guy flew two hours just to have dinner with me in the most romantic and exquisite restaurant in the city?

If anyone else but Tucker had come here tonight, I would've already called my best friend to tell her all about it. But since I didn't want to jeopardize anything before her big day, I chose to keep the news of Tucker being here to myself.

Flutters of excitement ran through me, and I slid myself into an Otto & Newhouse coral sheath I got last Christmas. One of my rare fashion indulgences I bet Tucker would approve of. It gave my boobs all the attention, without looking too desperate, and ended just above my knees.

I fixed my hair into a loose braid, curled my lashes, and applied two thick coats of mascara, wanting my eyes to look bigger and more awake than they seemed. Foundation, a spray of perfume, a pinch of blush on my cheeks, and coral lipstick. I smacked my lips together, ready to go.

Tucker gasped the moment I stepped into the kitchen, hopping on one foot to put a heel on.

"Wilde, wow," he said, his gaze slowly drawing over my figure with an appreciative nod. "Otto & Newhouse? It's like you speak my language. Looks great on you." His perusal weighed on my skin, causing shivers to appear. "All right, I can work with a braid." He winked. "Come on, let's go." His large hand pressed on my lower back as we made it to the door.

In front of the building, a car with tinted windows waited for us.

"After you," my date said, opening the door to let me in.

I angled my upper body to face him when he joined me in the backseat. "All of this for tonight?" He nodded. His eyes swam with a million things I wished I could name. "Why are you here, Tuck? Tell me the truth."

He stared into my eyes. And my body shuddered from the intensity of his gaze. "Told ya. To take you out on a date. You said you've been feeling off. Wanted to cheer you up."

I smiled while I studied him. A frown creased his forehead.

"Okay, fine. Truth then." He fished something from the inner pocket of his jacket. "Here. Wanted to give you those."

I accepted the envelope and opened the flap. Inside lay over twenty pictures of Nick at different stages of his life.

I swallowed, meeting his serious demeanor. "You flew here to gimme pictures? You know you could have sent them in an email, right? Or by mail."

He nodded. "Yes. But I wouldn't have had the pleasure of seeing you in person if I did. Don't look so surprised, Wilde."

"We're not sleeping together." The refusal passed my lips before I could think of the words.

A mischievous smirk painted Tucker's face. "I didn't come here for sex if that's what you are assuming. We said six weeks, and I'm sticking to my word. I flew over because I wanted to spend some time with the maid of honor before the big day. Get to know each other better. And because I was starving."

A warm laugh bubbled out of me, and Tucker's baritone joined in.

"Fine. I guess they don't have food in Chicago. Let's feed you, big guy. And for what it's worth, I'm happy to see ya. Thanks for coming over and cheering me up."

My heart flipped in my chest when a genuine smile

took over his face, but I ignored the pummeling and focused my attention on the view outside

His hand rested above my knee as if it was a natural thing to do, and I didn't push it away, loving the warmth that zipped through me where our flesh connected. And the flutters that leaped in my belly.

When my gaze drifted back to the man sitting next to me, the smoldering in his irises got me breathless. It sent my pulse into a frenzy, and I tried to shut it down before it could shatter my resolutions. And the safety of my heart.

Without a word, he knitted his fingers through mine, and I relaxed in my seat, my head pressing against his shoulder while I enjoyed the ride.

11

TUCKER

osmos was exactly how I'd imagined it to be. Dimmed chandelier lights, dark ceiling and walls, ocean oak tables and flooring. It was both romantic and chic. I pulled Addison's chair, and she flashed me a smile when she sat. That could send my heart tipping if I wasn't careful.

"Wine?" I asked when the server brought us the drink menu.

"Huh, one glass. Told ya I was having insomnia. Alcohol will just feed it. And I'm desperate for eight hours of uninterrupted sleep."

I turned to the waiter, pointing to a bottle of red before thanking him.

Addison rested her face on her folded hands, watching me. Like the ocean on a sunny day, her blue eyes sparkled under the low light. And sucked me in.

"Tell me. Why are you really here? You didn't come all this way to have dinner with me and bring me baby pictures of your best friend."

I cleared my throat and tasted the wine when the server poured some into my glass after swirling it.

"Perfect." I waited until he filled our glasses and left before continuing. "That's the truth. Heard great things about this place. Never had a chance to visit it. You're my only friend in town, Wilde. So, I thought I could check two boxes on my list with one visit. I won't tell you I've missed you if that's what you're afraid of."

I flaunted her my biggest smirk and winked, and she sighed, bringing her glass to her lips.

"Oh, this is good."

"It is, right? Anyway, to answer your question, I barely ever go on vacations. So tonight somehow feels like a little reprieve from work."

"Well, this is sad. I don't get much free time either, but still, everyone deserves to have a break once in a while."

A curve drew on her full lips, and my finger itched to trace the contour. And I yearned to savor them one more time, to reminisce about their taste and the feel of them against mine.

She raised her glass to mine as the silence between us charged with unsaid words and the blazing chemistry I shared with no one else. "Let's drink to your night off then."

"To us."

Dinner was exquisite, but right now, I couldn't tell if it tasted better only because the company was appealing. Seated beside each other, Addison and I ended up splitting all that we ordered, talking about anything and everything.

"Dumbest thing you ever did?" she asked as we shared a piece of chocolate-swirled cheesecake, her spoon floating in front of her mouth and curiosity swimming in her irises.

"Who asks that?" I teased with a lifted brow. "Usually

women wanna know the cutest or funniest thing I ever did."

"I'm not every woman," Addison said, her gaze fused to mine.

A loud, heartfelt laugh bubbled out. "Don't worry, I noticed. Got reminded quite a few times already since I met you."

"Thank you." Pride poured from every inch of her face.

"You're thanking me? Geez, you're weird. A nice weird, though." I shook my head, unable to hide the stupid grin breaking on my face. "Dumbest thing... Let's see. One night I was in a rush to get somewhere, followed a crazy girl's instructions, and ended up ripping my favorite shirt, spending my night dressed like a stripper, and throwing away my hotel keycard when I discarded the ruined piece of fabric."

She cupped her mouth and yelped. "Oh god. So dramatic. I hoped it ended better than it started. I bet she was worth it, though."

I exhaled loudly and rewarded her with a boyish grin I was aware ladies loved. "The girl made me share her bed. And the next day, we had some of the best sex of my life. So, I would say she redeemed herself quite amazingly. She's unforgettable."

I brought my wineglass to my lips and took a long sip, never breaking eye contact with my date.

"Still up for some *Wilde* adventures?" she asked, her eyes shooting devilish sparks in the dim light of the restaurant.

"Should I be?"

She stared at me with intent, the sound of her voice seductive. "It depends. How much do you like to get burned when you play with fire?"

"When the fire is addictive, I could risk my life for it."

We said nothing as we finished our dessert and I paid the check, fighting with Addison over it.

Outside, the summer breeze swept our faces.

"What time is your flight back?" she asked.

I checked the time on my watch. "In three hours."

She clapped her hands before her. "Awesome. Let me give you a tour of my city. After Nashville and New York, Atlanta is the next best thing."

I moved until I faced her and tipped her chin up with a finger. "Don't you wanna go back home? Get some sleep. You look a bit pale."

"No. You're here just for a few hours, and if this is the only time off you get this year, I want it to mean something. It must count." She laced her fingers through mine, and some sort of electrical discharge stirred in me from where our palms joined. Addison blinked, and I'd bet she felt it too. Instead of releasing her grip on me, she tightened the connection. "Follow me."

My gaze drifted to her heeled feet. "You're not seriously thinking of walking all over town in those, are you?"

"Nah. I'm much more technologically advanced than you think, big guy. We're taking those."

I followed the direction of her pointed finger.

"You're kidding, right? Tell me you are."

She nodded. With conviction. "*Truth always*. Remember?"

I perused my surroundings and forfeited the idea of a better option.

"Fine. But those things are way too small for a guy of my height."

Addison chuckled, her fists resting on her hips, "Stop trying to find excuses because you're afraid."

She used her credit card to rent the scooters, and we each hopped on one.

"You're gonna ride in this dress?"

"Watch me."

This woman. She would never cease to amaze me.

We rode for over an hour as she showed me where she worked, her favorite park, some tourist attractions, the college she attended. But the entire time, my attention was riveted on her. As if she were a magnet and I couldn't pull away from her field.

"See, you aren't injured. All safe and sound," Addison quipped.

"It's actually fun," I conceded.

We continued our tour, exchanging heated gazes and loaded grins.

Minutes later, she stopped in front of a fast-food place so suddenly, I almost bumped into her.

"What the hell, Wilde. Are you still hungry?" I asked as she fumbled with her scooter.

"This thing is broken. Or the battery is dead. Either way, it won't restart."

"Let me check." I failed at fixing it too. "Use mine. I can walk. I'm in good shape. I should be able to catch up with you."

Addison glanced at me. "I know. That's not the point. It won't be as fun," she said with a pout. She blinked, but soon her eyes lit up with a mischievous twinkle. "Got an idea. I'll hop on yours." She approached my scooter. "Make room for me, big guy." With her arms secured around my midriff, she pressed her front to my back, molding our bodies to perfection.

The sensation of her warmth against mine awoke the electric tingles I felt earlier.

It affected every string of my composure.

When we stopped on the sidewalk in front of her apartment sometime later, I breathed easier the instant she peeled herself away from me.

With the discarded scooter long forgotten, I cleared my throat as I checked my watch, Addison standing a foot from me. My eyes caught the movements of her chest, her breasts rising with each breath, enticing me. "I'll have to go soon." My words sounded huskier than intended, and I cleared my throat.

I ate the gap between us with a stride and used my hand to tuck the tendrils of her hair behind her ear.

Her lips trembled as she met my eyes, her expression shadowed by the streetlamp above her.

Our eyes fixated on each other for a minute, neither of us brave enough to break the enchantment that had settled between us.

"Can I kiss you?" I asked, enraptured by her lips.

She shook her head but leaned forward at the same time.

Addison Wilde was a tall woman, even more with those heels on. I didn't have to bend too much to claim her mouth.

She sucked in a breath when my lips grazed hers, and my heart skipped a beat at the contact.

The mere connection sent a gazillion shivers along my spine.

My fingers tangled in her hair of its own volition, angling her head to deepen the kiss.

At this moment, I felt alive. And fucking amazing. As if only her mere presence removed the dead weights that had been pressing on my chest forever. As if I could fly along with her.

My entire dark world brightened with colors.

I really had to see that doctor. Now I was certain something was wrong with me. No more doubts. Women never had this kind of effect on me. We used each other for pleasure. Or companionship for a limited timeframe. Nothing more.

My body hardened.

Before I could get in deep with her where I would be unable to leave, I broke the contact with her lips. Scratching my eyebrow, I muttered, "Sorry."

Addison averted her eyes, adjusting her sinful dress. The one I'd been dying all night to remove off her. The one that fit her curves like a second skin.

"I should go," I said. "Let me walk you to your place."

She bobbed her head. "Sure."

"Hey." I framed her cheek with my palm and forced her to look at me. "If we keep doing this, I'll never be able to catch my plane. You know how it went down last time." Hurt along with something else danced in her eyes. "I've always been honest about this. Bachelor parties and wedding flings with you are one thing, but we can't just fuck around for weeks without emotions getting involved. And I don't do relationships, Wilde," I whispered, the weight of my regret crushing my chest when I spoke the last sentence.

She reeled her hurt in without even blinking.

"I knew the specifics of this arrangement when I seduced you in Nashville. I'm not some innocent woman, Tuck. I can take care of myself. I'm not looking for a relationship either. Well, I am, but not with you."

Her words, even if they echoed mine, stung. They pierced a layer of my heart I never knew existed before.

That doctor's appointment couldn't come fast enough. While I was at it, I should also book one with a neurologist. Perhaps I hit my head and didn't realize it. I seemed to have inflicted some serious damage to my skull, and now the side effects were strangling my rational thoughts.

"Truth. The thing is, I'm not looking to get my heart broken. I'm playing with ya because you're a safe choice. I know better than to fall for a womanizer like you."

I arched one eyebrow.

"Okay, and because you're insanely hot. But no need to blow your ego out of proportion." She squeezed my hand, still pressed against her cheek. "And I'm the one who made the no-sex rule first tonight. I'll just have to relieve myself on my own, I guess."

"Wilde…I'm…we don't…"

She placed a finger over my lips to silence me. "I had a perfect night. Let's not spoil it with false promises neither of us can stick to."

I nodded because I was at a loss for words.

"I'll still walk you upstairs."

"I wouldn't expect any less from you."

At her door, I leaned forward, and my lips skimmed her cheek. I gulped a sharp intake of air to settle whatever was going on inside me.

One of my hands molded to her hip crest, holding her in place. Anchoring her to me. The desire to touch her was strong. We breathed each other in for a short moment.

"Thank you for doing this with me tonight, Wilde."

"Thanks for flying here to spend a few hours with me. I had a great time."

My hand drifted to the small of her back, and I tugged her to me. No way could she not feel how bad my body was attracted to hers. Addison ground her hips against mine, increasing the fire already kindling between us.

"Tuck—" Her voice, a breathless murmur, played with my self-control.

"Let's do this again some other time," I whispered, my lips buried in her mass of blonde locks.

She swallowed. "Let's not."

I let out a chuckle. "See you around then." I stepped back and spun on my heels before she could close the door in my face. "Sweet dreams, Wilde."

———

For the next week, Addison and I either talked or texted every night, sharing about our days, our jobs, or nothing in particular. Our little night chats had become the highlight of my days. Yes, I'd turned into that kind of guy. The heaviness of my work and my lonely life didn't matter anymore every time we were together. In person or hundreds of miles away.

Fresh from the shower, I changed into a pair of lounge pants and a long-sleeved T-shirt, grabbed a beer, and perused the time on my watch, waiting for it to strike nine. Seated on my bed, my legs stretched before me, I peeled the label off the bottle.

Seconds later, Addison's name was displayed on my screen, and I picked it up, unable to stop the curl growing on my lips.

"Hey Tuck. Miss me already?" she asked as a greeting, the smile in her voice contagious.

Even if I were tempted to say no, I knew I wouldn't be able to lie to her. "Always, sweetheart. How was your day? That fucker Reinart giving you trouble, or did you succeed in ditching his account?"

She sighed. "He actually came to the office today."

"Wow, he did?"

"Yep. And decided to flirt with me. As if that would convince me to work with him."

My hands fisted at my sides. Stupid used-cars guy. I wished I could tell him what was on my mind right now.

"Did it work?" I chastised myself when the words left my mouth, but no way could I take them back without sounding like a jealous asshole.

Her laughter filled the line. And my heart at the same time. "Nah. Too late for playing nice. I'm so over that account. I have better things to do with genuine clients who respect me as a graphic designer. And as a woman."

That's my girl.

Fuck. Did I really say that? I shut my lids, wishing I hadn't spoken aloud.

"Your girl?" Addison asked after a few infinite seconds.

Yep, I did say it. It wasn't just the one meaningless thought popping into my head. I had so many of them these days. Daydreams about her sporting a happy grin or watching me with a devilish glint. Addison spread underneath me, ready for me to ravage each inch of her body with my tongue. Or she in my arms at night or locked around me as I pushed into her in the shower. Things I wished to tell her. Or asking for her opinions on both trivial and life-changing decisions.

I covered my slip-up with a nervous chuckle. "You know what I mean. Don't make a big deal out of it. Anyway, I'm just proud you gave him a run for his money."

"Yeah, well. How about your day? Did that meeting go as expected?"

I cleared my throat. "Yes. But it will mean more work for me." I paused. "It's a good thing. But some days, I wish for a simpler life. I'm about to get a big bonus." I grimaced when I added, "It just doesn't have the appeal it used to."

"Perhaps you could try something else. Just a thought."

"What would I do?"

"Anything. Dahlia told me how gifted you are. You

could try your hand at anything. Like sky is the limit. Nobody has that chance in life."

I reflected on it. "I guess. Still, I've never imagined myself doing anything else."

"What would you do if you could reinvent yourself?"

I didn't even have to think about it. "I'd do something that brings people together. Whatever it means. Never really put too much thought into this."

"Like what? Organizing events? That's actually what I would like to do. Right after designing T-shirts."

"Quite impressive. Nah, I was thinking more like hosting events instead of organizing them. Or... I don't have a clue. I'd have to ponder it some more." I shifted on my bed. "How's the video montage coming? Think I'll be able to see it before the wedding?"

"I'm mostly done. There are some changes I wanna make. Give it a week or two at the most."

"Don't deceive me, Wilde," I teased, unable to hide the amusement in my tone. "I have great expectations from you."

"Please don't expect too much. I am trying my hand at it."

"I won't," I said, the teasing clear in my tone. "But after I noticed your creativity back in Nashville, I'm sure I'll be impressed."

We talked for a little longer, switching to video chat at some point.

"What would you choose as a superpower if you could pick any one?" she asked.

I considered the question for a full minute. "Fly."

"Why?"

"So I could come to see you right now and make sure you're really okay and not pretending for my sake."

I winked. And she appeared flustered. The pink hue looked good on her cheeks.

Addison bared an over-exaggerated all-teeth-display smile, and I failed at containing my laughter.

"Fine, you're not faking. Can clearly see it right now." We both burst out in chuckles. "We should hang up. It's almost eleven. Time flies with you, Wilde. And I'm not helping you kick your insomnia to the curb by keeping you up late most nights."

She didn't formulate a reply, instead watched me with a soft smile. My skin tingled, and my gaze got lost in the blue lasers trained on me.

"Thank you," she said after some time.

"Why?" I asked, almost breathless from the intense connection we shared.

"Just for being you. Night."

Her soft voice blanketed the loneliness that had been visiting me in these months, a protective feeling that I cherished.

"Night, sweetheart."

And for the next hour, I lay on my bed, unsure of what I had experienced in the last few hours, but longing for a repeat. Because my body and soul were now at ease.

———

The next day, I was about to leave for work when the concierge met me at my front door with a kraft paper package in hand. "For you, Mr. Philips," he said, handing it to me. Looping my messenger bag across my shoulder, curiosity had my fingers ripping the wrapping apart only to find a folded piece of purple cotton inside. Instinctively, I knew it was one of hers. A T-shirt Addison designed. Bracing myself for whatever message it conveyed, I unfolded it, her scent reaching my nose. The devil had sprayed it with her perfume. The crooked tilt of my lips occurred naturally when I flipped it over.

"Official Atlanta Scooter Club. Honorary member."

And this time, the size seemed like the right fit.

A badge and a certificate fell on the floor, the latter signed with "Addison Wilde, President." My lips stretched wider. She had gone all in, all Wilde, on this.

I tried to call her but hit her voicemail. Instead, I sent her a text.

Me: Got the delivery. I can't wait to show my colors to the people of Chicago. Think we could start a chapter here?

Addison: Oh, you're jealous of my president title, is that it? Let me think about it. I'm not against monthly meet-ups. Confirming my position as the head of the club.

Me: If you're the president, I'll be your vice.

Addison: You would agree to rule under me?

Me: Anytime, Wilde. That ass of yours is etched on my brain forever.

Me: Gotta go or I'll be late. Traffic is a bitch. Tonight at 8 still works for ya?

Addison: Yep. Later. Show your colors, big guy. Make me proud.

Instead of dropping the piece of clothing back in my

apartment, I shoved it into my bag after I took a whiff of it. A scent that coiled into my heart in a way I never expected. Today, I decided to bring a piece of her along with me, not a care in the world about how lame it might seem.

My phone rang at seven eleven that night. Forty-nine minutes before the time Addison and I had set for tonight's phone date.

"Hey you," I greeted her. "Everything all right?"

Addison usually called me at the time we pre-set, never late or early. The hitch in her breath hinted there was actually something bothering her. She remained silent. My pulse picked up at the thought she might be sad or upset.

"Wilde, talk to me. Or I'm booking the next flight to Atlanta and not leaving until you spill it."

She inhaled a shaky gulp of air. "You'll think it's silly," she whispered.

"Maybe. But you're not the type of woman to hide behind silliness and other people's opinion. Speak. I'm all ears."

I switched the call to video chat.

"Hey, I'm not answering that."

"Who's the baby now? Come on, let me see ya."

She sighed but ended up agreeing to it.

My mouth curled at the sight of her. Disheveled hair. Reddened cheeks. Dark outlines under her baby blues. A mix of cuteness and exhaustion.

A shadow lingered over her face, and I squared my stance, worry now tingeing my blood.

"Sweetheart, what's going on?" I asked, unable to hide the edge in my voice.

"I told Reinart to go fuck himself today. In person. In front of everyone." The air leaving her sounded painful.

"What did the fucker do?" I growled, ready to jump into my phone screen, my words clipped.

"He cornered me and palmed my ass. Called me *baby*, trying to seduce me while making me feel like a powerless piece of meat."

Fury, raw and blinding, rose in me, blackening my vision. I breathed faster, clenching my free hand at my side, the other one too busy strangling my device.

"Listen, don't ever say harassment is silly. The guy had it coming. He deserves every shred of your wrath. And telling him to go fuck himself is not enough of a punishment for acting like a jackass and manhandling a woman." I controlled the rage revving up in me with noisy inhales and exhales. "If it were up to me, his ass would be hanging from the Grand Canyon right now. Thanks to my soled foot, I have a sick right kick."

Addison's shoulders lowered, and a small bend of her lips graced her face. It suited her much better. And eased some of the murderous thoughts invading my mind.

She continued before I could finish plotting this guy's fallout. "These days, I don't recognize myself anymore. I'm either full-on happy or ready to kill with my bare hands. That's if I'm not about to bawl or pass out from exhaustion. And when Reinart got handsy, I froze. I'm usually a scary and feisty opponent when someone pushes my buttons. Not today. I should've kicked his butt to Alaska myself."

"He deserves more than a *go fuck yourself* from you. The dickhead has been acting like a jerk for weeks, and you've been putting up with him the entire time. I would've loved to witness you giving him a run for his money, though. Don't feel bad, but you've been working a lot lately. And with the last-minute wedding plan details and everything else, you deserve a break."

"I'm just... I don't know. Disappointed in me, more than anything else. Fighting back and delivering upper-cuts the Southern way is more my thing."

I returned her lopsided smile. "Please never let me be on your wrong side. I'd be scared for my life. And my balls. I'm never entering a ring to battle with you. Even though I like it when you're playing dirty."

Addison relaxed her posture, and some color returned to her features.

"Thank you. For having my back. And calming my mad self."

"I did nothing."

She shook her head. "Nah, you did everything right. You listened to me. And made me feel less shitty about my day."

Pinching my lips for a moment, I asked the question burning the tip of my tongue. "Why didn't you call Dahlia to hash it out?"

"She doesn't know about Reinart. She's in full wedding-preparation mode. And truth? You're the first person I thought of. It sounds stupid, but I knew you'd understand and not blame me for not ripping his balls out." She paused. "Dahlia would have driven here to give the guy a piece of her mind. It would've been ugly." A laugh bubbled out.

"Nah, that I don't believe. Dahlia's isn't scrappy like that."

"Don't underestimate her, big guy. We're Southern girls. We're tougher than we look. Don't forget she already threatened you."

"Yes, that. You've got a point. She was scary enough."

"See, told ya. Anyway, Becca offered to tag along tonight and get drunk after work. In the past, I would've done that—"

"What changed?" I asked, holding my breath.

"You. We happened. I wanted to tell ya. Don't ask me why. It makes no sense at all."

"Maybe it does," I ventured.

"Maybe. Anyway, thanks for listening to me. And giving me the space to vent."

"Always, Wilde."

We remained quiet for a long while, our gazes lingering, silence speaking more than words.

"By the way, thank you for the shirt. I'll start recruiting after the wedding. I'm pretty sure our Chicago chapter will put yours to shame. Just saying. Be prepared, sweetheart."

The tension vanished from her, the knowledge calming the jitters I'd experienced earlier.

"Hey Tuck?"

"Yeah."

"I really like this friendship thing we've got going on. It's important to me."

"Me too. It's actually nice to have you in my life. Never thought we would end up here, you and me. I never had any girls as friends before. You're the first one."

"I'm your first *girlfriend*?"

I sighed. "You know what I mean. Also, don't let it go to your head, Wilde."

We both burst into a fit of laughter.

"Gotta wake up early tomorrow. Night, Tuck."

"Good night, sweetheart. Hope your dreams are filled with me."

She giggled. "We'll see."

We hung up, and I stared at my phone screen for longer than necessary afterward.

"I miss ya," I said to my blank screen. Then I shook my head, trying to push away the words I just spoke. Because they made no sense. And they sounded foreign on my tongue. But right.

An invisible clamp crushed my stupid heart at the thought. More knots twisted my stomach.

I'd been lonely for a while, and now it weighed on me. Damn my stupid mind for mixing everything up.

12

ADDISON

Becca shook me out of my slumber two days later. "Hey Addi, are you still feeling off? You've been sleeping all day."

I lifted myself on one elbow, trying to blink my drowsiness away, so out of it, that I felt like I'd just landed back after a very long trip.

With a slow browse, I perused my bedroom. It felt both foreign and familiar as my brain rebooted at a lazy pace. I registered the vintage dresser set I had bought in college and repainted in a teal hue. The full-length mirror framed with recycled barnwood Dahlia gifted me when we were teens. I blinked again. My focus adjusted, and I brought my attention to my roommate.

"Been talking to Tucker till late last night. We were playing a stupid twenty-questions game and couldn't stop."

Becca's eyebrows reached her hairline. "You two have been spending an awful lot of time together after he came here a week ago. Anything I should know?" She waggled her eyebrows in the annoying way she always did.

I shook my head. "C'mon, Becca. We live a few states

apart. Nothing's going on. Don't make up stories. Fake news is so last year. We're just getting to know each other. Best man and maid of honor thing. It's easier if we work together than fight all the time."

"Oh god, you're attracted to him. Big time. You're blushing."

I pressed my hands over my burning cheeks.

"I'm not. Stop. Don't create a story that doesn't exist."

Becca raised her hands between us. "The next thing I know, you'll be each other's plus-one at the wedding."

I cleared my throat.

"Oh, you already are? Are you kidding me?"

I waved a hand. "It's easier that way, you know. No distraction. Better teamwork. We're doing this for Dah and Nick. It's nothing."

"Yeah, yeah, it's nothing. If you say it," she said, barely able to reel her smirk in.

"I'm not seeing anyone, and Tuck hasn't invited anyone yet. Why shouldn't we simplify our lives for once? Inviting other people means babysitting them for the day. Hard pass."

"Whose idea was it?"

"Mine. His. Who cares?"

"I do," my traitorous girlfriend said. "I'd pay a lot of money to be in your headspace right now."

"Enough. Let's not talk about the wedding. It's in a month. A lot can happen by then. Let's do something fun tonight. You and I."

Her amusement dissolved. "Nah, I can't. Ben got tickets for the ballet in town. I gotta get ready soon."

"Oh."

"Sorry, Addi." She winced. "Can I take a raincheck?"

"Yes. Don't worry. I'll catch up on my sleep. I've been working like crazy, and my insomnia isn't cured. I'm still

EMMANUELLE SNOW

struggling to not wake up in the middle of the night and toss and turn."

Becca clapped her hands. "You need your *non-friend* Tucker to rock your nights, girl. You've been having insomnia since you met him. So maybe he holds the secret key to the cure. Like he induces it and then heals it." She allowed the idea to settle in my brain for a beat, then added, "Yes, I bet it'd work."

"Oh God. Do you hear yourself? You speak nonsense."

"Do I? It sounds perfectly sane from my end."

I nudged her side. "Blah-blah-blah. Just go and get ready now. Ben hates being late."

My roommate left, and her words replayed in my head. *He induces it and then heals it.* What if her words were true? What if Tucker was the answer to my sleepless nights? To my restless body and mind.

Without thinking, I opened my laptop, surfed the web for a few minutes until I found what I was looking for, then closed it with a thud before retreating to my bedroom to gather everything I might need.

Four hours later, I landed at Chicago O'Hare Airport with only a small carry-on and my courage.

Pretending I had to send back the pictures through the mail, Dahlia gave me Tucker's address, and I recited it to the cab driver.

I kept my back straight the entire ride, hoping my plan would not fail me, or my humiliation would just skyrocket into space. Not that I cared normally, but I didn't want things to be awkward between us. Also, I was trying to forget I was riding in some stranger's car. Cabs were gross. Who knew what had happened in this backseat before?

"Lady, you look nervous," the driver said in a strong accent.

I rolled my shoulders back. "No. I don't do nervous. I'm rather excited. Or something close to it."

My stomach was tied in knots. Excitement wasn't the right emotion. My insides were a ball of nerves the closer I got to my destination.

I paid the fare, grabbed my bag, and with my chin high and back tall, I entered the impressive building that matched the address I noted on my phone.

A man in his sixties greeted me. "Good evening, miss. May I help you with something tonight?"

"Hi. Sure. I'm here to see Tucker Philips."

"Who should I announce?"

Nervous jitters awoke inside me. No, I didn't want this man to call Tucker and ruin my surprise arrival. Our daily phone talk was scheduled in less than ten minutes. I needed to up my game to not miss my opportunity window.

"Sir," I said, using my most convincing tone and smiling sheepishly. "Tucker is the groomsman at our best friends' wedding. We have things to discuss. It's kind of important. I was hoping to surprise him. I'll have him call you as soon as I'm up there, or you can ride the elevator with me to make sure I'm not some crazy ex-girlfriend."

"Oh, so you know Mr. Peterson?"

Feeling Lady Luck on my side, I added, "Yes. Nick is marrying my best friend. We're about to become this one big family, the four of us." An idea crossed my mind. I opened the photo app on my phone and swiped to the pictures of the bachelor-bachelorette party night. I flipped my phone to show the man pictures of the four of us and of Tucker and me in our matching T-shirts.

He studied me for a long beat. "It's not in the building rulebook to let anybody who's not on the list go unannounced up. Mr. Philips is a nice guy. And he's quite private too."

"He is," I agreed. "We're working on a video montage together. He's giving me pictures of Nick as a child. Do you have kids?"

The man's lips twitched, and he grabbed his phone from the inner pocket of his jacket. "Two. They're adults now. My daughter just gave birth to our first grandchild. Lela. She's two weeks old." He thumbed the screen and showed me the picture of a little pink-swaddled bundle.

"Oh, she's beautiful. And tiny. You must be proud."

"I am. She's an angel." He put his phone away. "What's your name, miss?"

"Addi."

"Listen, I'll make an exception this time and let you go up. In a couple of minutes, I'll call Mr. Philips to make sure everything is fine with you being here. You seem like a nice young lady, but I'm old and have witnessed a lot in my life. If you bullshit me, I'll have security remove you faster than you can spell my name."

My eyes darted to his nametag.

"Your name's Leo."

"Exactly."

"I promise I'm one of the good ones, Leo. I flew here to talk about the wedding business. And see Tucker."

He nodded, and after I thanked him, I moved forward to drop a chaste kiss on his cheek before entering the elevator, ready for the next phase of my plan.

––––––––

When the doors opened on the forty-sixth floor, I held my breath, desperate to calm the thundering of my heart. I didn't do nervous. No, I wasn't programmed to feel anxiety like the rest of humanity. Until now. For the first time in my short existence, my organs were playing pinballs inside my body.

Tucker always sent my heart into an exciting yet fearful dance.

I stopped in front of the mirror in the hallway to fix my hair, touch up my lipstick, and adjust my loose white top. Paired with denim cut-offs and ankle cowboy boots, I looked Southern-sexy. And hot enough to seduce the man living a few doors down.

With a white-knuckled grip on my bag, I padded toward the door number I'd memorized. The last check of my phone told me Tucker would be calling in... Five, four, three, two, one. Okay, he wasn't that punctual, but close enough. I waited for the device to ring and brought it to my ear after accepting the call.

"Hey big guy, you're late," I teased.

He hesitated for a second, no doubt checking the time.

"Three minutes. I wouldn't call it late."

"Three minutes is three minutes. I could've decided to not wait for ya."

He let out a chuckle. "Keep telling yourself that, Wilde. I'm certain you're addicted to me by now."

"You wish."

A grin took my face hostage as I knocked on the door.

"Can you gimme a minute? Someone's here. Must be the concierge."

"Sure."

He yanked the door open, his eyes searching the surrounding space before settling on my silhouette, as if to make sure I wasn't a figment of his imagination.

"Hey you."

His throat worked, and I found the movement enticing.

"What are you doing here?" he asked, a frown etching his forehead.

"Thought you'd like some company."

His dark irises surveyed the length of me. "How did you get here?"

"Plane. And cab. The usual."

Tucker blinked, his frown deepening. "Wait. You took a cab? On your own? To see me?"

I shrugged.

"I thought you said cabs freaked you out." His eyes searched my face. For a hint. Or anything he was dying to read there.

"They do. So?"

"Fuck, Wilde. I'm touched. You braved your fear of gross vehicles for me." His hand rested over his heart while he looked impressed with me.

I huffed. "I wouldn't call it a fear, but you're right. I did. In the heat of the moment, I almost forgot about it."

He stashed his phone in his back pocket and reached me in one stride. His muscular arms wrapped around me and lifted me up. And against him, I felt special.

When he put me back down on my feet, my front brushed his strong torso, and my body electrified at the contact. For a minute, we stared into each other's eyes, neither of us breaking the charged silence.

Until he cleared his throat. "Wilde, are you here to invite me on a date?" he finally asked, the husky sound of his voice reverberating through me.

I shook my head, my smile anchored to my lips.

"Are you here to give the pictures back?"

I shook my head again.

"Are you here because you missed me?"

I offered him a one-shoulder shrug. "Maybe."

His ringtone broke the moment. We both ignored it. But soon, it rang again.

"Oh. It must be Leo."

"Leo?"

"The guy downstairs. He's supposed to check up on me. To make sure I'm not a lunatic who forced myself onto you."

Tucker frowned. "Wait. Why?"

"Just answer. I'll explain later."

"Now that you mention it, how did you get up here?"

I offered him my most irresistible smirk. "I have my ways." I zipped my lips with my fingers.

He chuckled before answering his phone. After exchanging a few words with the doorman, he brought his attention back to me. His fingers intertwined with mine, and he reached for my bag with his other hand. "Let me show you around." He stopped and turned to watch me. "Are you spending the night?"

"It depends."

"On what?" he asked, his gravelly voice now sending shivers through my entire being.

"You."

His throat rippled, and something glinted in his eyes. He said nothing, but seconds later, I found myself in his room. He dropped my bag on his bed without an explanation.

"Let's talk about it later."

I nodded and followed him to the kitchen.

"Had dinner?"

"Nope. But I heard from a respectable source that Chicago can't feed its people. I'm scared I'll starve tonight."

"That's a shame. I wouldn't want you to go to bed famished. Remember, I have plenty on me I can feed you with. Too bad you're picky. If you change your mind, all you have to do is ask. And I'll stuff your mouth." He wriggled his dark brows.

Barely keeping a straight face, I tipped my brows in fake sarcasm and managed a rejoinder. "So generous and selfless of you, Tuck. Feeding Chicago's people with seeds and love juice, one woman at a time. Yeah, I can see the appeal."

"You don't know what you're missing, sweetheart." His shoulders bumped mine playfully. "Let me fix you something then, or we can order in. See, I can be a gentleman."

"Who said I came here for a gentleman?"

He smirked. "Touché."

We exchanged smiles, and I went along with him as he showed me his place.

"The view is magnificent from here," he said as we stared through the giant wall of ceiling-to-floor windows in his living room. "But after a while, it loses its appeal because I don't see it anymore. My eyes are used to the sight. It's a shame, though."

"I can't wait to see it in the daylight. I'm sure it's beautiful in the morning."

"So, you *are* spending the night." It was more an affirmation than a question.

"I guess I am. Careful though, I always sleep naked."

A groan left his lips. "I can work with that. Barely."

"Great." I couldn't stop grinning like a fool.

———

We sat cross-legged on the floor by the window, the city lights below trying to catch my attention. But the entire time, my gaze rested on Tucker. He had changed into normal-people's clothes, which meant a T-shirt, the one I sent him, which sent giddy flutters to my stomach, and a pair of what could pass as sweatpants. No Esteban Fu or Jaxon Arison in sight tonight. In my opinion, he looked even more incredible than in his usual dress-up attire.

"Why are you here, Wilde?" he asked as I battled him for the last chunk of chicken from the Chinese takeout we ordered. At first, we passed the containers back and forth, but now we were seated side by side, our chopsticks becoming swords, reaching for the best pieces.

"Are we playing the same game we did when you came to visit me the other night?" I asked with a lifted brow, plastering the most innocent look on my face.

He shook his head with a loud sigh. "Why won't you just tell me?"

"Because it's more fun this way. When you know nothing about my devious plans."

"Devious?" He mirrored my expression. "Will it get me in trouble? Again?"

"Maybe. Maybe not. Are you willing to find out?"

His Adam's apple bobbed, and I got entranced by the movement, missing his answer.

"What?" I asked, my voice so rough I had to clear my throat.

"Am I so handsome it's distracting you, Wilde?"

"Nah, keep dreaming, big guy."

His digit pointed at my face. "Tell that to the flush on your cheeks."

"Not blushing."

"Oh, you're just bothered. Fine with me." He wiggled his dark brows.

He moved in, his lips looking too freaking delicious for his own good. And mine.

Tucker Philips emanated an energy that was too powerful to ignore. At least, my body had a hard time staying indifferent. For once in my life, I enjoyed not being in control. And being chased after.

"Addison, why are you here?"

Oh my dear god. Goosebumps blossomed on my arms at his mere whisper of my name. No way could I resist this man. Was Becca onto something after all?

I swallowed, trying to grasp the remaining threads of my composure. "See, my roommate has this theory. About ya."

"About me?" he echoed.

"Mm-hmm." I paused, calming the skittish hormones that were desperate to get him naked. "She says you're responsible for my insomnia. That you induced it. After our little Nashville adventure. And that if I want to cure it, well, you gotta fuck it out of me."

"Fuck it out of ya?"

I nodded.

"Is this true? Do you need me to fuck away your insomnia, Wilde?"

Jesus, why did he always have to be so damn sexy every time he opened his mouth?

"I traveled all this way so we could test her theory. What do you say?"

"You know we're not supposed to have sex, you and I, right? We agreed."

I nodded again.

"And you know I'll get in deep trouble with your best friend if we get caught, right?"

I nodded half a dozen times. "Does it mean you won't do it? My sleep schedule is all over the place. I'm a tired shit show during the day and can't find a soothing position at night. Tuck, help a girl out. Desperate times call for desperate measures. Please. Fuck that curse out of me."

"Did I say I wouldn't?" He shot me a cocky sideways grin.

"Nope."

"So, Wilde, ask me again. With that dirty mouth of yours that gets me hard as a rock."

"Tucker Philips, would you please get me naked on the floor and fuck this state of insomnia you 'might have induced' out of me? Over and over again for the rest of the weekend?" I used my fingers to air-quote the words.

"When you ask it like this, so charmingly, how can I refuse?"

I grabbed the hem of my shirt, about to peel the fabric off me, when he stopped me with a hand.

Tucker inched closer, his breath caressing the shell of my ear. "Wilde, not so fast. I wanna seduce you first. We always skip the preliminary." He cupped my face, his gaze heavy on mine. Hot air filled every bit of space between us. Full of sexual tension. And lust sparks. His thumb traced the contour of my lips, his focus on my mouth.

"No. You took me on a date. We have daily hour-long chats. And we had a picnic just now. It counts for something. Told ya already I'm not here for a gentleman."

He pushed back, scooting away from me. "I'm a gentleman. I always am."

My breath caught midway to my lungs. "Show me then. Rock my world." My voice quivered. My senses heightened at the sight of him. The sexual energy emanating from him fueled my brain.

Tucker removed the bottle from my hand and placed it on the floor beside me. The hammering of my heart filled my ears as it rebounded against the walls of my skull. "You're gorgeous, Wilde. Just so you know, if you were my girl, I would never hurt you. You're too precious."

His words, even though I knew we would never be a

couple, made an impression on me. They meant something to me. Maybe not all men were heartbreakers. Or cheaters. For a second, I wished Tucker Philips was available. Because the friendship we had developed in the last two weeks was something I cherished. And something that did not occur often in a lifetime.

His hands gripped my waist, and he pulled me to him, his loud intake of air vibrating through me.

"How do you seduce a woman, Tuck?" I asked, breathless.

"Somehow, it's different with you. You're not just a girl I'll forget all about in the morning. You are…you."

"What does it mean?"

"You know things about me I've never told anyone. Even when we're doing this, it's not a game to me. Because I would never use you this way."

My words lodged in my throat. The sincerity of his words affected me. In a deeper way than I would've ever thought.

After swiping on his phone for a moment, soft music played from a sound system I couldn't see, and Tucker tightened his grip around my body.

"Dance with me."

I placed my palm on his free one, the other holding me against him.

I was so under his spell that I almost failed to recognize the song. My lips curled up as I leaned back to watch him. "Our song," I whispered.

"It'll forever be," he confirmed with a sexy wink. One I bet could set my panties on fire if they weren't already drenched.

Gosh, he was good at this. I thought to myself. I was the seduction queen, but right now, this man facing me was throwing me out of my own game.

**...Because all I wanted was to
call your name
All I wanted was to claim you
as mine...**

At this moment, I forgot our arrangement was just that
—an arrangement. Between two consenting adults. I
believed I could be all these things. And that someone
could love me, like really love me, for who I was. For me.

Tucker's mouth descended over mine, and he brushed
my lips in the gentlest of caresses. I shivered from head to
toe. A guttural moan escaped my mouth before I could
leash it in.

His hand released mine and pressed against my warm
cheek, the pad of his thumb grazing the corner of my
mouth.

"Fuck, Wilde. Why are you here again?"

"So you can fuck my insomnia out of me," I whispered, breathless, overwhelmed with foreign sensations.

His hands traveled down, and one digit traced the
length of the junction between my thighs. I sucked in a
shaky breath. Oh dear god.

A moan tumbled out of my mouth. This man. He had
a way to make my body sing every time he touched me.

Unable to contain the desire pooling low in my belly
and radiating to all my cells, I rolled my hips over his hand,
now rubbing me over the fabric of my shorts.

Tucker's mouth spoke next to my ear, his words a
murmur against my skin.

"Just like this, sweetheart. Come on, chase that pleasure." His breathing hitched, his movements growing
faster. "Yes, like this."

A moment later, I tilted my head back, my eyes closed,
chewing on my bottom lips, as elation built deep inside my

core. Then I pressed my forehead against his hard chest, barely able to drive some oxygen in. All the sensations swirling inside me captured my body and took me hostage as ribbons of pleasure coiled around me. My knees buckled as an orgasm hit me. Powerful and unchained.

My toes curled.

A loud whimper left my lips.

Tucker growled, holding me with both hands, as I tried to regain my control, weakened by the relief he provided me.

"Better?" he asked, his lips claiming mine in a dance I could easily lose myself in.

I nodded, unable to express anything in words.

His hard erection pushed against my lower belly, and I palmed it through his pants.

His hand entwined in my hair as he kissed me with purpose, eating my lips, savoring my tongue, starting a fire at my core.

We would combust together.

Right now, none of this felt like a fling. Like something we could wake up from. Because I had never felt this good in my entire life. As if I belonged in his arms. As if our minds, our bodies, and our souls were one. And nothing could come between us.

My fingers grabbed the hem of his T-shirt, ready to discard the piece of fabric away, when he stopped me with a hand.

"Addison, stop."

Something in his words—or was it his tone?—jolted me, and I jumped back.

Tucker blinked, and my heart skipped a beat at the torturous expression painting his handsome face.

"What?" I asked once I found my voice.

He rubbed his nape, shook one leg to relieve the

tension tenting his pants, and exhaled. "We can't... I can't... We said..."

"Can we make one exception? For tonight only. I'm so tired all the time."

"Wilde——" Uncertainty painted his face.

I blinked too. A lump appeared in my throat, and a rock pressed against my chest. The roots of rejection spread to every inch of me.

I ran a hand over my face, my eyes brimming with tears. I should've never come here tonight. This was a mistake. We said no strings attached and no sex, and then I traveled two hours to want to get fucked by a man who would never be more to me than a few nights stand.

I pivoted on my heels, ready to bolt out of there and forget all about this stupid idea of mine. Or Becca's. Yes, she was the one who put those ludicrous thoughts into my head. Why did I follow her advice? What was wrong with me? Nothing made sense in my life anymore. Did I fail myself so badly in my relationships with losers that I forgot who I was along the way? Had I become so desperate?

Exhaustion hit me and chased away the last flecks of lust still lingering inside me.

"Sorry. I should go," I muttered, not turning around to glance at Tucker one last time. I would never let him see the pain spreading across my face. No. I was Addison Wilde, strong and independent. I didn't need men to feel complete.

I hurried toward his bedroom to fetch my bag. I'd never been to Chicago before, but I'm sure I could find a hotel downtown and spend the next two days either locked in a room, throwing my stupid self a fueled-by-ice-cream pity party, or play tourist. I'd always wanted to see the Bean and eat a deep-dish pizza. Here was my chance. Yay.

I crossed the threshold of the master bedroom, using

the back of my hand to wipe the tears that now welled in my eyes.

Two muscular arms wrapped around me from behind.

"Wilde, wait." Just the sound of Tucker's voice appeased something deep in me.

"Let go of me. I need to get out of here," I said, carrying no conviction in my voice.

"Wilde, look at me. Are you crying?"

I cringed. How could Tucker always read me?

I clenched my teeth and spoke through them. "I am not."

Instead of releasing his grip around my waist, he tightened it.

"Tuck, let me go. Please," I begged. But soon my words turned into sobs I couldn't keep in.

Without saying anything, he spun me in his embrace, his arms circling my heaving shoulders and holding me against him.

He murmured into my ear, "Shhh... Shhh..."

I emptied the tear dam I had no idea existed over his shirt, his hand now brushing my hair and his lips kissing the crown of my head.

Once my sobs trailed away, he took a step back, using both palms to cradle my face, his thumbs erasing the traces of moisture left on my skin.

"Addison, I didn't push you away. I was just trying to not put at risk what we have. To not destroy what we've been building for the last two weeks. I want you. God knows I do. Every inch of me does. But I made a promise to my best friend. And failed to keep it twice already. And I made a promise to you too. That I can keep it in my pants for over a month. This isn't me. I'm the guy people trust. No matter how strong this pull between us is, I'm sure we can wait till the wedding. Doesn't mean I want you gone, though. You're my first girlfriend. Huh? Why do I always say it like this? You're the first girl I'm friends with. And it means something to me. I feel different around you. Good different. And your brand of crazy has grown on me. But we said no strings attached. The last thing I want is to hurt you. I've never slept with a girl I considered my friend before. This is all new to me. And truthfully, I'm not sure how we should proceed. Because I still wanna be your friend after the wedding. Even if it means no more sexual benefits from it. Let's not fuck this up. We agreed we'd have sex the weekend of the wedding and then stop."

I snorted.

Why did my first rebound have to be a nice guy?

13

TUCKER

"You should have been a jerk," Addison said, her voice throaty now after the tears she cried. "Then it would be easier to just move away and never talk to you again. Why do you have to be nice to me? It's fucking everything."

A warm laugh broke the tension that had settled between us as it left my mouth. "Sweetheart, don't repeat that. I have a reputation to uphold. Don't blow my cover."

Her eyes were still glistening, but a grin made its way to her lips. It eased some of the uneasiness that had taken over when she ran away from me after I stopped our make-out session. Still, I had a hard time justifying why I did it. All I craved was to fuck her the way she asked me to. Till the morning. And start all over again. But something inside me—call it the voice of reason surprisingly sounding so much like Nick—nagged me that it was a bad idea. That I'd regret getting too close to her. Too comfortable in our relationship. And I meant everything I said. Our nascent friendship was important to me. And I refused to jeopardize it. Because once the sex was done and over with, our relationship would suffer, no doubt. And I really appreciated the bond we shared now. It was unique. Nothing I'd ever experienced before. Easy and entertaining all at once.

Jesus, what was happening to me? First, my dick went on a sabbatical, and now this. Where did the voices in my head come from? I'd never invited them. And they played with my mind.

All my life, Nick had been my best friend, my brother, but also my confidant and family. I rarely opened up to people, but when I did, he was my go-to person. But somehow, in a matter of weeks, Addison Wilde had become the person I wanted to tell everything to. The one I wanted to call when I had a doubt or when I needed advice or a kick in the ass. Or the last voice I wished to hear before going to bed.

It made no sense, but hey, at this point, I had stopped asking myself *why*. We both had trust issues, and I could recognize a lot of myself in her. Or perhaps most of our friends were in serious relationships, and we, single people, had to stick together. No matter what, I relished her company and was in no hurry to oust her.

"Don't go," I pleaded. "Stay. You can either sleep in the guest room or share my bed. I won't have sex with you, but I could hold you. I've never done that before. But my gut is telling me this is what you might need from me. What we both need."

Addison averted her eyes. "Huh, I don't know. Not sure if it's a good idea."

"Think about it."

She yawned, and I followed suit.

"Tired?"

"Exhausted."

"Let's get to bed, okay? You need a good night's rest.

I'll watch over you. To make sure this insomnia stays away. What do you say?"

She offered me a small shrug.

"I'll take that as a yes." I tipped her face in my direction with one finger. "Were you serious when you said you sleep naked?" I asked with a wink, trying to bring back the flirtatious ease between us.

Addison burst into a fit of laughter, and the sight filled my heart with peace. Yeah, we would be okay.

"Maybe. Now you'll never know."

"Stay here. I have an idea." I went to my closet, grabbed a T-shirt, and handed it to her.

She quirked a brow, watching me with suspicion swimming in her vibrant blue eyes.

"Wear my T-shirt."

"Tucker Philips, you own mortal clothes?"

"Shhh, I told ya already to not spread rumors about me. But truth be told, I'm human. And since we're having a sleepover, I find it fitting I should lend you clothes. This way, you won't have to sleep naked, and we can share a bed. It's been forever since I had a friend over for the night"—I studied her face—"in my bedroom." The color had returned to her complexion.

"In this case, I'm flattered to be *the one*."

She moved to go to the bathroom when I clutched her elbow to stop her in her tracks. "Are we good? Tell me the truth."

Addison nodded. "We are. We will be. My emotions are all over the place right now. It's the lack of sleep. Sorry for being a train wreck. I'm usually not offended by many things." She smoothened the T-shirt I'd given her, rubbing the worn cotton between her fingers. "Thanks for this." She brought it to her nose and took a whiff before disappearing into the en-suite and leaving me on my own, wondering what I would do with her for an entire weekend.

We had already crossed lines in the past, and now I had no idea how to act, my usual game not helping at all.

Once she emerged wearing only panties and my tee, I almost fell off my feet. *Fucking fuck. God had to help me here.* I prayed to a few saints in my head, pushing down the tautness taking over the lower half of my body.

Addison paused in the doorway, one hand on her hip and the other resting on the frame above her head. "What do you think? Suits me?"

I swallowed. Freaking hot. The half-mast down below was now a raging boner, taking permanent residency, as my eyes traveled all over her gorgeous body. My fingers itched to familiarize themselves with each curve and dip.

Soft waves of her hair bounced with every step. With her makeup removed, her natural beauty was even more alluring. I couldn't seem to blink my eyes in case I missed a second of her dewy look. Her legs—those satiny, toned limbs—that I longed to have circled around my waist, had too much impact on me.

"Perfect," I croaked. Yeah, no other words would come out.

If I stood here any longer, my tent would rip through my trousers, wanting her touch. I rushed and locked myself in the bathroom. Once under the scorching stream of the shower, I fisted my cock, desperate to jerk off and relieve the tightness circulating in me, strangling my voice of reason.

My mind drifted back to Addison in my bedroom, and the gesture felt wrong. All wrong. My dick softened in my palm, and I showered quickly.

Something was happening to me, shattering years of existence and everything I ever lived by. First, I refused sex with a gorgeous woman I was definitely attracted to. And now, I refused to come into my fist, rather my body did, because of said woman. Banging my forehead against the wall, I cursed myself and all my they-make-no-sense resolutions.

When I exited the bathroom, Addison was already in my bed, under the comforter, looking like she belonged there.

Another surge of misplaced longing spread through me.

"You decided to sleep here," I teased, wrapping the towel around my waist tighter. My penis and my logic combated with each other, and I had no idea which one to listen to.

"Yes. Unless you've changed your mind—"

I hated the indecision I could read on her face. Turning my back to her and using the time to give my hormones a pep talk, I slipped my ass into a pair of boxer briefs and sprung on the mattress beside her.

"No, I haven't changed my mind." I flicked the switch and positioned myself on my side. "Now come here, so I can hold you and scare that insomnia away." And just like that, in the most natural way, Addison Wilde had tamed the wild part of my existence.

———

The rumpling of sheets woke me up in the middle of the night. I pulled the woman in my arms closer to my front, but she writhed away from my embrace.

"Hey Wilde, you awake?"

She rolled to her side until she faced me. "Sorry. Did I wake you up?"

"Don't worry about it. How long have you been up?"

Her finger traced the length of my chest, just between my pecs. A shiver zinged down my spine and stole my breath. "No idea. A while."

"Why didn't you wake me up?"

"You were sleeping peacefully. I love hearing you breathe. It quiets my mind."

I untangled myself from her and moved to my feet. Grabbing two hoodies from my closet, I handed her one.

"Huh? What are you doing?"

"Come on. Wear this and I'll show you."

She rose to her knees, slid her arms through the sleeves, and I closed in on her, pulling the hood over her head.

"Don't want you to get cold."

When I inched back, I noticed how perfect she looked dressed in my clothes. And some clamp tightened around my traitorous heart.

Her voice brought me back. "You know I'm still half-naked, right?"

I shrugged. "Just a sec." I offered her my sweatpants, way too big for her.

"Tuck, I can get a pair from my suitcase."

"No. I want you to wear these." I helped her into them and tied the cord at the waist as much as I could. I rolled the waistband and pant legs until she could walk and wouldn't trip.

Once satisfied, I held out my hand for her and pulled her toward the living room. I reached for the blanket on the couch and a few pillows and led her into the hallway.

"Where are we going?" she whispered.

"You'll see."

We took the emergency staircase and climbed four flights of stairs until we reached the fiftieth floor. Then we took another door that brought us to the rooftop.

"Whoa, this is—wow," Addison exclaimed as her eyes

busied themselves taking in the city. A soft breeze swept our faces as I tugged her to my favorite spot.

I set the pillows and blanket on a wooden deck where a few tenants were growing plants and herbs, and we lay on our backs.

"Pretend we're stargazing," I said as we stared at the inky sky, the lights from the city preventing us from seeing anything other than their glow.

We remained silent for a long while, Addison's hand nestled in mine, the sound of our combined breaths mixing with those from the busy streets below.

After a moment, she flipped to her side, and with her arm propped over my chest, she rested her chin on top of her hand. Her blue eyes bore into mine, and her eyebrows furrowed as if she was trying to read something I couldn't guess.

She sighed and motioned around with her free hand. "I'm sure girls love it when you bring them here. It's magical."

As if stung by a bee, I jerked to a ninety-degree angle, Addison sitting at the abrupt movement. "Wilde, you're the first person I've ever brought here. It's my secret spot. My *I-need-to-think* zone. Nobody ever has come here with me before. Not even my friends—" I shook my head and sighed, lowering my voice. "You're the first one."

Her eyes rounded, and she blinked a few times. "No, can't be. You're joking, right?"

I shook my head again and decreased the distance between us, pushing strands of her hair behind her ear. Sparks ignited at the tips of my fingers, and I yanked my hand away, rubbing it on my pant leg. "Nope. I would never lie to you. When I can't sleep, I come up here and let the calm of the night push my worries away. Thought it could do you some good too."

A pink hue colored her cheeks. And she looked younger and more vulnerable in the low light. "You serious?"

"Dead serious, sweetheart."

We watched each other for a fraction of a second, and it was enough to increase the tempo of my heart.

Addison rose to her knees, and her arms looped around my neck. She dropped a kiss on my cheek, her lips soft and warm against my skin. "Thank you, Tuck. It means a lot. I'm happy you trust me enough to share your special place with me."

We went back to the position we were in before, on our backs and our fingers knitted together as our eyes returned to the dark sky.

"Can I ask you something?" After the long silence, her voice sounded tentative.

I nodded.

"What happened in your life that made you decide you're not worthy of love?"

I stiffened at her words and shut my eyes, trying to wash away the barbs piercing my heart. How could this woman read me so well? How did she secure a key to my soul?

I cleared my throat, coughing to hide my discomfort. "Sweetheart, you're wrong. It's a choice I have made. And so far, I haven't regretted it. I don't feel like putting my heart out there. I prefer it safe and sound inside my chest. Not crumbled because someone else chose to smash it."

Thorns sprouted down my throat, and I breathed around their sharp edges to avoid choking. Would my simple explanation convince her to let go? And not pursue the topic?

Addison said nothing and tightened her squeeze

around my fingers. She brought our joint palms over her heart.

"Okay, fine. Don't tell me. Sorry I asked. You already know my story. Parts of it. I thought maybe you'd wanna share yours too. But you're clearly not ready, so when you are, remember I'm here. No judgment, just an ear to confide into."

She kissed my knuckles, never letting go of my hand. As if to tell me she was there for me. And that I could trust her. All I had to do was drop my guard, and she would genuinely listen. At that moment, I realized our relationship was not just physical. But a true friendship. Something to cherish. Something I had never experienced with a woman in my life. The sweet touch of her lips filled my heart with a warmth difficult to define, but powerful and soothing all at once.

"My dad," I finally said.

Addison said nothing, but by her alertness, I could tell she was listening.

"My parents. They met at seventeen and fell in love hard. And then had me. My mother was my dad's entire world. God, how he loved her. I was just a kid, and it was so evident to me."

I swallowed. I hadn't told that story in—well, never. Nick and Jace knew most of it because we grew up together, and I couldn't hide what happened from them. Yet, they never got to know every detail. The entire picture. Even when they asked, I would stay mute about it or change the subject. Because it hurt too fucking much to relive that year of my life.

Addison shifted closer to me. Everywhere our bodies touched, her warmth diffused through me. Reminding me I wasn't alone. And that she cared.

"A few months after I turned twelve, my dad caught my

mom with Ron, our neighbor. They were having an affair. It had been going on for a couple of months. I didn't know the specifics. Nobody told me, and I never asked. Anyway, it shattered my dad. Like I said, he loved my mom so much that he would have given her the world if she'd asked for it." I paused, reliving the most hurtful memory of my childhood. "Instead of kicking her out, my father tried to patch things up. To give their marriage another shot. But my mom wouldn't stop seeing Ron and asked for a divorce three months later. Anyway, my dad offered her two choices. Be a family, the three of us. Or to not fight him in court for my custody if she decided to leave him. Leave us."

I paused, trying to put some order in my emotions.

"But the truth was, she had just learned she was pregnant. With twins. And the babies were Ron's. She'd kept it a secret at first. But when my dad offered her two choices, that's when she dropped the baby-bomb on him. And it ruined everything. In the end, she chose her other family over me and my dad. Leaving him heartbroken. Leaving us broken."

"Oh Tucker, I'm so sorry," Addison said, now on her side, her hand cupping my cheek and her chin pressed into the crook of my shoulder.

"Afterward, I saw her for a month during summer vacations and four days during the holidays. That was about it. After a while, we lost touch. She hasn't been my mom in a long time."

"And your father? What happened? Did he ever remarry or something?"

"He started sleeping around. And drinking more than usual. Sometimes, he wouldn't come home at night. When I turned fifteen, I learned he often fell asleep at the bar he visited a few too many times each week. They started calling me when he passed out to take him home. When I turned nineteen, we had a chat. I told him I couldn't deal with his shit anymore. I was tired of being his dad, making sure he had clean clothes to wear to work and a stocked refrigerator. He finally accepted help and emerged victorious from his self-destructing cycle. He has a girlfriend now. Has been with her for almost three years. But I can tell even though he loves ever, she's not my mom and will never occupy the same place in his heart. Or maybe my mother fucked with his ability to love again."

Addison nestled herself deeper into my embrace. My arms wrapped tight around her, holding her, wishing we could stay like this forever. "I'm sorry it happened to you. But you gotta remember you're not your dad. What your mom did was wrong. I can't believe she pushed you away. No mother should ever do that to her children. But you can't punish yourself for her mistakes and for him hitting rock bottom. None of it was your fault. This had nothing to do with ya. You can't live your life expecting the worst to happen all the time. I've had my share of shitty relationships, and my heart has been broken too many times already, but love is precious. And I'll never stop believing I deserve it too. Because once I find the right person, it will mean all the past struggles and pain have led me to the one I'm supposed to be with. So, it wouldn't have been in vain. Just a part of my journey."

My lips lingered on the top of her head. Every word she spoke resonated in me. My heart banged loudly against my ribs. I blinked, chasing a foreign emotion away, not ready to assess its meaning.

"Thank you. It means a lot. Your words and you listening to me rambling about my childhood."

"Tuck—"

I silenced her with a finger pressed to her lips as she

cocked her head so we could look at each other. Past our bodies and into our souls. "Just so you know, I've never told the story to anyone before. Not in detail at least."

She sucked a sharp breath in. "For real? I'm your first again? Color me flattered." She paused, regrouping her thoughts. "Why did you then?"

"Because whatever happens between us in the future, I consider you my friend. You once told me I had trust issues with women, and I denied it. You weren't so wrong. And except for Nick and Jace, you're the first person who has figured me out. Whom I have let in. I can't explain it, but it feels right. I really thought I was doing a good job hiding that broken part of me."

"Sorry I unmasked you, big guy."

"Sure you are."

"Maybe I missed my vocation."

"Shrink? I'd come for a consultation, but you'd have to wear glasses. They'd look high-school-principal kind of hot on you."

She nudged my chest. "Pervert." She hesitated for a second. "I had a boyfriend I really loved in college. Shawn. I saw myself going the distance with him. He got me. We talked about moving in together, traveling the world, all those crazy dreams you have at nineteen."

"What happened?"

"One day we were touring apartments, and the next he said I was suffocating him. He left for Asia to backpack all summer, fell in love with someone, and I never saw him again."

"I'm sorry."

"Don't be. Most of my relationships have had tragic endings. For me. I got left behind and lied to more times than you can imagine."

"Oh. I get your anger toward men," I said.

"It's not really anger. Wariness would be a more accurate description. One day, I'll find *the one*. I just haven't met him yet."

I dropped a kiss on her forehead, and we lay there on the rooftop of my apartment building a bit longer. My confessions swirled around us. Some parts of me relaxed. Others got tensed. But that always was the case when I was with Addison.

"My parents separated when I was young. Phoenix and I—he's my twin brother—we barely saw our daddy for two years because he was dealing with stuff. Eventually, our father sought help, and my parents got back together. Phen lives in Europe now, so we barely ever see each other. My parents spend a lot of time there to help him out. He has twins of his own. One day, I hope we'll find our way back to each other. I miss him." She paused. "Guess, we have something else in common."

"What?"

"Twins run in our families."

We both remained silent.

"I know your weekend here is nothing like you planned, but I'm glad I told you about my parents," I said. "It was about time I got it off my chest so that it stopped eating me from the inside. Thank you for trusting me with your confessions too."

She tipped her head back to watch me with something akin to affection. Or an emotion not far from it.

Propped on my elbows, my gaze fixed on her. Neither of us said anything, the significance of our heartfelt confessions saturating the air. After a while, I said, "You know what? This little trick of yours—having me open up— helped me get rid of a pile of rocks that had been sitting on my chest for as long as I can remember. Thanks for being my friend, Wilde. I'm grateful."

We hugged a little longer until she rose to her feet and held out her hand. "Come on. Let's go to bed."

Hand in hand, we made our way back inside.

A new layer to our relationship had blossomed in the last hour. Now we'd forever be linked by the revelations of our pasts.

After we repositioned ourselves under the covers, Addison whispered, "Thanks for being my friend too."

Her breathing evened, and once I made sure she was asleep, I followed her, hoping we would meet again in our dreams.

14

ADDISON

Four days later, I dialed Tucker after I got home, showered, and changed, giving him enough time so he'd get my surprise delivery. We had our daily phone call all set, but today would be a special one.

He answered after the third ring. "Hey sweetheart. Why did I receive a Chinese food delivery under your name just minutes ago?"

I sat on my couch and grabbed the box of orange-glazed chicken and a set of chopsticks I'd picked up on my way from work.

Switching the call to a video chat, I perched my phone on the throw pillow. "I thought we could have dinner together."

"You thought great," he said, unwrapping his food. "I'm starving. You just got home?"

I let a long breath out. "Yep. I'm so tired. These extra hours I'm putting in are draining all my energy banks."

"And your insomnia?"

"Still having a blast disturbing my nights. Anyway, that's not why I wanted to ask you on a date tonight."

I chewed on a piece of chicken and almost orgasmed from the sweetness.

"Jesus, don't do that when I can see you, or I'll take the next plane out."

I snickered behind my hand. "You won't. It's not what we decided."

Tucker shook his head like he couldn't believe he agreed to this. "Now is the time to remind me I'm the stupidest man you've ever encountered."

"Oh Tuck. I'm fluent in stupid men, and let me tell you they look nothing like you. You're caring and funny and generous. They're not. See, two different universes. Back to my surprise. Give me a minute."

I opened the browser on my computer and linked a file that I sent via email.

"In a minute or two, you'll receive an email with an attachment. Don't open it until I tell you to."

"Is this some kind of torture you're inflicting on me? Or a plan that will put me at risk?"

I gestured *no* with my head, unable to restrain the stretch of my lips. "None of those. Just something I did and wanted to share with you. Listen, you're the first person I trust to see this. Consider yourself a beta tester. All constructive criticisms will be evaluated afterward. I'm open to new ideas. There will be another version coming in about a month with updates. Ready?"

"Always."

For the next three minutes and forty-seven seconds, we watched the video montage I made of Dahlia and Nick for their wedding. It included an acoustic version of a new song Carter wrote and scenes of him as he sang. He filmed it a few months back and sent me the footage. After the wedding, I would update it with pictures and clips from that night.

The song ended, and the last frame was a picture of the future newlyweds and Jack hugging under a tree with the words I added, followed by their wedding date.

> *To Dahlia and Nick*
>
> *You two are examples of courage, determination, and love.*
>
> *Being around you guys makes each of us a better person because you never stopped dreaming and moving forward even when things got tough. That's what makes you two the role models we should all aim to be.*
>
> *We wish you years of happiness. You deserve the best. Always.*
>
> *We love you with every bit of our hearts and are happy to be a part of your special day.*
>
> *Tucker and Addison -xx-*

"You signed my name?" Tucker asked, his voice lower than usual.

"Do you want me to remove it? I thought the words suited for both the best man and maid of honor since they are our best friends. And have been for so long."

"No. Don't remove it. I'm just touched you thought of including me since you did all the work, which, by the way, is incredible. Better be ready for people to shed some tears. This song—it's perfect."

"It's not ours, but Cart did a great job. I know it's not easy for him to see Dahlia getting married again, but he's grown so much since her last nuptial. Gosh, it's not my story to tell, but he was broken. And it affected all of us to see him hurting so bad. He's moving on. Slowly."

"Poor guy. I can't relate because I've never been so in

love that it split me open, but I can see how hurtful it can be. They share a special bond. Even I could see it the first time I saw them together."

"I think his last album was some sort of therapy. To let go of the past and move forward. He deserves greatness. Anyway, let's watch it again, and this time press pause when you have comments or suggestions. Bring it on, big guy."

———

Closing my office door behind me, I shot Tucker a quick text. It'd been a few days since our video date, and I crossed my fingers he was still in the mood to spend time together. Because this proposition I had for him was one nobody in their right mind could ever refuse.

And I was well aware I possessed something of great value in his eyes.

Me: Hey groom of mine. Miss me already?

He answered in mere seconds.

Tucker: Do you want me to miss ya, Wilde?

Flutters swirled in my belly. I could picture him sporting a cocky smirk and glints in his eyes, sweeping my body in a slow glance. I shivered as images formed in my head. *He's a safe choice, Addi. He isn't available. Just enjoy the company. For now.*

Me: Any plans tomorrow night?

Tucker: For you, I'll free my schedule. Wanna snuggle? I bet you miss my chest pressed against your back or my hard-on molded between your ass cheeks. Am I right?

I snickered despite myself. Tucker Philips, Chicago's womanizer, offering to cuddle with me.

Me: Careful, big guy. This could ruin your reputation if I start to blog about it. Are you willing to take the risk?

Tucker: Yeah. I'd love to be your dirty little secret.

Tucker: Your place or mine?

Me: Somewhere else. More exotic.

Tucker: Talk. Now.

Me: Are you sitting?

Tucker: Okay, this conversation isn't going in the direction I was hoping. Am I safe from any harm? Should I be afraid? Or hide?

Me: Are you sitting? I'm not telling you if you aren't.

Tucker: Yep. Alone. About to have lunch. Just survived a meeting.

I switched the call to video chat, and he accepted within seconds.

Tucker flashed me a ten-thousand-volt smile as he sat behind his desk, unwrapping a sandwich.

"Hey you," I greeted him.

"See." He motioned the space around with his finger. "Seated and ready for any news you deliver."

He curled his lips, showing a row of pearly whites, a contrast to his dark skin. The pink dress shirt he wore, rolled at the elbow, showcased his corded forearms and the watch around his left wrist. Tucker Philips possessed everything to make any male model envious. Pierce Reinart, my jerk of a client, should take a page out of his playbook before thinking he had a shot at piercing this industry, pun intended. Where Tucker was all masculine and projected confidence and oozed sex, Pierce was the cheap used model with no sex appeal, a chip on his shoulder, and a condescending attitude.

My eyes were trained on Tucker, and as if he could read the naughty thoughts swirling in my head, his grin grew bigger. And more devastating. For me.

I cleared my throat and tried to recall what we were talking about before I started ogling him.

His voice killed my fantasies. "What did you wanna tell me?"

With my fingers, I combed the loose tendrils of hair blocking my vision, doing my best to bury the butterflies invading my stomach.

"Oh yes, sorry. Got lost in my head," I muttered. *Smooth, Addi.*

Another smirk shaping his lips threatened to send me back to where I had just escaped from. Damn him. Mouthwatering handsome.

"You. Me. Tomorrow. Hockey game. Playoff. I got tickets. Nashville versus Chicago. My hood versus yours. Are you in?"

He blinked, put his lunch down, pretended to unplug his ears with his fingers, and adjusted his tie.

"Playoff tickets? Are you for real?"

I nodded. "Got my hands on a pair for the game in Nashville tomorrow. What do you say? I know it's last minute, but we can't waste those. They're worth a little fortune, but I got them as a thank you for a few hours of work I put in."

His nostrils flared. "Tell me they're not from that fucking useless car guy."

"No. A friend from high school. Mark. His dad owns a radio station in Nashville. Gave Cart and Dah their first break back in the day. Anyway, I reworked their logo and branding. Guess they were happy. Are you coming with me?"

"This is serious shit. You can't make jokes about tickets like those. Are you tricking me right now?"

I shook my head in denial, unable to keep my face straight at the excitement pouring out from him. "It's real." I watched the awe taking over him, and a chunk of my heart swelled at the sight. "You have exactly two minutes to decide, or I'll invite Nick. Dahlia doesn't care about hockey, even if hockey players are stupidly hot."

Tucker moved his phone so close I saw his face in high-definition. "Keep Nick out of it. I'm your guy."

I clapped my hands together. "Perfect. I knew you'd never be able to resist my charm."

I winked, and he burst into a warm laugh.

"Woman, you're a temptress. You don't need tickets for me to notice you. Let me clear my schedule for tomorrow, and I'll get back to you with an offer of my own. Still on for our chat tonight?"

"Sure. Gotta go, anyway."

We hung up, and before I could resume my work, my phone pinged with a message.

Tucker: Don't book transportation just yet. I wanna check something first.

I typed fast as a new set of jitters awoke inside me.

Me: Okay.

For the rest of the day, I worked on a dealership mid-year sale banners and social media campaign, humming Carter's newest song that was released yesterday. The one from his latest album, whose cover and promo material I had designed.

Becca knocked on my door after five when I was gathering my stuff, ready to bolt out of there. Tomorrow I'd work from home before leaving for Nashville.

"Hey girl," she said. "Don't wait for me tonight. I'm spending the next couple of days at Ben's."

"Soon you'll announce you two are moving in together. You're barely ever home these days."

She shrugged but couldn't contain her enthusiasm. "Yeah, I wouldn't be against it. I think he's the one."

"He is," I agreed. "You two are a perfect match. I'll be in Nashville this weekend, anyway."

She wiggled her eyebrows. "Did you get those tickets?"

I danced a little jig without saying anything.

"Oh, and am I wrong to assume you invited Mr. Chicago to join ya?"

"Nope. Not wrong."

"Addi, you have no idea what you're doing, right? I can predict him breaking your heart if you're not careful. I see it in your eyes. The yearning. You're not good at hiding your feelings." She stepped forward and hugged me. "Just be careful. I don't want you hurt."

"It's just a hockey game, Becca. Don't put too much thought into it. And I'm a big girl. My heart is safe because I know Tucker isn't available. But we're allowed to be friends and to enjoy each other's company. So, this is what it is. A friend-date. I heard Nick once say how much Tuck was a dedicated hockey fan. I can't waste these tickets on someone who won't appreciate their value."

"For hockey fans, tickets like these are equivalent to what a marriage proposal is for others. Don't you think he'll assume there's more to your feelings?"

"He is a no-relationship type of guy. Stated it many times already. The ticket is just that. A ticket."

She grabbed my hand in hers, and I followed her through the door.

"Just be careful."

"I will." The gleam in her eyes told me she didn't believe me. But I believed myself. Or was trying really hard.

We parted ways on the sidewalk after I promised to send her pictures because Ben was also a huge hockey fan.

Eight o'clock arrived, and Tucker called me on the dot.

"Be ready. Tomorrow, I'll pick you up after lunch. You and I, we're going on a road trip. Dress the part because Chicago is coming to your city, and we'll crush Nashville. The Honky-Tonks aren't good enough to defeat the Busters. If I were you, I'd skip the purple and dress in red. The color of victory."

Laughter shook me, and I wiped my damp eyes with my fingertips.

"Oh, you've clearly never been to a game with me, big guy. Let's see who's the biggest and most loyal fan."

"Deal," he said in a deadpan tone. "And by the way,

pack a bag because we're spending the entire weekend there. I never got a tour of the city last time. You owe me, Wilde. And I'm cashing out on it."

———

Tucker knocked on my door the next day, dressed in jeans and a Busters red jersey. He looked nothing like I was used to seeing, but this playful attire fit him.

"Nice jersey," he said as I twirled, showing him my purple Honky-Tonks top with number seventeen on the back, and fixed the cap on my head.

"You were saying?" I teased.

"You win, Wilde. Even if you're not wearing the right colors, the cap looks good on you." He bent to kiss my cheek. "Ready to go?"

"Yes. Let me just get my bag." He entered my apartment and went straight to my room to grab my stuff. "Thanks," I said, following him to his rental.

After he criticized all the songs I played on my phone and I disagreed with his musical choices, we let the radio pick the music for us.

"Top three best childhood memories?" I asked after we grabbed takeout and settled ourselves for the four-hour drive.

"Let's see." He reflected on it for a beat. "A vacation at the lake when I was about nine or ten. We rented a cabin. Nick came with us. My parents had to force us out of the water." The memory played in his head. I could see him get lost in his mind. "On Halloween, Jace, Nick, and I had decided to dress as one sea monster. We worked on our costumes for months. Jace's mom helped us sew some parts. Anyway, we won the school's best-costume award. It was epic. We received a gallon of candies as the grand prize. For a semester, I was part of the soccer team. Not that I wasn't good, but I preferred geeky stuff. Like reading. And numbers. But I enjoyed the workout part and started running for fun every morning before school. When my family crumbled, the daily exercise helped to keep my head in the game. Months later, I entered my first official sponsored run and gathered like two thousand dollars for a charity that helped kids with special needs. My cousin has a syndrome, something about his chromosomes. Anyway, the pride I felt after that day equals nothing else."

"Wow, that's impressive. I can picture you as a teen in my head. I have similar memories of Dah. She left on world tours twice, then got pregnant, married, and became a widow in a span of a few months, and the distance grew between us for a while. I was still in college, trying to figure out my future and remain active on the party scene, while Dahlia became an adult overnight. Growing up, I was the one not following the rules, always up for a good time. She was the mature one, the old soul. One decision changed the rest of her life. At twenty, she had plenty of money, but that came with a lot of obligations. I had student loan debts and an adventurous mindset. But she's my best friend. Forever has been. We've always found our way back to each other. She's more like a sister to me. Even when she was on another continent, she was still there for me. All the time. She's my favorite person."

"What's your best memory?"

"There are too many to choose from, but the day she walked on the stage for the first time and sang with Carter is a moment I will eternally cherish. They were just seven years old. I was a witness to every stage of their career. When she walked on the stage at Green Mountain Fest years later, I knew she'd make it big. We did everything together growing up when she wasn't with Carter. Bonfire.

Shows. Breaking curfews. Sleepovers. My memories of us are infinite."

I twisted on my seat, my back now against the passenger door, and admired Tucker's profile.

"What are you looking at?" he asked.

"You," I said.

"Why?"

I shrugged. "Because I like to. You're perplexing, but transparent at the same time. It's a combination I wanna crack." I paused. "And also, I'm wondering why you're not wearing the right color jersey. Purple is your color."

"Is it?"

"Yep. When you took me on that date, you wore a purple shirt. My ovaries overheated at the sight."

His lips drew up into a smirk. "Glad to know I had an effect on your ovaries."

"Well, I'm not allowed to fall for you, but I have no control over certain parts of my body."

"I'll remember that. Can I ask you a question?" I nodded. "Why are you dating guys who don't deserve you? Is it some sort of punishment you inflict on yourself, or do you enjoy the pain of a broken heart?"

"When I love, I love hard. And so far, my heart has led me down the wrong path. It's difficult for me to know when people have a hidden agenda. I'm a pretty open book. From now on, I'll be careful with who I let in. Hurting isn't something I like."

His hands squeezed mine, and I rotated my palm so our fingers could knit together.

"Thanks for the tickets, Wilde."

"Thanks for the road trip, big guy."

A comfortable silence settled between us.

"Would you mind if I shut my eyes for a little while?"

"Wilde, I'd be mad if you restrained yourself for me.

Sleep all you want. I'm watching over you. You're safe. I'll make sure of it. Gather your energy. Tonight will be the opportunity of a lifetime."

"I'm glad we're doing this together."

"Me too."

And before I could speak another word, sleep claimed me.

15

TUCKER

Before the game, we did not have enough time to go to our hotel, so we met Mark, Addison's high school friend and the one who got her the tickets. He and his buddies were having a pre-game happy hour at a bar on Broadway. The music was loud, the beer flowing, and the chicken wings spicy enough.

"Addi, you brought the enemy," Mark sneered, draping his arm over her shoulders and sitting way too close to her for my comfort, pointing in my direction with his chin. I scanned all around me. Yeah, I was the only one sporting Chicago's colors. But I'd never betray my team. The Busters were not only my friends, but also people I respected and the best team in the league. No argument could change that. "I can't believe you wasted a precious ticket on Chicago's fan club."

I sipped my beer, smirking behind my glass. "We'll see who's gonna cry himself to sleep later, man. I'm pretty sure my guys will crush yours before they can even understand the game has started."

His hand fucking lingered on Addison's back, and a seething rage erupted inside me.

On my feet, I moved into her space, my mouth an inch away from her ear. I heard her sharp intake of breath. *Move to another target, Marky-boy.* "Want a fresh drink?" She'd been sipping the same lemonade for the last hour.

"Please." She raised her glass, sucking on the cherry she fished from the bottom.

Mark studied me, his eyes forming slits, trying to get answers to the questions that popped into his head.

I shrugged and averted my eyes, bringing my attention back to the woman who was oblivious to what was in front of her eyes.

Feeling cocky and wanting to give this guy a warning without being too obvious, I dropped a kiss on her forehead. "Be right back, sweetheart."

His stare followed me, and I felt the burn on my back.

For some reason, I hated that guy. And I was generally someone who enjoyed the company of most people crossing my path. But Mark rubbed me up the wrong way. And his obsession with my date didn't sit well with me.

An hour later, we crossed the street and mingled with the crowd marching toward the stadium, chanting, a contagious cheerfulness soaking the air.

Addison intertwined our fingers, hopping with each step. "This is amazing. I've never been to a playoff game before. It hasn't even started yet, and I'm already pumped."

I fastened my hand around hers, and my heart hummed in my chest from the happy vibes she radiated.

We ordered snacks, soda for her and a beer for me, and took our seats. This day was surreal. Chicago hadn't played in the series for two years, and history was being created in Nashville. Exhilaration reverberated around us.

"Thanks for doing this with me," she said, seated on my right.

People jumped to their feet, clapped, and wolf-whistled when both teams entered the ice, and for the next hour and a half, we screamed and sat on the edge of our seats, the game in front of us wild and entertaining.

The Honky-Tonks mascot, a raccoon, came to us during the first intermission and kissed Addison's cheek, the episode displayed on the jumbotron, and the entire stadium erupted in cheers. The stupid animal pointed to my Chicago jersey and faked fainting, then returned his focus to the beautiful woman on my side. Her face tinted crimson, and she sipped her soda after smiling for the cameras.

During the second period, people, mostly assholes, walked past us, offering her beers that she kept under her seat with thankful nods, after they asked her on dates or offered to meet up with her later. *This woman is a catch. I'm well aware. Get in line, dickwads.* I curled a possessive arm around her shoulders, but they were either idiots or blind because none of them seemed to be deterred by it.

"Tuck. Do something. It's getting uncomfortable," Addison begged with rounded eyes after the ninth person came on to her, this time proclaiming his love, slurring his words.

My fingers brushed the length of her jaw, my body electrifying at the simple contact, and before she could argue, I claimed her mouth, sucking her bottom lip between mine. Her entire being stiffened, then relaxed as she locked her arms around my neck and pulled me to her.

I tried to break away, but Addison wouldn't let me, pushing her tongue into my mouth. All hell broke loose, and with the permission she granted me, I kissed her like I'd been yearning to the entire evening.

A throaty moan crossed her lips, and I stopped the kiss. Else I'd be at risk of humiliating myself the next minute.

Breathless, our foreheads pressed together. We hadn't noticed our faces being plastered on the jumbotron. The mascot on our right cupped his heart, his shoulders slumping forward with a saddened expression. People started laughing at his theatrical demeanor.

Second intermission? Did we miss most of the second period?

Addison buried her face in her hand. "Oh gosh, we always end up giving everyone a show."

I removed her hand and kissed her temple, tucking her under my arm. "Can you blame them? I'm pretty good-looking."

She slapped my stomach and rested her head against my shoulder.

"With anyone else, it would've been super awkward. Thanks for being here," she said, her body comforting against mine as we watched the third period.

With VIP passes around our necks, we joined Mark and his father near the press box.

The fucker kissed Addison's cheek—again—his hand splayed on her back. "How did you like it?" he asked, way too close to her face for comfort.

A permanent oversized stretch split her face in two, and her irises shone. "Best experience ever. I'll do any rebranding you guys might have in the future for tickets like these. Thank you so much." She attached her arms around his neck and hugged him. And Mark had the audacity to wink at me as she did.

As soon as he let go of her, I laced my fingers through Addison's and pulled her closer to me, kissing the crown of her head, just for good measure.

"Addi, we're having a private party later. Would you like to come?"

He dismissed me in front of her, not even being subtle about it.

"Sorry, man, we already have plans," I chimed in, without giving her time to answer. I led her away, and she braked to a stop right there, spinning to face me once we got far enough where the guy couldn't eavesdrop.

"Tuck, what the fuck. Couldn't you let me reply? I think I can speak for myself. Don't ever do that again. It was rude and unwarranted. We wouldn't be here if Mark's dad hadn't offered me the tickets. And if Mark hadn't vouched for me in the first place. So, play it cool. And respect my friend. Don't go all caveman on me." She angled her face to check on Mark and signaled with her finger. Wrath rippled from her as she waited for me to say something.

I dragged a hand through my hair and shook my head, glancing down, before I opened my stupid mouth. "The guy's in love with you, Wilde. Big fucking much."

She crossed her arms, death threats in her eyes. "No. We've been friends for years. Get your eyes checked. And don't come up with stories to justify your behavior. I'm not buying your shit. You were rude. Accept it. Say you're sorry. And move on."

"No, I'm not. Have you two ever dated?"

"What? No."

"He has a crush on you. I'm telling you."

"Stop. You know nothing about Mark."

"You believe you know what you're talking about. That's where you're wrong. I'm a guy, Wilde, and I know how guys think. With their dicks."

"Not everyone is superficial or led by their hormones," she countered.

"Oh girl, don't play ignorant. You're too smart to be that naïve."

She groaned, and this little fight of ours got me hard for her. Right now, I wanted to make her kneel and fuck her devilish mouth to shut her up. Nothing could ever look as hot and dirty as Addison Wilde giving me a head.

This woman had a way of getting under my skin. All the time. No matter what she said or did.

"I swear—"

"You swear what, sweetheart? Let me hear you," I pressed.

She muttered something I didn't catch, then added, "Nothing."

"It wasn't nothing. Your eyes are spitting venom, and you're flustered. What is it? Don't be shy."

A scowl painted her face.

"Since when do you shy away from your thoughts?"

"You're acting like a jealous boyfriend. I'm not yours, Tuck. I never was and never will be. Stop acting like a possessive jerk."

Her words rang true, but they sent my stomach spiraling with a foreign sensation.

"It's not. I-I'm not."

"Yes, you are. You can't decide who I flirt with. It's not your call. I can fuck whoever I want tonight, and you don't have a say in it. My body, my life, my choice."

Anger rose in my core. Her words made sense. I should be happy she didn't see me as boyfriend material. Didn't mean I had to agree. Or accept it. Imagining her having sex with the high-school loverboy sent chills down my spine. That meant nothing, but I hated the idea with a fervor I'd rarely felt before.

"Wanna fuck him? Go ahead. I'm outta here. See you tomorrow when I drop your ass back in Atlanta."

I swiveled on my heels, about to explode, when a small hand clutched my elbow.

"Tuck, don't go," she said. I turned to watch her once I reeled in some of my ire. Hurt flashed on her face, but she kept her lips pursed into a thin line, her eyes telling me she wasn't done with this conversation. "Wait for me. Geez. Let's just say goodbye and thank him. That's the least we can do."

We walked back to Mark, and he took his time kissing her cheeks and whispering in her ear. Addison giggled and tapped his chest. I saw red. Blistering firetruck bleeding red.

Without a word, I grabbed her waist to spin her around and kissed her. She pushed away after biting my lower lip hard on purpose, then skewered me with a scalding gaze while faking an upturn of her lips for those watching. A new surge of fury swirled in me. Matching hers.

This furious version of Addison Wilde made me harder.

Minutes later, we walked toward our rental. Neither of us said a word, our feet pounding on the pavement. At the reception of the hotel we'd chosen for the night, we both took our credit cards out at check-in. The receptionist's gaze traveled between us.

"Just to be sure, was it one or two rooms?" she asked.

"Two," Addison said while I barked, "One."

I angled myself to face her. "Come on, Wilde." My tone had lowered. "Don't punish me. Don't turn your back on us. We agreed to one room."

"There's no *us*, Tucker. I don't belong to anybody and certainly not to you. You made sure I knew from the start you were unavailable."

She said everything I wished she'd say, but no matter how I tried to process it, it hurt like hell.

"Don't ruin your weekend because *you* failed to notice your friend Mark has a crush on you," I said, fighting with all my instincts that told me to kiss her and promise her the world.

"We're not talking about this anymore."

"Fine. Let's get to our room. We're meeting the guys from the Busters in less than an hour."

Once upstairs, the tension between us still ran high. After showering, Addison dropped her towel in the middle of the room while she rummaged into her bag for a new outfit.

A groan formed in my throat. The mixed signals emanating from her disturbed my mind. She didn't want us to have sex. She told me she could bang whoever she decided tonight, but walked naked feet away from me without an ounce of shame or a second thought.

She hummed a song I didn't recognize, slipping her curves into lacy black lingerie, ignoring me the entire time.

I rubbed the column of my throat with my hand, at a loss for words. Did she want me to spread her naked on the bed and have my way with her? Or was she just playing me to see how long it would take me to break and make a move on her, only for her to refuse me afterward?

With my dick pulsing against the zipper of my jeans and my brain not working right due to the lack of blood flow, I tried to solve the puzzle that she was, with no right or wrong answer. I entered the shower, the hot stream flushing out some of the angst bubbling in me.

Refreshed and deciding to give Addison a taste of her own medicine, I walked straight into the room bare-assed, my chest still glistening with pearls of water, like I owned the place.

Our eyes met in the mirror while she was applying her makeup, and I saw a tug-of-war going on in her head. Her little naked act earlier had repercussions she hadn't expected. Pink covered her neck and cheeks. And now we were both aroused, but too stubborn to do anything about it. Because I'd made a promise to my best friend. And because we'd decided we shouldn't get together before the wedding. And because we were both too proud to put a stop to whatever this was.

We both got ready in our respective corners. When Addison neared me in a short black dress that displayed her toned legs and delicious calves, I forgot about our fight.

"Can you zip me up?" she asked.

I nodded, unable to speak, rendered speechless by the sight of her.

To add to my weakness when she stood before me looking like a dream, she smelled like summer and nights of endless pleasure. God, I was so screwed when it came down to her.

I pushed her hair over her shoulder, my finger lingering on the soft skin of her nape. Shivers licked her spine.

"Would you have preferred to have accepted his invite? To hang out with him? On your own? Be honest, Wilde."

"No. Never. We're here together. Who do you think I am? You thought I would just drop you at the hotel and party all night without a second thought? Seriously, Tuck, what is wrong with you?"

I exhaled the remnants of my doubts and looked away.

"I. Don't. Trust. The. Guy. Do you need me to spell it out for you?"

Anger laced her words. Addison turned in my arms, my digits still glued to her neck. "How did it become a trust issue? Did I do something to make you doubt me?"

"No," I grumbled through clenched teeth.

"Then stop with the nonsense. I'm happy to meet your friends. I wanna spend time with ya. If I was into Mark, I would have been dating him, don't you think? I'm not here with him; I'm here with you. I invited *you*. Stop being a jealous asshole. Grow the fuck up and don't meddle in my personal life if it doesn't concern you. I mean it."

"Understood."

We lost ourselves in each other's stares. Like two magnets, our mouths collided, and our hands traveled all over the other. Addison climbed me like a tree, rolling her hips over my engorged cock, whimpering into my mouth. My fingers tangled in her hair, guiding her lips where I wanted them to be while I feasted on the flesh of her neck and breastbone.

"I missed the taste of you so bad," I said between pants.

"Oh Tuck. Never stop."

One of my hands hitched under the hem of her dress, caressing the lacy fabric. My finger met her damp center, and she purred so loud it almost broke me right there.

With her body wrapped around mine, I stepped forward until I could press her back to the wall, granting me more room to eat her up the way I couldn't stop dreaming about.

Reality hit me. Like a cold shower dampening the electric passion.

Addison felt it too because she leaned back, her lipstick smudged around her mouth, her eyes glossy with desire, and her chest rising fast.

I let go of her, and she scrambled back to her feet, adjusting her dress that had bunched up around her hips.

"We said no strings attached. No sex until the wedding. We gotta follow our own advice. We can't keep doing this. Crash and burn together. Someday, the burn won't heal. And we'll be left with scars," she said.

"I know. I'm sorry. I had no right to claim you as

mine in front of your friend. Or here just now. You have a way of rattling my cage, and my control, Wilde. Two weeks to go and my dick would be all yours. For an entire weekend. You would own this playground. We're almost at the finish line. Let's not spoil it. And, by the way, I'd walk through lava to prevent you from getting hurt. And I won't let dickheads hit on you without fighting them away."

She hugged me, her head pressing against my chest, our breaths returning to normal, the taste of her still on my lips. "We just had our first fight. And makeup session. I don't like fighting with you. But this was hot."

My palm cupped her head. "Me neither. I hate that. But yeah, this was pretty intense." My lips lingered on her forehead before we broke apart.

———

Barry Hamilton, the best center in the entire country and my friend, greeted us when we walked into the penthouse the team had booked for tonight. After the Chicago victory, the guys had decided to have a small, low-key celebration since they had a strict curfew and low alcohol consumption rule during the playoffs.

"Hey man, I can't believe you are here tonight," he said, clapping my back and offering a beer. "Glad you could come."

"Addison, Barry. Barry, Addison," I said. "She's the one who made it possible."

He turned toward her and kissed her cheeks.

"Great game. Too bad you weren't playing for the other team," my date teased with a wink.

Barry's baritone laughter vibrated through the room, "Guys," he addressed his teammates, "the enemy is in the house. You have an hour to make her a Busters fan. Go ahead, seduce the woman."

We all chuckled.

He spoke into my ear. "I like her, man. Don't chase this one away." He clapped me between the shoulder blades and turned to welcome more people.

"Okay, I like your friends, big guy," Addison said once we put some distance between the team captain and us. "I think we'll all get along just fine."

I rested my hand on her lower back and walked her into the suite. "Ted Duffy, the goalie and a big fan of your friend Nick." She gave me a puzzled look and I added, "I'll explain later. Cory Black, Rory Dupont, Jeremy Butler, the best players in the league. This is Addison. Hands off, guys, she's with me."

My date shook her head, amused, and held her hand out to my friends.

They exchanged greetings and jokes as if they'd known each other for years and hadn't just met, and another layer of calm blanketed me. Yes, the team captain was right. Addison Wilde was a keeper. Too bad I wasn't looking to get settled down.

Hours passed, and I saw exhaustion taking over her features. Her lips didn't stretch as wide when she smiled; her eyes didn't shine as bright. She had been drinking only water and soda all night, yet she looked like she was about to pass out.

"You okay?" I asked, taking my place beside her on the couch when Cory Black moved to answer his phone and cut their discussion short. "You look tired."

"I'm exhausted. Sleep isn't too generous with me."

"Come on. Let's go home." She wrinkled her face. *Home? Why did I say that?* "To our room. Luckily, we're a couple of floors downstairs."

"Thank God. I'm not sure I would have survived a car ride."

We exchanged goodbyes with the guys, and Addison accepted the bag Ted handed her. "Hope we'll see you again. Now you'll never forget us, and maybe you'll become our biggest supporter," he said, pointing to the package I guessed was filled with merch and other Busters' memorabilia. "Don't forget to send me that custom shirt you promised. Tucker knows where I live. He'll give you my address." I had no idea what they were talking about, but by the enthusiasm pouring out from her, I had no doubt it was a big deal for her.

Rory Dupont neared us. "Addi, if things don't work out with Tuck, gimme a call." He winked. Fucker. He was aware it'd rub me the wrong way. I rewarded him with a murderous stare. And he smirked.

Most of the team knew about my no-dating rules, and tonight they enjoyed my presence outside my own comfort zone.

"Forget it, Dupont. She's too good for you. You can handle a puck in the big league, but you're still a novice with women."

He laughed it off.

"She's too good for you," he whispered, hugging me. "She can handle your sorry ass like a champ, though. Too bad you're not in the market for a relationship. Let me know when she's a free agent."

"Never," I said through clenched teeth.

"Oh, I see trouble in your future."

He exchanged goodbyes with Addison and walked us out before returning to his teammates.

The door closed behind us, and I squatted down. "Hop on."

"Tuck—what? Are you offering me a piggyback ride?"

"Come on, woman."

She giggled as she placed her feet in my palms while her arms curved around my neck.

"Thanks for tonight. I had a blast."

"The guys loved you. Now they'll ask about you every time we meet. You made quite an impression on them."

"Your friends are nice. They made an impression on me too."

Wearing one of my T-shirts at my demand and after she removed every trace of makeup from her face, Addison and I slid under the covers, our bodies molding together. My arm kept her close. She cocked her head to look at me.

"Night, Tuck."

"Night, Wilde." I inhaled her scent. "Am I still grounded?"

I heard the smile in her voice. "No, you redeemed yourself tonight. And I'm not sure I possess what it takes to stay mad at you. Tomorrow, we'll tour the city since we were too busy the last time you came to Nashville."

"I love it. You playing tour guide. Can we ride scooters again?"

"Ha, I knew you liked it the last time."

"I enjoyed spending time with you, and scooters make you happy. After all, you're the President of the club."

"Yes, I almost forgot I was at the top of the hierarchy. It's a date then. You better fight my insomnia away, though."

"Always, sweetheart. Lean on me. I have your back."

I kissed her nape, and together, we drifted to sleep. And I prayed in my dreams we could be more. So much more.

———

It'd been four days since I returned from Nashville, and I was in a hurry to get home to talk to Addison. I had sent her a special package, and according to the app on my phone, it had been delivered three hours ago. I had taken the time to paste a "Don't open without me" warning label before I mailed it. My meeting had lasted forever, and we had set our daily phone call for seven tonight.

The moment I crossed the threshold of my apartment, I loosened the tie around my neck and ditched my jacket. Summer was a week away, but the city was already sizzling under the suffocating heat. Looking at the time, I realized I had twelve minutes to spare, so I decided to jump in for a quick shower and change into more comfy clothes.

My phone rang as I slid the shirt over my head and scraped the remaining water droplets from my hair with my hand.

"Hey you," I said, excitement building in me at the thought Addison had no idea what that box contained.

"Miss me already?" Most of the time, she used this as a line of greeting. Little did she know I did. More than I ever expected to.

"Depends. Do you miss me, sweetheart?"

"Don't sidetrack, Tuck. The delivery guy dropped something earlier. And from the return address, it was sent from your city. Anything to do with ya?"

"It might. You'll have to switch to video chat to be sure."

Seconds later, a notification pinged on my phone screen, and I accepted the call.

Addison, dressed down in yoga pants and a tank top, filled my screen. To my greatest enjoyment.

Her smile widened when our eyes connected.

"Fine, I miss you," she said without missing a beat.

"Good. Are you ready for your surprise?"

"Should I be?" She clutched the box and shook it. "It feels like Christmas morning. I worked from home this afternoon, and I've been tiptoeing around it for hours."

"Patience, Wilde. You'll be rewarded soon."

"Can I?"

"Have you been a naughty or a good girl?" I teased, my words expressing much more than what they said.

"A good girl." Her gaze was glued to mine, and my heart skipped a beat at the fervor of our exchange. "Always. Being naughty isn't an option. For another week."

My throat worked. She followed the movement, her smile stretching bigger. Yeah, she got me there.

"Wanna play a game, Tuck?"

I shook my head with an equally wide smile. "Not before you open the box, sweetheart." Even through a screen, the sexual tension bounced between us. "Go ahead, dig in."

Through the screen, I waited for Addison to uncover what I sent as I sat on my couch.

Seated on her bed, cross-legged, she unwrapped the first item. "A lavender bath bomb." She rolled the ball between her fingers before bringing it to her nose to take a sniff. "I love it."

"Something to appeal to your senses," I said. "It is supposed to help you sleep better if you use it before going to bed."

"Wow, thoughtful and sweet. Can I continue?"

"Yes."

I studied her while she unwrapped a pair of bright pink fluffy socks.

"Something to keep you warm. And because your feet are always cold at night."

Her eyes lifted toward mine, and I read the realization in them.

"Observing and caring," she whispered. "I love your attentiveness."

Next, she pulled out a scented candle from the box.

"Something to set the mood," I said.

My pulse raced while I studied her.

The corners of her lips tilted up. "Charming and seductive. Up till now, you get a perfect score."

I high-fived myself mentally.

From her expression, I was confident in my choices.

Ripping the silk paper, she unwrapped a soft blanket.

"Something to curl into when I'm not around to cuddle."

She stared at me, speechless. "Tuck—" she murmured after a moment, visibly touched. "Considerate and warm. You couldn't be more on point. How can you know me so well?"

"You're a fascinating subject to study. Keep going. You haven't got to the best part yet."

Like a kid, she rummaged through the box and unwrapped the silk paper around a book.

"Something to escape into," I said. "I asked around at work, and the women told me it's perfect for a romantic heart like yours."

She flipped the pages, caressed the cover, and rested it against her chest.

"Generous and devoted. You asked around to get me a book?"

Was that moisture shining in her eyes?

I nodded. "I'd do it again just to see the elated expression on your face. It makes my day."

"Wow. Thank you."

She picked up a USB stick next. "What is it?"

"Something to soothe your soul. A playlist of love songs. We won't fight over this one."

Addison blinked and cupped her chest where her heart lay. "Kind-hearted and romantic. It's—I'm impressed, big guy. You're doing amazing so far."

Seconds later, she unfolded a red lace slip, rubbing the delicate fabric between her fingers.

"Tuck, this is exquisite. And provocative. You chose it yourself?"

I bowed my head. "Something to feel beautiful in," I replied, already picturing her wearing it.

Her fingertips padded the skin under her eyes, wiping away her emotions. Yeah, those were tears I'd spotted minutes ago.

"Wilde, I can't chase away your insomnia when we're far apart. I hope this will help you unwind."

She wet her lips with her tongue, enough to send me over the edge, if I pumped my dick one too many times.

"There's one last thing." My voice sounded rougher.

She opened the small black and gold box and was presented with a vibrating device.

"Something to help you relax," I said. "Orgasms are the best insomnia therapy. Better than any massage, in my opinion."

Addison said nothing. Her chest rose and fell in a quick tempo.

"All for me?" she finally said. "You handpicked every one of these yourself? For me?"

I bobbed my head. "Yes. I called it the 'Take It Easy Wilde Box.' I would really love you to get a few good nights of sleep. Dahlia needs you sharp and ready for the wedding next weekend."

"Thank you. It's the most thoughtful, naughty, and sweetest gift anyone has ever given me. I love everything. It's perfect. And I have no idea how to thank you the right way. You're too far for a hug. Or a kiss."

"One week. And you'll be able to thank me in any way that pleases you. Now, go. By the way, I already charged it. So, you're good to go whenever you're ready."

Addison's warm laughter did strange things to me.

"You thought of everything."

"I tried."

"Is it waterproof?" she asked with a quirked brow and that devious grin I'd come to love so much.

"Yep. You can read that book in your bath in candle-light after you give yourself the second-best orgasm while listening to a custom selection of romantic songs. Only to dress into something sexy while keeping your feet warm, and dreaming my arms are around you. How does it sound?"

"Like we need to hang up. Because I'm already aroused by the description. Unless you wanna join this little party?"

I cleared my clogged throat. "Not this time. For once, be selfish and think only about yourself." My dick hated me for being too rational. Again. He wasn't used to this altered reality. Neither was I. But I was starting to get attached to the new version of me.

"Okay, I will. This is really nice of you. Can we continue this conversation tomorrow as planned?"

"Absolutely. Go, exhaust yourself, Wilde. Let me know tomorrow how it went."

"I will," she said, her voice already lustful. "Hey Tuck? If this is the second-best orgasm I can get, what's number one?"

"One Tucker Philips can provide."

"I should've guessed. I'll let you know tomorrow if you're good enough to keep the top spot."

"Yeah, do that. I'm telling you I'm not even scared for my title. Night, Wilde."

When I fell into a deep slumber later, I could see her in my head as she moaned my name and abandoned herself to the pleasure only I could provide from a distance.

Sparks of excitement filled me. Sparks I could get addicted to.

16

ADDISON

My tongue swept my bottom lip as I smoothed the skirt of my maid of honor pale yellow chiffon dress a week later. Admiring my reflection in the mirror of what used to be Dahlia's bedroom in her old house, I twirled around. The gown was beautiful. Strapless, with a short train, it made me feel like a princess when I put it on the first time. Having a best friend owning a bridal and evening gowns shop had many advantages. Never again would I be wearing a dress that didn't fit me like a second skin. I had picked this gown a few months back and hadn't tried it again since. Admiring it, I fell in love with it all over again. Squirming, I adjusted the fabric over my breasts, annoyed about my upcoming periods making my boobs sensitive and swollen. Poor timing.

With a hand, I rubbed my stomach. My hormones had always been a crazy ride. And this time would be no exception. The wedding would be a crying fest if I didn't get myself under control. I had a tendency to be a hormonal crier. And booze would now not only feed my insomnia, but also my tears. I sighed. Getting drunk and making a fool of myself this weekend wasn't an option. Perhaps this was a good thing, though. My upcoming situation would also prevent me from jumping Tucker like a needy girl-friend the moment we met again.

The universe had decided to send me a message. A very clear message. For once, maybe I should just listen.

Or I could push the thought away and categorize it as nonsense.

Tomorrow was my best friend's wedding, and a glass—or two—of champagne wouldn't kill me. I deserved some fun of my own. Two glasses. Yes, I'd draw the line there.

With my phone in hand, I checked the time, an excuse to see if Tucker had sent me a text message. Nothing. His flight was scheduled to land sometime in the middle of the afternoon. I offered to pick him up from the airport since I got here in the morning, but he had a rental and was meeting Nick for some last-minute tuxedo adjustments.

I loved the friendship thing we got going on. Physical, sexual, intellectual. We had really bonded over the last six weeks. Inserting himself into my daily life, Tucker had taken over a huge part of my time. We clicked. No better word described us. And I cherished every second we spent talking and goofing around and confiding in each other.

We'd graduated from superficial conversations full of sexual promises and innuendos. Everything about Tucker Philips made sense to me now. His fears. His doubts. His insecurities. The only thing I still hadn't figured out was the shadow I sometimes perceived in his gaze. And my gut told me it was quite recent, nothing related to his child-hood. When he thought no one was paying him attention. But it languished there. In the darkness of his chocolate-brown irises. I noticed it. More than once.

Someday, I'd ask him about it. If our friendship

survived this weekend. Because we were supposed to have sex again. As a part of our agreement. My body tingled just at the thought of it. And the memories of that day when we singed the sheets of my hotel room. Even over a month later. His lips on my skin. His hands everywhere. The way he transformed me into an inferno, burning hotter for him the more we pleasured each other. And the promises of a repeat performance this weekend before going our separate ways. How could I not be obsessed with him? Still, I had no idea how we both kept things PG-13 both weekends we spent together considering the sizzling chemistry and undeniable attraction we shared.

The thought of never lying in his arms again after this weekend twisted my stomach. It'd be the end of many chapters we were writing together. And the end of that physical connection I'd never experienced with anyone else before him. And despite myself, I loved us together. Even when sex wasn't a part of the equation.

My heart rate accelerated. Something coiled my insides.

A million questions swirled in my head. And deep down, I feared if we got intimate again, it would put our blooming friendship at risk. And break the fragile equilibrium between us. I loved the chase. Our relationship. The restraint and the magnetism pulling us toward each other. Tucker and I were sexual people. We loved sex. A lot. And somehow, we both had resisted our number one temptation while growing closer. Pride danced in me at the idea we completed each other and could rely on the other when we lacked strength.

I inhaled, wishing it would calm the bouncing balls of nerves hitting the walls of my chest.

The way he held me when I visited him in Chicago and two weekends ago in Nashville, as if I mattered to him

—as if I were his whole world—gambled with my emotions. Now I feared I'd gotten attached to him more than I should. With someone else, a relationship, love, could be possible. But not with a man allergic to commitment. I would only set myself up for disappointment in the end. And another broken heart. And my heart had enough scars already.

Yeah, I'd ridden that rollercoaster before. We shared great sex. I fell in love. Then the guy decided I wasn't worth whatever attachment issues he struggled with. Result? Another Addison Wilde failed love story. Instructions? Start over and repeat. Until the parts of my heart, held only by a flimsy thread, healed while I vowed to a celibate life. No, thank you. I yearned for love spelled in giant glittery letters. The one you could never overcome because it rattled your core just thinking about losing it. The thing movies and novels were made of.

Since last night after we hung up, my heart and head had been debating if Tucker and I should go forward with our plan or forfeit it and continue to nurture our friendship instead. In a platonic way. One option kept my heart safe, the other put it at risk. Our relationship meant a lot to me. It defied logic. Even my own. But I wouldn't want to live without it for another day.

With my gaze locked on my figure, I twirled one last time, loving the cascade of the fabric as the dress fell back in place. I lowered the zipper, watching the gown billow to the floor at my feet before picking it up and hanging it behind the door. I caressed the bodice between my fingers, my mind drifting to Tucker. Again. A stupid smile curled my lips. My heart sang in my chest. Seeing him tonight signified making a decision. And my head and my heart hadn't settled yet. I required more time. Whatever my heart desired, the guy didn't do relationships. And he'd been adamant about it. Multiple times. Yes, I had to follow my head. Our off-the-charts sexual compatibility shouldn't be explored further. Okay, I would talk to him. Explain how I felt. And he would agree. Because it made sense.

I nodded, confident of my position.

Our insane chemistry should be put to better use.

Doubts crippled me.

How could I stay friends with a guy my heart ached for without risking it in the process?

A dreadful feeling washed over me, and I buried my face in my hands with a growl.

Why did it trouble all my cells thinking we wouldn't share any intimacy again?

Despite what I told myself, I couldn't imagine a life without Tucker Philips in it. One in which he called me every day, held me at night, chasing away the bad guys in my dreams or fighting my insomnia. The sight of him in pressed suits or his enticing smirks directed at me with barely contained lust got me giddy. And shot me with doses of calm. Even when I tried to lock my heart from the hurt, the man with dark skin and sparkling irises had stolen a huge chunk of it.

No. No, no, no. I refused to acknowledge what I already knew. I would fight this.

Closing my eyes, I counted to three, and leaving my new resolves behind, I grabbed my phone again, re-reading our last text exchange.

Yeah, I was that weak.

Tucker: Counting the days till I see you again.

Tucker: I lied.

Me: Why? When?

Tucker: It's more like hours, to be honest. Sweetheart, we've been patient enough. I want you. Under me. Over me. Sitting on my face. On all-fours. And in a dozen other different ways.

Me: Oh Tuck. I want you too. I want it all. That tongue of yours... Just thinking about it makes me wet.

The smile stretching my lips probably mirrored the one I had at the same exact moment we wrote this. And the anticipation tumbling in my lower belly had grown stronger over the hours.

Me: Tuck...

Tucker: What's wrong, Wilde?

Me: I'm happy. How did we get here?

Tucker: What do you mean?

Me: Us. How did we get so comfortable together? So close? Our friendship. It's significant to me.

Tucker: No idea. But I regret nothing. You've become the most important person in my life. With you, I don't feel like I'm stuck. I feel like I'm living.

Stuck? I had noticed the word the first time. Could it explain the shadow in his eyes? One day, I'd get to the bottom of it. Soon. Because I hated the idea that something was bothering him.

Tucker: Oh fuck. Can we talk later? I'll be late if I don't leave in like ten minutes.

Me: Sure.

Tucker: I'll see you soon, sweetheart. Don't miss me too much *winking emoji* And don't miss your bus or I'll come to get you myself.

Me: You wouldn't.

Tucker: Try me. I already did. Twice.

Me: I know. Wanted to hear you say it.

Me: See you later.

I laughed because I loved the idea of him coming to get me, all caveman-like, handsome and sexy, scooping me over his shoulder to carry me where I was supposed to be.

With a shake of my head, I cleared my stupid grin. My heart banged a little faster. That man... Gosh, I really missed him. A warm shiver zipped through me. And now I was lying to myself. Ohmyfuckinggod.

I sighed, cursing at myself, and rummaged through my suitcase to find something to wear tonight, trying to keep the images of him away to avoid transforming into a puddle of arousal. And locking the desire center of my brain to make sure it would not interfere with my new dedication. Keep our relationship platonic.

In an attempt to focus on something else, I turned my laptop on and lost myself in my newest designs. Much later, when I noticed the time, I fumbled to save the open file. "Oh no. And now I'll be late."

Dahlia and Nick had invited us for a pre-wedding dinner in an hour, so I should hurry. At least, I had left my naughty thoughts where they belonged—far away from here—for an afternoon.

See, I could do this. Be strong. And resist his charms.

I showered and applied my makeup, doing a great job at thinking about anything but the man I had no right to think about.

My mind drifted to the wedding the next day instead.

A new set of jitters swam in my belly. Flowers. Music. Food. Love. I placed a flat palm over my chest, calming my thudding organ, and gave a pep talk to my reflection through the full-length mirror on the bedroom wall. "Things will work out when the timing is right."

I firmed my back. Confidence slithered through the cracks of my vulnerability, growing roots.

Since I'd questioned it earlier, I was now aware I had to keep the man at arm's length. Knowing my heart would probably let him slither in.

With a little insight, Nick and Dahlia's warning was fitting. Maybe they knew me better than I knew myself. Would they agree to be the protectors of my heart from now on? Because I failed at the task.

Great, I was rambling in my own head. And thinking about asking my best friend and her future husband to micro-manage my love life. This was bad.

I bet they sensed Tucker and I would hit it off, and they knew us well enough to guess it could be disastrous if we ended up in bed together. Me the romantic. Him the guarded womanizer. Or ex-womanizer. A love story doomed from the start.

"See, Tuck? That's what spending too much time with you does to me," I said out loud. It fucked my mind. And my body. Not fucked. Confused. Confused my mind and my body. "See? It happened again. Why do you have to be so irresistible all the time? And smell so great? And be nice and caring. And freaking hot."

Dressed in a denim skirt and an off-the-shoulder white top, I climbed behind the wheel of Dahlia's car. The one she lent me for the next few days since I had traveled here on a bus. I checked my reflection one last time in the rearview mirror and fixed my lipstick before driving to my friend's place.

Carter and Jack were kicking a soccer ball on the front lawn when I pulled into the driveway.

"Hey guys," I said as the toddler ran into my wide-open arms when I squatted down.

"Addidi," he screamed when I lifted him and spun him around.

"Ohmygod, you're so tall. Did you grow a foot in the last month?" He bobbed his head as I lowered him back to his feet after hugging him. This kid owned a big slice of my heart. Jack Hills topped the list of my favorite human beings in this world. Right next to his mama.

"Hey you," Carter greeted me as we kissed each other's cheeks. "Dahlia said to meet her inside as soon as possible. Some maid of honor emergency, I think." He shrugged and picked up Jack to seat him on his shoulders, maneuvering the ball with his feet. They always looked so happy together. As if they belonged to a world nobody else had access to. Like he and Dahlia did when they were kids.

He kicked the ball in my direction, and I blocked it. From his perch, Jack applauded.

"Guess I should go. See you later, you two," I said as I made my way inside, adjusting my skirt.

"Hey girlfriend, I'm here. What's the problem?" I asked as my feet met the plank floor. I scanned the main level. It looked nothing as it did the last time I was here.

"Wow, you guys did an amazing job. I'm speechless. This is so beautiful. No doubt why you're getting married. You make a terrific team. Wow."

The farmhouse had been turned into a more modern version while maintaining the old dignity. The wooden floors and ceilings were the same but refreshed, and everything else had been changed. The kitchen and the living room had interchanged places. The walls that used to be a silvery shade of gray before were now white, giving a fresh vibe to the place. The old staircase had been sanded and re-stained the same color as the floors. Here and there were black and purple accessories. It looked country-chic, modern, and vintage all at the same time.

One day, I'd like to own a house. Just like this one. Some place warm and cozy. Some place to call home.

Dahlia met me in the kitchen and pushed a wineglass into my hand. I discarded it on the countertop, my stomach churning at the thought of an early drink.

"What's going on? Carter was being cryptic outside."

She took a seat beside me at the island.

"The lady who was supposed to come over to do our makeup tomorrow bailed on us. She had to leave town. An emergency. I was thinking, with your mama owning a beauty salon which means being a makeup wizard runs in your veins and your genes, if perhaps you'd agree to replace her. I know I'm asking a lot, and you have plenty of maid of honor and organizer's duties to deal with, but if you could find some time to do my mama's, mine, and Mrs. Peterson's makeup, you'd save my life."

I pulled Dahlia into a hug as tears filled my eyes. "Nothing would make me happier and prouder, girlfriend. You've always been my favorite model. Remember that time at the prom or at that music award show? I'm very flattered you asked." I leaned back to wipe my glossy eyes.

"Ohmygod, you're crying. Everything okay?"

I sniffled. "Wedding jitters. You getting married is making me emotional. I'm so happy for you. And Nick. But mostly for ya." Dahlia brushed my hair with her hand. We stayed in each other's embrace for a minute. My tears dried, and I straightened my back. "Anyway, I'm sure we can delegate most of my tasks to Tucker. No way will he be sitting around on his ass all afternoon drinking whiskey while we get everything ready. Consider it done. I'll deal with him."

Dahlia pulled back.

"Oh, Addi is back. You look good, girlfriend. I'm sorry I haven't been available lately. This craziness is almost over, and things will go back to normal." She hugged me a little tighter. "I've been yearning to ask. How is it going between you two?"

"Tucker and I?"

"Yes. You seemed to get along just fine in Nashville. Did you guys keep in touch? Did you convince him to take part in that secret project of yours?"

I swallowed before speaking. "Yeah, we're fine. We messaged a few times. Mostly wedding stuff." And one half-naked selfie. Two late-night raunchy video chats. One date. A weekend sleepover. A weekend getaway. Hundreds of hours over the phone. Too many text messages. But hey, mostly wedding stuff, right?

"Good. I feared you guys would either hit it off or wouldn't be able to stand each other. Both of you are much more alike than you think." A long pause. "How is it going with the *I'm-done-with-men* thing? Changed your mind already? Who is your mysterious plus-one?"

I let out a heartfelt laugh, my mini meltdown forgotten, and my best friend joined in.

"Fine. You knew I'd never go through with it, even if I

think it'd make my life easier and my heart much safer. I had lunch with Felicia, my college experiment, as you called her." I sighed. "It kinda sealed the deal. I'm not made for this. I love men too much."

Dahlia snickered. "Promise me you won't date the first one you meet, okay? You deserve someone great. Someone who will love you and put you first."

The door yanked open, and laughter reached us, cutting short our conversation. The one with a deep baritone sent my heart into a frenzy, and all my hair stood on end. This was bad. Very bad. I wasn't ready to see him just yet. And, for some reason, in the last half-hour, I'd convinced myself he would skip being here tonight. Or that his flight had been delayed. Just the idea of Tucker standing feet away from me turned me into a horny time bomb. Having him too close, while I was still debating the right course of action, was dangerous. Multiplied by ten, with our friends surrounding us. His presence destroyed my resolve. And toyed with my stupid hormones.

"Hey Tuck," Dahlia greeted, rising to her feet to meet him. "How was your flight?"

"Great."

"Remember my best friend, Addi, your *bride* and the woman you sang to?" she asked, half-smiling.

"Hey you," he said, staring at me for far too long. The column of his throat worked. His pupils dilated. His lips parted.

My skin tingled, and my face heated up under his heavy gaze.

Warmth shot through me, and desire welled up between my legs.

I shouldn't want him. Not if I wanted to stay true to the promise I made to myself to find the right person for me. No more one-night stands. I thought I could do rebound sex, but I was bad at it. My heart sometimes forgot about the no strings attached rules. Because Tucker Philips was the one my entire body longed for. My weakness. The man who should share my bed. And rock my nights.

He inched closer to me, stealing every remnant molecule of oxygen meant for my lungs.

When his lips connected with my cheek, I caught fire. His presence invaded my senses. My hand fisted his shirt, a reflex I hadn't grown out of, to preserve my balance. Goosebumps blossomed on my arms. My breathing picked up. My heart galloped in my chest.

Oh dear, catastrophe was about to happen. A collision of desires we had leashed in for far too long.

I took a whiff of him, closing my eyes as I savored the clean and manly scent he wore so perfectly. Ocean breeze. And him.

"Miss me, sweetheart?" he asked in a husky voice with an edge that only I could hear.

I nodded. Barely. But enough to see the dangerous twinkle in his eyes. A devilish smile broadened his lips.

Every cell in me throbbed at his proximity.

Nick touched his friend's shoulder, breaking the spell. "Whiskey or beer?"

I resumed my breathing. If we weren't careful enough, we'd get caught. And now wasn't the time to stress our friends with our antics.

Tucker cleared his throat, finding his composure back and stepping away from me. "Beer. For now. Anything for you, Addison?" he asked holding my eyes, articulating each syllable of my name in a way that made my legs weak.

Was my face all flushed? And my armpits drenched? I hooked a finger into the collar of my shirt and motioned it back and forth, bringing much-needed air to my combusting self.

"Water's fine. Thanks."

Tucker walked past me and whispered, so once again only I could hear him, "Am I making you all hot and bothered, sweetheart?"

I met his eyes for a flash second and looked away. "No," I murmured through clenched teeth. The game was on. I could imagine how we'd implode together. And yet, I was unable to stop the imminent clash.

He let out a low chuckle. "We'll see." He winked, then followed Nick. There. I almost lost the fight in me at that instant. Our connection had intensified since the playoff game two weeks ago. The stakes had gotten higher. And Tucker had transformed into an addiction whose sole mission was to ravage me. Mind, body, and soul.

Hours later, the five of us sat around the table, now that Jack was in bed. "To family," Dahlia said, her wineglass in hand. "You, my friends, are our family. We love each of you so much. Thanks for being here with us. It means more than you'll ever know."

The cook they hired for tonight brought us some fancy salad after we clinked our glasses. I was about to bring my fork to my mouth when warm fingers slithered their way to my pulsing center, sliding my panties to the side and gliding into the depths of me. I yelped and shut my eyes for a second, trying to act casual.

The sparks spiraling through me were foreign. And intoxicating. As if I was being touched this way for the first time.

A truckload of sensations, each more pleasurable than the others, washed through me. It took all I had to not roll my hips, chasing the friction between my legs.

"Are you okay?" my best friend asked, worry swimming in her hypnotic green eyes.

"Yes," I said, my voice stuck in my throat. I downed my water, trying to cool myself off. Beside me, Tucker pinched his lips, acting as if his fingers weren't buried inside me, playing me like a love song. The heel of his hand brushed my clit, and my blood turned to lava. Shudders infiltrated my entire body as it came alive under his expert caresses. Yeah, I had no self-control when he was involved. I chewed on a piece of lettuce longer than needed, unable to focus on the conversation going on around the table.

"Addi, you gotta settle this debate. What do you think?" Nick asked, his fork suspended mid-air, waiting for me to answer a question that I had no clue about. I blinked. Under the table, Tucker applied more pressure to my throbbing bundle of nerves. I clenched my thighs, trying hard to not squirm on the chair and moan at the top of my lungs.

"I think you're right."

Nick's fork fell to his plate, and he went "Ah, ah." I had no idea what I had just agreed to. Who cared? My body tensed. No way would I come right here at the table surrounded by my closest friends.

Tucker spread my wetness over my folds, teasing me, my body too sensitive to be fiddled with.

Pleasure blinded me while it pulsed through me, and I punched the table while all eyes drifted to me.

"You sure you okay?" Dahlia asked. "Your face is all red."

I nodded. "Yeah. Something's stuck in here," I said, massaging my throat.

She rose to her feet. "Let me get you more water."

A throaty "thanks" bubbled out.

The cook came to the table and asked Nick something, who stood to follow him.

As if pulled by a magnet, my head turned toward Tucker. His eyes gleamed. And he had a victory smirk hanging from his lips. The one I was dying to feed on. My cheek rubbed his sleeve. Did I transform into a pathetic aching puppy? Heavy lids and teeth biting into my tongue, I hid my face in the crook of his arm, angling my body to increase the friction between us.

"You guys are so bad," Carter stated, finishing his plate, acting as if nothing was happening three feet from him. "You could at least be subtle about it. It's written all over your faces you're sleeping together. Just a question, though. Where are your fingers, Tuck?"

I clenched my jaw as a first wave of pleasure hit me, strangling Tucker's hand between my thighs. A deep-throated groan whistled out of me.

Tucker kissed the tip of my nose.

I swallowed and blinked.

"Please, Cart. Don't say a word. They don't have to know." I gasped, my eyelids fluttering, wondering how long I could last without detonating.

My voice sounded so unlike mine.

Dahlia entered the room, and Tucker and I broke apart.

My chest heaved. I kept my gaze down, trying to even my shallow breathing.

She put a glass of water before me, and Carter rose before she could sit back.

"Dah, can I talk to you for a minute?" She nodded. "In private. I think Nick should come too."

She turned her head to face us. "Sorry, guys, it won't be long. Meet me in the den, Cart, I'll get him."

Carter fixed us for a long second and whispered,

leaning forward, "You have three minutes to finish what you're doing."

Now boiling with need, I pivoted on my chair until I faced Tucker again. He curled a hand around my nape and kissed me as if it'd be the last time, his fingers diving in and out of me at a dizzying pace. The orgasm built inside me, and in no time, I liquified around his expert touch. He removed his hand, and with his thumb coated in my arousal, he skimmed the length of my lower lip. The taste of me on his digit turned me on in a way no words could express. With the tip of my tongue, I licked his fingers clean while he watched me.

"Good girl. God, you're hot. I've missed you, sweetheart."

We fixated on each other for a long moment. Tension coiled around us, ribbons of pleasure tying us together.

After a beat, I found my voice. "Tuck, we're not supposed to. We said after the wedding, remember? Friendship and sex are blurring the lines."

"Fuck the wait. You want it as much as I do. I paid penance. I can't wait to have a taste of you later. It's all I've been thinking about. Taking you on this table. On the island in the kitchen. By the front door." He brought my hand over his erection, his dick twitching under my touch while I massaged it. "See? I'm not waiting another night."

"What about your words?" I asked, breathless, falling under his charm. "Our deal?"

The more he stared at me like this, with hunger and lust, the more I drifted toward him, unable to resist the pull.

"Let's talk about it later," he said as footsteps neared us, and we moved apart as if nothing had happened. I kept my head low, knowing my face was flushed, and excused myself from the table the moment everyone sat, needing a minute—or many—to regain my composure and leash my hormones back under control. And to cool off.

My body still pulsated, desperate for more.

In the bathroom, I splashed cold water over my face, doing my best to not ruin my makeup. I shook my hands, trying to infuse myself with words of wisdom.

Control yourself, Addi. You can do it. Just for a few hours. Remember what you decided earlier? Resist. Be strong. You can do this. He'll understand.

The door opened when my hand wrapped around the knob, and Tucker slid his tall self into the opening.

I startled back. "What are you doing here?" I asked in a whisper, my heart rate picking up at his closeness. My fragile composure slipping.

"Dahlia is wondering if you're all right." He shrugged. "I offered to come to get you." He flipped me around and nestled his hard length between my ass cheeks, grinding his hips against my backside. I whimpered, clutching the counter with both hands to prevent my knees from buckling. His palms ventured underneath my shirt and dragged upward until he cupped both breasts, my nipples stiff enough they could drill holes through his flesh. His lips traced the length of my neck. Okay, I was melting right here. On my best friend's bathroom floor. "Fuck, Wilde. I've missed ya."

I shook my head, unable to open my eyes, the sensations rushing through me and threatening my balance.

"No, Tuck. You can't miss me. The only thing you're allowed to miss is our friendship. Not my body."

I inhaled through my mouth, calming myself, and spun around between his arms now caging me. I tilted my head back to lock eyes with him, his warm breath sweeping my cheek. With one hand sprayed on his broad chest, I kept him at a safe distance.

"Wilde, this weekend will be torture if I'm not granted permission to touch you. To fuck you with my tongue. My cock. My fingers. Told ya, you're all I think about. All. The. Time. Help a guy out. We deserve our playtime. We've been reasonable long enough."

I shook my head. "Listen, we gotta stop now. We'll get caught. For the rest of tonight and the weekend, we better stay away from each other."

He blinked. "Is that what you want?" he asked, a perplexed frown wrinkling the contour of his eyes.

My throat closed. *No. Yes. For my heart's safety.*

I hung my head and looked away. "It's for the best. Being selfish and jeopardizing the wedding isn't smart."

He tried to meet my fleeting gaze. "Wait? You serious? This makes no sense. I missed you. I thought we agreed to spend this weekend together. When did you change your mind? Why didn't you tell me last night when we talked?"

Because it's all new. I realized I could easily fall for you. And it scares me because I know you won't reciprocate my feelings if it happens, and I'm being honest about how I feel. And our friendship is sacred to me, and no way will I spoil it. I've had too many failed relationships in the past.

I wiped my watery eyes with my hands. Why was I crying all the time? Dahlia's wedding was happening at the worst time.

Tucker's voice softened as he held my upper arms, leveling his eyes with mine.

"Hey, why are you sad? What's going on?" He pushed my hair away from my face, and I stared at a spot behind him. "Addison, talk to me. Last time we discussed it, you said you couldn't wait for the weekend to arrive and have me all to you. You even made dirty promises."

Worry billowed in his eyes. Why did he have to be so

damn handsome? And so caring? It wasn't fair. My dream man was a Mustang. One who could never be tamed.

I shrugged. "Nothing. Wedding jitters. This thing is making me all emotional. I love weddings. Always have. True love. Soulmates. They mean something to me. Something I aspire for. Someday." His knuckles brushed my cheek, but I jerked away from his touch. "Don't worry. I'm fine. Imminent period. Girls' stuff." I sniffed. "I'm okay. Now let's go back before our friends start wondering what we're doing."

He dropped his head and blew out a breath.

"Fine. You win. We'll do as you say. You'd tell me if something was bothering you, right?" he asked, shoving his hands in the pockets of his dark trousers.

"Yup. Everything's great. Better than great. Our best friends are about to get married. Yay," I said, pumping my fist. Tucker studied me for a long, fat minute, trying to read me. Or that's what it seemed like. I fixed a smile on my face, straightened my back, and exited the bathroom without another glance in his direction.

———

"How long are you in town, Tuck?" Carter asked when we were all seated in the den, the guys—except him—now sipping on whiskey, and Dahlia and I drinking tea instead.

"Two weeks maybe. Not sure yet."

My heart pounded at Tucker's words, and I couldn't even explain the reason.

"You never told me you accepted my offer," Nick chimed in with a frown.

"It will be fun to have you around for a little while. Where are you staying?" Dahlia asked next.

"For all I know, your old house. Nick offered it to me when he came to visit."

Dahlia winced.

"Is there something wrong?" he asked.

My best friend's gaze ping-ponged between us.

"Well, Addi has moved in for the weekend." She turned to face her almost-husband. "Babe, you didn't tell me you had promised it to Tucker."

Tucker's eyes moved to me for half a second before drawing back to Nick.

"You can stay here while Addi is in town. It's only for a few nights, anyway. Then you decide if you wanna move there instead. The offer to stay in town for a couple of weeks still stands. Your choice." Nick shrugged.

"Nah, I can't stay here. You guys need your space. You're getting married tomorrow. So, a hotel it is. No worries. I'll find a decent place in town."

"You could stay at Cart's," Dahlia suggested. With her mug nestled in her hands, her copper hair cascading freely over her shoulders, and her legs tucked under her, she looked relaxed about her next day nuptials. The opposite of how I felt.

Carter shrugged. "Sure. There are plenty of rooms if you're looking for a place to crash. I don't offer room service, but other than that, it's rent-free."

Tucker shook his head. "No way. Jack is going home with you, and you're all entitled to your privacy. I'm just an outsider here. The hotel is fine. And I'll decide what to do after a few nights."

"Or you could stay with me," I offered, not bothering to look at him, busy nipping at my fingernails. "There's enough room for the both of us. And like Nick said, I'm just in town for three days, anyway. Soon you'll have the entire place to yourself.'"

Nick's voice broke the awkward silence, and he scratched his temple. "Guys, I'm sorry we both offered you the house without talking about it first."

"Then it's settled. We're shacking up together, big guy."

"You sure?" His glance asked much more than his words.

"Yep." I looked away, but his stare burned the side of my head.

Carter snickered behind his hand and fake-coughed when my laser-beam eyes landed on him, ready to turn him into a roasted chicken.

My heavy stare pinned him on the spot, and he reeled his laughter in.

On my feet, I hugged my best friend. "I love you. I should go. Tomorrow is the big day. You should get some rest."

Tucker joined me. "Sweetheart, let me walk you to your car. It's my unofficial job as the best man to make sure the maid of honor is always safe and sound and accounted for."

I rolled my eyes, pretending to be annoyed, when little fireworks exploded inside me instead. Tucker had a way of making me feel special. No wonder women fell at his feet all the time. He and I never got into details about his past sexcapades. And I didn't want to know all the specifics, anyway. *No, thanks, I'll pass.* Still, I could recognize his power of seduction.

My eyes took him in, and I enjoyed the sight. The attraction searing between us didn't only come from Tucker's model-face or football-star physique. Nor from his panty-melting grin or the way he undressed me with his eyes. It was a mix of everything combined with his huge heart and sense of humor. And the caring and sweet side of his that he hid from most people. Altogether, it was a deadly combination.

If he was after my heart, I'd offer him the entire organ without second-guessing myself. Because that was how I was wired. Love and love hard. Trust and trust harder.

No, Addi, a voice in my head warned me. *Stop doing that. Take your time. Don't fall in love so quickly. Make sure whoever you entrust your heart to is the right person. Please, no more broken hearts.*

"Come on, Wilde. Let me do this." His words had more meaning than anyone else could understand.

I sighed and shut my eyes for a second. "Fine. But I'm pretty sure walking to my car isn't a hazard. Even if it's late."

Dahlia and Nick hugged us, teasing about how if we spent too much time together, we'd drive each other nuts, as Carter joined us, a sleepy Jack tucked in his arms.

"I'm ready, big guy. Show me the way," I said, pulling Tucker's hand. The warmth of his palm in mine propelled shivers down to my knees, then to my toes. My body woke up. Tingles moved along my vertebras.

Next to my car, he leaned in until his forehead rested on mine.

"Wilde, I can keep you company tonight. Just hold you. We're getting good at this cuddling thing. Or help you relax with whichever part of my body pleases you. All you have to do is say yes. I've missed you so damn much. Two weeks without seeing you is boring as hell. My bed is empty without you in it."

My heart flipped around in my chest at the sound of his breathing and closeness. He spoke the words I was dying to hear, but in another context.

Taking my courage in my hands, I motioned a *no* with my head. In contrary to the lust screaming from inside, begging him to take care of all my needs. "We better not. I shouldn't have let you touch me earlier. It was a mistake. I fucked up all the signals."

"Which signals? I want you; you want me. Don't complicate things."

I lifted a hand between us and rested it over his heart, relishing the strong rhythm underneath my palm. My fingers toyed with the fabric of his dress shirt as I avoided looking at him.

"This thing between us is getting out of hand. We gotta stop before it's too late. Hooking up will affect our friendship. How could it not? And I'm not risking it. Being your friend is all I can give ya. Or everything we are will shatter. You know I speak the truth. Over the last couple of weeks, I've got very attached to you. And very attracted to you. And I miss you like crazy when we're apart. You've starred in all my dreams too. Refusing you, *us*, is super hard right now."

And all I want is to protect my heart. Same as you do. Because knowing we would be together this weekend made me feel something I never thought I'd feel again. But bigger and rawer. It's precious to me. Being your friend is getting harder than I thought. Because no way are you supposed to be obsessed with your friends. Wishing you could see them every day of the week. Or sharing every insignificant detail of your life with them. Even the things that don't matter. Because their smiles are enough to make everything better. And bring you to a place where you're at peace.

"I'm that bad looking, huh?" Tucker teased me, breaking the trance I was falling into.

I shook my head, a small smile peeking out. "I wish." A lone tear escaped, and he used the pad of his finger to wipe it off. His lips, soft and delicate, erased the last trace of moisture, and right there, I almost forgot all about my stupid decision to stay away and nearly kissed him. My voice trembled as I spoke, "I'm so sorry. I know we had a plan. And I was really looking forward to it. But I'm afraid I won't be able to keep the 'no strings attached' from my end. You're not looking for a relationship, and I am. Well, not now, but eventually. I'm done settling for less than I deserve. It's best if we keep our distance so my heart can get tougher. It must harden up. Together, we're explosive, and if we're not careful, it'll all blow up in our faces."

He cleared his throat. "You have no idea what I want, sweetheart. You never asked."

"I don't have to. You've said your piece from the start. It's on me. I'm the one unable to follow the rules now. I thought I could, but I was fooling myself. It's over. Let's not make this weekend weirder than it has to be."

As if I'd poked him, Tucker jumped back, hurt flashing in his dark irises. "Fine. Message received. See you tomorrow, Wilde. I'll book a room at the hotel after all. Call me if you require help with the wedding plans." Without another word or glance in my direction, he stepped back, with his shoulders rolled forward and his hands deep in his pockets.

I swallowed the rock-hard lump sitting in my throat, slid behind the wheel, and drove away, feeling as if I'd broken something that didn't even exist.

17

TUCKER

Was she joking? Was this a prank? I blinked. And blinked again. Just to make sure I'd heard her right and this wasn't some nightmare I had agreed to partake in.

Addison left me high and dry in our friends' driveway without another glance in my direction. She. Fucking. Left.

Stunned, with mixed emotions brewing inside me, I watched her until the car turned the corner, and I lost sight of her taillights. With heavy steps, I trudged to my rental parked on the side of the road, kicking clouds of dust around me.

With a hand clutching the door frame, I glanced back in the direction she disappeared. Just in case she realized she'd spoken nonsense and decided to come back and explain herself.

I waited. One. Two. Ten minutes.

Nothing.

Twenty-four hours ago, we were both eager at the idea of finally being together again. And now, out of nowhere, she rambled about getting attached, panicked, and drove away.

I had my fingers inside her pussy hours ago, and back then, she didn't seem to be against the idea of us.

I plugged my dead phone into the charger. One text message pinged.

Addison: I'm sorry.

With my palm, I hit the steering wheel. The worst that I wasn't even mad at her. Not really. I was angry at the circumstances.

We spent countless hours on the phone over the course of the last few weeks. And each time we met in person, we refrained from having sex when we shared a bed. Even if we were both ripping at the seams in such proximity. And cuddled all night. Because that was the only closeness we indulged in. My dick sprang to wood in my pants, and I pushed it down. "Not tonight, buddy." Addison Wilde was the girl we both craved.

Driving to the outskirts of town, I booked a room in the only hotel around. Padding to the sixth floor using the stairs—I really needed to expel my frustration—I fumbled with the key card, my nerves getting the best of me. How much would I pay for a gym right now to exhaust my body and mind? Waiting for some miracle, a call, or a message, I didn't shower and lay on my bed, still dressed.

With my eyes closed, I played the last month and a half in my head. Where did I go wrong? Where did I miss a hint?

Nothing. I came up with nothing that could explain Addison backing out on us. *Us.* Why did I keep using this word? We were friends with benefits with *no* benefits. Not a couple. Not a thing. Just people enjoying each other inside and outside the bedroom. But without sex.

Yet, something felt like a mistake. My skin tingled. My stomach roiled. All signs I was missing something right in front of me.

With my phone in hand, I read her last message again.

Addison: I'm sorry.

"Me too, sweetheart."

I imagined a life without her. Or with her only being partially in it. Living in different states and barely having time to meet anymore. Not being each other's last call of the day.

I saw her, clearly as if she were beside me right now, holding hands with another guy. Kissing him. Fucking him.

Cold chills awoke on my nape.

Hell rose inside me.

A lump clogged my airways.

Sweat beaded on my temples.

I held my breath, thinking the sting would go away. That the hand tightening around my heart would let go. But it didn't. Instead, it squeezed harder.

As if someone had cut my air intake. My sole source of oxygen.

Then it hit me. Like a tidal wave, it crashed over me, seizing my airways. Emotions I had pushed down most of my life resurfaced. The sound of an internal alarm rang in my head.

I put my hands over my ears, trying to quiet all the evidence I was losing my mind. Big time.

My lips parted as I tried to express the words I feared. But they refused to pass the threshold of my mouth.

Could this be real?

Could I be that guy?

No. I shook my head. It was all a nightmare. A cry escaped my mouth. Darkness fell upon me.

Why couldn't I wake up?

I searched for an exit, an out. Nothing.

Springing to a sitting position, I ran a hand over my face, my lungs collapsing as I sucked a breath in. The burn wouldn't dissipate.

Was I asleep?

Was it all a dream?

My eyes perused the room.

It took a second for me to recall where I was.

Grabbing my phone, I looked at the time. Only minutes had passed since I lay on this bed.

What was going on with me?

I exhaled. My body shook with the realization.

Addison: I'm sorry.

My eyes were taken hostage by her words, flashing as if they were neon signs.

Sweeping through the pictures I took in the last six weeks, I stopped to look at every one of them where we were together. And the ones I snapped of her when she wasn't looking.

"Wilde, I'm in love with you."

The words left my mouth by themselves. And this time, they didn't hurt. They only sent a charge to my heart.

"I love you," I told a picture of her, wearing her Honky-Tonks purple jersey, focused on the game that night.

Jumping to my feet, I grabbed the car keys I'd discarded when I got in, only to retreat to sit on my bed again, my elbows propped on my knees and my face buried in my hands.

I couldn't go to her without a strategy. Some well-thought-out plan.

She was clearly emotional tonight, and I couldn't just spill the words to her like that. Without making sure she was in the right set of mind to receive them.

Fear crippled me. How would Addison ever believe I spoke the truth? She had been played by losers too many times already. And I'd been professing my non-commitment to her since the moment we met.

I peeled my clothes off, my body igniting.

Under a stream of cold water, I showered, hoping it would calm the jitters in my stomach and put order into my thoughts. I was Tucker Philips. I didn't do love. I didn't even have an idea what a committed relationship would ask of me.

I repeated the words, loving how they sounded and was getting used to them. "I love you, Addison Wilde." Blood flowed to my dick because he enjoyed her as much as I did.

I curled a fist around the girth, working him until I couldn't stop, and shooting my release became my only way out of the tornado I found myself spinning in.

Tremors shook my body.

I pumped myself faster.

I jerked my head back, cold water cascading down my face, the muscles of my jaw taut.

Prickles built in my spine.

My balls ached.

I increased the pace of my hand around my shaft.

My forehead banged on the wall, my lungs struggling to inhale any fresh air.

With one last flick of my wrist, I let go.

My load sprayed the floor, and some of my apprehension left me.

Oxygen made its way back to my brain.

My shoulders dipped forward.

Jesus, I was in love.

Bare ass, I went back to bed, tossed and turned for hours before I surrendered myself to sleep. In my dreams, I wished I could test run the idea of an *us*. Followed by a heartfelt conversation with the woman who had inserted herself into my heart and stolen a chunk—rather the whole organ—without warning me.

18

ADDISON

The next morning, I woke up with a stiff neck. I'd flailed all night, unable to find a soothing position. My insomnia had been back in full force in the last week. After the weekend I spent at Tucker's place and the confidences we exchanged, it had lessened. But now I spent my nights up, barely able to keep my eyes closed for more than two hours at a time. The realization I was falling for the best man didn't help. He occupied too many of my thoughts and dreams.

Today was Dahlia and Nick's wedding day.

My nerves bounced around in my chest. I tried to control my breathing. It didn't work. In addition to making sure everything ran as planned and being the maid of honor, I had agreed to be the makeup artist.

A fresh batch of jitters hit me, and I rose to my feet, rushing to the bathroom. I didn't remember the last time I'd been so nervous.

It's just for today, I reminded myself. *Everything will be fine. Dahlia hired that wedding planner to deal with the details so I would have time to enjoy the night I'd helped to organize. And Tucker will have my back*. Hopefully, he would put his hurt at being rejected on the backburner for a day.

Skipping breakfast for obvious reasons, my stomach still unsteady, I showered and got ready, humming the wedding march song as I did. Yeah, I was a sucker for happily-ever-afters.

Around ten, I arrived at Dahlia's, just in time for the hairdresser to tame the wild mane I'd kind of neglected since I woke up.

A server passed *amuse-bouches* around as I finished applying makeup on Mrs. Ellis, Dahlia's mother.

"Addison, you're still very skilled. Your mama taught you well." I air-kissed her cheek, my eyes filling with moisture. My mother owned a beauty salon back in our White Crest hometown. Dahlia and I spent countless hours getting pampered there as teens. I started working at the salon on the weekends at fourteen and had absorbed everything beauty-related. I would practice my skills on my best friend, from hair to nails to makeup trends.

"Thank you, Mrs. Ellis," I said, cupping my heart with both hands. My eyes drifted to Dahlia as her future mother-in-law helped to zip her gown up. The river down my cheeks intensified. I brought my gaze back to my best friend's mother. Tears shone in her eyes too. "Please don't cry, Mrs. Ellis, you'll ruin your makeup," I said in a teasing tone. She watched her daughter with so much pride as I continued, "She's gonna be okay. Dahlia is strong. She went through awful things and is still standing tall. Nick is perfect for her. He will pick up the stars for her if she asks him."

She nodded as she grabbed one of my hands, cradling it between hers. "She's been through a lot. I'm glad the storm has passed. Witnessing her hit rock bottom had been one of the hardest things I ever went through in my life.

My heart broke when she pushed us away. I'm glad Carter stayed beside her during that time. But I always knew she would come back to us. On her own terms. When she was ready. Look at her now. Radiant. And thriving. It's all I've been asking for. Everything I ever prayed for each night before going to bed. That my baby found her way back toward the light. Because her heart was in the right place. Always has been. Even when she had to make tough choices." She paused, using a tissue to dry her teary eyes. We both watched my best friend spin in front of the mirror, admiring her dress, a beatific smile tugging her lips. "Nick is good for her, I agree. They make a great pair."

I nodded, sniffling.

"Are you okay, Addison? You're all pale? Do you need to sit? Some water?"

I shook my head. "I'm just tired. And emotional. Nothing to worry about. Today is precious. I want everything to run smoothly. To be perfect. Because she deserves it." I turned to face Dahlia again. "Hey girlfriend, now that you're dressed, come here. I'll finish the work of art on your face." I winked at her, and she lifted one finger as if to say, "Just a minute," as she listened to Nick's mother.

Her mama reached for my wrist.

"Honey, you would tell me if something was wrong, right? We've known each other forever. I'm here in case you need to talk about it. Just remember that."

Her eyes fixed on mine pointedly. They said so much to my soul without her saying a word out loud.

It? What did she mean by—?

My thoughts evaporated as Dahlia joined us.

"I'm ready," she said, sitting next to her mother.

I placed a hand over my mouth. My tears resumed. "Ohmygod, you look so beautiful. Nick is going to go crazy. He's a lucky man."

She got up and pulled me into her arms. "One day, it'll be you, Addi. I promise. And I'll be your maid of honor."

I pushed my emotional overload away and focused on my task: helping my best friend be the most beautiful bride.

The ceremony passed in a blur. It took place on their property, just next to the barn Nick had built behind their house.

The entire time I was up at the altar beside Dahlia, I avoided looking at Tucker. I felt his heavy stare on me. Every second of the ceremony. We linked arms after the bride and groom kissed each other, and I kept my gaze trained in front of me.

My eyes drifted to the wooden garden chairs, the giant white bows linking them together to line up the aisle, the carpet of white petals. Long recycled barnwood tables were set up further on our right, decorated with golden plates, white candles, and more ivory white petals. I watched Jack squirming in Carter's arms. And the sight of them calmed my mind.

Carter and Dahlia's ex-bandmate, a great guy named Stud, was playing the guitar and singing a melody I couldn't hear, the beating of my heart deafening.

A makeshift dance floor was on our left, garden lights hanging from the tree branches above.

The set-up was magical. Perfect. Mesmerizing. And just as Dahlia had imagined it in her head. Months ago, I had submitted to the wedding planning team the sketches I drew, and under my watch, they did an incredible job of bringing her vision to life.

My grip around the bouquet of white roses in my hand tightened.

All day, I'd avoided Tucker, piling tasks on his to-do list.

Playing makeup artist earlier had ended up being the perfect excuse to avoid engaging with him.

"Later, can we talk about what you said last night?" Tucker asked, his mouth close to my ear. Tremors shook my body at the intimacy we shared. His scent invaded my senses, and I shut my eyes to force some control over myself. "Are you sad? I thought you were looking forward to this day. I'm used to you being full of life when there're people around. Mingling, chatting, and entertaining the crowd. Almost annoying with your *everything-is-a-celebration* attitude. So far today, you haven't come up with any wild plans, insane ideas, or silly challenges." He adjusted the tie around his neck. "You're avoiding me. The whole day, you've barely said a word to me, and you tasked me with supervising other people's work. You're fighting back emotions. Those tears can't be only wedding jitters."

I sniffled, refusing to look at him, patting under my eyes with a tissue I'd stacked in my bra, making sure my mascara didn't leave stains.

We walked up the aisle and stood on the side as we watched our best friends come our way, the small crowd cheering on them, their eyes locked on each other. My tongue swept my lower lip, and I plastered a bright smile on my face, clapping and ignoring the man whose eyes were on me.

"Tuck, I'm fine. Stop worrying about me for a sec," I whisper-yelled through clenched teeth. "Why is everyone on my case today? A girl is allowed to cry when her best friend is getting hitched for the second time after her first husband died and she thought she would never fall in love again."

Dahlia and Nick followed the photographer, Carter in tow with Jack in his arms, his face a mask of contained pain.

I supposed we all felt different about this day.

People spread out on the lawn, talking and drinking champagne. I pushed away from Tucker, desperate for a breath of fresh air. Away from him.

A few strides and he was on my heels, his hand on the small of my back.

"Wilde, we gotta talk. At some point, we'll have to discuss *us*."

"Tuck, no. Gimme time. And there's no *us*, remember?" I rubbed my temples, my lids sealed as I tried to block every stimulus from reaching me. "Just this once, let me be. If you wanna talk, we'll do it later. Now isn't a good time."

He said nothing for a while, then stepped back

The more distance he created from me, the easier I breathed.

The constant pull zigzagging between us jeopardized my dedication to stay away.

Anytime he stood too close, my entire self started reacting to his presence.

He returned to my side. "Wilde, I'm not buying it. Let's talk." His voice sounded more like a plea than a demand when he turned around to face me. One stride forward and panic swirled in me. Before he could catch up with me, I lifted the hem of my gown with one hand and ran toward the barn. My free hand covered my mouth, trying to confine my despair. My head and heart pulled me in opposite directions, and right now, I had no clue which one to trust. Once I slowed down, I glanced at him over my shoulder through the curtain of tears clouding my vision. His arms hung at his sides, and he looked defeated. And baffled by my rejection and refusal to engage with him.

A storm, agonizing and devastating, raged inside me as

I rested my body against the wall on the other side of the barn.

I felt lightheaded and sad. Hopeful and anxious. A confusing combination.

My emotions were all over the place.

With a deep sigh, I tried to regain my joyous state.

Mrs. Ellis joined me.

Her arms enveloped me when uncontrolled sobs poured out. Everything today appeared to be a bigger deal than it really was. And yet, I couldn't evade the over-whelming frenzy flowing in me.

My best friend's mom wiped my eyes with a tissue and held me until I calmed a little. With her hands gripping my upper arms, she leaned back, her eyes full of compassion.

"Honey, have you told him yet?" Her words passed through my foggy mind, and my brows creased, having no clue what she was talking about. "I can tell he's a nice guy. Last month, in Nashville, he couldn't take his eyes off you. Nor today at the altar. The chemistry you share is almost palpable. How long have you two been together?"

"He—what? How? Who?"

I rubbed a hand over my face and shook my head, trying to make sense of what she was saying. Because none of her words today did. Not to me at least. Was she privy to a secret nobody shared with me?

"Tucker. Addison, the guy is really fond of you. That much is evident. He looks miserable out there by himself." I cocked my head to watch him. Hurt painted his face. Raw sadness carved his features. "Did you tell him? If he messes with ya, I'll kick his shin myself. We Southern women must stick together. Did he say some-thing to upset you? I hope he'll take care of you. You deserve to be happy, honey. And loved. Especially in this condition."

She rubbed my back. As if to infuse me with the courage I lacked. And affection.

I stood there, my body tensed, and my brain not processing her words.

She must have sensed it because a soft smile curled her lips. Her fingers pushed strands of my hair away from my face.

"Oh, you didn't tell him. Am I right?"

I scratched the side of my head, my insides now tied in a series of knots.

A shiver ran through me.

I fanned myself with one hand. I was right. There was a secret. Fear grew inside me, crawling along my spine. What was I supposed to know and didn't?

So far, this day had been nothing as I expected.

Mrs. Ellis's thumb dried the last trace of tears from my cheek, softness brimming in her eyes.

"I-I have no idea what you're talking about," I murmured, my voice weak, and my body trembling.

"Addison, I think you're pregnant. I thought you knew."

I stood there, unable to move or speak.

My feet dug into the perfectly manicured lawn.

My throat closed. Not even a breath could come in or out.

No. Mrs. Ellis was mistaken. She had to be wrong. She knew nothing about me. Or Tucker. Or our relationship.

"You're wrong. I'm not—I can't be." I took a deep breath. "You're mistaken. Mrs. Ellis. I'm not pregnant."

She offered me a stern glance as her green irises focused on me, reminding me of Dahlia's eyes when filled with empathy. "Are you sure? All the signs are there. You barely ate all day; you scrunched up your nose every time there was food around. You're tearing up for nothing. I'm sorry to tell you that, but we've known each other for a long time. Honey, your breasts are fuller. That's an unmistakable sign. And I know for a fact my daughter wouldn't have outfitted you in a gown strangling your chest. You really had no idea?"

I shook my head. But it felt as if someone else did. Like I was in another dimension and this wasn't my body. Nor my life playing in front of me.

I tried to swallow but failed.

Balls of angst pinballed inside me.

She was wrong. Dahlia's mama was wrong.

"Addison, it will all be okay. I think you should tell him. By the look of it," she angled her head to watch Tucker, and I followed her gaze, "I'm pretty sure he'll do right by you."

My eyes lingered on him for a bit longer. He stood by himself, an empty flute of champagne in one hand, kicking the ground with his expensive shoe, his other hand stuffed in his trouser pocket, looking lost.

His usual cockiness was missing. Somber face, loosened tie, dejected expression. He reminded me of the night we spent on the rooftop. That was the time I saw the most vulnerable version of Tucker Philips.

"He worries about ya. He wanted to run after you, but I told him you and I had to talk first."

I nodded. Because what else could I do? Open and close my mouth like a stupid fish? No way. So I clamped it shut.

At that instant, I didn't feel like crying anymore.

The fear brewing in me multiplied, coiling my stomach in steeled bands.

I still believed Mrs. Ellis had no idea what she was saying. My period was due any day now. It explained every sign she interpreted as a pregnancy.

"It's the time of the month. It makes me bloated. And turns me into an emotional wreck. Nothing unusual here. And yes, I'm tired. I've been working long hours."

Mrs. Ellis rubbed my bare arm. "I'll leave you to it. You know where to find me. If you need my help, for whatever reason, just say the word." She turned on her heels but halted mid-step. "And for what it's worth, I'm pretty certain you love him too." She offered me a tight-lipped smile. "The same way I've always known Carter was in love with my daughter and that she had feelings for him, but not as strong as the ones she bore for Jeff. You're not as unreadable as you think you are, Addison. Your eyes speak the truth. They never lie."

She walked away.

No matter what I did, oxygen refused to reach my brain.

My legs wobbled. Back dots blurred my vision. I shut my eyes, unable to stand upright.

19

TUCKER

She rejected me. For hours, I'd been following the instructions she laid down in her wedding-planning notebook. Dahlia and Nick had hired people to take care of this, but still, Addison had requested I made sure nobody undermined her work. And since I couldn't refuse her anything, I'd been playing along all day.

Flower arrangements at the altar: *check*

Table centerpieces: *check*

Fairy lights over the makeshift dance floor: *check*

Rose petals spread down the aisle: *check*

Band setup: *check*

These last-minute tasks had helped me keep my mind away from everything, except for the conclusion I came up with last night. That I had fallen in love despite me, with a woman who was both my equal and my biggest challenge. My other half and my wildest dream. She fooled herself if she thought that by now I wasn't attuned to her. The glints in her irises were missing today. She looked paler and thinner than usual. As if life had given her a hard time lately other than her recurring insomnia. I wasn't aware of anything else eating her up. Last week, she couldn't stop gushing about the wedding, and now she appeared as if she wanted to be anywhere but here. Anywhere but next to me too.

We locked eyes from a distance after she hastened away. Something wasn't right. The space separating us last night had grown to a full-size canyon today.

Riley Burns, Dahlia's ex-manager whom I'd met at the bachelor party, came up to me.

"How is it going? Tucker, right?"

I accepted the flute of champagne he handed me.

"Good."

We chatted for a moment, and the entire time, my gaze did not drift away from the clearly upset maid of honor. Stud, the guy playing the guitar during the ceremony, stole Riley away after we agreed to continue our discussion later.

Whatever haunted the woman my body and soul recognized as mine, it affected me too. I longed to be by her side, transforming her rain into a rainbow and her frown into a smile.

"If you'd listen to me for one sec, I'd tell you how much you mean to me," I said, chugging the rest of the bubbly alcohol.

I was in love.

The concept didn't compute with me. But it didn't scare me. Even if I had no idea what it implied to be in a committed relationship and if the feelings were reciprocated. Unless we had that talk, I had no way to be sure.

Addison broke into sobs, and the sight devastated me. My feet strode forward, always going in her direction. No matter how hard I fought it, my body had a mind of its own.

Mrs. Ellis comforted her, and my chest deflated. Now I

was jealous of a middle-aged lady hugging my woman. Yep, over the last month and a half, Addison Wilde had become mine. To love and to care for.

The thought sent my heart cartwheeling behind my ribs.

Their exchange had heated up, and Addison now gesticulated, new flames I'd never seen before dancing in her eyes. The sight cut me deep inside. Could we be so connected that her pain became mine? That her struggles hurt me too?

I chased the displeasure taking over my face with a hand.

Yeah, I had no clue how to be in a relationship or to do love, but with her, I was willing to try.

Mrs. Ellis left her, and I was about to turn back on my heels to give her the space she'd pleaded for when I noticed her knees bending and her balance shifting.

"Wilde," I yelled, rushing to her side before she hit the ground.

20

ADDISON

Mrs. Ellis was right about something. I hadn't eaten all day, and now I felt weaker than I ever did. Two strong arms caught me as I was about to collapse to the ground.

Tucker.

My heart jolted back to life when I opened my eyes and saw him standing there, the trench across his forehead deeper than before.

"Thanks," I muttered.

"Wilde, enough already. Seriously, you're starting to freak me out. You almost fainted just about now." His grip around my waist tightened. His low voice, barely above a whisper, tickled the side of my face. "What's going on?"

"Food. And water," I said as he held me up, pressing me against his chest—my safe haven—his heartbeat rocking me to calm. And bringing me much-required comfort. I took a deep breath, hoping to send blood and air back to my brain.

"Come," Tucker said, his voice reassuring, laced with noticeable concern. "I've got you, sweetheart. I'm here.

Lean on me." Never letting go of me, he brought me to a shadowy corner of the yard, where the sunrays couldn't hit me too hard, and pulled up a chair. "Wait here. I'll be right back." He kissed my forehead and hurried away. A tiny piece of my heart healed at how he cared for me, and another one hurt as he put more distance between us. My gaze stayed glued to him. Tension had taken over his upper back, and he kept rubbing his nape as if to loosen the knots that had developed there.

At a distance, he cocked his head, and our stares fused. Even when I tried to avert my eyes, I couldn't, the magnetism emanating from him powerful and impossible to resist.

Minutes later, Tucker came back with a plate full of finger food and veggies and a glass of water and took a seat facing me. "Here. Eat."

I nibbled a carrot stick in silence, unsure if my stomach would hold it in, washing the small bites with water.

"How are you feeling? You're pale. Something is off. Don't bullshit me."

I pressed my lips together, avoiding his piercing dark irises.

"What did Dahlia's mom tell you? You seemed upset after she left."

"Huh, no. I didn't—I—it doesn't matter."

Tucker lifted my chin with a finger to study me, and my heart rate picked up.

Could he read me as much as I could read him? I glanced down for a long second, praying that he would miss my despair.

Instead of letting it go, he continued, "It matters to me, Wilde."

I slouched my shoulders as fresh tears prickled the back of my eyes. How could Tucker Philips be so in sync with my feelings? If I wished it hard enough, could I disappear right now?

"Tell me," he pressed.

I lifted my fleeting gaze to meet his. A don't-fuck-with-me expression lingered in his dark one. My pulse kicked up another notch. "It doesn't matter. Really. She talked nonsense." I shrugged, bringing a stick of celery to my mouth.

"Wilde. What did she say? If it's nasty, I'll chase her down. I don't care how old she is or if her daughter is royalty."

A tiny smile peeked through, curving my lips. I squeezed his strong forearm, feeling the cord of his muscles twitching underneath my palm.

"Stop. Don't go all Chicago on Mrs. Ellis. She's a fan of yours. She couldn't stop praising you," I said, avoiding his eyes.

Tucker dipped his head down and searched my face. His voice lowered as he continued, "Then tell me, Wilde. What did she tell you? It affected you, and I won't drop it."

I inhaled. I didn't have to tell him, right? Dahlia's mama had no idea what she thought she knew. A little *what-if* hovered over me. And I feared she could be right after all. No, she was wrong. So wrong. But Dahlia's mama had more experience than I did. Ohmygod. My hands quivered. All the thoughts jumbled inside my head. Tucker moved closer, erasing the distance between our heads, his warm cheek now resting against mine.

"Talk."

His big muscular hand cupped my bouncing knee.

I pinched my lips together. Dahlia and Nick's wedding wasn't the time for all the drama.

"Wilde." Tucker's voice grew impatient. Insistent.

Why did he have to push the subject?

"Talk. I know you're hiding something. If I did anything that hurt you, I'm sorry. But I can't fix it unless you tell me what it is about. Is it about last night? I didn't wanna push you. I thought we were on the same wavelength. I had no idea you changed your mind. Truth is, I'll never talk about us being together like this again if that's what you're afraid of. I promise. Now be honest with me. Please. We said *truth always*."

I spewed the next words, closing my eyes, not ready to face the emotions that would take over his grave expression. "Tuck, I don't need to be fixed. I'm not some project you gotta tackle. Since when do I owe you something? We're not even a couple, so stop acting as if you're entitled to know everything." My voice cracked. "Anyway, it's nothing."

I cupped my mouth as more sobs rocked through me. He didn't deserve my venom.

Tucker cleared his throat. "Don't try to push me away by using harsh words. It's not you talking like this. I've learned to know you well enough in the last month or so to call you on your bullshit. I'm not letting you off the hook until you confide in me. I know you don't owe me anything, but I can't stand you being sad. Suit yourself, Wilde. We're staying here until we get to the bottom of this. I'm being your friend right now. Deal with it."

I groaned.

He moved closer, squeezing my hand.

I sighed, not sure how long I could keep the doubt storming front stage in my head to myself. I shut my eyes and silenced the voices in my head as I delivered the news, not knowing the best way to do this. After all, being dramatic was my most endearing quality, no? That's what Phoenix, my twin brother, used to say growing up. He'd be so proud of me right now.

"She thinks I'm pregnant."

I pushed a hand over my mouth, hoping I wouldn't throw up as the words flew out of my lips before I could catch them back.

Tucker froze beside me. His grip on my knee slackened. His throat worked as his breathing quickened. He pinched the bridge of his nose, and his head tilted back.

"Wilde, is she right? Fuck. Tell me the truth. Here and now. Don't sugarcoat anything. Are you pregnant? Is Mrs. Ellis right?"

I shrugged. Because I had no clue. What Dahlia's mama said added up. But my upcoming period could explain most of my symptoms too.

"Wilde. Are you pregnant? I deserve the truth. Be honest with me," Tucker said, his voice more insisting this time.

"I-I don't know. It didn't cross my mind until she suggested it. My cycle is always all over the place, nothing unusual. Adding to the fact I'm under a lot of stress—"

His large hands framed my face, his palms hot, calming the tremors in my body. I could have fallen asleep right there, knowing nothing bad could happen to me with him watching over me.

"No reason to panic over it if it's nothing. We'll get a test and clear this up, okay?"

I nodded, lifting my eyes to stare at him, knots loosening in my stomach at the idea he'd take the lead. Something eased in his expression. Why wasn't he freaked out by all this? Inside, I was a storm. A volcano about to erupt. To devastate my life.

"No matter what, we'll do this together."

I nodded again. Like a robot. What else could I do? I must have looked so dumb.

"The morning-after pill...can it fail?"

"No idea." I fidgeted with the golden chain around my wrist. "I followed the instructions. It's supposed to be effective if taken within seventy-two hours. I took it well before that. I swear I did."

"Stop. Don't blame yourself. I don't. And I believe you."

His lips molded to mine. Warm and soothing. Soft and comforting. Protective.

"I love you, sweetheart. We'll be fine."

My lungs idled. Air couldn't reach them anymore. I swallowed. My pulse raced. What did he just say?

"Whoa. W-what?" I escaped his grip, but Tucker held me there, inches away from his face. "You're out of your mind. Are you crazy? This day is surreal. I'm sure I'm dreaming. What the fuck, Tuck. You don't love me. We spent like a dozen days together at the most. Are you high?"

My breathing returned. I inhaled a big gulp of air, needing to wake up my numb brain.

"Stop squirming, Wilde. Listen to me. For once. Just listen. I've never said those words to anyone before. There's something about you. I never planned for this to happen. You woke up something in me. The time we spent apart made me realize many things. While they made you rethink everything, they cemented something in me. Lately, you've become my best friend. The one person I can't live without. Don't ask questions because I don't possess the answers. How you did that, I'm still confused. But you took a big slice of my heart home after we went our separate ways the last time. Every day, you're all I think about. The only person I wanna call at any hour, just for the pleasure of hearing your voice."

The gears of my brain overheated.

"Tucker, you can't love me. I told you I'm not screwing

things up another time. You and I. Not happening. We can't. It's not…it's not…"

He firmed his shoulders. "It's not what, Wilde? It happened when we were in different states. Every moment I wait for our daily call. Everywhere I look, you're there. I dream of you every night. Slowly, each time we had one of our late-night conversations, you anchored yourself deeper into my heart. Believe me, I'm as much in shock as you are. I had no idea what it meant either. Until I saw you last night. And the more I think about it, the more I'm sure I'm in love with you. If it isn't love, then tell me what is this feeling? Because I have no idea how to get you out of my mind. I want to be with you all the time. Kiss you even if everybody is watching. Hold your hands and dry your tears. It was killing me to see you sad earlier without being able to touch you or comfort you. It was as if my own heart was bleeding and I couldn't stop the hemorrhage."

He scratched the side of his head while I sat there, speechless, the words locked inside.

"I never thought I'd ever feel this way about anyone. But here we are. This isn't how I imagined breaking the news to you. And by the way, I should run away. I know it, and with any other woman, I would have. And I'd be in denial. For some reason, with you, it's different. I can't hurt you, and I can't comprehend why I'm so fucking calm right now. Wilde, if you're pregnant, I'm pregnant. No way will I ever let you go through all this by yourself. And when you're sad, I'm sad. Please explain what spell you've cast on me because I'm bewitched by you. And it's powerful."

He lowered his head until his lips caressed mine with unsaid words.

I held my breath. Nothing he said stood to reason. But for a moment, his words made me feel better. They helped to lessen the tsunami raging in my core.

"We spent two weekends together physically, but hundreds of hours together over the phone or video. Sometimes over six hours or more at a time. Don't lie to me or to yourself. It's a lot of time to connect and to get to know somebody."

"But—"

"No but."

"There's something."

"Tell me."

"Always the truth, remember?"

He nodded.

"I lied to you last night. And it's eating me up from the inside. I'm horny all the time when I think about you. I have no idea where it comes from," I said against his lips.

"See, that wasn't hard," he whispered, his lips curling against mine. "We'll be all right."

Tucker's hand molded to my head, and he crashed his mouth on mine, tasting me. Owning me. The same way he did that first time in Nashville. But more potent.

I placed one hand over his heart, relishing the strong beating under my palm.

He sucked on my tongue, battled my lips for the upper hand, awakening flutters in me. My fingers fisted his dress shirt, keeping him close.

"Let's find out. Get a test. Nobody will notice we're gone. It will only take fifteen minutes. We'll be fine. I promise."

I nodded, deepening the kiss, taking all he could give me right now. Because it calmed the throbbing in my heart. And my overimaginative mind.

Words I kept inside emerged on their own. "I'm sorry I pushed you away last night. I didn't want to. I thought I was protecting us. From falling too deep."

"What is going on?" The sudden words disrupted the most intimate moment I'd had since forever.

Breathless, Tucker and I broke apart and turned our heads, our foreheads still pressed together.

Nick stood there with wide eyes, Dahlia hot on his heels.

"Tuck, what's going on? Man, we agreed on two rules." The groom shook his head, a million questions dancing in his eyes.

My heart leaped in my throat. I squeezed Tucker's hand, hoping he'd understand I would stick by his side.

"Okay, none of this is going as it should."

I sucked in a cleansing breath at his words.

"It's not what you think. I love her, man."

"Tuck, stop saying that," I said through clenched teeth, narrowing my eyes at him.

"Wilde, it's true." He dropped a chaste kiss on my forehead.

"You what?" Nick blinked.

Dahlia stopped at his side, her gaze sweeping between Tucker and me. Nick's lips parted, but nothing came out.

"Addi? What's this all about?" My best friend studied me, crinkles around her eyes.

Tucker turned around to glance at me.

"I love her. And we might, or might not, be having a baby together."

"Tuck—" I breathed out his name, more like a request.

A yelp exited Dahlia's mouth. Nick blinked, faster this time, watching me as if we had spoken another language.

"Addi?" Dahlia's silken voice brought me out of my trance. "Speak."

I moved both my hands up and lowered them to my thighs. "We have no idea. It's something your mama said. Anyway, it's a long story. I'll tell you more once I know for sure, okay? Sorry to rain on your parade, guys. You weren't supposed to find out. Not this way at least." I stared down, feeling a bit ashamed. My heart beat so fast I expected it to jump out of my chest.

"Addison Samantha Wilde, look at me," she said. Damn it, my friend meant business when she used my full name. As if it hurt, I motioned my eyes slowly in her direction. "Are you guys together?"

"We are," Tucker said at the same time I said, "No."

Our heads swiveled until we faced each other again. And I was tempted to believe him when he said, "Trust me."

Dahlia continued. "Are you guys happy? There's so much we missed. Last night, you two—" She sighed. "We'll talk about it later." Her gaze bore into mine. "Do what you must. I'm here for you. Always." She moved closer and enveloped me in her arms. Because Dahlia Ellis was the best. Always had been. And would forever be. "Go, get a test. And let me know if I'm going to be an aunt as soon as you find out, okay?" I nodded against her shoulder. "And while you're at it, touch up your makeup. You have mascara stains down your cheeks. You look terrible." She winked, and both of us burst out laughing. Yeah, I would be all right.

Nick traced his eyebrow with a fingertip, lost in his mind for a moment. "Keep us updated. Whoa. Never saw this one coming. When I think about it, I'm not even surprised..." He sighed. "Spare me the details of how this happened. You two are—I miss the words right now. Babe, we should have bet on it." He secured an arm around his wife. Devotion and unconditional love passed between them. He brought his attention back to Tucker and me. "Do what you gotta do. I'd say wrap it up, but I think it's too late."

"Come on," Tucker said after they exchanged one of their one-shoulder man hugs, helping me to my feet, lacing his fingers through mine. "Let's get out of here."

Dahlia snaked her arm through her husband's. "If we did, I would have won," she whispered. I shook my head, unable to hide my smile. "Let's go. I wanna dance," she added. Nick's stare focused on his best friend for a few seconds before he led his bride away and kissed her as if nobody else existed in their world.

Hand in hand, Tucker and I sauntered away, following in their steps.

"Wilde, no matter what, I'm not going anywhere. Lean on me."

21

TUCKER

In front of the bathroom door, I paced while Addison peed on a stick. Full breath in. Full breath out. In the last hour, I'd lost the ability to inflate my lungs on my own without reminding myself to. All my thoughts were a tight, disordered weave inside my head. My heart must have done a dozen flip-flops in my chest in the same amount of time.

I not only had proclaimed my love to the woman who might be bearing my child, but also announced my feelings in front of my best friend. Dahlia and Nick promising to love each other forever earlier had turned me into a soppy version of myself.

Fear crawled along my spine. I was just getting my head around being in a steady relationship and now I had to consider I might also become a dad.

Every word I spoke to Addison earlier sent my heart into overdrive as I replayed them in my head. On a loop. I meant them. Didn't mean they didn't terrorize me.

It wasn't normal for me to be this obsessed with a

woman. Being in love and the sentimental shit was Nick's thing. Never had been mine before.

I snapped out of my restless state and focused on the door.

For how long had Addison been in there? Who took more than one minute to pee?

I rapped on the wooden panel. "Wilde, come on. Give a man some slack. I'm dying here. Are you okay? Do you need anything? Can I come in?"

Not a word. Nothing. Resting my forehead against the closed door, I pleaded, "Addison? Let me in. And be there for you." Still nothing. Some heavy breathing sound—kind of a leaden snore—reverberated from the other side. My pulse throbbed. "I'm coming in, sweetheart. You ain't keeping me in the dark."

The doorknob turned in my hand, and I stepped inside the room.

The sight before me turned my blood to ice. Addison was curled in a ball on the tiled floor, her maid of honor gown spread around her in a chiffon puddle. At first, I thought she was crying. But when I realized she was actually asleep, my blood warmed up, and my heart swelled.

She made a perfect vision. Half her hair was braided in a fancy updo. A rosy flush covered her cheeks. Long, mascara-coated lashes rimmed her eyes. She resembled a doll. Her full lips formed a pout, one I was dying to tug between my teeth. And kiss senseless.

Black streaks lined her cheeks.

Fight had left her. She seemed at peace.

After going to war.

With my back against the wall, I slid down until my ass hit the floor, lifting her limp body into my lap. She stirred but didn't wake up. We stayed there for a long time while I brushed her hair away from her delicate face, my mind spinning. In her hand, Addison clutched the stick. Carefully, I tugged at it, the urge to know what it indicated strong. And wondering if life was about to send me on a ride I had never seen coming. One I wasn't sure I was prepared for.

She let go of the test when my fingers curled around it, and I pulled it free. A dark pink line appeared in one window. My throat closed, and it pained to swallow the lump growing there. My gaze scanned the second window, where I noted an almost invisible pink line. Was my vision playing tricks on me, or was it really there? That was the moment I stopped breathing. The moment I got dizzy and pressed the floor beside me with one palm to keep my balance, as if I were at risk of falling into a bottomless well and never seeing daylight ever again. I dragged a hand over my face. Fuck. I had no idea how this thing worked, but my gut told me my apprehensions would turn out to be real. With an extended arm, I grabbed the packaging set on the counter. Even after reading the instructions twice, I still couldn't confirm with certainty what the almost-invisible line meant. Deep down, I was aware I did know the meaning. But it was like my brain refused to acknowledge it.

Relishing her presence and craving her touch, I cradled Addison's body to my heart and closed my eyes, my head supported by the wall behind me.

With my eyes shut, I prayed the entire day was a dream, and Nick and Dahlia's wedding hadn't happened just yet. That I'd get a do-over. To make everything right.

"Here you are," a male voice said, bringing me out of my slumber. Did I fall asleep too? It took me a few seconds to realize the voice had addressed me. As if they had been glued together, I pried my lids open, wondering where I was when my vision returned. The sight of Addison, still deep asleep in my arms, dressed in her yellow gown, rebooted my brain. I stretched my neck, perused the room, and met my best friend's gaze.

He cleared his throat as he sat before me.

"So?"

I shrugged. "I can't tell. It's ambiguous." I pushed the stick I'd been strangling in my hand into his and watched him as he rubbed his jaw and twisted it between his fingers.

"How do women understand this?" he asked with a frown.

I sighed. "No idea. I read the instructions many times. I'm still not one hundred percent sure."

He sighed, looked at me, and breathed out. "Do you love her for real? What I mean is, what's going on between you two?"

"It's complicated." My eyes drifted to Addison, and I studied the pattern of her breathing. A lopsided smile grazed my lips. "There's something strong simmering between us. We've spent some time together. The connection is real."

"Wow. But I thought she annoyed the shit out of ya."

"She does. Most of the time. Or rather, she did. Now I can't resist her. I thought I'd seen everything. But she's wilder than me. And I never believed it could be possible. Her kind of crazy unleashed mine. I don't know how to explain it. It isn't just physical. It's chemical. I spent all my evenings at home in the last six weeks, waiting for her to call. One weekend, she surprised me and flew to Chicago. When she left, I missed her scent on my pillow, the way she tied her messy hair after she woke up, or her heartbeat when I held her at night. We spent another long weekend together. A jerk was all over her, and it drove me nuts. Never felt that kind of jealousy before. We met with Barry and the guys, and even they fell under her charm. She's special. All this time, it wasn't even about sex. So, yeah, I think this is real." I paused to order my thoughts. "Jesus, listen to me. I'm turning into you, man." I ran my free hand over my face as realization set in. "Damn it."

Nick furrowed his brows and offered me a pointed look. "Is it such a bad thing? Being me, I mean. Look, I'm happy. I just got married today to the most amazing woman I know. I have a family of my own now, a great business, an incredible little boy, friends. Being me is great, actually."

I tilted my head back and let out a silent chuckle. "Yeah. It could be worse. I guess." My laughter died. "What am I gonna do? I'm clueless when it comes to women."

Nick smirked. "No, you're not. You've been studying them for years. I think you'll figure it out. Just be honest if you can't commit, okay? She doesn't deserve to be misled."

I shook my head. "I would never. She's the first woman I'm not trying to get into her pants every time we see each other. Well, yeah, I do, obviously. But I like that we can chat for hours about other things. That our connection is even stronger outside the bedroom. It's not only about sex all the time. Just so you know, I may have broken rule number one back in Nashville, but in my defense, I don't recall it at all."

"How?"

"It's a long story, but we kinda bet we would each bring a woman back to the hotel. I have no idea how it happened, but when we woke up the next morning, we had hooked up together. You know the morning you barged in—"

"Fuck. She was the woman you trashed the hotel room with?"

"Yep. And neither of us can recall anything."

"And that unbelievable shower story?"

"That was part true. I helped her with her speech, we fell asleep, and I had to drag her to the shower to wake her up. But we spent the next day together. In bed. That's the only time I broke the rules willingly. Sorry I lied to you."

Nick flicked his hand. "You're both old enough to make your own decisions. I shouldn't have given you those rules to start with. It just—I don't know. Somehow, I feared the day you two would meet. You're very much alike. Dynamite. Amazing people. Loyal friends. But sometimes unpredictable." His eyes trained on us for a moment. "For what it's worth, Dahlia said you two are a match made in heaven. I have to agree. No pressure, man."

I snickered and shook my head.

"Anyway, it's almost dinner time. We would very much like for you two to join us. If Addi feels all right. She looked exhausted earlier. Heard pregnancy can do that."

"Give us a few minutes. I know she'll request some time to fix her makeup and stuff." I held my breath. "And I have no idea how she'll react to this," I said, pointing to the pregnancy test still in Nick's hand.

My friend handed it back to me and rose to his feet. "If you two are meant to be, I'm glad you're the one for her. She's amazing. And you're my best friend." He stopped on his way out and spun around. "Never would I have thought I'd see you sitting on a bathroom floor one day, caring for a woman with stars in your eyes. Somehow, it suits you."

He mumbled something else I didn't quite catch and left.

I blinked, still wondering if this entire day had been a dream after all.

Addison and I joined the rest of the wedding party, still unsure if she was pregnant or not. After she woke up, she read the instructions herself and stared at me with doubts in her eyes. Instead of panicking, we'd decided to take another test the next day. Besides, there was nothing we could really do about it tonight.

We sat by our best friends for dinner. Gave speeches. Stole glances. Kissed. And danced under the stars when the band started playing one of Carter Hills's hits. *Our song.*

I pressed my hand on her lower back, enjoying the feel of her body nestled against mine. "Whatever the test says, I'm not going anywhere. We'll find a way to be together. To work it out. If that's what you wish too."

Addison nodded against my chest as my lips skimmed the top of her head. "Thanks. For being here with me," she whispered.

My insides clenched at the sound of her voice. "Are you feeling better? I'm glad you ate. Mrs. Ellis warned me to keep an eye out on you."

"She did, huh? She worries about me. But I'm fine. Or I will be. There's still something bothering me, though."

I lifted her chin with one finger. "What is it? Ask me anything. I'll be your loyal servant."

She detached herself from me and rose to her tiptoes until her lips graced my earlobe. "I'm still horny. For you. Are you coming home with me afterward? My nap felt amazing, and now I'm ready to have some fun. And there's no point in avoiding you any longer. All my arguments are baseless now."

"Wilde, you sure?"

She nodded, her irises swimming in lust.

"You won't have to ask me twice. I'll be whatever you want me to be as long as you'll have me." I kissed the tip of her nose and pulled her closer to my chest, wondering what would happen next. And if our lives would forever be entangled—and changed—by the next morning.

"Two weeks without you was torture. I'm obsessed with that pretty mouth of yours." I slapped her ass, and she yelped. "And we succeeded in not tearing each other's clothes off for over a month. I've been patient so far. But every second I'm not inside you is agony."

"I know. And I'm aching for you."

"That's what I'm talking about, sweetheart." I held her hand in mine and brought it to my crotch. "Feel the effect you have on me."

She was flustered, her eyes flaring.

"Take me home, Tuck. I need you tonight. I don't wanna be alone. Rumor has it I may have a surprise for you," she said, mischief in her eyes.

Around midnight, Addison could barely stay up on her feet. We said our goodbyes before we both climbed into my rental car. My hand reached for her thigh and gave it a squeeze.

Her head rested on my shoulder, and I felt whole at that moment. As if, for once, the pieces of my life had a purpose when positioned next to one another.

I parked in the driveway of Dahlia's old house and turned off the engine. Unable to resist the maid of honor for another second, I pulled her to me over the console between our seats. My mouth found hers, our lips taking their sweet time, memorizing every detail. My hand curled behind her head, holding her in place as my mouth devoured hers.

She purred before pushing back, one hand attached to my biceps.

"Gimme five minutes, okay? This surprise I told you about. It's my best man gift to you."

I arched a brow. "I thought it was that T-shirt?"

A heartfelt laugh broke free. "Yes. And this. You'll see; you'll like it."

She exited the truck cab and waving at me, entered the house, turning the lights on as she made her way to the second floor.

I caught a glimpse of my ridiculous grin in the rearview mirror and shook my head at myself. I was becoming everything I always swore I wouldn't.

But somehow, right now, the idea suited me.

It only enlarged my smile. And calmed the thumping of my heart.

When the longest five minutes of my life ended, I made my way inside and locked the door behind me. I followed the trail of lights to the master bedroom upstairs.

In the doorway, I swallowed. Hard. And swallowed again. Addison was every man's wet dream, all sexy in the skimpy red lingerie I'd gifted her, tied to the bed, a selection of accessories lying around her barely covered body. I had no idea what the rules were, but now that I got sight of the playground, I was more than ready to have some fun.

Like a hunter, I stalked my prey. The one I knew the taste of, as it had lingered in my mouth for over a month. Her red-painted lips, resembling juicy berries, looked enticing. And forbidden.

My dick twitched in my pants, so thick and rigid that I had to push it down with an open palm to prevent it from dying from strangulation. Desire circulated freely inside me.

"Wilde, you're something else. I thought I had seen everything." I almost ripped my shirt apart as I removed it, the fabric burning my skin, and held my breath.

Unable to look away, I padded in her direction, losing myself in her mesmerizing blue eyes as they swallowed me whole.

"You can't ask a guy to not think about you when you do shit like this, sweetheart. You're perfect, and I can already predict we both won't be getting much sleep tonight." I blew out a long breath as I neared the bed, my knuckles sliding along her jaw. "I thought you were tired?"

She shrugged. "I was. But my need for you is stronger."

Now bare-chested and about to combust, I smoothed her bottom lip with my thumb. She shivered on the bed and moaned, making her even more irresistible. A guttural groan left my mouth in response. She sucked on my finger before releasing it with a pop. Spasms woke up in my spine, tightening my balls and firing through my body.

"Ready to play with me, *Tuuuck*?"

My throat worked as I tried to form coherent words.

My voice, sounding more like a growl, sent fresh, wicked twinkles to her eyes. "Tell me the rules, Wilde. I've been ready the past six weeks for a do-over."

I leaned forward, my lips finding hers, my hands on her hipbones, holding her in place as she wiggled underneath me.

She bit my lower lip, and I blinked when reality hit me.

"Wilde, we can't do this."

I stumbled backward, trying to escape her allure. With her hands tied over her head, there wasn't much she could do to keep me from moving away.

Her lips pursed as she watched me, hurt painting her face.

"Tuck. Don't go. We can talk about it. I thought— doesn't matter. We can just sleep. Or cuddle. Be with me tonight."

Was she thinking I didn't long for her? That I wouldn't do anything, short of selling my soul, for a taste of her. I scratched my temple and sat beside her, brushing her hair back. I didn't have enough eyes to admire her the way she deserved to be. And the way I craved to.

"No, it's not that. I haven't changed my mind. But if you're pregnant, we'll hurt the baby—*I'll* hurt the baby."

After a beat, Addison's clear laughter broke the silence of the night. "Tuck, if it does exist, it's like chickpea size." She almost pinched her thumb and forefinger together above her head. "This big. And even when it gets bigger, I don't know a lot about babies, but I know sex can't hurt them. No matter how impressive your manhood is. Stop fighting this."

I huffed, wondering if she spoke the truth.

"Tucker. Listen to me. You can't poke the baby. And there's a reason why pregnant women are horny all the time. It wouldn't be fair if we couldn't indulge in sex. Let's play now, okay? You can't leave a woman all tied up on a bed and do nothing about it."

A naughty grin formed on her lips, and it broke my restraints. Forgetting all about my fears for a few hours, I plunged forward with the intent of rocking her night. And making up for the things we hadn't done since the last time we had sex.

Later, entangled in the shower, our bodies were still vibrating with lust and endorphins. And contentment.

"Where did you learn that thing with your finger?" I asked Addison, still mesmerized by everything we had just done.

She shrugged. She just gave me the most erotic experience of my life, and she fucking shrugged. I shook my head, the tip of my spine still tingling, and my chafed cock aching for more. Usually a straightforward lover, I wasn't used to sex with toys, but Addison made the game enticing and exciting.

"In college, I experimented a lot," she said, motioning to the bedroom. "Hope I didn't traumatize you."

"Sweetheart, it'll take more than some balls and chains to scare me away. You should know that by now." My tongue trailed kisses down the length of her throat. "I think I could get used to this. With you."

She spun in my embrace and looped her arms around my neck, her eyes glistening.

"Want to go for a second round? We haven't tried the hot candle wax yet."

"We should get some sleep. Never thought I'd say that, but my dick is begging for some rest. You should too. Today has been quite an emotional ride."

She stared at me and sighed, her smile never faltering.

I kissed her pouty mouth as flashes of everything those lips had done to me in the last two hours danced before my eyes.

"We'll have a re-match tomorrow. I'm in town for another week at least."

"Tucker Philips, are you taking a vacation?"

I snickered. "Trying to. We'll see how it goes. Nick suggested I stay here for some time. I wanna indulge in a change of air."

"Awesome. Because, technically, I'm here for two more days. You better be a man of your word. I'm not done with you just yet."

My squeeze around her tightened. "Watch out, Wilde, or I'll fall for you." I winked, and we both grinned.

"I thought you already had?"

I palmed my chest with one hand. "Touché."

"Tuck, you don't need to sweet talk me. Or promise things."

"I'm not. I just want to be there for you. With you. No matter what, don't fight it."

I twirled her around and enveloped her with my arms, resting my chin in the crook of her neck. My hands lowered to her breasts. "I think these bad girls missed me."

Addison slapped my arm. She cocked her head to the side, and I leaned down, meeting her mouth halfway and forgetting about everything outside this shower.

For now.

22

TUCKER

The next day, we lingered in bed for hours after we woke up at ten and survived on sex and snacks, entangled in sheets. Addison lay by my side, still naked, our legs intertwined, her head propped over my pec, and her vibrant blue eyes fixed on me. She nibbled on her thumbnail, a confirmed sign I'd learned over the last month that something was bothering her. I stayed silent, waiting for her to sort her thoughts.

"What are we going to do?" She blinked and refocused on me, as if trying to read my mind. "If we're having a baby? I live in Atlanta, and you're in Chicago. I can't ask you to move across the country, and I'm not sure I'm made for the chilly northern winters. How would we even co-parent? How would it work? Like flying up and down the country every week with a newborn? That makes no sense. This is the worst-case scenario. How could a night we both can't remember lead to this? Perhaps it's a false alarm. Oh gosh and now I'm rambling. I'm Addison Wilde. I don't ramble. See, these hormones are already affecting my brain. And my sanity. I can't live like this for another eight months."

She closed her eyes and took a deep breath in. Held it for a second or two and let it out.

When her gaze roved back in my direction, I captured it.

"No need to make all those decisions before we take another test. Or get a doctor's appointment. But yes, I would move across the country to be with you." I pushed myself to a sitting position and lifted Addison with me, keeping her against my chest, my stare trained on her face. "Wilde, over the time we've known each other, you've become a huge part of my life. Things have been off, almost weird, it's hard to explain, on my side for a while now. I had been feeling my life was passing me by and had no idea how to fix it. Everything had lost its appeal. All my friends had moved on. I forgot how to be content until you came along. Every time we're together and you're beside me, it soothes all my doubts, all my insecurities. I don't feel lost anymore. And…I can't believe I'm saying this, but I worship the ground you walk on. Don't know how to explain the effect you have on me. But whenever we're together or whenever we talk, it all makes sense. Like I'm finding my true self all over again and that I don't have to hide behind some perceptions or play a part. That I can be me. Whatever it means. And nobody, not even my best friends, has succeeded in making me want to drop the act. Only you did."

A single tear rolled down her cheek, and I caught it with the pad of my thumb.

"Don't cry, sweetheart."

Addison watched me as if I held the answers she didn't possess. And my heart waltzed behind my ribs at the sight.

"Marry me."

She blinked. "What?"

I cupped her cheek and moved forward to catch her lips between mine.

"Let's get married. You and me. Make it official."

"But I may not be pregnant, Tuck."

I framed her face with both hands. "See, I don't care. I want you. All of you. Now. No matter what the test says. Let's not get influenced by the result. I love you."

Addison blinked again. A few times. As if to make sure she was awake and this wasn't some dream. "And I thought I was the impulsive one?"

A loud chuckle broke free. "I have my moments."

"You're still in shock about the pregnancy scare. Let's not rush things, okay?"

"Nick once told me, when you know, you know, when he was talking about Dahlia. And this is the first time I understand what he meant that day. Because what we share is real. And rare. And you're the only person who can tame my ways, who makes me yearn for more." My nose skimmed hers. "If you weren't aware by now, I'm a smart guy. Nothing I do or say is always as spontaneous as it sounds. Most times, I have plans. And rules. Or I used to. Not anymore. You shattered them all. And you freed me of some invisible ties. You stole the best friend title, Wilde. And I don't see it changing anytime soon. You just get me. You don't require a manual to understand how I work; it comes naturally to you."

"Wow. It's-it's a big commitment. You've become one of my closest friends too." Her lips searched mine. "Truth is, I've talked to you more in the six weeks we've known each other than all my friends combined in the last year. And Dahlia and I talk a lot. Seriously, we talk a loooootttt."

The ghost of a smile formed on her lips, still pressed against mine, her breathing sending shivers through me. "I can't believe I'm actually considering this. Am I awake?"

"Yes, I promise you are."

We kissed before she pulled back.

"Let's say we were to do this. Would you want a ceremony or to elope?"

I shrugged. "Anything that would make you happy. But since we never do anything like most people, in order or small, I'd vote for Vegas. Us, Nick, and Dahlia. Your parents if you want them there. And we could throw a reception later. For everyone else we didn't invite. What do you think?"

She nestled closer to me, and we lay back on the mattress, my arms around her. "I love how you think. The best of both worlds. Why am I excited about this?" She huffed, unable to hide the happiness setting in. "Let's do this. Tomorrow we'll pick a date."

In one skilled movement, I grabbed her wrists and flipped her on her back, losing myself in the deep blue sea of her eyes. My cock sprung wood, and while my mouth busied itself kissing the shit out of my *fiancée*—was that how I should call her now?—I pushed two fingers inside her, relishing the way her back arched and her legs opened to make room for me.

I trailed kisses down her throat, along her collarbones, in the spot under her earlobe. My tongue traced her jawline and found its way down to her perky breasts. I laved one nipple with circular strokes and sucked on it as she cried my name, her breathing fastidious, begging me to continue. With a hand locked behind my head once I released it, she positioned me over her other breast. And her silent plea made me cherish her second nipple the same way.

I lowered myself until I could kiss her belly and traced the seam between her thighs with the tip of my tongue. Her body trembled, and I moved back up, unable to wait another second for my dick to slide home.

Home. That's how being with this woman made me feel.

In perfect rhythm, we moved together, Addison whimpering each time my length rubbed against her sensitive spot. No doubt her fingernails left marks in my ass cheeks when she changed the angle of her pelvis, deepening our connection.

With hooded lids and rosy lips, she looked fucking fabulous.

"Mine," I said between slow thrusts, trying to lengthen the pleasure, not ready to be done just yet. "Addison Wilde, you're mine." My mouth found hers, our tongues entwining in an erotic number. Something had shifted between us. I could feel it in the way our bodies communicated. In the way we kissed. And the way we touched.

I nuzzled her neck, letting the fruity scent of her imprint on all my senses. Using my elbows to hold my weight, I leaned closer to her, every inch of me dying to touch every inch of hers.

"Oh god, don't stop what you're doing," Addison pleaded, her hips buckling and rolling. She reached for my hand, and we linked our fingers as I increased the pace.

Her other hand curled around my nape, and she dragged me closer. Until I almost crushed her under my weight. "Don't you dare stop."

A raw cry released from her luscious lips, and it almost brought me to a point of rupture. I had never felt this way before. And my entire self had a hard time comprehending the shift taking place in me. Without breaking eye contact, I pounded into her until we both went over the edge, undone and satiated.

I had never made love before, but this moment, what we just did, nothing else could define the connection we shared. The way I felt. The bubble we found ourselves floating in. The love enveloping us.

————

"Want me to get a test now?" I asked as Addison and I snuggled in bed later that afternoon. Except to grab food and use the bathroom, we hadn't left the bed all day.

She shook her head. "Nah. I still haven't got my Tucker fix. Don't go right now. Stay with me a little longer."

"I love Jamie for a girl," I said. "And Lucas for a boy."

She turned between my arms to kiss me. "Baby names? Really?"

"Why not?"

"Because we know nothing yet."

"Just a thought. I'm restless. My brain is thinking, analyzing."

"I can relate. Many unanswered questions. If we're doing this, then I agree with Jamie for a girl. And I love Jamieson for a boy. Anyway, let's not get ahead of ourselves. I'm not even late yet."

"Doesn't matter. I want everything with you."

"Hold me tight, big guy. I gotta catch up on some sleep."

And with the only woman my heart had ever beaten for against my chest, I concluded that no one night stand could equal the peace I experienced in that instant. The warmth swirling in me. With a cocky grin, I buried my face in the mass of her hair and dozed off in no time.

I woke up to an empty bed. One quick perusal of the

room confirmed Addison wasn't here. The sun shone low on the horizon, pink and orange brush strokes decorating the sky. I put a pair of boxer briefs on and made my way downstairs.

My feet refused to move forward when I entered the kitchen, the vision in front of me stealing my breath away. Dressed only in lacy panties, Addison's hips swayed to the rhythm of a country song while she busied herself prepping something. Her hair was piled at the top of her head —the way I liked—and her left shoulder bore love marks. Her skin, lightly tanned, glowed in the low light. Every delicious curve of her body, the ones I'd memorized by heart and could recognize in the dark, tempted me.

Seconds later, I had her back to my front, my arms around her waist, and my chin propped on her shoulder. "Is this what married life with you will be like? You cooking topless. Because if it is, we're flying to Vegas tonight, ditching any other plans we may have."

She spun to face me, her round breasts pressing into my bare chest while my hands descended to her ass, molding to its flesh. She yelped, and I swallowed it as my mouth feasted on hers.

"You still wanna go through with this insane idea?" she asked, leaning back to catch her breath.

"Yeah. Don't you?"

She shrugged. "I do, but it's big. And hurried. How do we know we're ready?"

I took a step back to study her face. "How did I become the one looking for a commitment and you, the one having doubts?"

She tucked loose strands of hair away from her eyes. "Marriage is sacred to me, Tuck. It's important. It means something. And in my mind, you don't do it twice. Unless your husband dies one night and leaves you pregnant and alone. Then you're allowed a do-over. I already told ya I've been burned in the past. A baby, a wedding, don't you think it's too much, too soon?" Moisture welled in her eyes. "See, again I'm an emotional ticking bomb. When will this stop?" She hid her face in her palms, her shoulders heaving.

The sight broke me, and I fastened my arms around her. Where she belonged.

"Don't cry. I don't know what to do when you do. It fucks with my heart. It breaks me." While the silent tears etched her cheeks, I held to her tighter. "I know it's a lot to process, but we won't do anything you're not ready for, okay? If you're pregnant, it's important to me that our baby has a family. A strong foundation. I told you about my parents. When I'm in, Wilde, I'm all in. I never do things halfway. You can't just have parts of me. Only the whole package deal."

"Thank you. For being understanding. And supportive. I promise I'm not always a weepy mess. And I love your package."

I kissed her forehead. "I know, babe. Whatever it is, we'll figure it out. And my package loves you too."

"It doesn't show right now," she pointed to her tear-stricken face, "but I'm happy and grateful that if we're having a baby, you're its daddy."

We finished prepping dinner together, the remnants of our last conversation permeating the air around us.

"Tomorrow we'll go to the doctor," I said after a long stretch of silence.

Addison nodded, her eyes still red, and a thankful, tight-lipped smile drawn on her lips. She was now dressed in one of my T-shirts, the one I gave her when she visited me in Chicago a month ago, bringing my undivided attention to her long legs.

Later, tucked under a blanket, we watched a movie, her head resting on my lap while I twirled the strands of her hair around my fingers.

"Thank you," she said, "for not thinking I'm a nutcase."

"I'm actually a big fan of your brand of craziness. Just so you know."

She poked her tongue at me and chuckled, and it eased the tension that had been surrounding us for hours.

That sound. I could listen to her laughter on repeat. Forever.

When I caught my breath, I dug out my courage. "Addison Wilde, would you be my girlfriend? I know it sounds juvenile, but I've never said those words to anyone before."

She nodded and moved to her knees, straddling me, her arms loose around my neck. "I'd love to be." She grinned. "I really do. I check *yes*. And for what it's worth, being your first is kinda exciting." She smirked. "You know you proposed before we officially started dating, right?"

I mirrored the tilt of her lips. "It's us. Get used to it."

———

The next morning, I woke up first. Little by little, I shifted my body gently away from Addison's arms, my heart heavy at the idea of leaving the bed, and got dressed in the dark. All my clothes were still at the hotel, so I did a walk of shame in the suit I wore for Dahlia and Nick's wedding two days prior. Real nice. On my tiptoes, I exited the bedroom and made my way downstairs.

Forty minutes later, I was back with breakfast, all my stuff, and two pregnancy tests, plus an appointment with a doctor Nick recommended for later that day. The lady at the drugstore gave me detailed instructions for the tests to make sure we would do it right this time after I asked her over a dozen questions.

The house was silent when I entered through the kitchen door.

In the hallway upstairs, I undressed, ready to slip under the covers again and take a nap with my body molded to Addison's until she woke up.

In the bedroom doorway, I stopped in my tracks. My eyes took her in, hair disheveled, shoulders dropped forward, sitting on the side of the mattress.

"Hey, you're awake. I had this plan to come back to bed for an hour or two. With you." I traipsed closer. "How are you feeling?" I studied her features closely. "What's going on?" I sat beside her and draped an arm around her shoulders.

The scent of her shampoo filled my nostrils. And I didn't find it as overwhelming as the day we met. In all honesty, I missed it every time we were apart.

"Tuck, I'm not pregnant."

"What do you mean, you're not pregnant?"

She dried her teary eyes with the sleeve of the hoodie she'd put on. "False alarm. My period started. I've been right all along."

"You sure?" I winced. "Sorry. Stupid question. Are you okay?"

She nodded. "It's for the best. We're not even a couple, and we're not ready for this. Baby, married life. It's better this way."

I swallowed, avoiding her eyes. Why were her words sounding like a death sentence right now?

Did she mean it? Sure, I had no clue what it meant to be in a steady relationship, to be a husband or a dad, but when my thoughts drifted to Addison, I always figured we could do this. Together.

"You must be relieved?" she asked, her head buried in my chest as my fingers combed her hair.

"No." My tone sounded harsher than I meant it to be.

"Well, I am."

I tried to argue, but the words got stuck in my throat. Were emotions making her say those things? Didn't she hear a word I said yesterday? I remained silent, unsure of how to approach the new turn of events. The temperature of the bedroom seared. The gears of my brain worked overtime, about to catch fire. A chill crossed my back. Before I could overreact or panic, I kissed her temple, untangled myself from her grip, and jumped to my feet.

"Gimme a minute, would ya?" I said, locking myself in the en-suite bathroom.

I ran a hand over my hair. Splashed water over my face. Paced the room.

As if someone had turned off the lights of my heart, I slumped on the bathtub rim, curving my back and resting my elbows on my knees.

The lining of my throat itched. My heart tumbled down my chest. My stomach felt as if it'd been filled with lead.

After a while, a soft knock on the door brought me out of my daze.

"Tuck, are you all right? You've been in there for over thirty minutes. Can we talk?"

I cleared my throat and pushed my emotions down. "Yeah. Coming."

I met her on the other side of the door and wound my arms around her frame.

"Don't be mad, okay? I changed my plans," Addison said, her voice trembling and her eyes low.

My heart pumped ice instead of warm blood.

"What do you mean, you changed your plans?" I asked, my fingers digging into her hipbones, fearing she'd vanish if I didn't hold on to her. All I yearned for was her warmth. Her love. And her affection. Anything she could give me.

"My bus is leaving at the end of the afternoon."

I jerked away and ran both hands through my hair. This was a mistake. A freaking joke. Did I hear her right? Was this entire weekend even real, or was my imagination playing tricks on me?

"Pause for a sec. You're leaving? Yesterday we were making wedding plans and believing we might have a baby together, and now you're ditching me? What about us? How do you see our relationship evolving? Are we doing long distance for a while? Do you expect me to move soon? Tell me what's the plan now because you lost me. I'm confused. Whatever we choose, I'll do my best to be available and make you a priority. But if you go now, I have no idea when we'll be able to see each other again. Or have this conversation. It's not something I wanna discuss over the phone. We've barely spent enough time together this weekend. After everything that went down on the last day, I'm not ready to let you walk away. Now that our friends know about us, we don't have to hide anymore."

Addison's fingernails traced lines over my shirt, avoiding my eyes. I frowned, unable to look away.

Was she kidding right now?

My heart cracked and crashed on the floor.

I scratched my temple, trying to make sense of her rejection.

Yesterday seemed like a lifetime away.

"Can we talk about it?" I pleaded.

"Yes. The last thing I want is to break your heart."

"You have a funny way of showing it."

She reached for my hand. "Let's have breakfast. I'll explain."

23

ADDISON

"Tuck, we're rushing into things. Every time in the past I jumped into something that wasn't meant to be, it backfired. You're too important to me to go down that road and compromise what we have. And I don't want you to force things at your end and become someone you're not because you think it's your duty or it's what I expect."

We faced each other on the couch, eating bagels Tucker bought earlier and sipping tea. "Because caffeine isn't good for you. Or wasn't," he had said.

"I agree I don't have any dating experience, but let me ask you something. How do we know the time isn't right if we don't give each other a chance?" His jaw slid back and forth. "I usually aim for what I want, not backing down but going all in. This is how I work."

"The thing is, we shouldn't have to try. It should come naturally. Not by rushing into things and getting married on a whim."

My words echoed the conversation I had with Carter the night we all had dinner on that rooftop in Nashville.

Don't push it. Be yourself. Let them come to ya. Right now, I couldn't agree more.

Tucker's palm rested on my cheek. "Wilde, you are the queen of impulsiveness. You make rash decisions and always rationalize them like they make sense. I know because I've been on the receiving end many times already. I've never told a woman I love her before. It's all new to me, but deep down, I know it's right. I wanna give it a shot. Be together. See where it takes us."

I shook my head.

"Why not? I hear what you say, doesn't mean I have to agree."

"Tuck, I've played before. And I've been played. My exes, I went all in without a second thought. See where it led me."

"To me," he said, a tremolo in his voice.

For the third time, I was presented with a vulnerable version of Tucker Philips. Placing my cup on the coffee table, I squeezed his hands between mine. "Tuck, you're a player, a womanizer." He growled. "Okay, a reformed one. But you proclaimed yourself as one. For the longest time since we've known each other. You never shied away from who you are. And I love that about you. Your authenticity. Your no-bullshit attitude. As much as we get along and I like you, I'm fearful of risking my heart. I've been burned too many times. My records aren't great in the dating department. My last two boyfriends were liars and cheaters. One was married, and I had no clue. Yep, I was the other woman, and the last one was a serial polygamist. Not my proudest moments."

"First, I'm nothing like those creeps. Second, I'm done with this shit. Already told ya." He inhaled. "I want an *us*. We're great together; you can't deny the chemistry. Wilde, you're the one complicating things right now. Not me."

Pain masked his face.

And my heart leaked. So did my eyes.

I ran the back of my hand under my nose. "Maybe we should back down and keep some distance for a while. Figure things out. Take the time apart to assess where we're at and where we're going. Not under the pressure of a surprise baby or shotgun wedding."

Tucker pushed away, and the distance he put between us sent a fresh batch of tears down my face.

He swallowed before speaking, his words drenched in emotions. "So, that's it? After everything that has happened this weekend and all we've shared, you're ready to move on and forget all about it? All about us?"

I tried to keep my calm as tsunamis and storms battled inside me.

I inched closer, but Tucker pivoted to avoid looking at me. Hurt radiated from his entire frame. And it broke another layer of my heart.

I spoke over the lump in my throat.

"That's not what I said. Impulsive decisions don't always turn in my favor. This time, I'm done playing it by the ear and forcing things that's aren't meant to be. If we're supposed to be together, life will make it possible."

"Sometimes, life needs a kick to get into motion. Destiny too."

A smile broke free on my teary face.

"Tuck—"

I clamped my fingers around his upper arm, and he resisted before letting go and facing me again. His glossy irises tugged at the strings of my heart. I felt so much for him. The last thing I wanted was to make it more difficult than it already was.

The heels of his hands rubbed over his eyes.

"Wilde, I'll show you that you're wrong. I'll prove it to

you. No way am I exposing my heart and having you slam the door in my face. I'm not that guy. The one who runs when things aren't perfect or get complicated. I love ya. Whether or not you wanna hear it, it doesn't change the fact, you're the one for me. Baby or not. Wedding or not."

"Tuck—"

He raised a hand between us.

"Don't. Don't say anything you can't take back. *Truth always*. I'm only alive when you're with me, and I'm not willing to take a chance at losing what we might have. What we already have."

Startling me, he gripped my waist and leaned in to kiss me. His tongue proclaimed his love. And his lips promised me we'd be all right. Nestled against him, I believed we could do this.

My arms looped around his neck, fusing our bodies together.

One of his hands traced my spine. The other descended to grab a handful of my ass. I purred against his lips. Tucker groaned into my mouth. Together, we were fireworks. But fireworks could be dangerous if not handled carefully.

"I'll drive you." It wasn't a question.

"For what it's worth, I'm sorry," I whispered against his chest. Strong arms wrapped around me, protecting me. Shielding me from the outside world.

"Don't be. It will work out. You'll see. I won't lose you, sweetheart. Told you yesterday, I have your back. And I'll make sure you find your way back to me and agree to let me care for your heart."

Emotions stirred inside me. Tucker spoke every word I ever wished a man would, but still, I couldn't seem to let my heart open up.

"I'm scared," I admitted after long minutes.

"Me too. But you don't have to be."

"I wish we could have more time."

"Stay with me. Until tomorrow."

I sniffled. "It's better if I don't. It's already hard enough. Our friendship is important, and I'll never risk it." I closed my eyes. "Thanks to my hormones, I'm a crier this weekend. I can't think clearly. The space will do me good. To assess my complicated feelings."

I prayed walking away was the right thing to do.

"Let's take a bath. Together. And enjoy the hours we have left before you gotta go." He arced a brow, asking for my permission, and I bowed my head. "Come with me, Wilde. Let me hold you for a bit longer."

24

TUCKER

"Wilde, I'm addicted to your kind of crazy. You could even say I need it in my life. Like a powerful drug that makes my body hum." Addison and I faced each other in the packed bus station. My eyes were on her, only her, as if the buzzing crowd around us didn't exist in our world. "You're everything I never knew I wanted. You're even crazier than I am, and I didn't think this could be possible. You branded me to you, and now I'll never want anyone else for the rest of my life. You stole my heart. Why can't you see it? You can either cherish it or crush it; it's your choice, but I'll never take it back. I can't believe I'm saying it out loud, but I'm gone for you. I love you, Addison Wilde. Everything I've said since yesterday is true. Have me. Love me. Torture me. Because I feel alive when you do. Don't go. No matter what, I still want you to be my wife. Let's figure it out. Here. Together. You're the only unpredictable variable in my life. The surprise of my days. The reason I've been smiling so damn much lately. The oxygen my body requires to function properly."

"Tuck, we already talked about it."

"I don't care. I've replayed everything you said this morning multiple times. What if we never find our way back to each other? Are you willing to risk it? You're the one for me, sweetheart. Fuck, I sound like my worst nightmare. Who cares, right? You're happier when you're with me. I can tell. Those clouds in your eyes clear up when we're together."

"Okay, stop. My life is in Atlanta, and yours is in Chicago. Except for our friends and maybe a common habit to do stupid shit, we—"

"We what?"

"What happened to 'no strings attached'? Now we go on with our lives. No harm done. And see how it goes." She paused, inhaling through her mouth, rubbing her hands together. "Let's trust life and see how it unfolds. I need time. As much as I'm desperate for love, I gotta be able to abandon myself completely to that emotion. This is harder than I thought it'd be."

Addison moved to her tiptoes and kissed me. Hard and soft. Offering me a new window to her soul. It confirmed what I was aware of, that we belonged together. Now my sole mission would be to show her just how much.

"There's nothing I want more than to surrender myself to you, big guy. It's not that I don't love you or care about you, it's just that I can't jump into this the way you're asking me to. I shouldn't have said 'Yes' yesterday. I'm sorry if I led you on." Her lips claimed mine once more, and I lost myself in the kiss.

"Wilde, I feel more alive gravitating in your orbit than I've been in the years on my own. And we'll be happy. I promise you."

She pinched her lips together, fidgeting with her hands. "It's not that I don't believe you. I'm much happier when you're around. My days are brighter when they involve you. I like us together. A lot. By now, I'm also aware you're a man of your word. Once I go home, I'll miss you like crazy. It's just… Tuck, it's all going too fast. I need time. To assess everything. To take a breath of fresh air on my own. The ride is scary, and I'm not sure I'm strong or brave enough to risk it all. That I'm ready to go blind without thinking it through."

"I know you're afraid, but I won't let anything bad happen to you or your heart."

"Gimme some time. To sort out my feelings." With that, she stepped back, gathering her suitcase and bag.

I sighed. "Go. For now. But don't run away."

She twirled on the balls of her feet, and I grabbed her elbow before she could get too far.

"I'll give you time. But soon you'll realize I was right. I know because I came to the same conclusion. And it was a shock at first. That I could fall so hard for someone else. And I'll come to get you, Addison. Call me, and I'll stop everything and fly to you. Anytime of the day or night. I'll sweep you off your feet and never let you go."

I kissed her one last time, my heart leaping in my throat.

My feelings hurt as I tried to hide my helplessness from her.

"Can we still talk at night?" I ventured, fearing she'd refuse.

Addison shook her head. "We better not. For a while. Clean break. No outside influence until we're both ready to have that talk."

Her refusal weighed heavy on me. "But——"

"Tuck, let's not complicate everything. Let's just take some time apart. Goodbye."

"No, no goodbye, Wilde. See you soon. It's way less dramatic."

"But dramatic is my trademark."

Her eyes brimmed with tears.

And similar dampness filled mine. "See ya around, Wilde."

She spoke again, but her words got drowned as she disappeared further into the noisy station. All I heard was "Big guy," and it drew a sad curve on my lips.

I watched her leave, and I felt as if something died inside of me.

My world turned a dull shade of gray, stealing all my colors.

How long would it take for her to come back to me? To realize she'd made a mistake? The other option, the one where we'd go our separate ways didn't sit well with me.

I kept my eyes trained on my heart walking away from me until it vanished, disappearing in the crowd without another look in my direction.

With a slouched back, I dropped to the nearest bench, my legs stretched before me, my insides turning into a pile of rock.

Unshed tears burned the back of my eyes. It felt as if I'd been skinned raw, my heart hung dry, bruised and weak, for everyone to see. A muffled cry broke through the rim of my lips. How could this hurt so fucking bad?

With the back of my hand, I chased my tears away.

Yesterday, Addison agreed to be my girlfriend.

And today, she quit on us.

"Mommy," I screamed. "Don't go. Stay." With all my strength, I pulled at the strap of the bag she carried. Sobs drowned my words. "Mommmmy."

Could she hear me?

Why wasn't she saying anything?

I tugged harder.

After a long moment, she kneeled in front of me, just before crossing the threshold of the front door.

"Tucker, men don't cry."

"Will you come back? Where are you going?" I asked through hot tears, fighting them, to be a man like she asked me to.

My mother shook her head. "Your father and I decided it would be better if I move out. But he'll need you."

"Where are you going?"

"Ron and I are moving out of town. It's for the best." She averted her eyes, worrying her bag strap. "You'll come to visit us. Later."

"When?"

"I'll let you know when I'm ready. It's hard for me to leave, but this is what is best for you." She kissed my cheek. "Goodbye, Tucker."

"No. No goodbye."

The door slammed behind her as she made her exit.

The memory of my mother walking out on me resurfaced. I hadn't thought about that day in such a long time.

Addison was all wrong. I loved her. And never again would I let a woman I loved walk away without a fight.

I shut my eyes, fighting the grief playing behind my lids.

My body shuddered. As if I was in the throes of the withdrawal effects of the drug I was the most addicted to.

Time ticked by.

I had no idea how long I'd been sitting on the bus station bench, but I had no inclination to move either.

All my thoughts collided in my head. I replayed every scene since I got here. Every word, look, or kiss Addison and I exchanged.

Her words made sense. That was what upset me the most. But it was her fear talking. Her past experiences of trusting other people with her heart. Not the woman I loved. Not the wild temptress who seduced me.

Or did she seduce me because she thought her heart would be safe, that she wouldn't fall for me?

Doubts swirled in me. Did I try hard enough? What else should I have done? Or said? Should I have run after her or locked her in the house until she gave in? Why was I questioning everything? My cracked organ dangled freely in my chest. Addison left. With a tiny flame of hope still burning, I watched people entering and leaving the station. No, she wouldn't come back. If she did, she would've already been wrapped in my arms.

Devise a plan. Win her back. And her complete love and trust. I would map out something. Not today, though. But soon.

A new wave of sadness shifted through me, pooling in my aching chest.

I was right the day I met her and said she would be the end of me. Addison Wilde entered my life and tipped over everything I thought I knew. Like a hurricane. Leaving me to deal with the aftermath by myself while she figured it out herself.

She made me see things from a different angle. And I liked the vision. I liked how she believed I could do things I'd be proud of. That had meaning.

With my hands over my burning eyes, I prayed for her to return, knowing with certainty it was like wishing for rain during a drought. Hopeful but not realistic.

Someone sat beside me, offering me a flask. I cocked my head to the side to meet my best friend's worried gaze.

"What are you doing here, man?" he asked, perusing the train station.

"Reflecting on my life. How did you find me?"

Nick clapped my thigh as the burning liquid lined my throat.

"Addison called Dahlia and told her everything. When you didn't answer your phone, I knew I'd find you here."

"Why? How?"

"Under your tough exterior, I've always known you are a softy at heart. Do you really love her?"

I shrugged. "Yeah. I do. But she's not here, isn't she? She left with my fucking heart in tow, leaving me bleeding."

"I'm sorry, man. Addison sounded sad when she called."

"Why do I bother with love? Is it really worth it? She never said it back, you know. The L-word. She acted like she loves me, but the confession never left her mouth. Occasional fucks are much safer and less complicated."

Nick took the flask from me and brought it to his lips.

"But they don't fulfill you anymore, right?"

"How do you know?"

"We've been friends for over two decades. I've noticed the differences in you. Even when I visited you last month, I could tell something happened to you. Your heart was less guarded. Your smile genuine. You had a spark I hadn't seen in years. I just had no idea at that time what it was." He paused. "Or who it was."

"Look at me now. Why bother? She's not here to take ownership of any of it."

"Give her time to miss you. To work on her confidence. To see the big picture. For what it's worth, love isn't all black or white." We stayed silent for a long while. "Both of you have worked on yourselves. Grown. For the best. She's a good one, and I stand behind what I already said. You guys are perfect for each other. At first, I believed one of you would end up hurting. Next time, I'll listen to my wife when she makes predictions. You and Addi have issues, but I saw how you watched over her on our wedding day and how she brightened up when you were around. Those things don't lie."

"Can you call Addison and tell her just that?"

Nick bumped my shoulder with his. "Don't be cynical. She'll come around."

"Man, the attraction was strong. Is strong. I can't explain it. My senses heighten every time she nears me. At your bachelor party, I tried to stay away. I did. But she was all I could see. All I could smell. All I craved. I would have spent my life inside her, just because it felt like home. Because I know that's where I'm supposed to be."

Nick ran a hand through his tousled locks. "I didn't know. No wonder you're hurting so bad. I'm sorry. I never thought I would hear you say those words in this lifetime. This updated version of you suits you much better. Welcome to adulthood." He rose to his feet. "C'mon. Let's go home. You are not spending the only vacation you've taken since you graduated in a bus station in Green Mountain."

My friend held out his hand, and I grabbed it, requiring his help more than ever to go through the rest of my day.

"Did you really ask her to marry you?" he asked with a sideways glance.

A loud laugh whizzed out from the deep end of me. "Would you be surprised at this point if I did?"

He shrugged. "Nah, nothing can floor me anymore."

"You really believe she'll be back?"

"Yes, I do."

25

ADDISON

I exited the bus, ready to go home, my stubbornness and fears hefty on my shoulders. And the suitcase rolling behind me, a dead weight in my hand. It carried my sorrows, my broken heart, and my fucking ego. Amongst other things. Things I wasn't ready to dig into or assess. Things that scared me instead of bringing me peace.

My eyes, raw from all the tears I'd shed, stung. Three and a half hours was way too much time to replay my last conversation with Tucker in my head—the pleas in his voice and the hurt in his eyes—and come up with millions of reasons why I should just turn around and gift him my heart like it begged me to. Like he begged me to. Because that's all I wished for, but my head got the last word. And it urged me to protect my weakest organ. How did we end up here? Tucker Philips was supposed to be a safe choice. A risk-free rebound.

He'd never been a commitment kind of guy. And considering my rap sheet, I always fell for the wrong ones. The unavailable ones. Or the ones with emotional baggage. I always jumped into love with no safety net. Quickly and without questioning the validity of the feelings of the other party involved. Bad habit. Now I knew better. And my heart would thank me one day. It would thank me to have protected it during a moment of weakness.

The pregnancy-scare precipitated engagements we weren't ready for. I wasn't ready for. As long as I stayed away, maybe the hurt could be contained. Tucker's confessions caught me off-guard. They exposed my feelings. We made promises we had no idea if we could go through with.

How could I miss someone I'd known for just a little over a month? How could I feel like my heart had been ripped open when I boarded that bus?

Distance would do me good. To give order to my complicated feelings. Yes, it would help me see things clearly. Without any pressure from exterior sources.

My pulse calmed—sorta—and I straightened my back and upped my chin. I convinced myself I was okay.

Sitting on the curb, I texted my best friend.

Me: Home safe. Well, not home per se, but almost there. Leaving the station right now. I'll talk to you later.

Me: Love you

She replied within a minute.

Dahlia: Thanks for keeping me updated. How are you doing?

Me: Same. Confused.

Me: Sad.

Me: Broken.

Dahlia: Can I tell Tuck you're all right? The guys got wasted. We had a barbecue, and he didn't say it, but he was clearly hurt. Talked about ya the entire time. Back in my old house now. Sleeping it off. I'll keep an eye on him.

Me: Again, I'm so sorry. You should be living in wedded bliss and having amazing married sex. Not dealing with my fuck-ups.

Dahlia: Don't worry about me. I'm getting all that. And more *winking emoji* When Jack is asleep. Anyway, you've always been there for me. When I was shattered and thought I'd die from a broken heart. I'll always support and love ya, girlfriend.

My gaze stayed glued to the little bouncing dots at the bottom of the screen.

Dahlia: But I'll say this because Tucker is my friend too.

Dahlia: I understand why you left. And I'm glad you're not jumping into something you're not ready for and taking the time to make sure you're doing the right thing. But don't lead him on, okay? If he's not the one you can see yourself with, be honest. He's a good guy. And he's proven himself over the weekend. And you guys looked good together. Sexy. Happy.

Dahlia: I know you've been hurt before. But I can tell you like him. A lot. And from what I've seen and heard, he really likes you too. He wasn't faking it. Take some time, decide if going for what you wish for is worth it this time.

Emotions bubbled in my throat. I typed but erased it. I had no idea what I should say. My best friend said it all.

Dahlia: Fine. Don't reply. I'm glad you made it home. I'll call you in the morning. Sleep on it. Our conversation isn't over. I love ya xx

With the tip of my forefinger, I jabbed the screen until I erased all traces of my previous reply and wrote a simple *Thank you. Me too* instead.

As if my feet had been stuffed with lead, I staggered to the nearest public transportation station to catch the train that would drop me closer to home. Once on the sidewalk, I slowed my steps, not in a hurry to find myself all alone in my apartment. Rebecca was at Ben's. I knew because I checked earlier. She had no idea the shitshow my few last days had been, and I had mixed feelings about her not being home tonight. I usually told her everything about my life, but this time, I feared her opinion about the whole pregnancy-scare slash Tucker-asked-me-to-marry-him followed by for-the-first-time-I-took-a-step-back-to-analyze-the-situation episode. Tonight, the company of my favorite movie and a tub of mint and chocolate chip ice cream would do. Not ready for another emotional breakdown fueled by alcohol, I ditched the wine. No, thank you. Sugar would have to be enough to up my spirit.

Tucker's proposal had been spinning in my head since the moment the words left his mouth.

"Let's get married. You and me. Make it official."

"But I may not be pregnant, Tuck."

"See, I don't care. I want ya. All of ya. Now. No matter what the test says. Let's not get influenced by the result. I love you."

"And I thought I was the impulsive one?"

He laughed. "I have my moments."

"You're still in shock about the pregnancy scare. Let's not rush things, okay?"

There. My reasoning had made an appearance. The little voice in my head was onto something. I should've listened to it at that exact moment.

"Nick once told me, when you know, you know, when he was talking about Dahlia. And this is the first time I understand what he meant. Because what we share is real. And rare. And you're the only person who can tame my ways, who makes me yearn for more."

But then he said just the right words to make me believe my feelings were reciprocated. Could he really do relationships? Could he leave his playboy ways behind for good? For me? For the chance of an *us*?

When he said... Tears welled in my eyes.

That man... I hiccupped, trying to keep it all in.

He bared himself to me... His heart. His soul.

Time apart would tell me if being together was a spur-of-the-moment commitment or something to explore and nurture further.

"Addison Wilde, would you be my girlfriend? I know it sounds juvenile, but I never said those words to anyone before."

"I do," I said out loud to myself, wiping my face with my sleeve. "But I'm afraid this can't be real. That it won't last. How do I prevent myself from getting hurt if it isn't?

How do we do this, big guy? How can we be sure it's meant to be?" I closed my eyes, straightened my back, and breathed deeply. "Universe, life, or destiny, whoever hears me first. Please make sure, if Tucker and I are supposed to be together, that you don't wait years to put us back on the same journey again. Show me a sign that I won't be able to deny or misinterpret. Please be on my side this time. Thank you for listening to me."

I opened my eyes and exhaled the remnants of my hesitancy.

This would have to do. For now.

Curled in the blanket Tucker gifted me—the one he sprayed with his mouth-watering cologne—I fell asleep, hopeful my love life would sort itself out.

———

The next two weeks bled into each other, and I went through the motions. My heart was still aching, but more than anything, I missed my friend. I had become used to talking to Tucker every night. To send him a dozen text messages a day sharing small details about my life or asking him if I should buy the blue or the purple dress. Indulge in tacos or pasta. Yeah, super important stuff. Because I liked to hear his input on every subject. Like it mattered to him and he took pleasure in advising and listening to me.

Becca knocked on the ajar door of my bedroom. "Addi, are you ready? We gotta leave in ten minutes." She moved closer. "How are you feeling?"

"Better. Still weak, but less dizzy."

"You've been spreading yourself too thin lately, trying to put Tucker in your rearview mirror. Is it working?" She folded her arms over her chest so as to say, "Don't bullshit me."

"Not really."

"See? I agree with Dahlia. Fainting at the office yesterday is the unmistakable sign you gotta start taking care of yourself. No more accepting too many projects, even if Joseph insists. It's not healthy. You're lucky you came back to your senses before I called nine-one-one, or I would've dragged your ass to the hospital, forcing them to inject you with some common sense."

"Who's dramatic now?" I teased, grabbing her hand. "Thank you for driving me. I'm sorry I scared you. I'm ready to get my blood work results back, though. My mama says it could be my iron levels. Or stress."

"I hope it is nothing serious. And I'm being your friend here, offering unsolicited advice. Call him. You're miserable. How has convincing yourself you're better off without him working for you so far?"

I shook my head.

"You two have unfinished business. Maybe he's the one. Or not. But unless you try, how will you know for sure?" I parted my lips, ready to argue, but she continued. "If he's still in love with you, give him a chance to show you how things could be between you two. What do you have to lose?"

What she said added up. Didn't mean I was ready or in the right set of mind to listen or agree. "My heart. The one every man I dated in the past stomped on and rolled in the dirt. When I'm with Tuck, it feels real. More real than anything I ever felt before. What if—what if he decides he preferred his old ways? I'll be the one heartbroken. Again. And I'm done. Done being that girl. The one who falls in love first. Who trusts without a second thought, who devotes herself to a relationship that has no future."

"Addi—" Becca said, pulling me in her arms.

"Love is messy, but it's not supposed to wound me so

bad. I don't deserve to be taken advantage of another time."

"I know. I know," she said, brushing my hair.

An hour later, I exited the doctor's office. My head and my heart were blank. Not processing the truth except for one thing.

That sign. I was the one who asked for it. Now destiny, life, or the universe just plastered it on my face so I wouldn't miss it. Guess the joke was on me now. Or rather, the doctor did. How long could I pretend he was wrong?

"What is it?" my friend asked, rising to her feet as I joined her. My sight was hazy, and my pulse ricocheted. Was my thorax big enough to contain my wild heart? "Addi, are you gonna pass out again? You're white as a ghost. Do you wanna sit down? What did the doctor say? I should've gone in with ya."

She gripped my upper arm and led me to a seat.

"Addison Wilde, talk to me. I'm freaking out if you can't already tell. Are you dying? Is it serious?"

The thoughts in my head interweaved. My lungs struggled to inflate on their own.

Tremors shook my fingers, and I pushed my hands under my thighs. My tongue darted out to moisten my lips, but it failed. My mouth felt dry as if I'd swallowed sawdust.

"Becca, it's my blood pressure. It's serious, but not terminal."

She sighed, relief evident on her features as I spoke further. "Huh, I fainted because it's too low and I gotta rest more, eat better, get up more slowly. Take vitamins."

"Oh, so you *are* iron deficient. Your mama was right. Mothers know best."

I shook my head and caught her gaze. "No. Becca, it's not my iron levels.

"No? What is it?"

"I'm…pregnant."

The ground opened under me as the words left my mouth for the first time. I'd been bawling at the sight of puppies for weeks, and now I had no tears to cry as reality hit me.

My friend brought a hand over her mouth. "Oh. Shit."

"Yep. Oh shit. Oh fuck. Or any other expression that you deem fine."

She neared me and wound her arms around my shoulders, bringing me the comfort I had no clue I required, but appreciated.

"Whoa. This is—this is—what are you gonna do?"

I offered her a pointed look.

"You gotta tell him, Addi. My words from earlier have a million times more meaning now."

"Yep. Let's say that's not how I imagined our reunion. I heard what you said. I had this plan. To seduce him all over again. To start afresh. Take my time. Date him. Enjoy us until I had no option of either being all in or out. It sounds silly now. We haven't talked in two weeks, and now I'm just supposed to announce he's gonna be a father? Way to kill the mood. Dahlia says he's not angry with me, but what if he changed his mind?"

"Girl, I'm aware you have a flair for drama, but this isn't a conversation you should have over the phone. Go to him. Meet him in person. You gotta decide if you wanna be with him. Live with him in every way. It's not just about you anymore. You guys will be in each other's lives for the rest of your days."

I dropped a kiss on my friend's cheek, the racing thoughts in my head popping all over the place. "Even if I hate to admit it, you are right. See, I can recognize it." My voice broke as more emotions battled in me and Tucker's hurt face flashed in my head. "The irony is that I told him

I didn't expect him to change for me. Now he'll have to because of circumstances. I'll talk to him, but don't rush me. Please. I might need a few days to process the news, okay?"

"Sure. Whoa. You're going to have a baby. Can I be in shock too for a second?"

"Yes. As long as you help me wrap my head around it." I let out a sarcastic chuckle. "It's my fault. I asked for a sign—"

"What sign?"

I flicked my wrist. "Never mind. Let's just tell the universe I got the message. Loud and clear."

One of my palms lowered protectively over my abdomen. I swallowed the barbs prickling my airways. I couldn't define how I felt. I had a fetus growing inside me. It all seemed so surreal. So right. And so wrong.

Becca nodded, her hand squeezing mine. "I'll help you. But then you'll put your grown-woman's pants on and face Tucker with the truth. And from what you've told me about him, he'll do the right thing. By you and the baby. Wow, you're going to be a mama." Her eyes glazed over. "I'm gonna be an auntie."

I inhaled a shaky breath. "But the thing is, I don't want him to feel obligated to move here or to marry me because I'm with his child. One day, he'll resent me if he's forced into this life. Or if he has to throw all his dreams and accomplishments away because we're in this situation together."

"Addi, you're asking for nothing. If he changes his life-style, it'll be his decision. Tucker thought you weren't pregnant and still begged you to stay. He still wanted to marry you." I gave her stinky eyes. "Okay, that was a bit precipitated, but still. Girl, he showed dedication."

"Or craziness. Oh god, I'm pregnant. There's a human

being growing inside me. How crazier than that can it get?"

"No overthinking. Don't push him away because you're afraid. What if he's the one you've been looking for all along? What if life decided to give you both a push forward in the right direction? It's not the scenario you had in mind, and it didn't happen the way you thought it would, but you're here now and must deal with it. Who knows, maybe that's exactly what Tucker needs to move on from his old ways once and for all. To free himself from chains and ties he's already disenchanted with. Have you ever thought about that?"

"Don't be right. 'Cause it unnerves me when you figure my stuff out before I do." I poked my tongue out at her, and Becca wrapped me in her arms.

"Yeah, yeah. I love you too. If you love him, give him a chance to prove to you he meant all he said."

That night, I watched my phone screen for hours, hoping it could ring and the one person I had to talk to would be on the other end of the line. Like he used to be. As if my brain could command some magic if I really put all my psychic abilities into it.

Sitting on the deck curled in the blanket he gifted me—in a way it was like he was there with me—I contemplated my options, addressing the pros and cons on a piece of paper. At one point, the tears that had refused to appear until now drowned my face, the shock fading away. It was a mix of all the emotions rushing inside me. Becca's wise words replayed in my head. And I reached the same conclusion.

For two days, I paced the apartment like a lioness in a cage. My body got tired, but my brain was restless. I was all over the place. At home. At work. At night. Knowing most of my symptoms were due to the pregnancy and not me going insane without any logical explanation eased my mind. A little.

On Friday morning, my agitated self was desperate to know how Tucker was doing. I grabbed my phone and did the same thing I did every few days.

Me: Hey, it's me. How are you?

Dahlia: Hey girlfriend. Awesome.

Me: Married life still good on ya?

Dahlia: It's the best *winking emoji*

I could picture her big smile in my head.

Me: Ready for your honeymoon?

Dahlia: Counting the days. Are you feeling better? What did the doctor say?

Me: Yes. No. Long story. We'll have to talk about it. Can I call you over the weekend?

Dahlia: I'm free in fifteen minutes if you are too.

Me: Nah, I have a full day.

And I can't tell anyone before I tell Tucker. But how I wish I could get your advice right now. Having my best friend in my corner would be a relief. She went through this all by herself. She had more insight than I did.

Me: How is he? Is he still in Green Mountain?

Dahlia: Left last night. Said he had things to deal with that couldn't wait anymore. Have you talked to him?

Me: Not yet. I will. I'm done avoiding him. Gotta go. Love ya xx

Dahlia: Love you too. I'm so happy you're giving you guys a chance. He's a keeper. Be safe and call me as soon as you can.

Tucker was back home. For my plan to unfold, he had to be. No way would I have this conversation in front of our friends.

Five days later, after I put my plan into action and made the necessary arrangements, I packed a suitcase and booked the first flight to Chicago.

Doing the right thing started with informing the man I knew, deep in me, I loved and prayed he still loved me back, that we were having a baby together.

I wasn't ready to jump into a relationship, but I was dedicated to spending time with him and seeing where it'd take us.

Baby steps.

All pun intended.

"Oh Tucker, you're in for the surprise of your life."

26

TUCKER

I packed my belongings, zipped my suitcase, and surveyed the room after I made the bed, the odor of fresh laundry permeating my nostrils. Addison's scent infusing the sheets was gone now. The thought of it sent a weird zing to my heart. It'd been about two weeks since she boarded that bus and left me to deal with many questions I had no answers to. Sure, her heart had been skinned alive by jerks before me. I had many flaws, but I never treated a woman badly. And I'd always been honest with my intentions, never leading one on for no reason. No, my style was to be upfront and respectful.

We'd been apart for two weeks. Two weeks, for Christ's sake. And still, my vocabulary lacked the words to explain how being away from Addison Wilde made me feel. How empty and colorless everything around me seemed when she wasn't there to add her own colors to my universe.

My phone rang before I could exit the bedroom. *Nick.*

"Hey man, still in town?"

"Yeah. Was about to stop by your place to kiss your

wife goodbye. Hug your little boy. And maybe see you too while I'm at it."

"Yeah, yeah. I know you'll miss me too."

I let out a loud chuckle. God, I forgot how good it felt to laugh.

After Addison left, I kinda cursed at the world. And drowned my sorrows for a day or two. Until I decided to do a little introspection and think about what I really wished for and where my life should go from this point.

Two things I realized after a whiskey blitz, other than she had a point when she claimed we were jumping on that *us*-wagon too fast, without thinking it through.

First, I spoke the truth when I told her my player lifestyle was behind me. Doing the same shit I'd been doing for a decade didn't satisfy me anymore, living the same days over and over with no surprises. Except for a different woman between the sheets. I aimed for more.

Second, what I felt for Addison Wilde was called love. It hadn't faltered during our weeks apart. Since I lost sight of her at the bus station when she blended into the crowd, I'd been searching for her every minute of the day, hoping she would appear and tell me she was done being afraid and would trust life and give us a chance. I lost count of the number of times I checked my phone in case she sent a message. Even in the middle of the night when I woke up with a start, thinking she was lying beside me or had spoken to me in my sleep.

My father used to say actions spoke louder than words. Than any promises.

And thus, my stay in Green Mountain had jumpstarted my plan, the promise I made, to prove to her I had changed. That my bachelor antics were in the past.

Dahlia was on my team, and every few days, she updated me on her friend's whereabouts.

EMMANUELLE SNOW

"I know you love me," Nick said, bringing my attention back to him. "You'll never leave town without a proper hug. No shame in saying so, man. I love you too."

"Oh Jesus. Married life is taking a toll on you. You've become a clingy motherfucker."

"Look who's talking," he added with a laugh. "You're in love, and you don't even hide from it. Times are changing. Tucker Philips is evolving. Finally being true to himself. I never thought I'd see this day. Still going forward with your plan?"

"Can't wait to start redefining my life and my priorities. Tucker 2.0 is coming to a town near you, my friend."

"Bring your ass over here. We're having brunch. Dahlia saved you a place at the table. Jack can't wait to see you too. What else will you do, anyway? Your plane is leaving only at three."

I breathed out my relief. Yeah, this new version of me was growing on me. "I'll be there in twenty. Tell Jack-Man, Uncle Tuck will be right there. He better line up his toy trucks. I'm ready for a rematch."

I finished cleaning up the house, and once I put my suitcase in the trunk of my rental, I slid behind the wheel.

Addison's and my song started playing on the radio. My pulse quickened. For some reason, even destiny was on my side on this one. I relaxed my stance. Yeah, I was going to win her heart back. Every fragment of it.

And then I'd claim those chunks as mine. Yes, I felt confident. Addison Wilde would be mine. Soon.

———

After spending all this time in Green Mountain, where life was as laidback as it came, surrounded by people I cared about and who enjoyed my sorry ass too, my apartment seemed blah. The overpriced decor missed the cozy vibe of Dahlia's old house. The neighborhood missed the charm of Main Street. And my bedroom missed the presence of the woman I hoped I'd share it with.

The place I'd been living in for the last three years felt strange. And foreign. As if I'd walked into someone else's bachelor pad. It lacked personal touches. And warmth.

A tiny smile played on my lips. The updated version of me was blooming. And I was ready. Excited even.

In the bathroom, I watched my reflection in the mirror after I exited the shower and wiped the steam on the glass.

"Tuck, today is the day. One action every day toward your goal. You can do this. And you'll win the girl back. I believe in you. Stick to the four-step plan. It can look scary, but it will all turn out fine. You've got this."

I fist-bumped my reflection. Like a fighter about to enter the ring, I stretched my neck on both sides, jumped up and down, rolled my shoulders back, increasing my confidence and cheering myself mentally.

Dressed in a suit—something I hadn't worn since the wedding night—I entered the high-rise building where I worked. Zion, the security guard checking our IDs, welcomed me.

"Look who the cat brought back. How was the vacation, Tuck?"

I handed him the two-milk-one-sugar coffee I got him on my way here.

"I missed this while you were gone," he said, lifting his cup to thank me.

"Vacation was great. I feel like a new man." This wasn't far from the truth. I now had objectives and goals. I was focused on my newfound mission. And it filled me with a sense of hope.

"It's been a long time since I saw a genuine smile on your face, son. It suits you."

I returned his grin. "Yes, I feel much better. Alive."

I entered the elevator car, and a small hand stopped the doors before they closed. A girl from an accounting firm in the building I'd encountered a couple of times before flashed me a wide smile and inched closer.

"Tucker Philips. I missed you," she purred, her fingernails tracing the length of my arm. A chill crossed my body. In the past, I would have relished the attention. Now it made me feel weird. I took a step back to escape her proximity, but instead of giving me my space, she moved forward. "A while back, you promised me a date," she said with a suggestive wink. "How about tomorrow night? Your reputation precedes itself. I can't wait to test the merchandise." Her eyes lowered to my crotch.

I swallowed and shut my eyes.

How did the old version of me live only for this? Everything about this woman touching and seducing me felt wrong. My blood cooled down in my veins. The opposite of what it used to do when a good-looking woman entered my peripheral vision in the past.

I loosened the tie around my neck.

Did the thirty-seventh floor get higher while I was gone? And why did no one else enter the damn car, forcing her to back away?

Jerking my arm away from her grip, I stepped aside.

"I'm sorry. This ship has sailed."

Her eyes wrinkled, and she watched me with a stunned expression, collagen-filled lips drawn in a pout. "Huh. What do you mean?"

"There's someone in my life. I'm not doing this," I motioned with a finger in the space between us two, "anymore. I'm done. Retired from the game."

She blinked. "You what? I must have heard you wrong. Sasha told me you weren't the settling type. Unless it's me. Aren't you attracted to me?"

I turned to face her. "It has nothing to do with you. I swear. I met someone. She stole my heart; we're meant to be. End of the story."

Anyone who knew me would think I was talking nonsense. And yet, it brought me peace.

Jace would roast my ass now. He had no idea how much my life had changed in the last two months.

The doors finally opened on the thirty-third level. The woman offered me one last puzzled look before stepping out. "If you ever change your mind—"

"I won't."

And I wouldn't. No matter how this thing between Addison and me turned out.

"See you, Tucker."

I nodded, stuffing my hands in my pockets. "Sure."

I let out a long exhale when the doors closed again. And at that moment, it confirmed I was doing the right thing. There wasn't any lingering doubt in my mind.

"Whoa, I didn't see this one coming," Steven, my boss, said after I revealed my new career choices half an hour later. "You sure?"

"Yes. I've been mulling it over for weeks. This is what I must do."

He bobbed his head. "Can you gimme a week to transfer your smaller accounts to simplify your workload? I think the transition would be smoother if you'd do it yourself. Your clients trust you. You're one of the best in this profession."

"Sure. I'll give you five days at the office. And after that, I'll work remotely." I scratched the side of my face. "Steven, I wanted to thank you. For giving me the opportunity. For believing in me. Right from the start. It meant a lot. I wouldn't be here without you, and I appreciate everything you did for me. I couldn't have found a better mentor. You kept me out of trouble and jumpstarted my professional life."

He rounded his desk and stood before me. I held my hand out to shake his, but he pulled me into a hug instead.

"Tucker, you've always been like a son to me. I saw the potential in you, even when you were still in college. I'll miss having you around. But I also understand your desire to follow your heart. Mindy and I have been married for twenty-one years. I get the feeling. Remember, my doors will always be open if you change your mind along the way or if you miss me so much that you have to visit."

"Thanks."

"And that woman of yours is a lucky gal. I hope things work out." He shook his head. "I'm like a proud papa bird watching his offspring fly off the nest."

He let out a warm laugh, and I joined him.

"I'll keep in touch." He gripped my upper arms and nodded as I added, "I'm around for five more days. Maybe you'll be happy to get rid of me by then."

"Never."

I waved and made my way to my office and closed the door and the blinds, requesting a little privacy to get on with my day. Even if it was the right decision, I still required time to process the idea my life was about to change.

Work remotely. *Check.*

———

Elisa had agreed to meet me in the pub that used to be our Friday night watering hole during our college years. I waited for her in a corner booth with a bottle of red and a basket of chicken wings and taquitos. She was a fundamental part of my plan, to put the next step into action.

"Gosh, I'm having a date with the famous Tucker Philips. Women are going to throw daggers at me now. How are you doing?" she asked after I rose to my feet to greet her and kiss her cheek.

"Great. You look beautiful. I swear you look younger than me now. What's your secret?" I wiggled my eyebrows. "Hamilton?"

She slapped my forearm and laughed, tilting her head back. She resembled her brother so much right now.

"Why do I feel I'm right?" I teased.

Her laughter died, and she shook her head. "Tuck, you have a special talent. It's like you can always tell what I'm up to. Seriously, how do you do it?"

"No talent, just observant. I spent the evening with Barry last month after a playoff game, and the entire time, he couldn't stop gushing about you. I just put two and two together." I shrugged, and she failed at hiding her smile, seated before me, her chin propped on her closed fist, a love-induced expression in her eyes.

Barry Hamilton, the star of the Chicago Busters, was Elisa's long-time friend from college.

"Fine, Barry asked me out on a date. We've been spending more time together in the last year. I'm just not sure what to make out of it. We've been best friends for a long time. He's friends with Jace too. I'm not sure if getting together is the right thing to do. For all parties involved."

"What is it that *you* want?"

"I wish it was a simple question," she lamented.

"It is. Or it should be." I paused. "And in his defense, you won't know unless you give it a shot."

Yeah, I was rocking this new Tucker 2.0 *I'm-fluent-in-relationship-drama* persona.

She took a sip of her wine and leaned back in her seat.

"I guess you're right. When did you grow up? Become reasonable? So full of wisdom? Where's the guy only looking for a quick romp in the sheets and a fun time?"

I pasted a cocky smirk on my lips. "I have my moments," I teased.

"Fine. You got me. I had feelings for Barry back in the day. And I know he did too. But he got recruited in the league and said he didn't have a place for love in his life. Timing wasn't on our side."

I nibbled on a chicken wing. "Things change. People change. Life goes on."

"The rejection was hard, even if it made sense at the time. I got burned. My heart got crushed. It was hard after that, being just friends with him."

Her confession reminded me of Addison's. Elisa poured more wine into my glass, and my attention snapped back to her.

"I knew a guy just like that. Afraid to commit. Actually, that's part of the reason why I wanted us to meet."

She offered me a pointed look and folded her arms over her chest. "Tell me more, Tuck. I'm curious now. You were mysterious over the phone. Talk. The last time you asked for my help was at the fundraiser when you were being stalked by that unhinged woman and we pretended to be madly in love for a few hours."

"Oh, that was an epic night." I shook my head, unable to get rid of my stupid smile at the memory. "Jace wanted to kill me when he thought you and I had slept together. Came to my place, challenging me to a fistfight."

Elisa cupped her mouth. "Oh God, I didn't know about that. My brother can be a tad protective sometimes."

"Like I said, epic." I sipped my wine. "Be honest, though. We had fun."

"Yes, being with you is never boring. That's why you've always been my favorite. Shhh. Don't tell Nick," she added with a wink.

I drew a cross over my heart. "I won't. Your secret is safe with me as long as you don't tell Jace I love you more than I love him."

Elisa chuckled and held out her hand. We shook on it. "Tucker Philips, we have a deal. Now tell me why I'm here."

"Nothing bad, I promise. You won't have to save my ass this time. Or pretend anything. You'll actually be proud of me."

"Shoot."

"I met a girl. And I fell in love."

My smirk doubled in size while Elisa spat her wine and covered her mouth with a napkin, her eyes big and inquisitive. "Okay, say it again, and don't mess with me this time."

In between catching up, I told her about Addison.

"That's the woman Barry told me about. Said you two looked cozy together and that she could hand you your ass without blinking. She made an impression on the team."

"Hamilton has such a big mouth." Laughter crossed my lips.

"We've been telling each other almost everything for as long as I can remember. It's a gift and a sin all at once."

I cleared my throat. "Yes, I've become accustomed to the feeling."

"Tuck, will you take me to your place?" she teased with a quirked brow when we exited the pub three hours later.

With my palm resting on her lower back, I walked her forward. "You bet."

"Can't wait to see how huge it is. I've heard great things about it. I hope the rumors are true. I would hate to be deceived if it doesn't meet my expectations. Or the ideas I've formed in my head about you. And your place."

I winked. "Woman, be prepared to be astonished. Tucker Philips never does anything half-assed. He always gives his best shot."

Elisa's contagious chuckle warmed my insides. I loved being able to joke around with my friend.

"Lead the way." She snaked her arm through mine, and side by side, we made it to my condo, four blocks away.

27

ADDISON

y heart lurched into my throat as I stood on the sidewalk, my suitcase at my feet and tears brimming in my eyes. I should've known better. And the worse was that I couldn't be mad at him. I knew who Tucker was when we started this thing between us. And he never shied away from it. He'd always been honest with me. But at some point, my stupid heart imagined we could be more. Somehow.

Now shame on me. Because it didn't take him a lot of time to replace me. For a guy who wanted us to get married, raise a baby, and have a happily ever after, it certainly didn't take long for him to mend his broken heart.

It began to drizzle, and I tilted my head back, enjoying the rain as it mixed with the moisture filling my eyes.

A protective hand covered my belly as the rain picked up.

I watched the man I loved as he tucked a strand of dark brown hair behind the woman's ear. They exchanged a knowing smile, and she lifted to her tiptoes to kiss his cheek. He shook his head, and one of his hands cradled her face. Her hands pressed into his chest while they shared a moment. One I wasn't supposed to witness. My heart died right there. And I only had myself to blame.

"I'm sorry, baby. I promise your daddy is a great guy."

The downpour intensified, and chills traveled through me. I rubbed my arms, trying to inject myself with some warmth, unable to avert my eyes from the train wreck happening in front of me.

My breath lodged in my throat when Tucker's head pivoted in my direction. As if he could sense me here, watching him through the wide glass of his building lobby.

Our gazes locked for half a second. His lips pursed. He blinked, as if wondering if he was seeing an illusion or if I stood there for real. He looked handsome in a pair of dark jeans and a simple long-sleeved black shirt. More like the Tucker I'd grown to know. No suit to conceal the vulnerable side of him. The one I got to witness on multiple occasions.

He dropped his arms at his sides, said something to the woman, and I used this distraction to stalk away, my suitcase in tow. I pushed through the few people on the sidewalk, staring at him every now and then over my shoulder.

Rushing outside, his eyes searched the night. He tugged at his hair—a bit longer than what it used to be—and screamed something I couldn't hear from where I stood.

Tucker kicked a puddle of water, splashing around him, and seconds later, my phone chimed. I pulled it from my back pocket, trying to shield it from the rain.

Tucker: Wilde, tell me I didn't dream of you being here. Fuck, tell me I'm not going insane.

My heart leaped. The image of him and that woman

flashed in my head.

Ping. Ping. Ping.

More messages came in, and I ignored them all.

Opening an app, I booked a cab, ready to get away from the man crushing my heart.

My phone rang, but I declined the call. It went off again, and I declined it a second time.

Exhaustion weighed on my shoulders.

The day had been long, and nothing had gone as planned.

Ping. Ping. Ping.

Unable to stay indifferent, I read the feed.

Tucker: I know it was you. Don't deny it. I can feel ya. I always know when you're around.

Tucker: Stop running away. Let's talk.

Tucker: I'll search every hotel, every restaurant, camp at the airport if I must, but you're not leaving before we have a real discussion. Again, why are you here?

Tucker: Don't you think it's a bit childish to avoid my calls? I saw you. You saw me too. Pick up.

Tucker: Fuck, Wilde. What are you so scared of? Why come all the way here just to avoid me?

Tucker: Fine. We'll talk when you're ready. You know my number. You know where I live.

Tucker: Night. I hope you're somewhere safe. Don't do anything stupid, okay?

28

TUCKER

If Addison thought she could outrun me, she had no clue who she was dealing with. The rain intensified, and the instant I secured my phone in my pocket, I spotted her by the side of the road, looking for an exit. Anger filtered through me, but decreased as I took her in, my steps carrying me in her direction. Blonde hair glued to her scalp, a see-through white shirt, thanks to the downpour. I was grateful for the early darkness the gray clouds provided.

When my eyes found her, a renewed surge of happiness waltzed through me. She came back. For me. To me. But then she did her little disappearing act, and the specs of joy turned to wrath.

This woman.

How could she infuriate me so much and yet call to my heart like nobody else ever did before?

I sighed.

Before she could climb into the cab that halted before her, I circled her waist with my arm.

"Not so fast, sweetheart," I whispered into her ear,

relishing the shivers that worked through her body. *Fuck, I've missed you too.*

My pulse quieted.

My entire body relaxed.

Yes, we were both still in sync with each other.

She cocked her head until we faced each other. "Let me go."

I encouraged the driver to keep going after I slid a twenty-dollar bill into the half-cracked window. "The lady doesn't need transportation."

Addison tried arguing, but the driver sped away after I tapped the rooftop twice.

"Wilde, where did you think you were going?"

"Home," she said, fighting my arm around her.

"Home? Not a chance. Why are you here?"

She closed her fists, fury illuminating her blue eyes.

I huffed my annoyance before releasing her. "Fine, you're free." I lifted both hands in surrender. "Better?"

She adjusted her now-fully-transparent shirt, her eyes throwing flames at me, singeing me down to ashes.

Heat, wild and untamable, rushed through me.

I softened my tone. If it were just up to me, I'd have been already balls-deep into her. "Can you please explain why you're in Chicago right now? I don't recall you telling me you were coming."

She clenched her hands tighter, raised her chin, ready to launch an attack on me. "Oh, so you'd have had time to hide your side-piece. Nah. I prefer to learn I've been replaced sooner than later."

I raked my fingers through my hair, unable to reel in my laughter. Addison Wilde had a jealous side, and for a reason I couldn't explain, it boosted my ego. And my desire to get her naked.

"Geez, you think it's funny?" Her irises turned into

missiles. "Lots of promises, few kept. The guy I fell for said he'd find his way back to me. You sure were convincing. You got me hooked, almost believed you for a while. Enjoy the destruction, big guy."

"Are you done?" I asked. The entire time her rant lasted, Addison had eaten every bit of space between us. Yep, the connection hadn't faded. Whatever she fed her mind, her body knew better.

A groan left her mouth, and she swiveled to leave, but I clutched her wrist. Her pulse hastened, and I felt every thump.

"Wilde, you said you fell for me? Care to tell me more?"

She cursed under her breath. "No, I didn't say such a thing."

"Pretty sure you did. Want me to play it back to you?"

Her eyes doubled in size. "A replay? Are you high? Stop with the nonsense."

I mimicked her stance and rested my fists on my hips. "Am I? Talking nonsense?"

Her arms flew to wrap around her. "Enough. Not having this discussion with you. I didn't fall for ya. Now move. I'm outta here."

"Where would you go? You know no one else in the city except me."

"Wrong again. I have friends. Anyway, as I said, I'm going home."

"Jesus, you can't fly back tonight. Not in this state," I said, gesturing to the length of her drenched self. "Names?"

"Names of what?"

"No. Who. People you know in town."

"None of your business. Go back to your lady friend."

I raised one brow. "Lady friend?"

"Would you prefer fuck-of-the-day?"

"Fuck-of-the-day? Wow, I'd like to see how Jace's sister would react to be called that. Go ahead and ask her boyfriend if you wanna know if she's worth it."

Addison blinked, confusion clear in her expression.

"Ask him. You two already know each other, anyway."

"Stop sidetracking. I saw you two together."

"Nah, you think you saw something. It's an imagined deduction. Your personal spin on a situation you're not privy to. For your personal knowledge, Elisa is Barry Hamilton's girl."

"Oh."

"Yep. *Oh*. Never assume things about me, sweetheart. That's not how I pictured our reunion to be. You've said your piece. Coming home with me now?"

"This conversation is over. I'm out of here."

She attempted another escape. We were both soaked, and I craved a hot shower and dry clothes. Before she could step away, I scooped her over my shoulder, balancing her suitcase in my free hand.

"Tuck, put me down." She kicked the air, and I only tightened my grip around her.

"Houdini, you're done acting-out tonight."

"Tuck," she growled. "Let me go."

"No."

Minutes later, we entered my building, Addison still cursing down my back, punching my ass cheeks.

"Go ahead, sweetheart, get that angst out. The way I see it looks a lot like you spread naked on my bed with my face between your legs. If that's your definition of preliminary, I can work with it. We should try roleplay next."

Leo, the concierge, held the door open for us. "Welcome back, Mr. Philips. Hi, Ms. Wilde. I'm happy to see you again. I wish you two a great night."

"I'm not staying," she barked.

"Well, we'll see," I said, pressing the button to my floor after we entered the elevator car.

Only when it started moving did I lower my furious woman down to her feet.

"Happy?" she asked, her face flushed and her wet hair all over the place.

I grinned. And my dick stirred in my pants. "Absolutely."

She punched my chest, but I caught her wrists on the second attempt. "You can't do that. Take me hostage," she screamed.

"I beg to differ. I know how much you enjoy the chase. And the game." Her dilated pupils offered me all the confirmation I needed. "Stop pretending this fight didn't turn you on as much as it did to me." I pointed a finger at her chest. "Tell me. Why are your breathing so fast, Wilde? Do I bother you that much?"

She groaned. "I gotta go."

The elevator door opened to my floor, and baiting Addison with her baggage in my arms, I got her to follow me inside my condo.

Puddles of water pooled at our feet.

"Gimme a sec."

Moments later, I returned with towels and handed her one. "With or without?" I asked.

She frowned.

I explained. "Shower. With or without my company? There's this trick I've mastered that always helps to put a smile on your face. And my dick has tricks of its own you can't seem to resist." She rolled her eyes. *What's with the attitude?* "Fine. Tonight, you do you. Just tonight, though. You get one free pass."

Before she could argue, I took her suitcase to my bedroom.

"I'm not staying," she repeated.

"Wherever you must go, you can't, soaked in a see-through shirt."

She gasped, taking in the sight of her red bra through the fabric for the first time. With her arms folded over her chest, she spun until her back faced me.

Stepping behind her, I locked my arms around her waist and kissed the back of her neck. Addison went rigid before relaxing against me.

"Whatever the reason you're here, I'm glad you came." Chills lined her back. My lips connected with her moist nape once more. "Go, shower. I'll make some tea to warm you up, and we'll talk."

Fight left her on hearing my words. She nodded and murmured a "Thank you," breaking the silence. In my closet, I fished for a sweater.

"Here. Wear this."

She rummaged through her suitcase for a pair of shorts. "I brought clothes."

"Wear this," I repeated, my tone not open for discussion.

Addison closed the bathroom door behind her without another word. Hurrying to the guest room, I showered in the en-suite in record time and returned to the kitchen.

Multiple questions popped into my head. Why was Addison in Chicago? Who were her mysterious friends? In the hundreds of hours we talked and opened up about ourselves, she never mentioned anyone.

Dressed in a pair of cotton shorts and my sweater, Addison joined me. Every remnant of my ire died at the sight of her. She looked both beautiful and vulnerable. Her hands stayed inside the arms of the shirt, and she avoided my eyes and went to stand in front of the floor-to-ceiling windows to admire the city. The rain had decreased in intensity, and we could make out the lights of the buzzing nightlife below.

Taking the spot next to her, I breathed at ease in her presence.

We stood there for a long while, both of us looking at the dark body of Lake Michigan in the distance.

After a moment, I cleared my throat. "Her name is Elisa. We've known each other forever. She is Jace's sister. We had dinner together."

She said nothing, glancing away, sipping her tea.

"We met because I asked for her help. Not because I was looking for my dick to get sucked. Already told you my words are important to me. Don't picture me as the villain in our story because I'm not." I heard her sharp intake of air as I explained, "She's a realtor."

Addison remained silent, and I sidestepped until I faced her and blocked her view.

"Wilde, you're something." I exhaled my annoyance. "Jesus, I'm moving. Selling this place."

"You are?"

"Yes. Because I have plans. For the future. Let's talk about you first. Why are you here? You never said." For the first time, I noticed dark flecks near her pupils. "Or perhaps you missed me too?"

She closed her lids, pushing me out, preventing me from seeing the expectations in her eyes. Or reading her inner thoughts.

She scrunched up her face and finally spoke. "Just know I'll be okay with whatever you choose to do. No pressure. We can discuss it. Don't go overboard or make crazy promises you won't be able to follow through."

I erased the gap between us and tipped her chin up.

"Open your eyes, sweetheart. Look at me when you tell me what you flew here for. I gotta know, Wilde." My lips were a hair's breadth away from hers. One tiny move forward and they could be mine. We shared the same air, and heat spiraled around me.

I drew in a cleansing breath meant to calm the excitement bouncing inside me.

With a large smile painting her lips, her next words changed the course of our lives forever.

"Congratulations, you're going to be a daddy."

29

TUCKER

My heart stopped. It literally stopped. My knees wobbled. But then reality—and Addison's words—hit me, and I regained control of my body. Without thinking, once my brain processed her words, I lifted her in my arms and spun her around, nuzzling her neck and breathing her in. *Congratulations, you're going to be a daddy.* That was really what she said. We were having a baby. I lacked words to express the amalgam of questions and emotions swirling inside me.

When I lowered her to her feet, Addison watched me with a stunned expression.

"Wait. You're not upset? This time, I had no idea how you'd react."

"Upset? Me?" I pointed to my chest.

"Huh, who else?"

"Sweetheart, with you I would—" I rubbed her forearm, but she escaped my touch.

"Stop. Now. Don't sweetheart me. We gotta talk."

My fingers itched to brush the skin of her face. To

prevent myself from touching her, I clamped a hand around my nape.

"Wanna sit?"

She nodded, her features strained and impossible to read. At that instant, I wished she'd let me in.

On the couch, I kept a safe distance between us and angled my tall self in her direction.

"Do I ask questions, or do I let you talk?"

Addison closed her eyes, inhaled, and met my gaze when her pupils drifted in my direction.

"Questions. But let me just say that first." She paused. "I'm keeping it. Whether we're together down the road or you've changed your mind or whatever, this baby is already a part of me. Of us. I moved here so we can prepare together. If that's what you still wish for."

I lifted a hand. "You moved here?"

"Yeah. Can we talk about it later? I'm tired. These hormones are still tampering with my sleeping schedule."

I rubbed the column of my throat, twisted with chains of emotions.

"Fine. Let's see. I'm not a pregnancy expert, but I'll try. How far along are you?"

"Eleven weeks."

"Eleven? Our little Nashville bet was like nine weeks ago. I might not be a hormone genius, but I'm a math nerd."

"That's how they calculate it. From the last period. Back in Green Mountain, the bleeding... The doctor says it can happen in the first few months, and I shouldn't worry."

"Oh. It was my next question. What about that pill you took?"

"It failed. Big time," she said, pointing to her abdomen.

"Oh." I regrouped my thoughts.

She lifted a finger and rose to rummage for a piece of paper from her purse and handed it to me.

I unfolded it. A dark square fell, but I ignored it as I read the results of her blood work. One word stood out. *Pregnant.*

Sensations foreign to me invaded my body. Pride? Anxiety? Fear? Contentment? How could I define the cocktail simmering in me? Tingles transformed into goose-bumps. Now I had the written confirmation I'd be a daddy. *I'm going to be a daddy.* Whoa, I'd have to rehearse saying it when I was alone. Until my mind came to terms with the fact that it was real.

Addison wrapped herself with the blanket I kept on the couch end, and seeing her at ease in my home sent my heart into a frenzy. How could she have no idea how perfect we were for each other?

Our stares fused, and something powerful and raw passed between us. Emotions filled my eyes. I blinked them away. My throat constricted, crushing my vocal cords.

She gestured to the square of paper that had landed on the rug, and I picked it up.

If I thought seeing the word *pregnant* would shatter me, nothing had prepared me for the black-and-white picture of a tiny bean that I guessed to be my baby. *Our baby.*

My heart beat fast. It jumped in all directions.

I scratched the column of my throat and tried to swallow.

"Wow," I mumbled, my eyes fixated on that colorless form. "Why didn't you tell me sooner?" Hurt seared in me at the idea she kept me in the dark about something that concerned both of us. "By now, I thought I'd proved you could trust me and that I'd have your back."

"I'm sorry for all the back and forth. I really thought I wasn't pregnant. Until I lost consciousness at work. At first,

I put the fault on long hours, lack of sleep, and low mineral levels. The doctor told me it happens."

"Fainting?"

"Yes, that. Due to low blood pressure." She fidgeted with her hands. "Just so you know, bleeding instead of periods at the beginning, well, it's not uncommon. And it's also a side effect of that morning-after pill. Unless I had taken that test you got, I couldn't have known. I'm sorry." She twisted a strand of blonde hair around her forefinger, her gaze barely meeting mine.

"How are you doing? For real? Other than the fainting and exhaustion parts?"

"Under the circumstances, okay. I'm still a bit shocked, so it's hard to tell. I'm not sure I realize it fully yet. On the other hand, I'm already attached to this little peanut. It's a part of me. Hard to explain."

I moved closer to her and grabbed her hand, squeezing it in between mine.

Using the tip of my digit, I traced the lines of her palm. "Where do we go from here? What are we to each other? How will this work?"

Addison pinched her lips together. "No idea," she said after a long beat. "Already told ya, I wanna be with you. But no pressure. Can we take our time? Learn to be with each other without being a couple? See how we can work together. Learn each other's habits, what drives us crazy, who we are in this relationship, and decide if we can still stay together when we get on each other's nerves or fight. If we're better as lovers or friends."

"What you say speaks to me. Doesn't mean I'm over-joyed with being only friends with you. But we can try. If that's what you wish. Be warned, I'll be here. Every step of the way. Whatever we are to each other."

By now, I had a permanent stupid grin etched on my face. I could tell by the stretch of my lips.

Without being aware, Addison and I had come up with very much alike plans. It confirmed the validity of mine. I'd just have to adapt the moving-to-Atlanta part. But it all had a purpose now. Greater than just getting the girl back.

"What about your apartment?" I asked.

"Becca's boyfriend agreed to move in at the end of the month if I decide staying here is what's best for me. For us." She locked her eyes on mine. "They were already talking about it, so it makes sense. I'm working remotely for now. But I have an offer to join a marketing firm in town next month if I stay. It's a lot to deal with. Also, I have my first planned sonogram in a few days. And I thought you'd like to be there. My ob-gyn referred me to this great doctor in Chicago. Said we'd be in good hands."

More sparks of joy packed my chest.

And I lacked the words to express how I felt.

"So…you agree…with everything?" Addison looked at me with a lopsided smile, her gaze filling with what could be defined as hope. Or expectation.

"Sweetheart, I wanna do it all with you. I haven't changed my mind. We'll go slow, help you find your pace. But I'll be right there by your side for all of it."

I leaned in to claim her lips, but she cocked her head, and my mouth connected with her cheek. I startled back.

"Sorry. Too much too soon. Can we wait and see how it goes?"

My throat worked, and I barely contained the flecks of annoyance rising inside me. "Platonic relationship. Understood."

She flicked her hands between us, her smile fading. "No. Yes. Friends with no benefits. For now. Don't be mad.

Please. Give us a little more time to adjust. Gimme a little more time because it's a lot to take in."

I let out a chuckle, and she stared at me with an arched brow. The curve of her lips did wild things to my dick. I had to focus and not listen to the bastard for once. But god, it felt good to know he was still well and alive around her.

"How long have you known?"

"A week. And telling you face to face was the right way to go. I couldn't have dumped the news on you over the phone. But I couldn't tell you right away because I had a few things to deal with before and also...well, I had to wrap my head around it. To be able to have this discussion with you."

"Thanks. I appreciate you coming here." I said, still stunned by the news she had delivered.

"Are you all right?" she asked. "I unloaded all this on you."

I nodded. "I will be. Are you moving in? You should have told me, I would have... I don't know, but I would have made room for you."

"I'm not. We need our respective space to make sure if we jump into this, we do it right. For our baby's sake."

My breathing quickened. Knots tightened my stomach. A million questions circled in my head. I had to know. "How do we see us being an *us*?"

Addison pushed loose strands of her hair away from her face. "Like I said, I wanna be with you. I do. But I'm not willing to rush it. If we do this, we do it right. Take our time. Learn to be together."

"Why do you wanna live anywhere else then? Stay here." The next words burned the tip of my tongue. "In the guest room. Or wherever you choose. I'll never kick you out."

"I already have a place. It's better this way. For now."

She cocked her head, and her eyes rounded with curiosity. "Wait. Didn't you say you were selling this place? Where would you go?"

I huffed. "Atlanta."

She blinked.

"To pursue you. To show you I'm serious about us."

"You were? For me?" A lone tear flowed down her cheek, and I caught it with my thumb.

I nodded. "Always for you. The last three weeks without you have shown me just how much I enjoy your presence in my life. I've missed you, Wilde. That's the ugly truth."

Scooting even closer, I pressed my forehead to hers.

"I've missed you too. I'm sorry for making things complicated. But for once, I just wanna do it right. Because you're precious to me."

"We'll be okay. We'll find our normal." I splayed a hand over her belly. "Before Mini-Wilde is born." The small gesture encompassed all that I was feeling. Like being the protector of the two most important people in my life.

"Thanks for understanding. For being you."

"You sure you don't wanna stay here? With me? I just got you back. I have two of you now to watch over. And I'm not sure I can sleep peacefully, knowing you're some-where out there and I have no say about it."

Addison's laughter warmed my heart. "Don't be all possessive. I'm living like ten minutes away from you. We'll make it work." Her lips stretched into a yawn. "I gotta go. Some of my stuff is being delivered in two days. I want to make the place mine. Set it up. And today has been the longest day ever."

I moved to my feet and shoved my hands into my pock-ets. "Sure. I'll drive you."

"Tuck, you don't have to—"

"I do. You're the woman I love and the mother of my unborn child. Jesus, saying that out loud makes it seem even more real."

She poked my shoulder with a fingertip. "Get used to it. It's happening."

Twenty minutes later, we were in my SUV as I followed her instructions to her new place. The rain had stopped, and the dark cab of my truck felt more intimate as I blanketed her hand with mine, resting it in her lap.

"Next light, on your right," she said.

"You picked nice. It's a wealthy neighborhood. I thought you'd have rented an apartment. I'm feeling a bit better knowing you'll be here rather than in a two-room shithole in a sketchy neighborhood."

"A shithole was all I could afford in this economy, but a friend of mine offered me his pool house for as long as I would need it. It's way better than living with some roommate I've never met."

"I prefer you somewhere safe. Funny, though, Rory Dupont lives here. You may run into him."

I turned right. Then left. Then stopped in front of a massive red-bricked house with a black-iron gate.

My eyes zoomed in on the address plate twice. Then I looked around, making sure we were in the right place.

"Thank you for driving me," Addison said, fetching her purse from the backseat. "We'll talk later. Find time to be together. Date, like couples do. Get to know each other better. Like we used to do."

None of her words registered. Specks of anger lodged in my throat. With a strained voice, I perused her features and barked, "Are you staying at Dupont's? Is this a joke?"

With a stiffened back and tightly pressed lips, her demeanor told me she knew I'd be pissed.

"I was talking with Ted—"

"Duffy? The goalie? Why were you talking to my friend?"

"As I was saying before you interrupted, I was talking to Ted about a second custom shirt he ordered and told him I was moving here."

I harrumphed despite myself.

"Don't act all jealous and stuff. Anyway, Ted said Rory has a pool house on his property nobody uses and since he's barely ever here, I could live in it rent-free and house-sit his home when he's away. Don't be a jerk about it. I'm not technically staying with him."

"Semantics."

She waved her arms in the air. "Oh, c'mon now. Are you serious? Let's leave it at this for tonight. We'll talk about my living arrangements later."

She motioned to open the door when I pushed the lock button. Twice. For good measure.

"Tuck—"

"Fuck no. No way. You're not staying at Dupont's when I'm in town. No. Not happening. My woman. My baby. Never."

Her small fists balled. "Tuck—" My name sounded like a warning on her lips.

"I know my friend. And the answer is still no."

I put the car in reverse and pulled away from the driveway before I could say something I might regret. And before Addison had time to escape my truck. She crossed her arms over her chest, a pouty expression taking over her face. One I wished I could kiss away. And turn into a smile. Aimed at me. Not fucking Dupont.

Once I calmed a little, I gave it a try. "How in hell did you think I'd be okay with you living at another guy's house, pregnant with my child? Tell me, Wilde. I'm confused right now. Even though he's my friend, he's still a guy."

"Tuck—"

"Both of you are staying at my place. End of discussion. Sleep in the guest room. In my bed. On the sofa. As long as it's not at another man's house, I'll be reasonable. And give you all the space you requested."

She sighed. "Geez, I had everything planned."

"Well, I did too. I had a four-step plan. To win you back. But you showed up here unannounced before I could make it to step three."

After a long moment, Addison asked in a softer tone, "What's step three? And what were steps one and two?"

My wrath dissolved. Bit by bit. "Sell the condo. Work remotely. Move to Atlanta."

The ripple of her swallow filled the silence.

"And step four?" she asked, her voice barely above a whisper, her eyes glinting with suppressed happiness.

"Get the girl."

I turned my head to gauge her reaction, but before I could, her focus switched to the busy city streets through the passenger window.

My heart lodged in my throat. Did my confession scare her? Or was it what she hoped I'd say? Silence fell upon us. Thick and intense.

Addison Wilde usually had a ready comeback or fight in her. But now she said nothing. Not a word. I dragged a hand over my face. All I wanted to do was to kiss her senseless, fuck her till the morning, make her mine, and never let go of her. Because, through her craziness, she brought me peace. And it still made no sense to me most of the time that I craved a relationship, but we hadn't seen each other in almost a month, and my thirst for her hadn't decreased. It just multiplied. And now I was condemned to sit on the sideline until she decided she was ready to give us a chance.

I could push her, but I doubted Addison Wilde would react positively to being pushed. And the last thing I wished was for her to backtrack and leave town because she felt pressured to a relationship she wasn't ready for.

So, I'd be patient. And wait. Prevent anger or disappointment from getting between us.

"Hungry?" I asked after a beat.

She cleared her throat. "Yes. I haven't had dinner yet."

I stopped at a red light and rotated in her direction. "I'm no doctor, but not eating while you're pregnant isn't the way to go."

"I'm well-aware. I wanted to ask you out on a date when I first got here. I had this idea in my head. Then I was going to set up my new place. Make it mine. You made sure this wouldn't happen." Her words sounded more exhausted, and sad, than angry. "You had your way. Twice. And now I can't even throw myself a moving-in celebration."

"Wilde—"

"It's fine." Tremors filled her words.

"Pizza. What about the deep-dish you like?"

"Sure."

"You can still celebrate you moving into your new place. In my condo. Until further notice, it's your new address. And I hope you'll make it yours."

She sent a lopsided smile my way but added nothing.

And it bothered not only my heart, but also my soul that I ruined her plans.

———

Seated by the window overlooking Lake Michigan, the same way we did the first time when Addison surprised me with a visit, we indulged in pizza on paper plates. Neither of us said anything, silence bouncing between the walls.

"What about your needs?" I asked once I flushed the last bite with a sip of water. "How do you take care of yourself? I'm aware of the intensity of your libido, woman. And it's explosive. And insatiable. I'm curious."

I hated the distance that had fallen upon us. A lighter topic of discussion could perhaps kill the elephant in the room.

Addison rolled her eyes at me. Yep, she did. Again. "FYI, I can relieve myself just fine."

I offered her a noncommittal one-shoulder shrug. "The offer still stands if you ever need help."

It worked. The air surrounding us was instantly loaded with explosive verve.

She tried to dissimulate the hunger in her eyes when they wandered onto me but failed. I saw the flames of lust burning when she gave me a slow once-over, chewing on her bottom lip while trying to avoid my eyes.

"No. All fine. I just filled my spank bank with brand new images. Thank you very much."

"If you ever change your mind, just say the word."

Her cheeks flushed darker. Yes, I still had a lot of effect on her.

"Our story is skipping chapters, and we gotta figure out how to write the missing parts together. Stop trying to fuck my brain."

A smirk curled my lips. "It's not your brain I wanna fuck, but sure, if you're offering."

Addison backhanded me. "Tuck. Not funny. Keep your dirty scenarios to yourself. I'm trying to act like the grown-up here. And you're trying to pervert my train of thoughts." She shook her head. "Clear head. Not drenched panties. That's my new motto when it comes down to you."

Jesus, I'd missed her so damn much.

"Drenched panties?"

"Tuck—" she voiced, unable to hide the amusement playing on her face.

I raised my palms between us. "Fine. No more sexual innuendos. I forgot you were a prude. My bad."

Her arms flew in the air over her head. "This isn't funny. I'm confused right now. Sex is my therapy. Usually. Not this time, though. If you didn't know, you're supposed to be supportive, and right now, you're not helping the case."

I cupped her face. "I can't wait to see how long you last."

She closed her eyes, did some meditation thingy with her fingers, and breathed in and out a few times.

"Is it working?" I asked.

Her lids opened one at a time. "Shhh. Zip it." Her eyes shut again, but that curve of her lips never dissolved. "By the way, I'm still mad at you. Kidnapping is a felony in the state of Illinois. And everywhere else."

"In my recollection of events, you're the one who handcuffed yourself the last time we were together. It's fair to say you're a willing participant in a kidnapping scheme. You just lack a way of expressing your gratitude."

I cleaned up our dinner, and it was my turn to avoid her gaze. Addison stood in front of the panoramic window, and I stepped behind her while she watched the city lights below.

"Won't you miss this view?" she asked.

"Maybe. But I stand behind the decision to sell this place. I love it here, but I've overextended my stay in this bachelor pad. Thanks to you, who opened my eyes, I wish for more from this life than a career and expensive shit. Chicago isn't the place where I wanna raise our baby." I wrapped my arms around her waist, my palm over her stomach. After a beat, she rested her back against me as I whispered, "No matter what, we'll be all right. I promise."

With a cock of her head, Addison's eyes found mine, trying to read my intentions. And my soul. No one guarded the door when it came to her. She had full access. The only VIP key that ever existed.

"What if we can't be together?" she mumbled after a minute.

"Time will tell. For now, I'm more than happy that my friend is back. Because I freaking missed her over the last three weeks. I had no one to send random text messages to or to call late at night when I was home alone."

She snorted. "Glad to know I'm so useful. Were you really moving to Atlanta if I hadn't come here?

I nodded. "Yes. Nowhere else would I rather be than around you." And as I'd been dying to do for weeks, I pulled her against my heart, my lips resting on the crown of her head.

Calmness washed over me, and my heart resumed its beating, at peace for the first time since the day following Nick and Dahlia's wedding.

———

"Do you maybe wanna share a bed?" I asked Addison after I showered and met her in the kitchen. She was having a late-night craving and eating peanut butter toast. I studied her face, wondering if I'd pushed my luck with my offer.

"Sure you don't want one?" she asked with a mouthful, a square of toast in her hand. I shook my head, smiling.

She looked so damn cute, dressed down, her hair braided over her shoulder, pregnant with my child—not that she showed yet, but I knew it, so it was just as fucking hot. I couldn't wait for her to get bigger, to feel the baby kicking. "It may blur the lines even more than they already are."

I shrugged and got closer. "I've missed you. We'll just cuddle. That's our thing. I wanna hold you. Have you two with me. Protect you. And make sure you being here isn't a dream. Just for a few hours. Before you freak out and start running again."

We exchanged grins. The friction in the air had dissolved. We were back to being our usual selves, the fight forgotten. "For your information, I won't. Soon I'll be too fat to run, anyway."

"No, you'll be perfect. To me, you already are."

The smile she aimed at me settled every inch of me. It lodged in my chest.

She chuckled. "No wonder you played the scene. You always have the best replies."

I propped my elbows on the kitchen island until our faces were inches apart. "Yeah, but this time I mean every word. It's not a ruse to seduce you. You're already under my charm."

Addison pushed my chest. "That's a hell of an ego you've got, big guy."

I took a step back and pumped my fist. "Ladies and gentlemen, Addison Wilde is back."

I winked and saw her squirming on the bar stool.

One day, she'd be brave enough to tell me she loved me. Because I could tell she did. All the signs were there. The way she watched me and grinned when she thought I didn't notice. The tilt of her lips, her dilated pupils, her flushed cheeks. How she always found a reason to touch my hand or hug me a little longer than required. Nonetheless, and most importantly, she'd moved across the country to be with me. It had to count for something.

After not many arguments from me, we both climbed into bed, and before we positioned ourselves, I pushed the covers back. "Can I touch you?" Her eyes flared and her breathing accelerated. "Your belly, I mean. Let him or her know I'm here."

Her fingers combed my hair, the tingling in my scalp addictive and playing with my weakened composure.

"Tucker Philips, you're an amazing man. You see, that's the problem. You're too good, and I'm not ready for you. At least, not fully yet."

Staring into my eyes, she lifted her shirt, exposing her bare stomach, and in that moment, all I wished for was to make her mine. In every meaning known to humankind. My body pulsated. My breathing picked up. Everything about Addison Wilde enticed me. Her beauty. Her vulnerability. Her energy.

Her fingers continued brushing my hair, and one fact was engraved on my soul: I would forever love this woman. She'd delivered me from the prison my life had been since a long time. Freed my heart. She added colors to my black and white existence. And glitter to my days in the way she shone. And no matter what brought her back into my life, she came here. She came to me.

Dipping my head, I peppered kisses all over her flesh. "Hey baby. It's the first time we're really meeting. I'm Tucker, and I'm your daddy." Swallowing became harder. All those feelings overwhelmed my chest. I closed my eyes for a fraction of a second. Never before had I felt the way I did at the moment. And it was impossible to define it. The corners of my eyes leaked, but I kept going. "I have no clue if you can hear me or not or how this works, but from now on, you'll hear my voice every day." My voice cracked on the last word.

"Tuck—" Addison's voice sounded rough, laced with emotions.

I inhaled through my nose to be able to deliver the rest of my message to my unborn child. "Baby, I promise you here and now, in front of your mama, to do my best. Even when I mess up, remember that I love you. That I'll always be there for you. Can you do that? I'll never make you feel like you don't belong or you are in the way. We'll make it work. From now on, your mama and you will forever be the center of my universe."

Addison's hand froze over my head, and when my gaze drifted to hers, she dried the silent tears cascading down her cheeks with her other hand.

"Oh, one more thing. 'Cause I don't want you to ever believe otherwise. I love your mama. Very much. We may have to remind her frequently because she isn't ready, but I'll prove to her I'm worthy of her love too. And that I'll step up. Be there. Support her and her devious plans, cheer on her when she has had a bad day, or rock her to sleep when the insomnia kicks in. She's the most amazing woman I've ever met, so be gentle with her. She has the wildest spirit and biggest heart I know. She's funny and crazy at times, but in the best ways. You're lucky to have her. I am too. And, to be honest, I didn't believe in love before her."

I kissed Addison's belly once again, not ready to move away.

"Tuck? Did you mean everything you said?" Addison's voice, soft and strained, brought me up to her face.

"Yep. And it's just the beginning."

I adjusted her shirt back over her stomach, pulled the

covers up, and flipped to my side until I could hold her in the way I was yearning to.

"Now sleep. I'm watching over you two." I kissed her nape, imprinting the fruity scent of her shampoo on my senses, and closed my eyes, relishing this moment and knowing I would for the rest of my life.

In the middle of the night, I woke up, my phone telling me it was almost three in the morning. I patted the bed around me and wondered for a few seconds if I had dreamed of the entire night. Addison. The baby. Us sharing my bed.

With my fists, I chased the sleep from my eyes.

Tingles rose over my nape. I could still feel her energy around. Her presence here was real, not a figment of my imagination.

Where was she?

A clamp tightened around my heart at the idea. No, she wouldn't leave, right? I jumped to my feet, slid my limbs into a pair of cotton pants, and padded through my apartment in search of her.

My pulse deafened the more I looked around and saw no trace of her being here. I dragged a hand over my face as I reached the guest room where I put her stuff in earlier.

I huffed a long breath and relaxed my shoulders when I spotted her unzipped suitcase on the bed. But no sign of her either. In the doorway, I scanned the room, waiting for my heart to settle.

"Wilde?" I called out as I returned to the living room.

No answer.

I tried again. And again.

It was like she had vanished.

I pressed my fingers over my temples, dread running in my bloodstream. Spinning on my heels, I went back to my bedroom and grabbed my phone to call her number.

It rang, and I found her device on the kitchen counter.

Where was she?

That's when I noticed the missing blanket and pillow from the couch.

My gut told me where to find her.

The rooftop.

Two by two, I climbed the stairs until I reached the door leading outside.

There she was, lying on her back, one hand over her abdomen, and the other bent under her head. I came closer, and her snoring curled my lips.

Careful not to wake her up, I slid underneath the blanket and circled her waist with one arm, nuzzling her neck.

She wriggled beside me. "Hey you," she said after a moment, setting between my arms. "How did you find me?"

"I looked everywhere for you. My bed is empty when you're not in it. Thought for a second you'd disappeared on me."

She kissed my cheek, and I could've died right there. "Tuck, we're linked for life now. I'll never leave without telling you first. I swear."

Her words brought heat to my core.

"Truth? I'm scared."

I brushed the side of her visage with my knuckles. "I know. I am too."

"But you said—"

I gave her a small shrug. "It doesn't change the fact I have no clue how to be a father. You didn't plan for this. And I didn't either. And if it had been with anyone else, I would have freaked out right about now. But somehow, with you, it's different. You're different. You bring me peace. And I believe together we can achieve anything. We can achieve greatness."

"Why do you have so much faith in me? In us?"

"With you, it goes over simple attraction. It's much bigger. Much of everything. I can't explain it, so I trust my instincts. The same way I trust you."

"But—"

I framed her face with both hands. "No but. Lean on me when it gets too much, and we'll be just fine."

"Thank you."

We stayed in each other's embrace for a little while, all the words we spoke enveloping us. Linking us for life. And healing more layers of my previously bruised and thick-walled heart.

"Just so you know, when I joined you, you were snoring. I heard you. Loud and clear."

Addison's laughter resonated in the inky night, and she pushed my chest. "No, I wasn't."

"Ask this baby of ours, and you'll see it'll team up with me on this one."

"Shut up, big guy."

"Never." I paused and sucked in a breath as our eyes, in the dim light of the rooftop, promised things we hadn't discussed yet. Things only our souls could recognize. Something had switched between us. "Come to bed. It's late."

She nodded and gripped the hand I offered her after I moved to my feet. My eyes widened. She was dressed in the hoodies and pants I wore earlier. And it shot me with so much pride. And a smidge of possessiveness. Addison Wilde would be mine. Someday.

"I see you're wearing my clothes," I teased her as she made no move to remove her hand from my grip.

"You told me once they looked good on me, so..." She shrugged.

I moved closer, and the air soared between us. Time stopped. My heart banged against its cage. Addison's breathing picked up. She licked her bottom lip with her tongue. I followed the motion with my eyes, entranced by everything that was her. Vibrant and mesmerizing, her eyes darted to mine. They traveled to my mouth as she stepped closer. And I just lost it. Tilting my head, I kissed her lips. Slow and torturous at first. Starving and hungry afterward. Addison melted against me when my hands molded to her hip crests. Our tongues touched, and she gasped, and gravity left me. I tangled my fingers into her mane, devouring her sweet lips, wishing to keep her as close to me as possible.

"Tuck. We shouldn't," she said between breaths, the air surrounding us catching fire. "But for some reason, I can't seem to stop. I lied to you earlier. Thinking about you when I come is not nearly enough. And now you're here. Next to me. I want you so bad. I always do."

"I know, sweetheart, and I don't want to stop either. I've missed you so damn much."

Our bodies engaged in a conversation that required no words.

We kissed. For what felt like hours. Taking our time. Playful. Both of us, teasing and starving.

"The truth is, I'm sex-deprived. Can we have sex and still learn to be with each other without actually being together? Or will it complicate everything?" she asked, detaching her mouth from mine, breathless.

"Right now, I'll do whatever you ask of me, but please, don't take this away from our relationship. Our connection is more than physical. And considering we're both sexual people, it feels wrong to remove this perk from our friendship agreement. And I believe it's important for the baby to sense his parents enjoy being with each other. Making each other feel good is the root of it."

Addison smiled against my lips. "Oh, you didn't just go there. You can't use the baby to convince me. It's called emotional blackmail."

"I did," I said in the cockiest way I could muster. "My sidekick and I will be an unstoppable force. And I take one for the team."

My tongue tasted the flesh of her neck, the length of her collarbones, the lobe of her ear.

Her hips ground against mine in an erotic tempo.

"Okay," she said in a throaty voice that powered up my entire body. "Only to relieve the tension and calm my crazy pregnancy hormones. For now."

I nodded because, at the moment, I would've agreed to anything to bury myself in the woman I loved and who was the mother of my unborn child.

Somehow, through the daze of kissing, we made it back to my place and tumbled on the bed, panting. My greedy self longed to touch Addison everywhere. Every delicate inch of her. The ones I memorized. Those I knew by heart. The ones I'd been deprived of cherishing for weeks now.

Hungry for her breasts, I peeled the hoodie over her head and dropped forward. Her puckered nipples looked darker than I remembered. I sucked one hard tip, trying to tame some of the thirst for her searing at my core. Her back curved, and she let out a loud cry.

"Sorry. My body is hypersensitive. I should've warned ya."

I kneaded her other breast under my palm, the fullness heavy in my hand. "Want me to stop?"

"Nah, never. Don't ever mention this silly idea again,

you hear me? I don't care how painful it gets. You offered to be the man for the job. Just put those fingers inside me now because I'm throbbing down there, and I'll throw a fit if you don't draw an orgasm out of me soon."

"Jesus, Wilde, you kill me with your words only. Your suffering ends now."

On my knees, I yanked the pants down her legs, and my tongue licked that moist junction of hers, my hands clutching her ass cheeks. She trembled when my tongue entered her and moved in and out.

"Tuck—I—oh god." She jerked her head back. "More. So much more."

"It's just the beginning, sweetheart. Now relax and enjoy the ride." I plunged two fingers inside her tight channel and sucked on her clit. My digits, back and forth, dragged the pleasure out of her. Addison rolled her hips, increasing the friction, moaning as her walls clenched around me. My tongue pressed harder against her bundle of nerves as I enjoyed her sweetness. I increased the tempo. She was close. I could feel it. My hand reached inside my pants, fisted my dick, trying to relieve some of its painful tension. Addison's thighs pressed on either side of my head, preventing me from moving until she exploded in a climatic bliss. We both sighed, staring into each other's eyes. "Wilde, you taste too fucking good. I missed this. I missed you."

She surfed the wave of pleasure while I got rid of all my clothes, about to rip them to shreds in my hurry. Soon I had her pinned under me, her legs spread.

Her hands brushed my skin and awoke flutters in me.

Squeezing and pumping me, her grip unrelenting, she became its sole owner. My cock and I made a pact right there. To surrender ourselves to this woman. No matter the cost. Because, against all odds, she possessed advanced expertise of my body. In one swift move of her hips, she positioned me at her entrance. Spellbound, I watched her engulfing each throbbing inch of me in one long, slow thrust, her slick wetness now my demise. And salvation.

Her eyes flared when my girth embedded itself inside her tight channel.

She shivered, and the look of lust filling her face broke me. In the most animalistic way.

She smiled, and there was no going back.

Using my tongue, lips, and teeth, I devoured the flesh of her throat, marking her as she cried out her satisfaction. Once I sampled every inch of her, I thrust my hips, delivering the promise I made. To rock her world and satiate all her hormonal despair. And brand her as mine.

"Fuck, you're so hot."

She watched me, sweat beading along her hairline, her pupils wide, and all hell broke loose.

I rammed into her until neither of us could suck a full breath in, and we both went over the edge, crying each other's name.

I slid down her sinful body and trailed kisses from the sensitive mound between her thighs to the valley of her breasts.

"Wilde, I'm taking the job. I'll be your sex slave whatever be the time of day or night. Just say the code word and I'll take care of all your needs."

"And what's the code word?" Her husky voice had some amazing effect on my dick, bringing it back to life all over again.

"Pineapple."

Addison burst out laughing, the sound resonating through each cell of my body. "Pineapple?"

I nodded. "Yeah. You're both nectar and spikes."

We washed ourselves and fell back under the covers,

where my arms fastened around her. I had no idea what Addison and I were, but I would take whatever she was giving me for now. Until all her fears melted. Until we became each other's entire world.

"Night."

She buried her face in my chest. "Goodnight, Tuck."

30

ADDISON

"Are you gonna sit and eat with me?" Tucker asked, stepping closer. "We've been living together for over two months, and you barely ever make it to the table, always perched on the countertop or eating while you walk around." He kissed my cheek. "Were you always this restless growing up?"

I spoke through a mouthful. "Pretty much. Now that the tiredness from the first trimester is something of the past, I've got all my energy back. And more in bank. Sitting is a waste of my time. I'd much prefer to do anything else. Want me to redecorate your place?"

"What's wrong with the decor?"

"Nothing. I'm just looking for a new project to tackle."

"Wilde, you work full time for that marketing firm, work over twenty hours on your own business, and find time to housesit Dupont's place. And you're pregnant."

I rolled my eyes. "Stop being dramatic."

"I'm serious. Don't you think you're already burning the candle at both ends, and sooner or later it will bite you in the ass?"

"I just possess all this pent-up energy. Meditation helps, and I don't want to start running around the block or going to the gym. Not my style. I prefer keeping myself busy."

"Fine. But if I think you're overdoing it, we'll reopen this conversation."

Placing my empty bowl on the counter next to me, I jumped off.

Tucker eyed me. "Where are you going?"

A piece of me loved the caring version of him. It spoke to my heart whenever he worried or got all protective of me in the sweetest way.

"Hilary, from next door, invited me to her book club meeting."

"When did you find time to read a book?"

"Saw the movie. And Dah told me about the missing parts, so I'll be fine. I can pretend and talk my way through it. Don't worry about me. I don't have girlfriends here because all your hockey player friends are single and never in town, and you still haven't introduced me to Pam."

"Forget it. I won't. She's the devil. Don't want her around my child."

"But it's not even born yet."

"Still. Not up for discussion." His hands found my waist, and he pulled me to him. "Will you join me for that barbecue on Saturday? It's an off-work event. A family gathering, so you'll meet people."

"Sure, I'm free. I have a yoga class in the morning, but other than that, my schedule is empty."

A frown etched into Tucker's forehead. "Yoga? Since when?"

"Last week. Trying to be zen. For the baby's sake." I searched his face. "Since you're not moving out of town, are you going back to the office, or are you continuing with the remote work?"

"For now, remote is perfect. I even decreased my hours because I have that other project on the side."

I gave him my best puppy dog eyes, but he didn't relent.

"Nope. Not telling you. Not until it's ready. Forget it."

I sighed.

"Anyway, until we decide what we'll do with us, the baby, and where we'll move to, I prefer dealing with my schedule on my own terms." He crossed his arms over his chest with this decision.

Tucker and I looked like a couple. We acted like a couple. We bantered like a couple. But we were just friends for now. Anyway, that was our official title to describe our relationship. We slept in the same bed at night. And we cuddled, but we were taking things slowly.

"And I have to pick up after you," he said with a shake of his head. "I can't believe how sloppy you get. Exhausted Addison had an excuse to be lazy. Energetic Addison doesn't have any."

"Life is already stressful, so don't add another layer. I'll do the dishes later. When I return. Nothing says it can't be done in a few hours. There's no rush. It will get done when I am in the right state of mind. Don't worry."

"I hate when the place isn't clean. Cleanness eases my mind."

"Coming from the guy who orders his ties by color, I understand the frustration. Let go, big guy. It's good for you to learn to relax."

His lips connected with mine. "That's not how I relax." His hard body pressed against mine. Air charged around us. All my cells vibrated at the promise in his voice. "Got other ways. You sure you wanna go to a boring book club meeting?"

I nodded and spoke against his mouth. "Mm-hmm. It will be fun."

He took a step back and raised his hands. "Fun?"

"That's what I said."

"Suit yourself then. I'll go back to my dinner."

My body froze at the withdrawal. What Tucker and I shared couldn't be explained. But it was real. More real than anything I ever had before.

As if he sensed the broken connection too, Tucker spun me around, his front to my back. With a skillful gesture, he billowed my shirt around my waist and yanked my panties down. The sound of his zipper being drawn down awoke flutters in me. I shivered when his burning dick traced my lower back and embedded itself between my ass cheeks, and he thrust up and down.

"I changed my mind. Dinner can wait. You sure you wanna go?" he asked in a husky tone that sent all my hair standing on end, his lips sucking the flesh between my shoulder blades.

"Yes."

His fingers gentled on my belly and lowered between my legs. The mere pressure on my clit was enough to send my head spinning.

"You want me to fuck you, Wilde? To brand myself on you so you remember me all night?"

I bobbed my head, weird sounds escaping my mouth as he increased the pace of his fondling.

"Please."

Pushing me forward with a hand until my upper body rested on the countertop, Tucker asked in my ear, his voice pure lust that electrified my cells, "You want me inside you?"

"Yes," I croaked out, my voice not sounding like mine.

With purpose, his fingers spread the lips of my sex apart.

"You're so wet."

He inserted himself inside me to the brim with no hesitation until a soft yelp broke the silence of our combined, rushed breathing.

His hands gripped my hipbones, and I disconnected from the present. My world had narrowed down to the flesh pounding into me and the waves of pleasure surfing in me.

Tucker rammed hard. The sound of his flesh against mine increased the arousal dripping from me.

I pushed the countertop with my hands, trying to keep my body from dissolving underneath his. With one hand around my shoulder, Tucker increased the contact, his thrusts harder and faster.

"Want me to punish you for going to that stupid club?"

"Do it," I screamed. "Fuck me like you hate me."

Gliding out of me and lifting me in his arms, he spread me on my back on the kitchen table. The cold surface sent chills through me, but I enjoyed the contrast under my heated skin, Tucker burning hot as he resumed his pounding inside me.

The taut expression on his face reminded me of the guy who fucked me for hours in my hotel suite back in Nashville that first weekend.

Animalistic. Unapologetic.

The pad of his thumb rubbed circles over my clit.

I detonated against him, but he never reduced his pace. He pummeled into me with more conviction, never giving me time to surf the climax that worked through me.

"Want more, Wilde? Want me to fuck you so you're

late and all flustered and everyone knows I got my way with you?"

I nodded.

He leaned over me, locked my hands over my head, and his gaze turned darker. Growls exited his throat. He attacked my mouth with bruising kisses. My tongue darted out to battle with his. I bit his lips. He nipped my tongue. I hollered as more pleasure traveled through me.

"You're lucky you're pregnant, or I would have spread you on your front."

A twinkle passed through his eyes. Directed at me.

He stepped back, and moving to his knees, he assaulted the flesh he'd just speared into with his tongue. His licks weren't gentle. They were meant to rob me of my common sense, of everything in that moment that wasn't him.

My ankles linked behind his neck, and I squeezed his head there, forcing him to continue his ravishing of my center.

He pushed a digit in, and a second orgasm hit me. I let go of his head. Wiping his mouth with the back of his hand, he resumed his standing position. He entered me, and chasing his own release, he drove in me ruthlessly.

His body went rigid, and I sensed him coming inside me. A split second later, he slid out, and his palm pumped his cock a few times. With his free hand, he pushed my top up just in time to shoot his load in the valley between my breasts. The warmth of his semen soaked my bra and heated my skin.

Tucker watched me, panting, a satisfied smirk grazing his lips.

"Mine," he muttered before leaving me there, barely able to land back from the rush.

He returned a minute later and washed my chest with

a warm cloth. His lips and tongue traced my skin, licking where his cum had just been erased off me.

"Have fun tonight," he said with a wink.

I tried to pull his mouth to mine, still hungry for him, but he moved away. *Tease.*

The realization I was almost ten minutes late hit me. Hurrying to my feet, still dizzy and living in a world far from here, I put my panties back on, trying to smooth my wrinkled clothes with my fingers the best I could.

Tucker was right earlier. I'd be flushed all night. And I would never be able to conceal the pleasure circulating in my veins from anybody. When I caught my reflection, I enjoyed the image presented to me. I looked high on sex. High on love. And that sent a discharge of euphoria to my heart. For once in my life, could I be on the right path?

"Hey Wilde," Tucker called out before I could leave. I spun to face him as he walked up to me, his expression relaxed but serious, and his lips drawn upward. "I was thinking. Would you marry me? I haven't asked you yet this week."

His cockiness made him so attractive. His confidence. That smirk. He played with my reasoning. Even more after what we just did.

I mirrored his smile.

"Let's not rush it. We're not there yet." I winked. Because that was what he'd do if the roles were reversed.

Every week, or two, Tucker Philips asked me to marry him. It started as a game, but the more time we spent together, the less a game it had become. And we both knew it. Every time I gave him the same answer, to which he assured me, "One day, you'll say yes. Because we both know I'll call you Mrs. Philips before our baby gets here."

"Perhaps I wanna call you Mr. Wilde."

"Fair enough. I'll take your name anytime, sweetheart."

He dropped a kiss on my lips, and I made my exit.

"Come back to me."

His words bore more weight than anyone could ever tell. But I knew better.

"Always. I'm yours. You made sure of it, and you're stuck with me for a long time, big guy."

"I wouldn't want it any other way."

———

"What's wrong?" I asked, pushing an arm inside the refrigerator to grab a bottle of water, forcing Tucker to step to the right. He was cursing, his back tense, looking agitated. "Anything I can do to help? You've been cleaning this fridge for the last hour."

He spun away from me. Anger radiated from him.

In the three months we'd been living together, I recognized that cleaning-obsessed Tucker usually had something on his mind.

"Hey, talk to me. What happened?" I rested my hand on the middle of his back, but he yanked away from my touch.

"Nothing," he finally said in a harsh tone.

"Liar. I call bullshit."

He turned around, and specks of hurt swam in his eyes.

I grabbed his hands in mine. "Talk to me." He averted his eyes. One of my palms shot up to caress his cheek. "Be honest with me. Truth, remember?" A surge of annoyance washed through me at the sight of him.

"It's you," he said, not meeting my gaze for a long second.

"Me?" I asked, pointing to my chest. "Why?"

He stuffed his hands in his pockets, looking unsure for the first time. "We've been living together for a while. And I still don't know where we stand. I'm not a guy who likes labels and always thought I didn't. But with you, it's different. Call me alpha or whatever, I don't care. But I wanna stake a claim on you. I wanna be able to tell people we're together. That you're mine. A third guy from work asked me earlier when I went in for a meeting if you and I were still *friends*," he said, quoting the word with his fingers. "Presenting you as my friend at that barbecue that day was wrong. They all think we're just roommates having a baby together. Like it's no big deal. Collin asked if I could give him your contact info. The guy wanted to ask you out. Who's bold enough to—never mind."

"Tuck, you should've told me. We gotta talk about this."

"You keep saying you're not ready for a relationship, yet we spend all our time together. We have sex almost every day. We sleep in each other's arms, but as soon as we're outside the bedroom, we're more like roommates. And it doesn't sit well with me anymore. I thought it would. Because everything you said when you moved in made sense. But maybe it's because I've never been in a relationship before, but—forget it."

"No," I almost screamed. "We'll talk about it. I understand. And I agree. That's why we shouldn't have added sex to the equation. It complicates everything. But we'll find our way. I swear. Gimme a little more time, okay?"

"Yeah. Sorry. I shouldn't have dumped all this on you. Not now. You're trying to meditate and stay put for more than five minutes, and I've added stress to your day. Not my intention."

He gave me a tiny lopsided smile.

"Anything I can do right now to make it better?" I offered.

"Yes." His hands locked around my waist. I stared at the ripple of his Adam's apple, the lust shining in his irises, the darkness of his gaze. And I almost lost it right there. To put all the voices in my head to rest and give myself to him, heart, body, and soul, without restraint. "Turn that meditation music down. It drives me nuts. That bowl thing you hit with that wooden wand, I hate it."

Okay, that's not what I thought he had in mind.

"And stop shuffling around the contents of the fridge. Please make an effort to put stuff back where they're meant to be."

I let out a loud chuckle. "Where's the fun in that? Rotation is better. You get to see the food in the back that you otherwise forget about."

Tucker shook his head. "No. Not convincing enough."

"Please," I begged, joining my hands under my chin.

"Sorry. The answer is still no. You're, without a doubt, the messiest person I know."

"But it's a part of my charm, right?"

His arms wound around me. "I guess."

"If it annoys you too much, I'm sure Rory will take me back into his pool house."

"Not a chance. You're mine. Whether you know it or not. Now come here." He pulled me to him, the beating of his heart strong against mine, his chin resting on the top of my head, and my round belly caged between us.

We stayed in each other's embrace for a while.

"Sorry if I'm too much sometimes."

"Nah. I love how you turn my life upside down. It's refreshing. Occasionally, it's hard for me to adapt, but I will. Except for Nick, back in college, never before have I lived with another human being. But unlike you, he cleans after himself."

I punched his chest, and his arms tightened around me as we shared a laugh.

"You really hate my singing bowl?"

"Hate it."

"Fine, I won't use it anymore when you're around."

"Oh, and another thing I hate."

I tilted my head back to look at him.

"When you put on clothes to do your yoga. If you were my girlfriend, or my wife, I'd want you to do that downward facing dog pose naked."

"Good thing I'm not your girlfriend then."

Tucker's loud chuckle resonated through the condo. "Yep. You get a free pass."

We stayed like this for a bit longer, just enjoying the comfort we brought each other.

"Wilde, will you marry me?"

"Let's not rush it. We're not there yet. Let's enjoy the time together."

"One day, you'll say yes. Because we both know we can't escape our destiny and you'll walk down the aisle before our baby gets here." His lips grazed my forehead. "I'm not taking no for an answer, so I'll ask you again later."

"And I hope you will." I paused. Just to make sure I wasn't mistaken. No, this was it. Now I was sure. Because it happened a few times in the last two days. "Tuck," I said, putting some distance between us. "I agree I'm untidy. That I can be hard to keep up with. And that the meditation music sucks. But still, I have a surprise for you."

"You do? You didn't need to. All that I care for is in this room right now."

"Believe me, big guy, you'll thank me for this one."

With my fingers laced through his, I led him to the bedroom.

"A new kinky trick? Or a head? I'm down for both," he teased. "I changed my mind. If it's your lips servicing me, bring on that surprise."

Peeling my shirt up over my breasts, I lay on my side and beckoned him with my finger. "Get over here." When he positioned himself behind me, I placed his open hand on my stomach, glancing at him over my shoulder. "It moved. I felt it. At first, I thought I was dreaming, but no. If we're lucky, it'll do it again."

Tucker blinked, his eyes filling with a layer of moisture. "Are you serious?" I nodded, and positioning me on my back, he leaned forward, his mouth inches away from my stomach. "Hey baby, it's me. Daddy. Your mommy said you're moving. If you could do this once more, it would make me so happy."

We spent the next hour in bed, waiting for our little peanut to flutter in my belly. And it did. Just a tiny, barely perceptible movement under Tucker's palm.

"Was that—?" he asked, his voice congested with emotions.

"Yes."

"Wilde, we created this. Together."

His mouth fused with mine. And every word our hearts bore mixed into that kiss. Our tongues found solace with each other. Our hearts beat to the same melody. Yes, our baby was in there, growing every day, turning us into a family even when we still hadn't figured out our own definition of it.

His hand massaged my sensitive breast, and a purr left my mouth at the contact of his flesh on mine.

"I'm so gone for you," he said, breaking our kiss to gulp some fresh air, then his mouth returned to mine.

Before I realized it, we were both naked, hungry for each other. Both his palms cupped my face. "This was amazing."

I agreed, my eyes clouding.

My fist curled around his manhood, working him, my thumb rubbing the moist tip and relishing the jerk of his hips at the movement.

"Wilde, I don't wanna play. I just wanna be buried deep inside you. And feel you around me."

Hovering over me, our hands linked together, Tucker stationed himself between my thighs and pushed inside. I gasped at the contact, loving the way he filled me and electrified my core.

He halted there, watching me, his smoldering gaze turning me into molten clay underneath him.

And this time, Tucker and I connected on a new level. And that was the moment I knew that whatever I did, I was his, and he was mine. No matter how hard I was trying to fight this, our bond was stronger than anything we could define with words.

The three words were on the tip of my tongue.

Before I could utter them, he rocked his hips, pushing deeper, and I lost all sense of gravity.

Tucker pumped inside me, and my legs wrapped around him, keeping his body as close to mine as possible, the friction driving me insane. My arms looped around his neck, tugging him closer, and I wished my mouth could translate the words I couldn't speak yet but felt for him. The ones I couldn't escape or hide from anymore.

I kissed him with all the passion in my heart.

We were branding each other.

He pistoned into me with abandonment.

And I joined him thrust for thrust.

His hands brushed my hair away from my face, his eyes

lancing into mine, with promises to never let me go. To love me with everything he was. To cherish me for eternity.

Sobs clogged my throat.

It was beautiful, life-shattering, wonderful, and scary all at once.

My knuckles skimmed the side of his face, and I tipped my head back, hoping he could read me. Down to my soul. That he could understand I was ready to give myself to him. Entirely. That I wanted to be his. And to love him. And let myself go as long as he was there to catch me on the other side.

We moved together in a slow tango, our mouths never breaking apart.

His lips devoured mine. And I treasured his.

We had become this unstoppable force.

Our movements turned more frantic, both of us chasing our release.

Tucker pounded into me faster. Hard enough that he had to hold me so I wouldn't fly upward. He anchored me to him. My legs fastened around his waist, and my fingernails dug into the skin of his nape.

My whimpers mixed with his groans.

Both of us could detonate any moment.

His hands molded to the back of my head, making sure our mouths wouldn't separate. I felt our kiss in each of my cells.

"Wilde, I'll—"

"Come," I said. "I'll—let go."

His body stiffened. Scorching heat spiraled inside me. He rolled his hips faster. His tongue swept mine with shorter strokes.

His teeth pulled on my bottom lip while I cried out my climax, my head tilting back and vision blurring.

"Tuck, I'm—"

He pressed a finger against my sensitive lips. "I know, sweetheart. Not tonight. Let's just enjoy this moment."

As if he hadn't kissed me in years, his mouth returned to mine, possessive and demanding. I lost myself in the comfort of him. In his love.

Without a word, once he softened inside me, Tucker led me to his glass-paneled shower. Neither of us said anything. As if words could burst the bubble of bliss we found ourselves in.

A serene expression painted his face, but the gleam in his eyes broadcasted how much happiness waltzed inside him. And it mirrored mine.

He took his time to wash each curve of my body and to lave me with his tongue, imprinting himself on me. Spinning me until I faced the wall, my hands on either side of my head, his digits ventured between my legs, sliding back and forth in lazy strokes, building pleasure deep in my core. I could barely stay upright, my legs wobbly and knees weak.

From behind, Tucker held me up with one arm around my waist, his torso pressing against my back, the firm wall holding me still.

I turned my head, searching for his lips. We collapsed together. Deeper than ever before. A series of moans escaped me, the echo bouncing against the wall of the shower. The hot stream enveloped us. His fingers played me.

It stole every breath from me.

My pulse raced.

Adoration filled my chest.

Pushing my forehead against the wall to help with my balance, I grabbed his throbbing length from behind, but he pushed my hand away.

We needed no words to understand each other.

Tucker pressed his head between my shoulder blades, hastening the gliding of his fingers inside me.

I couldn't breathe. Or think. Or process anything else other than his body taking mine hostage.

His thumb rubbed against my clit.

My eyes closed, unable to decipher all the sensations invading me.

Unable to fuck me with his fingers the way he wanted to, Tucker squeezed himself between the wall and me and kissed the length of me until he sat on the floor. Clutching my ass cheeks, he maneuvered me until I sat on his face, his mouth sucking on my clit. One hand returned between my legs, his fingers resuming their actions inside me. My body shook with tremors. It was too much. And too little. Too hard. And too soft. Too fast. And too slow. I lowered myself until there was no space between us. The friction sent black dots dancing in my vision. I was riding his face, about to collapse at any moment. He replaced his fingers with his tongue, but after a few strokes, I wiggled, wanting more. His digits went back inside me.

With my hands pushing against the shower wall, I let go, unable to resist any longer.

I had no time to come back from the rush when he moved back to his feet, standing behind me. I heard him work himself, but I was too dazzled by the orgasm that tore through me to do anything about it.

Without a warning, Tucker entered me in one push and emptied himself with a jerk of his hips. The contact and fullness of him surprised me, his erection pressing exactly where I longed for him. I gasped, and he released a guttural, animalistic sound that drove me over the edge for a second time.

———

My phone went off, and I accepted the call, unable to hide my happiness at the face lighting my screen.

"Hey girlfriend," I greeted Dahlia.

"How are you? Is Tucker taking good care of you?"

"Yes. Always," I said with a clear laugh.

"He better." She sighed. "I'm sorry it took me two hours to call you back. Jack was having a tantrum. And Nick is away for two days. Some construction project in Nashville. He went to check on his guys to make sure they were on schedule. Jack is reacting to him not being home. It's like, except for Cart, Jack and I have been on our own for so long, and now that Nick is a fully in our lives, my baby can't get enough of him. Their bond is strong, and it's all I ever wished for. It's beautiful. I know Jack is missing him right now, but instead of using words, he has decided to go evil on me."

"Sorry, Dah. I know it's a lot."

"And he's started to call Nick *daddy*. Not sure how Carter will react to this one."

"Oh," I exclaimed.

"Yep. Oh," she echoed. "He'll be in town in a few days, so we'll see. Jack will stay with him three days a week for a full month."

"I think it's cool. How the three of you make it work. My nephew is the luckiest kid."

"We do our best." She sighed. "Anyway, it's all good now. He's drawing a picture for me, so I'm all yours."

"Listen, I wanted to talk to you about something." I breathed some courage deep inside me. "Did you...well... hmm...did you have any body insecurities while you were pregnant with him? It's just... I'm not usually shy about my body and everything, but I've gained so much weight that I can't see my toes anymore. And this pregnancy is far from over."

I swallowed, not sure if I should open up about what had been eating me up lately but needed another mother's opinion.

"I did at the beginning. People asking me my age when they crossed my path. Like it was illegal to be pregnant at twenty. Like I did something wrong. But after Jeff died, in my grief, I could barely eat, and I started losing weight. The doctor worried. I had to get additional checkups to make sure I was healthy and the baby wasn't suffering from my lack of appetite. But what I learned is that it's all temporary. You bounce back. The truth is, you'll never be exactly the same, but you'll be amazed at what your body can go through. Don't be too hard on yourself."

"It's difficult to look at myself. Today, I had two ladies asking me if I was pregnant with twins. And yesterday, someone in the grocery line congratulated me for the triplets. Twins run in my family. Do you think they could have missed a baby at the sonogram?" My sarcastic laugh turned into sadness. And I used my fingertips to dry my cheeks. "I'm sorry for breaking down. My emotions are a tangled web."

"Hey, it's okay to have doubts. And to need time to accept all those changes. We never know how pregnancy will affect us, mind and body, so it's a day-to-day acceptation. I'm here when you question everything, okay? Or when you're not sure you'll be able to go through with it. Because it's happening now, and it will happen again after the baby is born."

"Thanks," I croaked out, my voice weak, sobs now rocking through me.

A loud bang resonated on the other end of the line. "Oh no, Jack just broke something. Baby, don't move." Her attention returned to me. "Can I call you back? I'm sorry. The timing is all wrong today."

I sniffled. "Yeah, sure. Go take care of it."

"I love you, girlfriend. I'll call you later. Don't be too harsh on yourself, okay?"

"I'll try."

Sitting on my bed, cross-legged, I caressed my belly, lost in my head.

"This is all new to me," I said to my unborn child. "I'm happy you'll be tall and strong like your daddy. It's just hard on me right now. But none of it is your fault. It's I who is having a hard time getting accustomed to my body. I just wanted to be honest in case you hear me panicking or if I'm sad and you can't comprehend what's going on with me."

The tears resumed in my eyes as I caught my reflection in the full-length mirror next to the door. All my insecurities bubbled up to the surface.

"Hey, what's going on?" Tucker asked when he entered the room sometime later.

I tried to hide my meltdown. In vain. I couldn't fake it around him.

He sat next to me and draped an arm around my shoulders. "What happened to you? You missed me too much?" he asked in a teasing tone. "You knew I was at the gym downstairs. You could've come to join me. I would've loved the vision of you in spandex."

"Do you think I'm too fat and I should go to the gym?"

Tucker's eyes snapped in my direction. "What? Why? How? Wilde, what is this all about?"

"It's this," I said, pointing to my stomach. "And what people have said... And how I look when I glance at myself in a mirror... It's just... Forget it. It's silly."

"It's not silly. If it was, you wouldn't be crying about it. Talk to me."

"My emotions are ruling my life nowadays. When I was a little girl, my daddy—"

Right there, I almost confided about my father's struggles, but for some reason, I feared it would affect the way Tucker perceived me, so I changed the subject.

"I don't fit in my clothes. And this belly is ginormous. Today, it all seems like a big deal." The little bent of his lips sent warmth through my bloodstream. "Don't look at me like that," I said, backhanding his chest.

"Like how? Like I'm in love with you? Or I wanna eat you up. Yeah, you're right, it's so wrong." His arms pulled me to him. "I'm here, Wilde. When you need a pep talk. Or a hug, come to me. Always. Okay?"

I bobbed my head, and he dried my teary cheeks. "Yes."

"Come on, let's take a walk. Clear your mind. Fresh air will do you good. It's Saturday, and there's a craft expo not too far. You love those. Gimme time to shower first, and I'll come with you."

I hugged him close to me. "Thank you." My lips met his. My heart flipped in my ribcage. Tucker Philips was the one for me. I just have to fetch in me the courage to be honest about my feelings once and for all.

We strolled around town, and the sunlight bettered my mood. Sitting on a small eatery deck, we ordered lunch. The waitress flirted with Tucker. A wink here, a touch on his shoulder there. It grated on my nerves. Every time he addressed her, she fake-laughed like he said something funny. He ignored her for the most part and only offered polite smiles, yet she was relentless, complimenting him on anything and everything. From his eyes to his food choice.

In the past, I would have sucked my date's tongue for everyone to witness or sharpened my claws and staked my claim. This pregnant version of me, moody and lacking confidence, felt insecure instead. Throwing my napkin across the table, I stood and hurried away, pushing the server as I stalked toward the exit. I heard Tucker say something and seconds later, he had cornered me on the sidewalk.

"Wilde, stop."

"Don't Wilde me," I said, through gritted teeth.

"Hey, hey, hey. Come here," he said, enveloping me in his arms. "It's okay. I'm with you. No one else. She is not even a blip on my radar."

I jerked away from his touch, requiring some space to breathe. "Your old self would have gotten her naked within the hour. You would've fucked her."

His lack of immediate answer confirmed my apprehensions.

"See? You can't even deny it."

He grabbed my hand. "I'm not that guy anymore. That version of me was hiding from his feelings. He didn't thrive. Or love. It was just a front. This version right here, with you, does all these things."

I shook my head. "She acted like I didn't exist. How can I be invisible when I am this big? It is rude. Hitting on some other woman's date. Can't believe she flirted with you in front of me. I'm pregnant, for God's sake. With your child."

"You're not invisible. Not to me. And it has nothing to do with your pregnancy. I saw how she scrutinized you when we took our seats before she even laid eyes on me. She was rude because she was jealous of you. That much was evident."

He kissed my lips, and I relaxed in his embrace.

"Where's the Addison Wilde who would have given the woman a run for her money? That Addison is fearless and can kick some asses."

"I'm still here. Somewhere. Buried behind Mini-Tucker." His lips drew into the smile that was intended only for me. One that tipped my heart. "Fine, I should get her back. You're right; she's a badass. Thanks for reminding me I'm not lost."

"I prefer you feisty. Come on. Let's enjoy the rest of our day."

———

"I'll be back in two hours tops," Tucker said the next day, leaning in to kiss my forehead. "Do you think we'll know the sex of the baby?"

"At this stage, we're supposed to. Do you wanna know?" I twisted my fingers and winced. "See, I'm not sure I do."

"You don't?"

"Nah. I love the mystery," I said.

Tucker huffed. "I want it to be a surprise too. Like it's been since the beginning."

"That's what I had in mind. Glad we agree."

His arms held me against him. "I love it when we think alike. Can we still look at the monitor, or will it be too obvious?" he asked.

"Pretty sure we'll be safe. It's all black and white and blurry lines. Except for the head, arms and legs, I'm not a pro sonogram reader. Neither are you. Unless you have special powers I wasn't aware of."

"All me, babe. Except for being able to extract multiple orgasms from you, I possess no other superpower. The appointment is at three thirty. I'll be home by three. Wait for me here. I'll pick you up, and we'll go for a celebratory dinner after."

"What are we celebrating?"

He shrugged. "Us. This," he pointed to my belly, "all of it."

"Awesome. Be on time, big guy."

"Always."

He left, a grin spreading on his handsome face, his pupils brighter than usual. Flutters invaded me. Yes, having Tucker in my life made more sense every single day. He fitted into a slot in my heart as if he was born to rest there. And I reveled in sharing my days—and my life—with him more than I ever thought I would.

"Where is he?" I asked out loud, talking to my baby, pacing the kitchen floor. Tucker was never late. It was three-fifteen, and I still hadn't heard from him. I called his phone, his office, both went without answer. I texted him a dozen times. Nothing. I bit the tip of my thumb, unable to stay still. One breath in. I refused to go into panic mode and imagine the worst. One breath out. Did he say we'd meet at the doctor's office, or was he supposed to drive me? No, he said he'd come to get me. Where was he?

Three-twenty.

Voicemail. And no answer to my five additional text messages.

I hauled my pregnant self into a cab, unable to wait any longer for the man sharing my life.

Around five, I left the doctor's waiting room where I'd been camping for the last hour, praying Tucker would show up. With a hand splayed over my baby belly, as if that could protect it from whatever else was going on in my life, I walked back home, using the exercise to quiet the voices in my head. Jitters now assaulted my stomach. I still hadn't heard from Tucker. His office phone line was still busy. And his phone went straight to voicemail each time I called. Dread spread through me.

Back at the condo, I removed my makeup and changed

into pajama pants and one of Tucker's shirts that fit my new form much better than my clothes and called my best friend.

Silent tears slid down my face. Maybe it was my hormonal state, but Tucker being missing really got to me. And I imagined all the worst scenarios in my head.

"Hey Addi, how are you doing? How was the sonogram? Did you get a picture?"

My lips quivered. Tremors shook my hands. "Dah, he's missing."

"Girlfriend, who's missing?"

"Tuck. We had a baby appointment. He was super excited about it. He'd been talking about it for days. This morning, he said he'd pick me up and never did. He had everything planned for tonight. I called his office, his phone, sent texts, all the things that a perfectly clingy girlfriend would do, and I still haven't heard from him. It was five hours ago. The guy is punctual. Dedicated. It's not like him. I'm sorry I'm dumping all my shit on you. Again. I'm on the verge of a panic attack. Do you think Nick can help me? I'm helpless here. This city is too big for me to search for him by myself, and I have no clue where to start. What if something happened? At what point do I call hospitals? Or the police? My baby's father is MIA."

"Slow down. Breathe. Let me get Nick. We'll find him. He'll show up."

Her husband joined the conversation, and I explained everything that had happened since Tucker left earlier today.

"Let me get back to you," he said. "I won't make you run around town, alone and pregnant. I'll make a few calls and get back to you."

I nodded, even though he couldn't see me. "Thanks. Do you think he's okay?"

"Yes. Usually, when Tucker goes missing, it's because he needs time to think."

"Oh-okay."

We hung up, and I continued my pacing of the condo, halting in front of the giant window I liked so much and wishing the door would open and Tucker would walk back in. Back into my arms.

My heart knotted in my chest, unable to keep a steady rhythm as its other half was nowhere to be found.

My phone rang twice. An unknown number. Holding my breath, I picked up.

"Hello?"

31

TUCKER

With my elbows resting on the sticky wooden top of the bar, I swirled my glass and downed my fourth whiskey. Or was it fifth? Maybe. I had stopped counting after two. Drinking had been a rare occurrence in the last few months. Since Addison moved in. In fact, I hadn't numbed myself since the day she left Green Mountain with my heart months ago.

Nothing in my actual life reflected a hint of my old habits. No more booty calls, late night drinking, or bar hopping on Saturday nights looking for my next fuck. This was the new updated version of my life, the antipode of its previous one.

I wasn't complaining. I was thriving. I spoke the truth when I told Addison I preferred the life we were building together to my bachelor existence. The only thing I missed was the woman. I had her, but not the way I wanted. Still, she slept in my bed every night, with my arms around her body. No one else. That, in itself, felt pretty damn rewarding, to be the one she shared her daily life with. I had hoped soon enough we'd be more. Much more.

I flicked my hand to catch the bartender's attention and gestured for another drink.

A surge of all the thoughts I tried to bury with alcohol made its appearance and nagged me. My face descended into my open palms, and I massaged my skull with my fingers.

A hand clapped me from behind. In the past, I would've thought it was Nick out looking for me. But he wasn't in town. The only other person who could find me here was Jace.

"Hey man," I said, not even turning to acknowledge his presence. "What are you doing here?" I took a sip of the fresh drink laid before me on the bar top.

"People are worried about you."

I let out a sarcastic laugh. "How did you get mixed up in this? You've become the champion at being unavailable since you married that...that...Pam," I said, choosing to pick my battles.

My friend sat next to me and ordered himself a drink. "Stop blaming me for being happy in my personal life, Tuck. It's shitty. And juvenile. I love her. Pam. She gets me. And I don't care if you think she's a headcase or if you two don't get along. Sure, I'd like for my friends and my wife to be on good terms, but I'll choose her all the time. Hold your grudge; it's fine. Because it's my life. Not yours. Have you heard me calling your girlfriend nuts or giving her attitude? No. My wife is flawed. We all are. But I'm happy. Just be happy for me. That's all I'm asking."

I lifted a hand. "Since you got together with her, you've been hurting your best friends, man. Guys like Nick and I who've been by your side your entire life. It's not how brotherhood works."

He sipped his drink, taking his time to answer. "Tuck, you and Nick aren't less my friends because you can't stand my wife. And I'm sorry I missed his bachelor party. And his wedding. It wasn't what I had planned. Something came up. I'll make it up to him. You two are my brothers. For life. It's just not easy to always juggle my time between all of you without getting complaints from one side or the other. But I hear you, and I'll do better. Maybe not tomorrow, but I will."

"I've missed you, man," I said, pulling my friend into a hug. "I need you right now. My life is slipping through my fingers."

Jace hugged me back before he let go of me. "I thought everything was great. Last time you said—"

"Earlier today, it went to hell. Made me question everything. I'm not wired to be a father. I thought I would be at least good at it, not perfect, but manageable, but life proved me wrong. Now I'm not sure where I stand. It all went down so fast. Addison has been telling me we should take things slow. I didn't agree. But now—now, I think she may have a point. I—"

A soft voice broke through my confessions. I'd recognize this voice amongst thousands. Even though I hadn't laid eyes on her yet, just the sense of her being there filled me with calmness. And peace. Addison Wilde had that effect on me. I chugged my drink, trying to dissipate the overpowering influence of her sudden appearance.

Jace moved to his feet. "I'll let you two discuss," he said, placing a bill on the counter next to his empty tumbler. "Call me if you need anything. And I'll do my best to be more present. Gimme some time to adjust. And for what it's worth, I have no doubt you'll be the best father to your baby. It already suits you. This new role. Don't lose faith in yourself. You've got this. I can tell."

I nodded, my throat clogged with knots that refused to dissolve. "Thanks," I croaked before he walked out after exchanging a few words with my woman and making sure she was fine driving me back home later.

Addison took his empty seat and ordered a glass of water. I glanced at her sideways. Her hair was piled at the top of her head, her face bare, and she wore one of my hoodies over a pair of flamingo-patterned pajama-set. She looked adorable and so out of her element in our little corner bar.

The one where my friends and I always came when things got tough and we weren't in the mood to chat. The last time I was here was when Nick mourned Derek. Over a year and a half ago.

We drank in silence, both of us keeping our gazes trained forward.

"I was worried," she said after a while. "I've been trying to reach you for hours. You missed the doctor's appointment."

Reality hit me. Like a slap in the face. "Fuck, Wilde. I'm sorry," I admitted through a booze-induced numbness. "Jesus, this day is a disaster. I screwed everything up."

She spun in her seat to watch me. "What do you mean?"

I shook my head with a loud sigh. "I'm not sure I can do this. With you," I said, my stare darting to her abdomen and shame filling me. "Not sure I possess what it takes to be a daddy. A good daddy."

Addison blinked. "Whoa. Stop. And rewind. Can you explain yourself? Now. And what made you change your mind? A baby isn't something we can return to the store because things are not working how we expected them to, Tuck. What does this mean—I'm not sure I can do this? After you promised we'd get through this together, after you asked me to marry you, after you forced me to move in with you, now you're telling me you're not fucking sure?"

I shook my head, avoiding her piercing stare, her angry tone poking holes in my heart. "I've had the worst afternoon."

"I'm sure there's an explanation. A lot can happen in a short amount of time. We've already talked about this and agreed it's okay to be scared. Because I am. And I have no clue what I'm doing either. You said we'd figure it out together. And I believed you."

"How can you have faith in me?"

"Because I see you. I see every day what you're made of. What you can achieve, your dedication, how selfless your heart is."

"Wilde, you've only witnessed the good side of me so far."

"Then show me the bad, and let me decide if I can handle it," she said. And my feelings for her multiplied when she spoke those words. "Let's go home, big guy. Then you can tell me all about your day."

I pushed my half-empty tumbler and motioned to stand, feeling wobbly on my own legs.

"Where's your phone? I've been trying to call you for hours?" she asked, urging me to lean on her for support as we stumbled out of the bar together.

I fished the plastic bag containing raw rice and my ruined device from my jacket pocket and waved it before her puzzled expression.

"It's a part of my shitty day. I'm sorry I missed the appointment. I was really looking forward to it." Dampness blurred my vision. "I wanted to be there. I'm sorry I let you down."

Hauling myself into the passenger seat of my truck, I shut my lids as Addison drove the ten blocks to my building. We made our way to our floor. By then, the liquor I drank, my conflicted emotions, and Addison caring for me had turned me into an emotional volcano about to erupt. Everything I felt dangled at the edge, ready to burst into the open.

As soon as I kicked the front door close, I fell on the floor in a puddle of limbs, exhausted and bearing more mixed feelings than ever before.

Addison made some tea and joined me, sitting beside me, her legs stretched before her, her belly impossible to conceal anymore.

"Drink this," she ordered in a gentle tone as I accepted the cup she placed between my hands.

We remained silent. The air thickened around us.

"What if I'm genetically programed to be like my mother? A lousy parent? How do I know I haven't inherited her selfish ways?"

"Tuck, you're nothing like her. You're good to me. To us." Her thumb indicated her burgeoning stomach. "Our story isn't your parents'. It's ours. And we can write it how we wish to. There's no rules, no limits. Whatever happened before doesn't define us and has nothing to do with us."

"Today was a test. And I fucking failed. Even I would be afraid of my parental abilities."

Her arms wrapped around my biceps, and she rested her cheek on my shoulder. "Tell me all about it. I'll judge for myself."

Moisture hung to my lower eyelashes, and this time, I didn't blink it away. "You'll throw my sorry ass away. Today, I got checkmated by a two-year-old."

She said nothing as I recalled my afternoon.

"When I got to the office to drop those documents, I had to consult with Smith about a client, but he was on an important phone call. His wife came with their son, you know, Theo. You met them at the picnic." She nodded. "Well, Theo's nanny was sick, and Lacy was dropping him at the office because she had a meeting herself. The three of us have known each other since college, so she didn't hesitate to entrust me with her son when I offered to watch him until his dad freed himself. Anyhow, Lacy handed me Theo and a diaper bag and told me it would be good practice before our baby's birth, then hurried away. With no other instructions."

I scratched the top of my head. My memories were a bit blurry, considering the amount of alcohol I'd consumed.

"It started great. I was confident in my abilities. I've watched Jack in the past, so I thought I knew what I was doing. We sat in an empty office with his toy cars. But Beverly, the secretary, walked in and didn't close the door after her. I was rummaging through my bag to find the document she was asking for when I spotted Theo running toward freedom through the opening. And let me tell you, two-year-olds are freaking fast. By the time I started chasing after him, he thought this was a game and ran straight into Brittany's empty chair that bumped into her desk and sent her fresh extra-large mug of coffee flying all over her desk, soaking piles of documents and her keyboard. I caught the kid and gathered paper towels to wipe the damages the best I could, seating him on that evil chair. Next thing I knew, he was unsteady on his feet, standing on that stupid piece of furniture and dropped my phone. Which, for the records, up to this moment, I still have no idea how he got. It landed into the turtle desktop pond Brittany keeps on her desk, splashing water all around and creating a second mess."

Addison gasped. "Oh, that explains the rice."

I grumbled and continued. "The tiny devil was driving me nuts, but I ended up taking control of the disastrous situation. We were back in peaceful territories. Until I learned the coffee slash turtle-pond clusterfuck had short-circuited something under Brittany's desk and the entire office ended up with an internet outage. It crashed the presentation with investors from Japan in the conference room and the entire phone system."

"Oh," Addison said.

"Yep. Thirty minutes with a toddler. And that's how it turned out." I felt like a failure. And the idea I'd be like my mother had been haunting me since, weighing heavy on my upper back. And crashing my hopes about this whole paternity adventure I was about to jump into and never questioned until today.

"Explain me how is it is linked to what your mother did? I can't see how they're related."

"Addison, I gave up. This was too much. I saw red. The whole office went nuts and instead of helping out or making sure Theo was safe, I handed him to Brittany. Without a second thought. And I walked away. I just left. Not a care in the world if the kid was okay or if Brittany could take care of him. Lacy trusted me with her son. I failed her too. What if I fail you? Or get overwhelmed and just dropped our baby to the next available stranger because I can't deal with something?"

"Tuck, listen to me. It's just one day. One episode in your life. It doesn't define who you are and your abilities as a father. You should learn from today, not draw a conclusion on your fatherhood aptitudes."

The tears I'd been reeling in now leaked freely.

"That's the thing, Wilde. I'm not sure I can do this. I'm not sure I'll be any great. Or that I'm what our baby and you need. What if I'm such a failure I put his life in danger? Or I fail you both. I would never forgive myself."

Doubts crawled along my spine.

"You're not alone. We're a team. You think you're the

first parent asking himself if he's good enough for the job? Wondering if he'll get through this? That's why there are two of us. So, we can take the lead when the other is down. Or when we have no idea how to proceed."

Desperate for her proximity, her heat, and her love, I grabbed Addison by the nape and pushed my forehead against her. Nothing I did or said helped to keep the tears I'd been holding in at bay. In a way, it felt liberating to just let them out. Draining my sorrows and insecurities away.

"The first time I babysat Jack, I put his diaper all wrong. And it made a—you can only understand if you were there. Little babies are cute and look innocent, but they can cause devastation, I'm telling you. Anyway, thinking it was just a mishap, I bathed him, changed him, and cleaned everything. Only to start over again later because I had no idea that his penis should be pointing south, and things got chaotic a second time. By that point, my clothes were ruined, and I smelled like baby pee. And last year, when Dahlia and Nick went to Carter's concert, the one you bought him tickets for, that evening, I babysat Jack again. He fell and bumped his head. You should have seen the bruise on his forehead. Quite impressive."

She cupped her heart at the memory.

"It was just a bump. Nothing serious. And I could've just decided there that I wasn't fit to be a mother. Or his aunt. But I didn't. Those things happen. With kids, they always do. Dahlia taught me that. One day, ask her about the stories when she was a single parent at twenty. Things weren't easy for her. And she had the means to afford a nanny and anything the baby needed. Yet, it turned out to be a challenge. No parent is immune to this."

"I hear you. What if I'm the exception to this rule? I've only been taking care of myself in the past. I've never been in charge of another human being's life."

Addison shook her head. "You won't be. We've been living together for months. And I've witnessed you interacting with Jack. The boy loves you. I'm his Addidi, but you're his Uncle Tuck. Children are perceptive. If you were bad news, he wouldn't want to be around you and follow you everywhere. Or pretend to call you on the phone when you're not there. Your connection with him is real. It will be stronger with your own blood. It already is."

Her lips brushed mine in a featherlight kiss.

"Let's get you to bed, big guy. Sleep on it. Tomorrow will be better. And I'll hold your hand. Every step of the way."

My brain went blank as my woman took it upon herself to undress me, removing my shoes and helping me out of my trousers. She peeled my shirt from my torso after unbuttoning it, her hands caressing my bare skin. Shivers zigzagged in me. A new layer of comfort descended upon us.

Once in bed, she positioned my head on the ridge between the curve of her breasts and her belly, combing my hair back with her fingers.

"Don't shut me out again. We're in this together. I wanna be there for you when you have doubts. And I want you to be there for me when I'm the one who's unsure about everything."

The beating of her heart combined with her soft breaths acted like a lullaby, and I fell into a deep slumber.

———

The next morning, when I cracked my lids open, I watched Addison getting dressed for work. Fragments of last night's meltdown flashed before my eyes.

"Hey. How are you feeling this morning?" she asked.

"Fine. How bad was it last night?"

Wearing only a bra and a pair of maternity jeans, she slid herself into my arms. "Nothing we can't overcome."

"Again, I'm sorry I missed the appointment. I'm not like that usually. I'm the guy you can count on."

She traced my pectoral muscle with her finger. "I'm aware. We're allowed a slip-up here and there."

"Still."

"I never doubted you. Let's get you hydrated before I gotta leave."

"Did my mind play tricks on me, or did you really pick me up in a bar dressed in night clothes yesterday?"

A heartwarming laugh crossed her lips. "I did. For you, I would do it again. And even go naked. You really scared me. I thought something happened. An accident. Or—"

"I'm sorry. That kid. It just brought back bad memories. And doubts I've been trying to avoid dealing with."

"When something bothers you, promise me you'll come to me. And if it's that bad, I'll pour the drink myself. Deal?"

She looked at me with a mix of warmth and patience, and something potent I could get addicted to.

"Deal," I echoed, my lips tasting hers before I pushed back, concluding I probably had alcohol-tinged morning breath.

Addison found my eyes. "Tell me the truth. Are you okay?"

"I will be."

"Awesome, because I have a surprise, and I think you'll like it."

I arched one brow.

"I couldn't get myself into having the sonogram yesterday. You weren't there, and it felt wrong to enliven the experience on my own. If you're free during lunchtime, the doctor said he could squeeze us in. What do you say?"

I blinked.

"For real? You did that?"

"Yep. I'm a pretty amazing partner, no?"

I locked my arms around her. "You're an amazing woman, sweetheart. And thank you for rescuing my sorry ass last night. I'm sorry I worried you."

I kissed her again, but she pushed me back. "Teeth. And a shower."

Laughter bubbled out. And it felt good to just share my life with her.

"Wait for me, Wilde. I'll be right back. Don't go yet. I'll drive you to work."

"Hurry, big guy. I'm not going anywhere without you."

———

A couple of days later, I left early to run some errands while Addison was still asleep. On my way home, I picked a bouquet of white roses, Thai food, and a maternity C-shaped pillow. A co-worker had recommended it, and I believed Addison would love some additional comfort while sleeping or just relaxing.

With excitement pouring out from me, I entered my condo, ready to surprise the woman I loved, but halted at the sounds coming from the bedroom.

I swore they felt to be sobs, but maybe Addison was watching some TV or that she was sleeping and those were snores.

Setting my purchases on the kitchen island, I tiptoed to the bedroom. Now I had no more doubts. She was crying.

I knocked on the door. "Hey sweetheart, it's me. Can I come in?"

She mumbled something I interpreted as a yes.

The sight before my eyes broke me apart. It fractured a slice of my heart.

Addison sat on the floor in one of my T-shirts that hugged all her pregnancy curves. She had mountains of discarded clothes and used tissues scattered around her.

I pulled her into my arms. "What happened? Did someone try to raid your side of the closet?" I asked, trying to infuse some humor into my words.

I handed her a tissue that looked clean, and she blew her nose before answering me. "Nothing fits anymore. I have nothing to wear except your clothes. How am I supposed to go to my book club meeting tonight if I can't get dressed?"

"For the records, you look beautiful as is. And fucking hot in my shirts." She offered me a death stare, and I lifted my hands before me. "Just saying. How about that dress we got last month?"

"Too small."

"And that new pair of jeans you like so much?"

"Don't fit into them anymore. I'm telling you, I got bigger in the last twenty-four hours."

"Let's be real then. Living naked has its benefits." I jumped to my feet, undid my tie, and proceeded to remove every single piece of clothing from my body until I only had boxer briefs on.

Addison let out a warm chuckle as I sat back down next to her. "Tuck, don't be silly."

"I'm not. You go naked, I go naked. Unless we go shopping. Your call."

She shook her head, that smile now anchored to her face. "You'd walk around stripped to the boxers with me if I ask you to?"

"Always. We're in this together."

"Ohmygod, we're so weird."

I turned until my palms cradled her face and my thumbs could erase the last drops of moisture from her eyes. My lips descended on hers. "You're stuck with me. So what will it be? Shopping spree, running around town naked, or wearing my stuff from now on?"

"Perhaps I'm being a bit overdramatic. Before we go to buy a new wardrobe, I'm sure I can find something that still fits for tonight. I just really wanted to wear that dress. And I got upset." She motioned around the bedroom with one hand. "And then this happened."

"How long have you been here, on the floor, in this state?" I asked.

"Over an hour. I tried calling Dahlia, but she didn't answer. I got really sad. Like *really, really* sad."

"Wilde, next time you call *me*, okay? You're the one person I would answer the call even if I was being tortured or was drowning in the middle of the Pacific."

"You better save yourself first. Then answer my call." I kissed the tip of her nose and she grimaced. "I'm serious."

"I know you are. Come on, let's sort this out. I'll help you. But first I got you something."

"Did I forget an anniversary or a birthday? I'm telling ya, mommy brain is a real thing. Those women claiming they can't think clearly when they're pregnant aren't joking. My head is filled with jelly most days. My thoughts are enveloped with fog."

"You forgot nothing. Since you're the one pregnant, you deserve some pampering." I shrugged. "And nights of good rest."

Holding her hand in mine, I led her to the kitchen.

Addison's eyes took in the pillow and flowers. "For me?"

"No one else."

She hugged the pillow to her heart. "I heard about this. Supposed to be amazing."

"That's what I heard too."

"Tuck, you're the best." Her eyes filled up with a fresh batch of tears.

"Hey, if you don't like the color, we can go to the store and exchange it."

Her crying resumed. "It's not that. Damn hormones. I'm happy. I swear. See? I can't even be thankful without shedding tears anymore."

I pulled her into my arms and kissed her lips. My hand entangled in her hair. "I'm not scared by the hormonal version of you." I grabbed a handful of her ass cheek, and she ground her hips to mine. "Here. Being hormonal can be a big turn on too."

"Pervert," she whispered against my lips.

"Only with you. When is that book club meeting?"

"Seven tonight."

"Then let's go. We'll go for a walk and grab food on the go. Fresh air and sunshine will do both of you good."

"What about the food you brought over?"

I shrugged. "We'll put it in the refrigerator. It can wait."

"Tuck?"

"Yes," I said.

"Thank you. We're good together."

My lips connected to her forehead. "I know."

Addison got ready, and I studied her from a distance. I didn't like seeing her so distraught. It occurred more frequently these days. Her glossy eyes and the firmness of her lips were undeniable signs that whatever troubled her before wasn't quite resolved.

Our eyes glued together, and she mirrored my smile. We'd be okay. Or I prayed we would.

32

ADDISON

"**D**o you need anything before I go?" Tucker asked. I watched him over the bowl of soup perched on my impressive five-month-old pregnant belly—yes, our baby would have Tucker's stature, no doubt—the spoon halfway to my mouth. "Want me to refill this?" he asked with an adorable cocky smile gracing his lips. Yeah, he knew me too well at this point.

"Yes, please. And can you bring me a pillow? My back has been hurting me today."

"Sweetheart, all you gotta do is ask when you're down for a massage or a bath. Or an orgasm."

"No, I'm good on all those counts. I've already come thrice today. I should be able to survive until tomorrow. Any news about that secret business project you're working on? I still can't understand why you won't tell me anything about it."

He shook his head. "Nah. Nothing to announce just yet. Don't worry about me. I've got everything under control. I'll tell you when the time is right. Be patient, Wilde. It's a virtue."

"I consider myself super patient, big guy. Look at me, less than four months to go. It feels like I've been pregnant forever."

I'd had only a handful of meltdowns in the last few months. Some days, darkness coiled tight around me, and everything looked bleak for a moment. Then it dissipated, and I returned to my usual cheerful mood. Since the day Tucker caught me crying on the bedroom floor with piles of clothes around me, I'd been careful to hide the emotional tumult my off days brought from him. I saw how worried he got even though he said nothing about it and tried to cheer me up. And I didn't want him to be concerned about my sometimes, temporary lack of enthusiasm.

"You're wonderful. Beautiful. And sexy." He filled my bowl and brought me a few crackers that he set on the coffee table before locking his lips with mine. He was always showering me with attention and compliments. As if he could sense I needed his reassurance.

"Do you wanna see what I've been working on lately?" I asked, adjusting myself. I had a hard time dealing with the weight gain so far, which was more than most women packed during their entire pregnancy. The insecurities about my body skyrocketed the days I didn't feel at the top of my game. Or when I studied the stretch marks in the mirror after a shower. Except that time I broke down, I hadn't mentioned them to Tucker per se, but he could tell because he complimented me every day and always made sure I felt pretty when I was having an off day. He could read me so well that sometimes I avoided looking at him, just in case he could tell what I didn't speak out loud.

"Always." I pointed to my laptop perched on the kitchen table. Tucker sat and powered it on. He opened the file where I'd stored my shirt designs. A loud whistle left his mouth. "Wow. You did this?" He scrolled down, his eyes trained on the screen.

I failed at holding in my pride. "What do you think? I got inspired. To try something new. Mini-Tucker is triggering the creative side of me. Maybe I should wait until he or she turns eighteen and make them partner in my business."

Tucker spun until he faced me. "Wilde, these are amazing. I'm ordering them all. When they become available. In every size. Our little one will be the most fashionable and cute baby out there. I'm telling you."

I snickered as he turned the laptop off and joined me on the couch.

"You're very talented. When did you have time to work on those?"

"Every day when I have a few minutes to spare. I love designing clothes. Wish I could do it full time. Or planning events. Both, actually. I don't know." I sighed. "I haven't planned anything since Dahlia and Nick's wedding, and I miss it. One day, I'll be my own boss. And do all the things I've always dreamed of doing."

"I know. And I'll be there to help you reach your full potential. Whatever it is you wanna do. Some time off when the baby arrives will do all of us good. I could also resign and be your handyman." He wiggled his brows. "I heard I'm quite skilled with my hands. And other body parts. Just sayin'. There's this girl I'm spending all my time with. She could vouch for me. She'd be a great character reference." I snickered. Amusement left his features. "Seriously, you should catch on some sleep, though. Don't exhaust yourself. Please."

"I won't. Stop worrying about me."

"It's my job." Tucker rose to his feet. "Call me if you need me. I won't be long, okay?"

"I will." He dropped another kiss on my forehead, and I melted inside.

"I'll see you later."

"Sure. Any dinner plans tomorrow?" I asked. "I was thinking we could go out after I'm done with work."

He nodded. "Count me in."

He let himself out and closed the door behind him. I heard the lock being engaged right after. And the same way it always felt every time we were apart, a heavy mass grew in my chest, crushing all my organs.

So far, Tucker had proven himself to be the most dedicated father-to-be. He made himself available every minute of every day in case I required his help. Or company. Initially when we had regular sex, satisfying both our needs, our relationship had mostly stayed in the friend-zone. But since we made love, the first time the baby moved inside me, things had been different. And I waited for the right moment to tell him how much I loved him. Because now there were no more doubts in my mind, and I was done being scared or not trusting my gut.

Dahlia called our living situation a modern arrangement.

Now I craved the real thing. I was done denying Tucker my love any longer. I wouldn't waste more of our precious time.

Yes, I would be honest with him about my feelings. Soon.

A shiver of excitement traveled through me as I tucked the fluffy blanket off the couch around me.

Trepidation jolted my heart as my mind drifted back to Tucker. Unable to restrain myself anymore from what I truly wished for, I dialed him, hoping he hadn't left the building yet.

"Miss me already or can I help you with something?"

I snickered. This man. He'd evolved so much in the months I'd known him. He was still irresistible, cocky, and handsome, too much for his own sake, but he had a calmness about him that wasn't there before. A serenity. I bet barely anyone noticed, but I did. Because it mattered to me.

"You know I always miss you when you're not around. Even if it's just for an hour. This place feels too empty without you. I know soon I will pray for silent nights, but until then, it's better when you're here."

"Don't be shy. It's okay to think I'm irresistible. I agree with you."

"Oh god, that ego of yours." We both burst into a fit of laughter. "Where are you meeting Jace? You never told me."

"At the same pub we went last month."

"Oh, I can still taste that burger. And now I'm hungry. Can you bring me one when you come back?"

"Yep. With the spicy mayo you like?"

"Double portion, please. On another note, I gotta tell you something. I'm sorry for always keeping you at a safe distance. It's not what my heart begs for. Since the beginning, we've been doing all the steps in random order. One-night stand, make a baby, become friends, marriage proposal, break up, have a baby together, become friends again, sleep together, being together while not being together. It's hard to keep up. What I'm trying to say through my rambling is that I wanna try for more."

"Wilde, I don't wanna try. I have the certitude you're it for me. The last couple of months just confirmed it. You're either all in or we keep doing what we do, this dance, but at one point, it comes with an expiration date. It's not fair to any of us, or to our baby, to be one foot in and one foot out."

I sighed and rubbed my eyes. "Maybe I didn't make it clear enough. I'm ready for more. With you."

I swallowed the panic rising inside me.

"As lovers or—?"

My belly tensed, and it stretched up to my back. "Oh fuck. Gimme a sec," I gasped, cutting him short, using both hands to caress the tightening muscles of my abdomen.

I heard the door open, but ignored it, too focused on my breathing, wishing for the tension to dissipate.

Two muscular hands wrapped around me, and Tucker's gaze locked on mine. "Better?"

I bobbed my head as the contractions lessened. "How? I thought you'd left?"

He offered me a non-committal shrug. "Nah. Wasn't feeling like it. I texted Jace before you called. I didn't wanna be away from you guys. I was hoping you'd call and beg me to come back, so I sat by the door and played silly games on my phone, deciding what to do. I was just about to go and grab you that burger to eat."

I blinked. "You did?"

He nodded.

Tucker held my face, kneeling between my legs. "So, about what you were saying before our peanut decided to interrupt you, were you serious?"

"I've been ready for a long time. I didn't want to admit it to myself. And to tell you the truth, I tried once. But then I was too chickenshit and missed the opportunity. We're already a couple. No matter what I tell myself. You are mine, Tucker Philips, and I wouldn't want it any other way."

He crashed his lips on mine, his hand curled around the back of my head.

"I'll make you the happiest woman on Earth."

"You better, because I wanna make you the most satisfied man in the universe."

"Wow, woman, it's a big commitment. Are you up for the challenge?"

"I was born ready. And I possess a few skills that make me irresistible, you'll see."

"I can't wait." He sat on the couch beside me and pulled me into his arms. "Later. Let's just watch a movie or something. I wanna hold you when you fall asleep. It's one of the best moments of my day. When you surrender in my arms, trusting me to watch over you. Unless you're hungry."

"Nah, just an indulgence I can live without."

Tucker slid under the blanket and repositioned it over me, and with my head resting on his lap and his fingers toying with my hair, we enjoyed being with each other. No more *what-ifs* hovering over us.

"One thing though before I agree to date you."

"What is it?" I asked, tilting my head back.

"One. Stop using my towel to wrap your hair after you shower. I hate when it's damp. Two. Naked yoga and meditation as often as possible. So, I can enjoy the view."

"I thought you said one thing."

"Changed my mind. I make the rules," he said, echoing the words I spoke when we first started having our night chats months ago.

Bile rose at the back on my throat. How could I tell him the idea of parading naked sent a wave of discomfort through me? Sparks shone in his eyes as he watched me. One by one, they killed all my doubts.

"Big guy, you got yourself a deal," I said before I changed my mind.

We kissed to seal the accord.

Now at peace, with my head giving up its fight and

allowing my heart to take the lead for once, locking all my pregnancy reservations far away, a wave of contentment washed over me. I drifted off to sleep feeling his caresses deep in my core.

———

The next day I woke up, strong arms banded around my body, shielding me from the rest of the world. I took a moment to inhale and enjoy the ease we'd had fallen into last night.

"Morning, sweetheart," Tucker's husky voice said from behind as he peppered kisses over my bare shoulder.

I squirmed against him, his short stubble tickling my skin. "Stop. We gotta talk."

His mouth now sprinkled kisses along my spine, his hands covering my belly. The baby kicked as if it agreed with our new commitment. "I don't wanna talk. We did that enough last night. For now, I wanna love my girlfriend. Now that we're official, I wanna show her just how happy she makes me."

"Babe, I'm serious. I forgot to discuss something. It may change the way you feel about me," I said between laughter as his hands traveled all over my naked flesh and lodged between my thighs. I gasped as he inserted one finger inside, my hips rocking of their own volition, unable to stay indifferent to his seductive touch.

"Call me babe again," he pleaded, positioning me on my back, his lips now tasting my breasts.

My hips moved faster. I panted, trying to infuse my brain with oxygen to recall the words that had deserted my mind seconds ago.

"Sweetheart." Tucker captured my mouth with his, hungry and insatiable, as his lips covered mine with lust and a million promises to make me feel good. My arms locked around his neck, and he balanced his weight backward, positioning me over him until I straddled him, and we moved together, our bodies in sync.

I was about to come undone when the words I'd been selfishly withholding emerged. "I love you, Tucker Philips."

He halted underneath me, his gaze taking mine hostage. He blinked, and his Adam's apple bobbed while he stared at me.

"I love you. I didn't tell you last night. Or all the times before. But I do." I exhaled. "It feels good to finally put it out there. To let go of my fears."

He cleared his throat, and his eyes illuminated with something I'd never seen before. "She said she loves me," he screamed.

I nodded, now smiling like a fool.

"I've been waiting to hear those words for so long." Ache laced his voice.

My palms rested on either side of his face. "I'm sorry. It's not that I didn't feel it. It just scared the shit out of me. All the times I spoke them in the past, it turned ugly soon after. But I'm done being afraid. You're nothing like the men I dated before. I wanna be yours. I love *you*. And I'll tell you every minute of every day until you believe it. I'll climb the Everest for you and holler it from the top."

Tucker watched me with a seriousness that sent my heart rate into a sprint. My hair stood on end over my arms. Knots tied my stomach. Did I say something wrong? Did I fuck up everything between us by voicing my feelings?

I blinked, trying to keep at bay the tears that were now threatening to fall. When I tried to remove my arms from around his neck, his hands moved to hold them in place.

"Don't." He paused, averting his eyes for a long second

that seemed infinite. "You know, other than Nick when he's feeling emotional, it's the first time in over a decade that someone spoke those words to me. I haven't heard *I love you* from a woman since I was twelve years old, I think. Before the shitshow hit my family." He swallowed hard, and I followed the undulation of his throat with my eyes before bringing it back up to his. "Do you know how happy I am right now? Do you realize what you just did?" He crashed his lips on mine, unapologetic and starving. "She loves me," he repeated when our mouths detached. "Finally, she said it."

My heart broke for the kid in him and for the man who never got close enough to somebody else to hear those words. The ones that mattered. The ones powerful enough to transform war into peace and tears into smiles.

"I love you, Tucker. You'll see. I'll say it enough you'll grow tired of hearing it."

He nuzzled my neck, kissing my skin. "Never. I'll never get tired of anything when it comes down to you. You're my best friend. You get me. You make me wild and tame me. Even when you drive me nuts, I can't resist you. And when you're black, I'm white. Together we're the perfect shade of gray. Every single time. And for your information, I knew. All along."

I slapped his chest as we shared a laugh. "How?"

"You're not as subtle as you think you are. Or I'm very good at reading you. But don't beat yourself up. I was waiting for you to realize it. Maybe I would have given you hints soon enough, though."

"How?"

"Anonymous text messages. Sticky notes. Here and there."

"What would they have said?"

"Addison plus Tucker. I love Tucker. Tucker is the one

for me. Tell him you love him already. Why are you being so stubborn? L-O-V-E. I'm in love, and I'm the only one who doesn't know it…Things like that."

I tilted my head back, laughing. "I prefer simpler declarations. Perhaps you should have tied the ribbon behind the airplane or the diver in the shark tank at the aquarium. Or the lip dub. Those kinds of things."

He kissed me hard. "You crazy woman, I love you. Now let me make you come until we reach another galaxy together."

"I'd live in space with you anytime. And I'm calling in sick today. We're spending the day together. To celebrate."

33

TUCKER

A ddison and I couldn't detach ourselves from each other. The idea of the two of us dating for real was a powerful aphrodisiac. We made love in bed, against the kitchen counter, in the shower—this one turned out to be a bit more complicated now, the space a tad small for both of us.

We were eating lunch, half-naked on the couch, her legs sprawled over me, when she moved to her feet with a wide grin.

"What is it?" I asked, flushing a bite of pasta down with a sip of water. "I haven't seen those devilish sparks since the night of the wedding." My body heated up just at the memory of her tied to the bed, wearing nothing but the red piece of lingerie I got for her. "Should I be worried? Or run for my life?"

Her contagious happiness bled on me, and I was now smiling like an idiot too. I sprang to a ninety-degree angle.

Tingles lined my spine. Yes, Addison Wilde being wild excited me. Because I had no idea what to make of it all.

She paced the living room, dressed only in one of my

T-shirts showcasing her burgeoning belly, and I zoned in on the swell of her ass as she walked back and forth. "My eyes are up here, big guy," she warned with an even larger smile.

I swallowed. "Yep. There's just something incredibly hot knowing you wear nothing else underneath that piece of cotton. Just trying to sneak a peek."

I felt my cheeks warming as if I'd been caught doing something bad.

Addison offered me a sharp stare. "You've had both hands, tongue, and dick deep in the candy jar earlier. Now focus if you wanna be granted another visit later."

I bobbed my head. "Yes, ma'am."

"See, I was thinking. It's the first time I feel like myself one hundred percent in so long. No more fears, secrets, or denying myself everything I crave. I wanna immortalize this day. We have very little time before Mini-Tucker arrives. Let's go shopping for the nursery, pick paint swatches for the walls, and get matching tattoos."

I chuckled before joining her, my hands resting on her hipbones. "I love you. Nothing will change that. But I have to stop you from getting tattoos. Not that I'm against the idea, but you're five months pregnant, sweetheart. Nobody is going to poke a needle into you. Not right now. Not under my watch. We'll discuss it again in a few months."

Her lips turned downward in a pout, and I kissed it, unable to remove the curl from my lips.

"But I really wanted to do this. With you," she grumbled.

I framed her stomach with my hands. "Can't you do something else for now?" The baby kicked at that exact moment. "See, Mini-Wilde agrees with me. No ink and needles for you two."

As if another bright idea had just landed, she blinked

and cocked her head fast, forgetting all about the tattoo. "I know. There's something I've been thinking about doing for a while now. But didn't do it, no idea why, though."

"Does it involve alcohol, stunt, needles, raw fish, bungee jumping, car racing, or putting your life or the baby's at risk in any other way?"

She shook her head. "None of the above. Nothing dangerous or reckless involved. And it won't be permanent, so if we don't like it, it'll go away. At some point."

"Intriguing. Can I have hints?"

She shook her head again. "No. Maybe. Because you're cute. Makeover. That's all I'll say. I'll need about two hours here to put it together. And once I'm done, we'll go on our date as planned."

I tugged her against me, our little bundle of unborn joy pressing between us. My lips claimed hers in a slow sizzling kiss, to show her just how much she meant to me.

"Are you shaving your eyebrows? I heard it's a thing."

Her warm laughter enveloped me. "Nah. I would never dare. Not sure it'd be a good look on me."

I let out a dramatic sigh. "At least we agree on this. Not that it would or wouldn't fit you, but I can't see the appeal. I prefer you with brows."

"Great, because I'm keeping them. Let's go. We have a lot on our to-do list for the rest of the day," she said, pulling away.

"We'll get you something new to wear tonight. After all, it's our first date as a couple. And I want it to be perfect. Been waiting for this day for a long time. I'll make a reservation."

"You'll see, big guy, it will be fabulous." She clapped her hands together. "Can't wait. This is so exciting."

My hand smacked her ass. "Go, get ready."

Addison strode toward the bedroom but pivoted to

watch me. "Tuck? Thank you. For always having my back. And loving me." She paused. "Have you talked to Elisa lately? Did the couple who were interested counteroffer after you refused their first bid?"

"They're supposed to come back with a final figure within a day or two."

"If we can't stay here, we should talk about relocation. You said Chicago isn't an option, and as much as I love you, I won't oppose it because damn, it's cold. And windy."

"Wanna go back to Atlanta?"

"Nah. Too big a city. Except for the weather, it's not much different from here. But it has great suburban areas."

"Green Mountain?" I proposed.

"Don't you think you and I would get bored in no time? Sure, it's peaceful and the scenery is to die for, but other than that, there's not much to do. Let's think about it for a little longer. And once the baby is born, we can decide. I can't wait to meet Mini-Tucker. And be a family, the three of us."

Slivers of excitement spiraled through me.

I inched closer, lifted her in my arms, and twirled her around. "Can we forfeit all our afternoon plans and spend the rest of the day in bed instead?"

She beamed, joy radiating from her. And she looked so perfect. Mine. I wouldn't joke around about marrying her anymore because the next time I asked, it would be the one.

"No," she said. "Not that it doesn't sound appealing, but remember, I have a makeover to tackle. And you said something about getting a new dress. Love the idea. I'm looking forward to our first date."

"If this place sells sooner than later, we should look for a townhouse in the meantime. Somewhere that requires no elevator when we wanna go for a stroll, and the car is

parked in front instead of a concrete basement underground. And a place which isn't downtown. I'm still
working remotely, and you'll be on maternity leave for
quite some time, so neither of us will have to commute
morning and night. What do you think?"

"I love it. Our own place. Starting afresh. We, the
urban folks, living in the suburbs. If you had told me I
would do so last year, I'd have never believed you. Look at
us. Becoming so mature."

I lowered her down to her feet. "I'll ask Elisa if she can
come up with a few listings. We could rent. Until we figure
out our next step."

Addison lifted herself onto her tiptoes to kiss my lips.
"I'm supposed to have lunch with her next week. You
could join us, and we could go over options."

"And gate-crash your girls' time? Nah."

"No big deal. Think about it."

Addison and Elisa had become close friends since she
moved in with me. They worked a block away from each
other and often met for lunch.

My woman disappeared into the bedroom, swaying her
hips, aware of how crazy it made me. The night we met,
later in that bar in Nashville, she kept doing it and
laughing every time she glanced at my erection that my
trousers couldn't conceal. Addison Wilde was a temptress.
My temptress.

———

Around six, I knocked on the door with a hint of
nervousness and loads of exhilaration. First date meant
chivalry and excitement, and I relished the jitters filling my
stomach as I waited for the woman I loved to let me in.
The dress we chose was royal-blue, knee length, hugging

all her pregnancy curves, and offering a glimpse at her cleavage. Perfect. Just like the woman wearing it.

The door opened, and I held my breath.

"Ta-da!"

"Wow. Wilde. Wow. I'm speechless." My gaze traced the length of her. Black ballet shoes, a delicate gold bracelet around her wrist, and that blue Otto & Newhouse dress that emphasized the ocean color of her eyes. One I convinced her to try on as it reminded me of the night we toured Atlanta together on scooters. My eyes stopped their ascent at her head. I blinked, unable to speak.

"Oh, you don't like it?" she asked, uncertainty taking over her features.

"You're kidding, right? I love it. A lot. You look fierce. You can't look this hot and expect me to keep my hands to myself all night. Unless torturing me was your plan all along. In that case, take me hostage right now; make me your prisoner."

Her clear laughter warmed my insides.

"Turn around. Let me see you," I ordered, my voice husky. Addison executed herself. "Fuck, how can we go out now? I want all of you to myself. All those fuckers are gonna check you out."

She smirked, pride and love pouring out from her.

"You're doing this on purpose because you enjoy the effect you have on me. How are you the only one who can bring me to my knees?"

Her tongue swept her painted lips. That devilish-looking woman was a maneater, and I wished nothing more than to be her first and last course. "I might take extra pleasure in watching you lose your mind."

I stood there, admiring the woman about to become the mother of my child.

"You did it yourself?"

"Yeah. Told ya my mother owns a beauty salon. I've learned a few tricks over the years."

Unable to resist any longer, I captured her mouth, one hand sliding into her shorter mane. The other one taking a handful of her ass. Goodbye, long blonde locks. Addison now wore her hair in a mid-length bob with bangs. And she looked gorgeous and sexy. And I promised myself I'd tell her all night. And for the rest of my life.

"Where are we going?" she asked as I circled my SUV to open her door.

"Dynasty. Got us a backroom booth. And there's a pianist playing tonight. Dark room. Dim lights. And a date looking like a queen."

All night, we ate, chatted, and laughed like we always did. Addison had a new peacefulness about her since this morning. And nothing could express how thankful I was for having my best friend, and the woman I was unable to resist, in my life full-time. All of her. Plus, being granted every delectable inch of her without restriction anymore.

We were almost done with our main course when her hands slithered up my thigh. Cupping my junk under the table, she leaned to the side, her lips millimeters away from my ear. "See, I know it's a first date and everything, but I'm pregnant and full of naughty hormones, so it gives me the right to put out tonight."

"Agreed," I whispered, breathing fast, her hand rubbing my pulsing hard-on, toying with my mind as I focused on not coming in my pants.

She pressed her breasts against my ribs. "And I was thinking, we could play a little game. You look so damn hot and smell divine, it would be a shame to see all that go to waste. Or to push away the unavoidable."

"Yes," I panted. "Anything for you, sweetheart."

"Remember that night when you made me come under

the table in front of our friends? I kept my cool, trying to act unaffected, and it worked. For the most part."

Her hand turned greedy, and I tried breathing at a normal pace.

A traitorous smile peeked through my lips at the thought of Carter Hills calling us out on that night. "I do."

"See, you have an advantage tonight. Nobody is sitting at the table with us. There's music playing, and it's dark. Let's see if you can come before the server takes our dessert orders, okay?"

I caught a breath when she unbuckled my belt and unbuttoned my trousers and her hand slipped inside my boxer briefs to fist my dick.

She worked me a little, and I closed my eyes, trying to shoot oxygen into my brain. The pad of her thumb rubbed the tip, and I squirmed with a groan, my ass buckling from the seat.

"Two can play this game, big guy. How well can you hide the fact I'm about to bring you to your knees?"

"Wilde, you should be the one on your knees right now," I said through clenched teeth.

"Later, Tuck. This game isn't over yet. If you win, you'll be able to ask anything from me."

I planted my fork in my steak with more force than necessary, stabbing the poor piece of meat. Even chewing became painstaking as she pumped me faster under the table, eating her chicken salad next to me as if nothing was happening. As if I wasn't about to explode all over myself.

My willpower, no, my sanity, only held by a flimsy thread.

"How are you doing, Tuck?" Addison gave me a side glance, and the animalistic beast in me begged to unleash himself, flip her over the table, yank her panties down, and ram into her until the next morning.

I inhaled, flexing and unflexing my fingers at my side. "Great. No idea what you're talking about."

She moved closer, her tongue tasting the flesh of my neck. I loosened my tie, suffocating with need.

"Getting bothered, Tuck?"

"Nah. Just hot in here. Wanna go for a walk and ditch dessert?"

Her smirk reached her eyes. And mischievousness filled them in the low light of the restaurant.

"Never threaten a pregnant woman to forfeit dessert." Her squeeze on me intensified.

"Jesus, we should go."

"Are you forfeiting? If you do, I win. The last time we made a bet, it had an unexpected repercussion." She gestured to her abdomen. "And I believe I won."

My hand curled around her neck, and I crashed my lips on hers, hungry and unable to resist her any longer. "I won," I murmured against her lips. "I got the girl, didn't I?"

Addison moved to her feet and discarded her cloth napkin on the table. "Meet me in the restroom by the back door in two. I'm calling it quits tonight. You get a free pass. This time only, though. Don't get used to it." She winked, and it almost killed me on the spot.

Having Addison in my life meant living precariously, and as always, I was all in for the danger. For every wild side of her.

———

"If we accept this offer, we gotta move out within two weeks, is that it?" I asked, just to make sure I heard Elisa right.

"Yes. The offer is more than the asking price. Not sure

we'll get another one like this. You two can talk and decide if you'd like to move forward. We must give an answer by tomorrow at noon." She placed a stack of papers in front of us. "Go through it, sleep on it. I'll be in touch in the morning."

She left, and I sat back beside Addison at the table. "What do you think?" she asked, stars in her eyes. "It's incredible."

"Babe, I'm gonna make a counteroffer. Buy us more time. You're seven months pregnant. No way are we moving so soon."

She rose to her feet and straddled me, her fingers toying in my hair and massaging my scalp. "Tuck, you're not refusing this. Unless you've changed your mind and wanna stay here, which I don't mind, or there's something else that bothers you about their offer. Otherwise, don't refuse because of me. And before you suggest a moving company, I'd like for us to do this together. Pack boxes. Put labels on them. Do normal couple-moving-in-together stuff. The movers can take care of the heavy lifting because obviously, I won't be able to do it. But we've already talked about it. I wanna set up the nursery. Paint the walls, assemble that crib, and buy tiny clothes. Together. Start this new chapter."

I rubbed my palms over my face, trying to be cool-headed about all of this and think without involving my emotions.

"If we do this, and I said *if*, you're decreasing your weekly work hours. No more overtime. A move is tiring. You need rest. The doctor warned you. You look like you're about to pop any minute, and you still have eight weeks to go. I'm serious, Wilde."

She leaned in to kiss my lips. "I love it when you wanna make sure I'm safe and sound." With a hand caressing her belly, she stared at me. In the way I could never get enough of. "Do you wanna sell this place?"

"I do."

"Then it's settled. Everything will work out how it's supposed to. Trust life."

"I trust you."

"Well, it's even better," she said, "because I want what's best for us. Let's call Elisa back. You know that townhouse close to where she lives? I can see us living there for a little while. It even has a backyard and a park across the street."

I picked up my phone and dialed my friend.

Addison's hands traveled under my shirt while I tried to have a coherent discussion with Elisa, her fingers tracing the ridges of my stomach. Her sensual perusal of my body electrified all my nerve endings. Her tongue teased the corner of my lips. My body powered on at the sensations traveling through me.

Dropping to her knees, Addison unbuttoned my pants, and her hand reached into my boxer briefs. Before I could stop her, she licked the length of my dick and purred as she wrapped her lips around it. *Jesus fucking Christ.* I tilted my head back, struggling with my breaths and my words. She worked me faster, her tongue and hands busy on me, and I offered her a pointed look as I asked Elisa to repeat what she said for the third time.

"Fuck, Wilde," I mouthed.

She dug her fingernails into the back of my thighs and gave me that devilish look I always failed to resist. When she sucked on me faster, the bobbing of her head drove me insane. And toward my release.

I hung up and stopped Addison with a hand. "Wilde, it's a very dangerous game you're playing right now."

"You love it when I play dirty," she whispered before moving to her feet and licking the length of my chest, followed by the side of my face, and offering me a sheepish grin. Standing up, she hurried away from me. Jumping over the couch, I caught her and enveloped her in my arms, and we tumbled onto the piece of furniture in a mess of tangled limbs, my body shielding hers to soften the deliberate fall.

Shifting position, I caged Addison underneath me, teasing her with the delicate pressure of my mouth on hers. Her tongue darted out to entice mine, but I leaned back.

"Tell me what you want?" I asked, panting as if I had just run ten miles.

"You."

Before I could add anything, she tore my shirt open, and buttons flew around us.

"Hey. I liked that shirt."

"With the sale of your condo, you'll be able to afford a new one." She winked. Devil. Not missing a beat, I used both hands to rip her sweater from the front.

"Hey. I loved that sweater."

I winked. "With the sale of the condo, I'll buy you a dozen more like this one."

Her round, perky breasts allured me, and I balanced over her, ready to indulge in them.

Her curious hands ventured under the ripped fabric over my chest, and she squeezed my nipples. "Has someone ever told you that you have great nipples?" she asked, her voice laced with lust.

"A woman. Once. And she seems to have some rip-up buttons fetishism. I always end up naked when she's around."

"Oh, what a vixen she must be."

Her eyes were a dark sea of blue now.

Her cheeks bore a light flush.

I attacked her mouth. "You have no idea."

Her fist returned to my dick, and she pumped me with world-shattering strokes.

A knock on the door startled us before we got too far lost in each other.

Addison frowned, and I soothed the wrinkle between her eyes with the pad of my finger.

"Elisa," I forced out. In our little make-out session, I totally forgot I had called her back.

Another knock.

Forcing ourselves apart, I went to open the door, thinking Addison had retreated to the bedroom to change. But Elisa walked in on us.

"What happened to you guys? It looks like you've been mauled in the fifteen minutes I was gone. Am I in the right apartment?" She shook her head. "Never mind."

"Give us a minute," I said.

I led my woman to our bedroom and pushed her against the closed door after I kicked it shut. "When we're done here, I'll make you pay for ruining my favorite shirt." I kissed her harder, and she became putty in my hands, kissing me back with fierceness.

Plunging my hand behind the elastic band of her jeans, I ran one finger against her center, rubbing it back and forth just to monkey around with her composure.

With hurried movements, I slid her pants and panties down her legs, then freed my pulsing dick.

A gasp left her mouth. In one slow thrust, I entered her, not a care in the world about our guest waiting in the kitchen.

She rolled her hips, tightening her grip on me.

My teeth nibbled the length of her throat as she tilted her head, her back arching, her swollen breasts begging to be cared for.

I bent down to lick the swell of the skin overflowing from the lacy cups.

Once I got her ready and needy, I pulled out.

"Tuck, no," she whined. "Give it to me."

"It's a promise, sweetheart. To finish you later. Give me twenty minutes and you'll be screaming my name so loud people on the rooftop will wish they were you, or they will call the cops on us."

She strangled my cock with her hand and used just enough force to get me to submit to all her wishes.

"Good boy. You better deliver."

I pressed my mouth to hers one last time before breaking apart. "I will."

Rummaging through my closet, I called, "Have you seen my gray shirt?"

"It's in the hamper of clean laundry."

I shook my head. "Wilde, how many times do I have to say this? My suits and dress shirts, dry cleaning. I love it when they're pressed and ready to wear, not wrinkled balls."

A new surge of desire pulsed through me as I watched her in nothing but her jeans and that suggestive bra.

"Oops. Tuck, you're too high-maintenance. You must learn to let it go. Laundry is laundry."

I sighed and picked a simple T-shirt from a drawer. "I like my clothes a certain way."

"And your housekeeping. Your fridge. Your car. This baby of ours won't care if your couch is leather or the rug is an import that cost a pretty penny when it throws up or spills milk. One day, you'll thank me for helping you be less stuck-up."

"Stuck-up? Me?"

She kissed me.

"Yes. But you're getting better at it. I still have faith in your abilities."

From the moment we met, I always knew Addison Wilde would be the end of me.

Now dressed and ready to move forward with our life, we joined Elisa in the kitchen perched over that stack of papers she left earlier.

Me, stuck-up? Nah.

————

Two weeks later, we were waiting for our stuff to be delivered to our new house—well, our temporary house a twenty-minute drive from the city—finishing the second coat of soft moss-green paint on the walls of the nursery. As predicted, moving had been rushed and exhausting, but now that my bachelor lifestyle was officially behind me, I felt lighter than I had before.

"We never really chose names," I said, stepping back to admire the work.

My woman had on a denim overall, with no shirt underneath, because I forced that new rule after she compelled me to work shirtless, a bandana tied around her head, her ocean-blue eyes vibrating as she scanned the room.

"I thought we did. That time in Green Mountain. Have you changed your mind?"

"No."

"Me neither. See, settled. Super easy." She paused and turned to face me, her blinding smile contagious. "We did it. I'm proud of us."

Before I could stop the words from pouring out, I got down on one knee and said, "Marry me. I'll never love anyone else the way I love you."

I braced myself for the words that always followed my proposal in the past. But this time, I hoped it'd be the right one. I felt it in the marrow of my bones. I really wanted Addison to be my wife.

"Tuck—"

My heart free-fell down my chest while she stared at me with a mix of surprise and something unknown in her eyes.

34

ADDISON

I blinked, my heart racing in my chest as the words I'd been waiting to hear for a while rushed out. Like a complete idiot, I stood there, frozen, trying to process everything they implied.

Tucker's eyebrows bunched together, and the fear that crippled his expression shattered me. Hurrying in his direction, I kneeled—well, more like slouched—on the floor before him and circled his neck. "Yes. A thousand times, yes."

My lips danced against his.

"You sure? Last time you said yes, you freaked out afterward and ran away."

I brushed the side of his face, leaving a blotch of green paint on his dark skin.

"No more running away ever again. You're stuck with me now. For better or worse." I kissed his chin, his jaw, the corner of his mouth. "Tucker Philips, I wanna be your wife. Let's stick to the original plan."

"Which means?"

"You, me, our closest friends, Vegas. And a party once the baby is born."

"Jesus, I love you so much. Once this little nugget comes out of the oven, we'll set a date."

"Oh geez, are you trying your hands at *poetry* now?"

"Maybe."

I exploded in a train of giggles, which ended in a contraction. "Forget it. Hope poetry isn't your mysterious project. With practice, you'll get better. Or not."

"No offense taken. I'll forgive you. Someday."

Tucker plunged forward, his tongue cherishing mine in luscious strokes, his hands all over me.

"I wanna marry you now," I whispered. "Don't you think we've waited long enough. No doubt, you're the one for me. I've known it the first time I laid my eyes on you. And after you sang that song to me, I was a goner. Big time."

"And yet you resisted for months."

"You can't deny I was worth the chase," I said in a teasing tone. "It would have been boring had I made it too easy on you. Gotta keep up with my rep."

"Woman, you're the most perfect headcase I've ever met. Lucky for me, you're my headcase. Are we really getting married?"

"Yes. And we're not waiting until Mini-Tucker is born. We're a family. Let's make it official."

The next morning, we were having breakfast when I surprised my man with two plane tickets to Vegas. He rounded the table to secure his arms around me, one palm splayed over my middle, the same manner he did every day, his chin propped in the crook of my shoulder. Our little one was having a blast in there, kicking and stretching.

"Oh, so you two have been planning this nuptial behind my back?"

I grinned. So big it hurt my cheeks. "Yeah. No. Not really. Remember, I had a debt to pay."

Tucker remained silent, waiting for me to explain.

"Vegas. Our bet in Nashville. I thought neither of us actually won, but a while back, you said you did. In all honesty, you're the only one who brought a girl back to the hotel that night. And since you had to wait months for me to admit my feelings to you, I'm awarding you the win. This time only, though. Don't get used to me accepting defeat so easily. I'm usually a much-tougher player. Today, this is me paying my dues. Two tickets. Presidential suite with a view of the Strip. Flight is tomorrow morning. If you agree to elope, Nick and Dahlia will join us to be our witnesses."

Tucker blinked, holding my hands in his. "Yes." He pushed my hair back and bent forward to kiss me but stopped midway. "Question. Are you sure it's safe for you to fly?" he asked.

"I called Dr. Pettyfer two days ago. Said everything looked good at the last check-up and as long as it was a short flight, he wouldn't object, even less, if it was to make an honest man out of ya."

"Wilde, you secretive woman, you planned this. When I asked you yesterday—"

"I had already planned to ask you this morning. You just beat me to it."

"Sorry I ruined your proposal."

I flicked my wrist. "Even though I looked forward to asking you, I love the idea you did it first. I've been thinking about it for a long time. Finally got the balls to reach for one of my dreams."

His mouth descended on mine, tasting my lips. "I love

it." He trailed kisses along my jaw and down my throat. Shivers passed through me. Arching my back, I gave him the unspoken agreement to play my body the way he wanted to. "Let's reward you with an orgasm, my second-place prize offering, and then we'll go dress shopping. You're going to be the most beautiful bride ever."

His lips returned to mine, and I shook my head against his mouth. "No. The groom isn't allowed to see the bride before the wedding day. It's bad luck."

"Tell me you don't believe in that shit?"

"Nah, but it's still fun to get you worked up over what I'll wear. Dahlia and Nick arrive tonight. She's bringing a few options from her store. We'll spend the evening at her hotel, so she can make some adjustments."

Tucker grabbed my ass cheeks, and I purred, unable to resist him as I rubbed myself against him.

"That's perfect. Nick will be able to help me put together the last details of the nursery. In case you go into labor sooner than later, it will all be ready tonight."

"Who knew talking crib and rocking chair could get me soaking wet?"

His fingers ventured under the straps of my overall, but I pushed them away.

"Not so fast. Wedding night, Tuck. No sex until then."

"Jesus, now I'm happy we're getting married tomorrow. Not tasting you until you're officially mine is kind of a big turn on."

I kissed him, deepening the connection, as I fastened my arms around him. "Wilde, there's something missing in that genius plan of yours?"

"What?"

He released me and left the room, only to come back two minutes later.

Dropping on one knee, he opened a white velvet box

showing me two matching pink-gold bands. I always knew pink was his favorite color. "Addison Wilde, would you marry me tomorrow?"

I cupped my mouth, tears flowing down my cheeks while I nodded. "Yes, I will."

———

I was saving my Mini-Wilde newest design when a contraction hit me. I exhaled and pressed each side of my thirty-eight-week baby belly with my palms, rubbing the taut skin, trying to dissipate the discomfort. When I met with my ob-gyn two days ago, he said he believed I wouldn't make it to forty weeks. Mini-Tucker already weighed over nine pounds, and I looked like I could explode at any time if someone poked my stomach. Yes, I had gotten that big. And I blamed my husband for all of it. Every time I went out, people still asked me at least once a week if I was carrying twins. Or triplets. The new story of my life.

"If you could please stay put for a few more hours," I told my unborn child, caressing my baby protuberance in a protective manner. "If I want this onesies collection to be a success, I gotta finish it before you decide it's time for you to get out. Or I won't be able to order samples for you to show them off on time. Daddy asked for one of each in all available sizes."

My baby kicked, the imprint of his feet, elbows, or knees tenting my skin. I pushed it, and he pushed back, both of us relishing our little private game. Soon, it would be a different one, and I felt more ready each day for this new challenge.

A mix of excitement and anticipation to meet this little

human that Tucker and I created together danced in me every minute of each day.

On my feet, I printed my newest design with the special printer my husband got me—I still couldn't believe we were married—and plugged in the iron press to heat it up, ready to see how it would look in real life on a blank onesie I bought for our baby. *A Little Wild* written in colorful letters looked amazing on the tiny piece of cotton fabric. I covered my stomach with it.

"This one is yours. The first tangible item of my baby collection." Pride filled my heart, and flutters invaded all my senses.

I moved to return to my seat when another contraction hit me. Stronger and longer than I'd ever felt before. Bent forward, I balanced my weight with one hand propped on my desk and another massaging my tense belly.

"Guess you love it," I said through gritted teeth as I calmed my breathing. "There are nicer ways to show me your approval, you know?" The tension left, and I went back to work. But soon, another contraction hit me. Then another.

I swallowed the pain and called out, "Tuck—" Okay, they were closer and closer in time. "Tuck," I screamed again.

He came running, storming into the room and squatting between my legs. "What's wrong?" His palms closed around our baby in a maternal gesture. "Mini-Wilde giving you trouble?"

"I think it's time," I said.

He watched me with furrowed brows. "For what?"

"This baby wants to come out. Now." Another contraction.

"For how long have you been having those?" he asked once it relaxed.

"Since yesterday, but they were far apart, and I thought they were just the fake ones. But now they're less than ten minutes apart, and they fucking hurt."

"Why didn't you say something?" He pushed my hair back and kissed my forehead. "Let me get your stuff, then I'll come for you. Can you wait for me for a minute or two?"

I nodded. Tears pooled in my eyes. *I am going to be a mama.* Reality crashed into me, and for a second, I forgot how to breathe on my own. This was the most exhilarating and scariest thing I'd ever done. I knew the endgame, but nothing about all the suffering and pain to get there.

Tucker wiped my teary eyes. "Hey, I've got you. We'll do this together. You're the strongest woman I know. Everything will be all right. I promise."

He jumped to his feet, and I grabbed his hand before he could walk away.

"Thank you. I can't do this without you. You're my rock, Tucker Philips. I love you."

"You're my inspiration, Addison Wilde. I love you so much right now." A wide, ridiculous smile painted his face.

"Just right now?" I teased.

"Nah. Always and forever."

———

After the nurse checked if I was dilated enough, the doctor told me to get ready. Our baby would come within the next few hours. I watched Tucker watching me with a too-large-for-his-face grin.

"Wilde, you've given me things in life I never would have gotten anywhere else. A family. You've made me a husband, and now a father. You showed me how to love. How to trust someone even if it meant risking my heart because the endgame could be worth it. I'll never be able to thank you enough. All I can say is that I love you so freaking much."

He kissed me before helping me change into a blue hospital gown.

He snapped a picture with his phone. "This is the last mile. The finish line. And you look beautiful."

"Tell me that later when I'm all sweaty, my hair disheveled, and ready to murder someone."

"Deal."

The doctor came back to check on me for the umpteenth time almost eight hours later. "The effacement is slower than what we expected. Even for a firstborn," he said, throwing his latex gloves into the nearest trash can after he examined my cervix.

"What does that mean?" my husband asked, worry coating his tone, his hand holding mine with a strangling grip.

"The baby is large," the doctor said, scanning Tucker from head to toes. "Let's say it doesn't surprise us, but your contractions aren't strong enough, and your cervix hasn't dilated as it should have. Before we give you drugs to speed up the dilatation and give strength to the contractions, I'd like you to walk for at least the next hour. Or until your condition changes. At this stage, I can't send you back home, and it's too early to be talking about C-section."

Fears tangled around my heart. But exhaustion made it hard for me to process all his words.

"I'm so tired. How can those contractions not be strong enough? They hurt so bad."

"It happens. Let's just do this, and we'll reassess the situation afterward. There are other things we can try. As long as the baby's vitals are good, there's no reason to worry or expedite the delivery."

"Okay," I agree, too weak to argue.

Tucker helped me to my feet, and after I went to the bathroom to empty my bladder, he secured the hospital gown at the back. Knitting our fingers together, he led me out of the room.

Tears rolled silently down my cheeks.

"Hey Wilde, it will be all right, you hear me? It happens a lot. I asked the nurse while you were in the bathroom."

I nodded, too exhausted to even stop the flood blinding my vision.

For the next sixty minutes, we paced the hospital hallways, only pausing when a contraction hit me. Each time, Tucker massaged my lower back, easing the pain.

An older woman stopped us as we passed the room where family members waited for their loved ones to give birth.

"Oh, lucky you, you're expecting multiple. Are they twins or triplets?"

A new surge of tears drowned my eyes as I pivoted to bury my face in Tucker's chest and broke into sobs. I blocked the conversation while Tucker explained to her there was only one baby in there.

"I'm so fat. I don't wanna be pregnant anymore. Can you get this baby out? My entire body hurts. I'm so sleepy I could fall asleep anywhere if it weren't for those damn contractions ripping my belly in two."

My husband's comforting hands rubbed circles over my back.

"Shhh, it's fine, sweetheart. I'm right here with you. I know I can't do a lot, but I'm not leaving your side."

As if I got stung, my head jerked up. "No, it's not fine. How can it be? We fucked while we were both wasted, and I took the morning-after pill, yet this baby found a way to stick in there. What are the chances? We're either the luckiest or the unluckiest people on Earth. I took the fucking pill, and it still decided to stay. Now I look like a whale, and people keep reminding me how fat I am. And to just fuck it out a tad more, this baby has now decided it won't come out."

"Addison," he said in the softest voice he could manage. He rarely called me by my first name, only when he was being emotional. Or overwhelmed. "You're neither fat nor a whale, you're pregnant. And that weight won't stay on forever. We already discussed it. And the doctor told you to not worry about it. I know it must be hard, but even if you can't see it, I'm telling you, *you are* beautiful. Take my words for it. I'd never lie to you."

I pressed my face between his pecs and let his words sink in.

"We'll get that baby out today. Or tonight. We're not going home without our little one." He lowered down before me in the hospital hallway, pressing both palms to my belly. "Baby, I love you. You know I do, but let's come out. I wanna meet you. Give your mama a break. Do we have a deal?"

As if the baby could hear him, it kicked, followed by another contraction.

Tucker returned to his feet and kneaded the tension in my back. "You walked long enough. Let's see what the doctor thinks." His strong arm held me up against him, supporting me, while we returned to the room.

In bed, I surfed between different conscious states, barely registering the nurse strapping the fetal monitor back around me and reading my pressure.

"The heartbeat is strong," she told me, rearranging the pillows under my head and the covers around me. "You're doing great. Sleep while you can. I'll be right here if you need me."

She exchanged a few words with Tucker, but my drowsy state couldn't make up their conversation.

Every two or three minutes, the contractions felt like lightnings ripping me apart, but in-between, I found some rest.

Tucker woke me up with kisses peppered on my forehead and soft caresses over my tense abdomen. "Wilde, the doctor gotta check you up now. Can you move to your back?"

I nodded, having a hard time escaping the dreams I lost myself in.

He helped me flip around and intertwined his fingers with mine.

"Okay, here's the thing," the doctor said, a somber expression drawn on his face. "We don't want you or the baby to exhaust yourselves too much, but I think we should try the medication before deciding for an emergency C-section. I know you're against the epidural and you asked for a natural birth as much as possible, but this is the next logical step. I must warn you those contractions will hurt. They'll be closer in time and stronger."

"Okay," I said, the enthusiasm in my words missing.

"Both vitals are good. I'm confident we can get that full dilatation. If there's no progress within a few hours, we'll reevaluate your options. For now, considering the baby's size and the width of your pelvis, we'll deem you a high-risk pregnancy. It's not uncommon, nothing to be alarmed about. We'll just monitor you more closely. Do you have any questions?"

I shook my head, unable to comprehend what he said or the gravity of the situation, my brain not registering any of it.

Tucker's lips descended on my forehead. "I'll be right back." Witnessing the pained turn of his lips sent zings of discomfort through me. Tucker would sort it out. Whatever it was, he'd make sure neither I nor the baby would get hurt.

I nodded and let go of his hand when the space between us increased and our fingers couldn't touch anymore.

We'd been here for over twenty-eight hours when I gave the last push, almost fainting from exhaustion. Tucker smiled through his tears. I forgot all about my sleepless nights, the rocky ride of the last day to get to this moment, my sore inner thighs, and everything else when the doctor handed him our son after my husband cut the umbilical cord. Tucker placed him in my arms, and the sound of my baby's first cry evoked a primal need to protect him deep in my core.

Yeah, I'd be a tigress mama. An emotional surge I had no control over whirled inside me, and I cried like I hadn't done in a long time as I counted his toes and fingers. Twenty. The count was good.

"All there," I croaked.

My own tears flooded down my face.

Tucker and I'd created this little human being together.

"Good job, mama," the nurse said, her hands cupping her heart. "You did amazingly well."

My gaze never left the small bundle lodged in my arms while my finger stroked his cheek.

My tears came from pure and raw happiness. From a joy I had no idea my heart could contain. The look on my husband's face as his eyes ping-ponged between me and our baby boy took my breath away. It broke me. And revived me. And I knew, at that instant, everything would be okay as long as we were doing it together.

I pushed the top of my gown down, and the nurse positioned the baby, only dressed in a white knitted hat, his dark skin rosy and his eyes round, on my bare skin.

Tucker leaned in to kiss me. "I'm so proud of you, sweetheart. He's perfect. And he has your eyes. You did great. Today sealed the deal. You're definitely the strongest woman I know." Yes, our baby was indeed perfect. Tanned skin, dark hair, and blue eyes.

"I love Lucas," I said, deciding on the name Tucker liked the most.

"No. He's a Jamieson. A Southern soul. You were right."

"You sure?" I asked, drying my wet eyes with my fingers, the tab still running.

He bobbed his head fast. "Jamieson Nicholas Philips. It sounds fierce. And badass. Just like you."

35

ADDISON

We secured tiny Jamieson in his car seat. Tucker adjusted the knitted cap over his head and the pacifier in his mouth that he sucked like his life depended on it. Watching them, my eyes leaking with still more tears, I breathed out a nervous puff of air. The moment we left the parking lot of the hospital, I would be on my own, responsible for most of the caring of our child. Tucker was present, but he wouldn't understand all that I was going through, the disconnection that had permeated my entire being.

My emotions were a tangled web growing inside me. In the hospital, every time I held him, Jamieson wouldn't stop crying, whereas with Tucker, his tears would dry up in a second. A nurse had nicknamed him the baby whisperer. And the entire staff agreed. How was I supposed to take care of someone who couldn't find his comfort with me? My baby spent nine months in my womb, and it was like he couldn't recognize me or the intimate link we shared. My husband and the nursing staff said it would get better.

Nobody understood the feeling of failure that washed through me every second I was alone with my child.

"You wanna sit beside him at the back?" Tucker asked, pointing to the open car door with his chin.

"No. I'll sit in the passenger seat," I replied in a thready voice, my eyes welling. "Next to you."

"Wilde, are you okay?" he asked with a frown. He wiped the drop of water rolling down my cheek. "What's wrong?"

"I-I don't know. It all just seems like too much." I waved my hands before me. "All this... I can't explain. I just feel like crying. My nerves are scraped raw. Everything sounds like a big deal right now."

Tucker pulled me into his arms, strong and powerful, as if he could shield me from any harm. "Sweetheart, what you went through is fucking hard. You're exhausted, and you've barely slept in three days. Let's go home, and I'll put you two to bed so you can recover and find your footing. It'll be easier with a rested mind to deal with all of it. Lean on me. I'll always catch you. Let me play nurse for the day."

I nodded against his chest, the leak in my eyes unstoppable.

My husband's comforting hand linked with mine as he drove us home, to our new life as a family.

My head pressed against the window, and I stared through it without registering anything. Maybe the rest would help me. A surge of chaotic emotions washed over me, and the tears I drained out turned into heart-wrenching sobs.

He stopped the car by the side of the road and pulled me to him. "Shhh, Addison. Don't worry. We'll find our balance." Could he read my mind? "The doctor wasn't joking when he said it was a difficult delivery. But you did good. Amazing, in fact. It's okay to be emotional. Anybody would be in this state." He kissed my temple. "Wanna go home?"

I nodded against his chest.

His lips lingered on the top of my head until I calmed down a little.

For the rest of the drive, his squeeze on my hand never faltered, and he brought our joined hands to his lips, kissing my knuckles.

"We will be okay. Don't ever doubt it."

"I know," I said, sweeping the back of my hand under my runny nose. "I love you."

"I love you so much I'm not sure my heart can contain it all." We parked in the driveway, and he turned to me before opening the door. "Ready?"

"I think."

Tucker exited the truck and circled it to help me out. His arms sheltered me. "Sleep a while once we get in. Husband's orders." My head rested in the crook of his neck. "We'll do great, Wilde. I promise."

I nodded, the weight of the world heavy on my shoulders.

When we stepped inside our home, everything looked different. So foreign. Perhaps Tucker was right, and sleeping would erase the heaviness inside of me. When we left for the hospital a few days ago, excitement had bubbled inside me. And I was ecstatic at the idea of coming back as a family of three. Right now, I couldn't feel those sparkles of joy. I dragged a hand over my face, my eyes swollen with the tears I did not shed.

Tucker walked behind me as I stopped in the doorway of the nursery, one arm winding around my waist and his cheek pressing to mine after he lowered the car seat with Jamieson at our feet. "We did it, Wilde. I can't wait to introduce him to his room, to everything we are."

I scanned the space we poured so much of our hearts into. The one we decorated with love. And anticipation. Right at this instant, coils of fear wrapped themselves around me. As if walking into the nursery would mark the end of me and all that I was. The room felt like my personal prison. One that I will never be allowed to leave. My throat worked hard, swallowing the strictures of unease lodged there. The abyss I was falling into was growing bigger by the second.

As if on cue, Jamieson started wailing, and I shut my lids, hating the idea I would have to breastfeed again so soon. I had just done that before leaving the hospital.

A battle rose in me.

Saved. That was the only word my brain came up with. My stance relaxed, and I breathed out my relief that I wouldn't have to step into the nursery. Not today. Because we agreed that, for now, I would breastfeed in our bed.

"Lunch time," Tucker said, his voice teasing. "Come on, sweetheart. Let's open the baby buffet," he joked, without realizing how much his words grated on me. Maybe he should feed him. Then he would know what I went through. I shook out my thoughts and with heavy steps, followed him to our bedroom, my resentment building in my chest at the idea of my nipples being sucked dry until I could scream in agony.

I knew I was responsible for feeding our son, but nothing could describe the hour of torment. All I wished for was to be away from here.

I forfeited the idea of sleeping until the next day, and going through the motions, I lay on my side on our bed. Tucker placed the baby in front of me while I unhooked my bra so Jamieson could suckle on my sensitive nipples.

The pain when he latched on sent a chill through me. I gritted my teeth, trying my best to just send my thoughts on a journey far from here, to evade my own mind. And body. Tucker, with a proud smile, lay behind our son, one protective hand on my hip bone, showing me, in the simple gesture, just how much he cared for us and how involved he would be in the entire process.

I blinked away the tears burning the back of my eyeballs. Was this how motherhood would be? Hurtful. So far, since my contractions started, nothing had been a pleasant experience. The labor had been long and filled with intense pain. Every moment in the hospital had been agony. And even at home, the ghost of the events haunted me. The nurses told me I would forget all those excruciating incidents once I held my baby. They lied. Nothing made the pain go away. Well, it did, for a few hours, only to return with a vengeance once some of the ecstasy settled down.

I sighed and brought my attention to the present, when I had to switch breasts so that Jamieson could latch onto my other nipple. An hour later, I studied the men in my life, Tucker looking at the tiny bundle in his arms in awe, as he patted his back and burped him. Why was his awe not directed toward me? I had fed him, raking over the coals of fire with every suckle. I was nowhere present in the world that was inhabited by father and son.

Something snapped apart in the depths of me. A fissure, that I never knew existed, cracked my heart in two. Instead of a bottomless outpouring of love at their bond, my emotions evaporated. I felt nothing. It felt as if I was standing there in front of them, but neither could see me. They appeared to be a thousand miles away. Far from me. Or was it I who had moved away? My mind was a fuzzy fog I couldn't breach to go back to my physical body.

For an instant, I wished I could disappear. That I could just quit. And find solace elsewhere. How could my mind conjure these thoughts? I was supposed to be overjoyed. Ecstatic. I was loved and had a family of my own. One I had wished for so many times in the past. Still, no joy passed through the barrier of my heart. Even though I tried, I couldn't find it in me to feel contentment.

Tucker turned to me, a dozing Jamieson nestled in the bent of his elbow, and kissed my cheek. "I'll put him to bed. Rest. I'll be right back to check on you."

Through my half-lidded eyes, the silhouette of him with our baby secured in his arms disappeared through the door. He looked like a natural. Like he was born to care for him. They belonged with each other. I was just the milk factory.

A stray notion crossed my brain and hooked on it. No matter what happened, Jamieson would be safe with Tucker. Nothing bad would ever happen to him. Besides, he preferred his daddy over me.

A pinch clamped my heart at the thought I couldn't see myself as being a part of this picture.

Fresh soul-crushing thoughts popped into my head.

Since the day I delivered, they appeared every now and then.

Tucker raising Jamieson on his own, me watching them but not being able to be near them, locked in a dimension I couldn't escape.

Tucker, living in a house with a picket fence and a swing set, laughing his heart out with another woman in his arms who looked nothing like me.

My life slipping away and nothing I could do to get a grip on it.

A fresh batch of hot tears brimmed in my eyes.

I suffocated, air burning my lungs on its way in.

Was I even awake, or was it all a dream?

Before I could come out of my distressing thoughts, muscular arms that always made me feel safe held me. Words were whispered into my ear. Kisses peppered on my temple.

This reality felt like a daydream. And so distant.

"Wilde? Wilde—"

Tucker talked to me, but I couldn't make out his words.

"Addison," he barked, worry lacing his tone, and I snapped out of my funk.

I blinked, trying to bring my mind back to the present.

Through a curtain of tears, my eyes drifted to his. His fingers pushed my hair away from my face.

"You okay, sweetheart? It's just a dream," he said, his voice lower now, protective, familiar. "No matter what it was, it wasn't real. I'm here."

I nodded, unable to speak, sobs clogging my throat.

"I'll stay here with you. Watch over you. Sleep now." He fumbled with the knob of the baby monitor by the side of the bed, molded his tall self to my body, and before long, sleep claimed me. Calmer this time.

When I woke up to Tucker caressing my cheek, I felt like he was pulling me out of some place far away. A dark cave I'd disappeared into and where I found my peace.

I opened my eyes to Tucker and Jamieson watching me. The smile on my husband's lips should have been burned in my memory forever, gladdening my heart. It was a mix of reverence and unconditional love. But for a reason I couldn't name or explain, I felt nothing. It was like it was intended for someone else than me.

"Hey you," he said. "Dinner is ready. You slept for over three hours. Our little man decided to be on his best behavior too to give his mama the rest she needed. But now he's hungry and about to suck on my tits if you don't feed him soon." My heart sank at his words. Feeding again?

The intoxicating smile that split his face in two didn't have the desired effect on me. Instead, it caused my being to quiver in fear.

I had to nurse the baby. Again.

Pushing my discomfort down, I pasted some sort of curve on my lips and placed my hand in Tucker's as he helped me to my feet.

I swallowed. "Gimme a minute. I'll join you in the living room," I said, my voice gravelly from sleep and shed tears.

He gave me a quick kiss, then his mouth lingered on Jamieson's fluffy hair.

"I love you, Wilde," he said.

"I love you too," I croaked on a rote.

In the en-suite bathroom, I locked the door and faced my reflection in the mirror. I didn't recognize the woman I saw. Dark circles around her eyes, engorged leaking breasts sensitive to touch, floppy skin over her stomach. There were no sparks in her eyes. No satisfactory grin shaping her lips. No sign of the woman I used to be. I buried my face in my palms.

What happened to me?

Jamieson cried, and I turned the tap on to drown out the sound.

Motherhood was worse than everything I thought it would be. My gaze returned to my abdomen. Unable to watch my reflection any longer, I pivoted until my back faced the mirror. No way would I ever be able to live with myself looking like I'd stepped into someone else's skin. A body that no longer felt mine.

Crumpling to the bathroom floor, I let out the tears I couldn't stop anymore.

"How will I do this?" I asked to no one. "How can I go through with this?"

Rummaging through Tucker's wardrobe after I dried my face, I chose a pair of sweatpants to hide my bulging stomach and thighs and one of his x-large T-shirt to cover the ugly nursing bra. Using his clothes to conceal my new unwelcomed form would do the trick until I found a better idea. If I didn't see the revolting bits, perhaps I could forget about them. For now.

Infusing fake happiness in myself and drawing my features into a neutral expression, I joined my men in the kitchen, Tucker rocking the fussy baby in the crook of his arm, singing to him.

In the doorway, I stared at them.

My baby had the best daddy I could ever ask for. That I was certain about.

But where was my place in all of this?

Feeling bad about the dreadful thoughts my mind had conjured, I chased my uneasiness away and looped my arms around him, praying it would heal all my invisible scars.

———

I stood at the edge of the precipice, debating if I should jump, craving the freedom. Could I fly if I put my mind to it? The breeze swept my face, and the sun warmed my skin. It looked so peaceful down there. Silence. I could hear nothing but the sound of my own breathing. Calmness filled all my senses with peace. For afar, I could see the line of trees and the blue sky. Extending my arms around me, I greeted the freedom. Nothing could disrupt my happiness here. I was safe from any harm. Nature shone brighter here. Closing my eyes, I let the world around me imprint its beauty on all my cells. I had become the wind and the sun.

A murmur resonated from far away. Disrupting my peace. With my hands over my ears, I blocked the sound. I would let nothing get to me.

I glanced down and asked myself once again if I'd fly if I jumped.

My feet brought me closer to the edge. I bent down to get some momentum when soft lips sprinkled kisses over my cheek, and I woke up from my slumber. I wouldn't fly today.

"Wilde, time to go. We have yours and Jamieson's first post-delivery appointment in two hours. I let you sleep for as long as I could, but if you wanna be ready in time, you should get up. It's almost ten, and our little one is famished."

My body felt like it'd been carved in concrete. Heavy and inflexible.

With my fists, I rubbed the sleep from my eyes.

Tucker lay beside me and kissed my neck.

I kissed him back, but listlessly. I couldn't seem to feel anything for him too. His requests reached my ears as orders or demands. For the last few days, I'd hoped the doctor would prescribe me magical pills that would give me back my energy and happy demeanor. The one I lost after giving birth. That he would tell me it'd get better. Because I missed the Addison who was ready to be a mother. Who worked her ass off to make sure everything would be perfect the day she welcomed her bundle of joy into this world.

"Can you feed him while I take a quick shower?" my husband asked, handing me our son.

"No." I took a step back, recoiling, twisting my arms behind me, but quickly recovered and shrugged.

"What?" Tucker watched me with a confused expression.

"Huh, sure. Never mind. Gimme a minute. I'll meet you in the living room."

"Don't you wanna do it in the nursery?"

I shook my head and pinched my lips to avoid grimacing. I couldn't walk into that room without feeling a clamp around my stomach and hyperventilating. Even though it'd been two weeks since I was back home, the feeling only grew instead of dissipating. I decided to avoid it, but I wouldn't tell Tucker because he would worry or ask questions, and I was in no state of mind to answer them because I couldn't explain whatever was going on in my own mind.

Pretending I had to get a glass of water, I shunned holding the baby for a little longer. Only once I was seated on the couch did I ask Tucker to bring him over.

With the baby set on a half donut-shaped nursing pillow pressed against my chest, I fed him. Even after two weeks of doing it every few hours, the entire thing still felt oddly uncomfortable and unnatural to me. My fingers itched to brush Jamieson's soft hair or rub his back, but I couldn't bring myself to touch him, to connect with him the way I should.

I kept my hands at a safe distance, close enough around him to make sure he wouldn't roll off the pillow, but not so close that I would have to feel his warmth under my palms.

In the doctor's office two hours later, I put my best face on and answered his questions with as much enthusiasm as I could muster. He wouldn't pin me as an unfit mother. Not today.

"I was just wondering," I said, inhaling deep to find the courage to open up about what bothered me. "Is it normal that I'm so tired all the time? Getting out of bed is hard. I mean, really hard. My energy reserves are low. And my emotions are all over the place."

"Addison, giving birth is not easy. It takes time for your body to adjust. You went through a long and difficult delivery. It can explain your symptoms. Some mothers need a little more time than others to recover. Postpartum is a personal journey. Don't be too harsh on yourself, just take it easy. As long as you rest and eat healthy, you'll be fine. And your husband seems like a hands-on father."

"He is."

"Then lean on him when it becomes too much. A lot of mothers put pressure on themselves and get overwhelmed because they can't do it all. Take it slow. Jamieson looks healthy and is growing according to charts. You guys are doing it right. Take some time off for yourself when it becomes overwhelming."

His words instilled flecks of hope in me.

It wasn't me, just my body taking longer to adapt to the schedule of feeding a newborn every couple of hours. For the first time, I believed I'd be all right. Time. I needed more time. Things would get easier.

In a better mood, I offered to grab food on our way back home.

"You look beautiful," Tucker said as we entered our home. "Let's put Jamieson to bed and spend some time together. I've missed having you to myself."

Tucker and I lived on an opposite schedule. And the few hours daily I was awake were to feed our son, so we never got a chance to be together anymore.

His hands looped around my waist, and the image of the loose skin there made me take a step back. I had no time to reel in the scowl on my face before my husband caught a sight of it.

"Wilde?" Tucker asked with a wrinkle between his brows. "What's wrong?"

I swallowed. "Nothing. Just hungry. Can we eat now?"

He scratched his nape. "You sure? You'd tell me if it was more than that, right?"

I forced a curl to my lips. "Yeah. Sure."

The deep-dish pizza didn't taste like usual. I forced a slice in, washing the small bites with water so Tucker wouldn't bitch about me not feeding myself enough.

I put the dishes in the kitchen sink, and when he attempted once more to wrap his arms around me, I decided to not pull away, before he got alarmed by my change of behavior and my refusal to indulge in the affection he provided me.

Minutes after we settled ourselves in the living room, my head dropped to his lap, and before I knew it, I fell asleep, wondering how long it would take for me to get my groove back. When I woke up hours later in our bed, I couldn't recall him putting me there.

The next week passed in a blur too.

It'd been three weeks since I gave birth and instead of feeling energized with every passing day, I felt more exhausted. Even showering now got harder every day.

I only woke up to nurse the baby or feed myself the bare minimum, my stomach in a knot almost full-time.

When I crashed after breakfast, I begged my dreams to take me to that cliff edge. Where I felt free. And at peace.

Slowly, each day, I drifted further away from my own life.

36

ADDISON

"Please make the baby stop crying," I asked out loud, trying to bury the annoying sound as I put my hands over my ears and retreated to our bedroom.

Tucker followed me close and grabbed my elbow to spin me around. Frustration blistered inside me when his grip forced me to look at him.

"Babe, he's twenty-six days old. He's not a robot. You can't just turn the switch off." I groaned something while he continued, "And he's not *the baby*. He's our son. Jamieson. He has a name. I don't understand how you can't say it. You chose it. And it fits him perfectly. Why do you call him by any other name under the sun but his?" He sighed. "Talk to me, Wilde."

I gestured around me. "I'm exhausted. That's all. And my tits are leaking. Gimme a break, okay? I'll get better at this *mommying* thing. You're not the one who popped him out of your body. Time. I need some fucking time of my own. Not attached to a milk-sucking human twenty-four-seven."

"Addison—"

The look in Tucker's gaze broke me. But I really needed to be on my own. Sleep it off. And just be in the moment. Was it too much to ask?

"I'm tired of people telling me what to do. Didn't you hear me? I'm not just a milking machine."

"I never said that." He restrained his annoyance. I could hear it in his tone. "Where is this coming from?"

I threw my arms over my head. "Just forget I said anything."

He inched toward me. "What's going on? Talk to me."

"I'm fat and ugly. I look like I have just gone through war. Or left an asylum. I need time. This entire thing is asking too much of me."

His hands rested on my upper arms. "Why didn't you say something sooner? We gotta talk about these things."

I stepped back and escaped his touch. "I don't wanna talk. I wanna sleep. And go back to how things were. Before the baby. Before I became—"

The baby's cries intensified.

"Coming, Jamieson," Tucker said as he turned on the balls of his feet. He stared at me over his shoulder. "This conversation isn't over. I understand everything you're saying, but it doesn't make it okay. Or acceptable."

"Whatever," I said, entering the darkness of our bedroom—I didn't even bother opening the curtains in the morning anymore—and slamming the door behind me.

Once alone, my breathing resumed. The knots in my stomach loosened. The weight pressing down on my shoulders cleared. And the suffocating prison I felt closing in on me released a little.

My clothes were rumpled, my hair dirty and tousled, but I didn't have a care in the world. All I wished for was to sleep for a day or a dozen. Tucker could feed the baby. I had pumped milk like a stupid cow for hours earlier. And he could do the night shift. Sue me, but I disliked the bottle, diapers, naps, and do-it-all-over-again routine. Elisa came over yesterday to play nanny for the afternoon and ended up doing my makeup and helped me change into real clothes. A much-needed upgrade to the sweaty-and-stained-shirts look I wore lately. Still, I refused to let her see my abdomen, too ashamed about how it looked at the moment. So far, it hadn't given me any hint it would go back to a respectable shape anytime soon.

I scrolled on my phone for a little while, and once Tucker got the baby to stop hollering, sleep claimed me, and I just abandoned myself to it.

In my dream, I found my way back to that edge of the precipice. The only place I found serenity. And peace washed through me as the breeze swept my skin.

The morning light filtered through the crack between the curtains as I stretched my arms beside me.

The sheets were cold on the left side of the bed, which meant Tucker had been up for a long time already.

Feeling less groggy, I took a long and hot shower, letting the stream wash away every remnant of my sleep. I had become quite good at avoiding my reflection and looking at my postpartum body. As long as I didn't acknowledge it, my brain could pretend it didn't exist.

I put on black pants and a loose-fit off-the-shoulder shirt and met my husband in the kitchen, hoping wearing clothes that belonged to me for once would make me feel good about myself.

"Wow, you look great," he said, placing a cup of tea in my hand and bending over to kiss my lips. "And smell great too. Feeling better?"

I shrugged.

The baby cooed in the seat he had set on the counter,

and my gaze fixed on him for a second before my focus went back to the food in front of me. Using my fork to avoid my husband's heavy stare, I played with the scrambled eggs, pushing them around. I could sense the questions, the annoyance, the incomprehension all pouring out from him.

Not hungry, but refusing to engage in a discussion, I brought the food to my lips. My stomach churned at the scent. My gag reflex engaged as I tried to swallow down.

"Sweetheart, you've been eating almost nothing since you gave birth. You gotta fuel your body with something other than caffeine. And Dr. Pettyfer said it would help with the milk production too."

My fork hit the plate with a loud bang as I pushed it away, done with breakfast.

"Don't call me sweetheart. I hate it. And I already told you I'm not a milk-factory. They sell baby formula at the store, so if you're unhappy with my services, feel free to buy some."

Tucker pulled the seat next to me and angled himself so we'd face each other. He grabbed my hands in his, and even though the gesture repulsed me, I exhaled and plastered a fake smile on my lips, trying to not start another war. Yeah, war. Because all we did lately was argue.

"Since when do you hate me calling you *sweetheart?* You never complained before." He tipped my chin up with a finger, encouraging me to watch him. "I think we should make an appointment with your physician, just to make sure everything is fine."

I sprang to my feet and jerked away from his touch. It felt as if millions of needles were prickling my flesh every time our skin connected.

"I'm okay. Exhausted maybe, but fine. No need to worry." I went to get heels and my purse and applied some lipstick, looking at my reflection in the entryway mirror. Our place was beautiful. Wide windows, hardwood floors, archways. Everything I'd adored when we first moved in. Now I couldn't care less about where we lived.

I smacked my lips together and fixed my hair, ready to bolt out of here.

Tucker joined me, a sleeping baby nestled in his embrace, alarm flashing in his dark eyes.

"Where are you going?"

"Work. I missed enough weeks already. I sent my boss an email two days ago, and he said I could come back whenever I was ready. Don't wait for me. I may come home late. I have a lot of work to catch up on."

The baby woke up, and his blue eyes found mine. I cocked my head, wanting nothing else than to escape this prison I lived in.

Tucker's broad shoulders blocked the doorway.

"Let me go," I ordered.

"No."

I folded my arms over my chest. "I gotta go. Move."

He handed me the baby. "Take him. Here and now, take your son. You haven't entered his bedroom once since we came back from the hospital. You nursed him only a handful of times. And every time, your features are painted with disdain. You've never changed a diaper or given him his bottle yet."

If I had steam coming out of my ears, Tucker would have been able to visualize how upset I was right now.

"You don't kiss him, hold him, or comfort him. Never. Not once."

"I'm tired," I said.

"Stop. It's your go-to excuse to justify you not bonding with him. Stop feeding yourself lies. I understand giving birth hasn't been easy. In addition, you have to go through all these physical and psychological changes, and your hormones are all over the place. You've been bleeding for over two weeks straight too. It's not easy. I'm aware. But that doesn't explain why you're not connecting with our son. Why you keep us at arm's length."

I shook my head as shame hung heavy on it. Why did I feel like such a failure right now? Why did I feel like I'd win the worst-mama-of-the-year award? Before Jamieson was born, I was looking forward to be a mother. I had always been envious of Dahlia and Jack, and I'd been wishing to be a mama for as long as I could remember. But the images I'd pictured in my head looked nothing like the real thing.

I'd always thought I'd be the mother taking long walks through the park, happy to push a stroller around. I believed breastfeeding in my bed, lying on my side like those pictures in maternity brochures, playing dress-up with my little one, and singing lullabies every night would make me happy.

Nope. Reality looked nothing like those fantasies.

"My breasts weigh tons. My nipples are too sensitive. I have to wear absorbable, thick granny panties. The skin of my belly is still saggy. My hair is falling. The shadows under my eyes aren't fading. You can't relate to any of these things. I'm the one who carried him for nine months. Who thought I would be getting torn in two when he finally got out of me? Through my fucking vagina. After over twenty-four hours of unbearable pain. How would you understand any of this, Tuck? Enlighten me. Sorry if I am not jumping around with overflowing joy. Not that I could, anyway. My bladder is probably screwed as we speak. Get in line if you wanna wreck my existence too."

Right then, I just emptied all the gloomy thoughts that had been swirling in my head for weeks now.

After I gave birth, I fell in love with our baby. Hard. I would've given my life for him. Hours later, a distance had grown between us. After we got discharged from the hospital, I'd convinced myself it was normal to feel a bit out of it after what I went through. Thanks to a new set of hormones, my emotions went crazy. I was exhausted, crying for nothing and everything, and sore. Then we got home, and that gap widened. Before I could comprehend the reason, all the excitement of being a mother died in the routine. And I lost the connection I shared with the baby. I didn't recognize him as a part of me anymore.

I slept for longer hours, trying to go back to the blissful state I'd experienced at first. In vain. The more days passed, the more lost I became. And larger the distance between the baby and me.

Now he felt like a stranger. Not the one I carried around for nine months. Not the precious little in-construction human being who kicked my stomach and whose knees and elbows I pushed back when they pressed against my taut skin. The baby resembled Tucker and me in the best of ways, yet I felt nothing while around him. No, all I felt was emptiness. And the desire to get the hell out of here.

Tucker lifted the baby against his torso, rubbing his tiny back. Deep down, I prayed to be as much of a hands-on parent as he was because I could perceive my husband was doing a remarkable job so far. He was a natural. This man turned out to be the most amazing father.

But right now, it didn't seem important.

His lips descended to kiss the fluffy dark hair of the baby. No, I couldn't say his name. No matter how hard I tried, it refused to cross my lips.

"Addison, we're having this talk right now. Why didn't you confide in me? I've been patient and have given you space, but it is getting worse every day. The more you close up on yourself, the harder it will be to get out of your shell. I'm not going anywhere, Wilde. So, better get used to having me around and in your business because I'm not letting go this time. Perhaps you really can't see it, but I know you. And this"—his finger motioned to the length of me—"isn't you. I'm not asking you to be a perfect parent, but I need to at least see you try. Now you're not even doing shit-anything. Sorry, Jamieson. You can't fail at being a parent because you're not doing it. All you do is stay out of it, keep a distance. Completely. I heard everything you said. And you're right, I didn't deliver a baby or carry one around. And I can't understand how leaking tits feel. But I'm willing to learn and to put myself out there. Whatever else is bothering you, please talk to me about it." His tone hardened. "In case you still have doubts about me and my involvement, I won't let you down. You better be honest with me. Truth, remember?"

I wished I could cry, the emptiness inside growing deeper with every passing second, but even the tears refused to come.

Tucker brushed my hair with a gentle hand. "I'll put him in bed. Wait for me, don't go. Gimme a minute." He paused. "Okay?"

I huffed and nodded, walking back toward the kitchen. I filled a cup with a dose of caffeine—I'd never been that much of a coffee drinker, but now it had become my drug of choice. The idea to add a little pick-me-up to my cup crossed my mind, but I didn't have the energy to reach for the liquor cabinet by the back door. Why were all these thoughts popping into my mind? Now I was considering adding booze to my morning drink. Great. Tucker refused to turn into his parents, but so far, I was the one about to score high in the bad-mother charts.

My husband came back and sat next to me, stopping my train of gloomy thoughts.

I hoped I could see hatred in his eyes. Or fury. So, I'd feel something. But all I read were love and concern.

Neither of us spoke for a long minute.

I sucked in a jagged breath, breaking the tense silence.

"Back when we started hanging out together, we said *truth always*. Here's the thing. I don't love him, Tuck. I know I'm not supposed to say that, but that's the truth. When I look at him, I feel nothing, except for maybe annoyance and disdain. He's only crying or sucking at my tits. I need a freaking break. Some fresh air away from him. He's always in my space. I'm suffocating. I got some time to think, and I feel I wasn't meant to be a mother. You're way better at it than I am. So, kudos. You win in whatever this is between us. And I won't argue with ya. You wanna spend time with him, deal with all his needs? Fine, go ahead. But I'm not gonna do it. And I want nothing to do with all this baby crap. Happy now? I've put all my darkest secrets on the table. Can I go?"

How could all these words exit my own mouth?

When did I become a robot, unable to feel anything?

I moved to get up, but his muscular hands kept me seated.

"Babe, I know you're not serious. You're not speaking with your heart right now. Nobody said having a baby would be easy. That you'd get everything right on the first attempt. For god's sake, I've ruined a dozen diapers, and shit spread everywhere before I figured out how to put it on the proper way. And every once in a while, I forget to burp him after he's finished with his bottle. But I don't pretend to claim I'm perfect at it. But I'm doing my fucking best. I'm trying. I'm putting myself out there."

"You don't get it, do you? I don't care. I prefer going

back to work than spending more time at home. I feel useless. And I'm not interested in the job. I just want to be left alone."

How could Tucker be so good at being a hands-on parent? How could he connect in the same way I disconnected with the baby?

I always thought mothers were instinctively better at nursing their children and understanding their needs.

Why was I so incapable of loving the baby the way he deserved to be loved?

Why was Tucker doing a better job than I since day one?

Warmth enveloped my chest. Awesome. Now my breasts were leaking, and I was soaked. I was uncomfortable and sore.

I crooked a finger to pull my bra away from my chest to give my breasts some room. A new feeling of failure coiled around me.

I wanted to tell Tucker he was right. Because a part of me knew he was. But those confessions died at the tip of my tongue.

I had turned into the worst version of myself I could be.

Darkness swirled in my brain. Tiredness washed over me.

Unable to stand any longer, I kicked my heels.

"Happy now? I won't go to work because I'm already too tired to even get there. I've turned into a sloth. Even pregnant at thirty-seven weeks, I had more energy. I could have run a marathon. Or built a house. Now it's fucking hard just to get out of bed or take a shower. And that sound. Gosh. That high-pitched sound he makes when he cries for no reason, it gets on my last nerve."

Tears should have come. They should have flooded my

face. But no, they refused to show up. Instead, anger bubbled inside me.

Tucker pulled me against his chest. The same way he had always done every time I needed his love and confidence in me in the past. But just now his arms around me were fuel for murder.

I pushed him away, but he just tightened his squeeze.

"Stop. Relax. I miss you, Wilde. So damn much. You're pushing both of us away when you should lean on us instead. To get through whatever you're going through. Jamieson and I, we love you. And all we want is for you to get better. To come back to us instead of living a parallel life like you're there but not there at the same time. It's too soon for you to go back to work. I object."

"No. It's not your call. I'll be happier there. Being here is asking too much from me. I told ya already. And the baby—no, I'm no mother material."

"Addison, Jamieson is your son."

"Maybe. But I didn't choose to be a mama. It just happened. And I blame you."

"Okay, so now I'm guilty of the best thing that has ever happened to us."

"I don't have a dick, so I didn't put him inside me on my own. The semen was yours. Can I go now? There's a happy hour after work tonight. Don't wait up for me."

"Wilde..."

"Don't Wilde me. If you wanna be a father so bad, just take care of him yourself. After all, he's your child too. See that as bonding time. All books I read say it's important for the father to get involved in the child's life from the beginning. Go ahead. Enjoy your time together. I'm out of here."

"No."

"Why do you make everything so complicated? You should just let me go."

"Never. You're stuck with me forever. Remember those vows? Because I do. *Addison Wilde, in front of our best friends, I promise to love and cherish you forever. You're my soulmate, my other half, my best friend. When you have doubts or are afraid, I'll be by your side, holding your hand. Together, we're it, sweetheart. We can face anything. We can be anyone we want. We can accomplish great things. I love you. Here, always and forever.*"

The first tear hung from my lower lash as Tucker recited his wedding vows. My heart cracked. Breathing became harder. Wrecking sobs escaped as my husband held me against him.

"Shhh. Cry it out. It's okay. I'm here, and I've got you."

I shattered in his embrace. I'd poured my heart out to him, and nothing about it made me feel better. Only worse.

My own words replayed in my head. *I don't love him, Tuck. I know I'm not supposed to say that, but that's the truth. When I look at him, I feel nothing, except for maybe annoyance and disdain.*

How did this even come out of my mouth?

Who was I? What had happened to me?

Lucidity and shame hit me all at once.

Tucker and the baby would be better off without me.

I had already failed them so much in just a few weeks. No newborn deserved a shitty mother. A mother like me. A mother who just couldn't care.

When Tucker's arms slackened around my shoulders and my tears ran out, I rushed to our bedroom and locked the door behind me. With my back pressed against the wall, I pondered my options. I had very few choices. And the only one that made sense told me to run. To set them free from me. To get the hell out of here.

Tucker turned the knob. "Addison, let me in. We're not done."

I wiped the tear residues off my face with my sleeve and swallowed the giant lump at the back of my throat.

The baby started crying, and I thanked him in my head for forcing Tucker to leave me alone.

"I'll be back."

I breathed easier.

"Shit," I heard him say under his breath before he added, "coming, sweet guy. Missing me already?" The softness lacing his voice, the tenderness, the love, I wished I could master that too.

Left to myself, I grabbed a bag from the closet and filled it with basic necessities. I changed into sweatpants and put tennis shoes on.

Tiptoeing out of the room, I reached the entryway, slid my purse over my shoulder, and penned a note on a piece of paper.

I'm sorry. You'll both be better off without me.
  Addi

I removed my wedding band and placed it on the console after kissing it.

A split second before the door closed behind me, my husband's panicked voice resonated from inside our home. "Wilde, wait—"

Once on the sidewalk, I sauntered away fast, almost at a running pace, as I made my way toward the nearest train station. I had no clue where I'd go, but anywhere far from here seemed like a safe choice.

I walked for minutes, or maybe hours. At one point, I had no idea where I was, lost in my drowning thoughts. The sun shone at its zenith in the blue sky, and I kept my head low to avoid being blinded by the sunrays. A car slowed beside me, but I ignored it.

"Addison Wilde, get in the car. Now," Tucker's harsh voice spoke. "Enough with the running away. You told me once you'd never do that again." I kept my eyes trained forward, refusing to meet his gaze.

"Addison, we'll get you help. You're usually a bubbly, crazy number, and these days, you're a shadow of yourself. Can't you see something is off?"

I kept my mouth shut, refusing to acknowledge any of his words.

"My mom left. She ruined me for the longest time. Until you came along. I won't let you do this to our son. Never, woman. Whatever it is, we'll figure it out, but you won't leave him like that. And you're certainly not leaving me either. We're a team. None of this makes sense. Get in the car."

I continued. And just then I realized I'd been walking in a circle. Great.

Tucker passed me and parked on the side of the road. He jumped out of the car to meet me, gripping my upper arms as I averted my eyes.

"Where do you think you're going? What do you think you're doing? Enough now. Get. In. The. Car."

From the corner of my eye, I noticed the baby watching me through the window from his car seat. His big blue eyes fused with mine. He smiled at me, unaware of all the commotion around us, as if I mattered to him. How could he? I hadn't been his mother in so long. Like ever. But still, he didn't break eye contact, as if to tell me he believed in me or something. Hurt stabbed my heart. And for the first time since we left the hospital, something passed between us. Something I couldn't name. Except it brought fresh tears to my eyes.

Tucker caught me just when I thought I'd crumple on the sidewalk, drained.

"Wilde, I've got you. Here, lean on me. Come back home. Come back to us."

The baby let out a loud, happy cry as if he agreed. Could he really sense everything going on? Could he feel me fading away?

"Will you accept my help?" Tucker asked, his arms tight around me, and his mouth kissing the top of my head.

I nodded.

I had almost left my baby. I had almost walked away from my own life. From my heart.

"Tomorrow you could go to the spa, get pampered, and catch up on some rest. I called your doctor. He'd like to see you next week. Pregnancy is hard and delivery, harder. And you're exhausting yourself. You don't have to return to work so early. We talked about it. We have enough money for you to take time off, to enjoy Jamieson's first few months. For us to be a family."

I held on to him like a lifeline. "Don't lose faith in me. Please. Don't—" And once again, I became a sobbing mess as my husband hugged me before helping me inside our car and buckling my seatbelt, my hand shaky and my body too numb to take care of itself.

37

TUCKER

I drove us back home and put Addison to bed before feeding a hungry Jamieson. With him strapped to my chest in one of those baby wraps, I cleaned the kitchen and set myself behind my laptop, working on the secret project I'd been keeping from my wife for the last few months. Something for her. For the three of us. I had no idea if she'd like it, but my instinct told me she would. And with everything going on right now, we all needed an escape. A place in this world to call ours.

While I lost myself in work, it prevented my mind from worrying about how my life had taken a turn for the worse in the last few weeks. Our fairytale came with a sour after-taste. My son snored against my torso, and I relished the sensation of our bodies connecting and comforting each other. In the last month, he had become my anchor. My rock. The one thing keeping me sane.

Right now, my baby required my love and care more than ever, his mother unable to provide for him the way she should be. And I wasn't even mad at her for zoning out, too worried about her mental and physical health.

Always questioning myself every second of every day, wondering how to find a way to reach her, to help her, to heal whatever it was that made her refuse to give Jamieson the attention he deserved.

But the weight of all of it had grown heavy on me.

I pinched the bridge of my nose, fighting to keep my breathing steady, a truckload of emotions whirling inside me.

But I couldn't lose it. Jamieson and Addison both required my support. My unconditional dedication. I just never imagined doing this parenting thing all by myself. Sleep had become a luxury I couldn't afford. Between work and taking care of the people I loved the most and everything around the house, I could barely hold it all together.

When I talked to Addison's doctor earlier, he said something about depression. Could that be it?

My heart sunk low in my chest as I grabbed a framed picture of us on our wedding day. My wife looked so beautiful in her long white dress, cradling her huge belly, her hair curled, and her smile genuine. The sparks in her eyes didn't lie.

How did she go from being radiant and full of hope to being sad, disconnected, and miserable?

How did all the zest for life illuminating her gaze transform into empty abysses?

My finger traced her silhouette.

"Whatever it is, sweetheart, we'll find a way back to you."

I turned the frame over and read the words she wrote there, the ones I knew by heart.

To my husband
This last year has been a rollercoaster I never

saw coming, but I wouldn't change the ride because it brought me to you. And you're everything I've ever wished for.

I'm sorry I've been stubborn for the longest time, but now I'm certain that I wanna spend the rest of my life with you.

We never do anything in order, but that's what makes up so perfect for each other.

I love you now and for the rest of my life. And I can't wait for us to be a family of three.

Your one and only sweetheart, A. xx

I reread it a few times, a smile etching on my lips and tears burning the back of my eyes.

With a protective palm caressing my son's back, I dialed my best friend.

"Hey man, how is it going?" he asked when he picked up.

The emotions balled in my throat, blocking my airways.

"Is it Tuck?" Dahlia asked. "Put him on speakerphone. Or better, ask him to switch to video chat. I wanna see my nephew."

I said nothing, fighting to keep my tears at bay as an incoming notification for a video chat filled the screen of my device.

"Hey guys," I said, plastering what I hoped would resemble a sign of happiness on my lips. "How is it going?"

"Oh, he's sleeping," Dahlia cooed. "He's so tiny. How did I forget Jack was that small once? Oh god, they grow up so fast."

My smile reached one side of my mouth, and I rubbed

the column of my throat, trying to ease the commotion storming inside me.

"Yeah. So small."

I glanced at my best friend, and he watched me with a wrinkle across his forehead.

"Tuck, don't bullshit me. I know the look. Something's happened. What is it? If it has anything to do with your secret project, I went there two days ago. It looks amazing. It should be done by the end of the month. My guys are doing great work. We should pay a visit together soon. A boys' road trip. With our sons. Wow, I love the sound of it. Both of us dads now. Who would have thought? Anyway, it's been a long time since we did something together."

I mustered another smile, the words stuck in my throat. I liked his idea, but for some reason, it made me wanna curl into a corner and bawl my eyes out. Not the answer he was expecting.

"Fuck, it's not that," Nick said, question marks in his eyes.

His wife backhanded his chest. "Careful, tiny ears close by."

"Sorry, Jamieson," my friend said. His focus returned to mine. "Do I need to fly to Chicago to get it out of you, or are you gonna tell me what's wrong? You look defeated. Stained and wrinkled clothes. I know for a fact something is wrong."

I didn't want to complain, to draw my friends into this, but I had exhausted all my resources, and I was tired. And I had to confide in someone. Or I'd burst at the seams.

In a way, I had Addison to thank. In all the months we'd been living together, she showed me I could let go, that a schedule could be modified, and rules could be bent. And that a shirt that wasn't pressed or a pair of paint-stained jeans were not the end of the world. I was grateful she did, or I'd never survive this chaos right now. I sometimes felt that unconsciously she knew this would happen and that she had prepared me.

"It's Addi," Dahlia stated, more like a fact than a question.

Moisture rose in my vision, and I nodded, unable to keep my suffering to myself any longer.

"Tucker," Dahlia said, her voice gentle and comforting. Fuck, I missed comfort. And love.

"She ran away earlier. It's bad." My voice cracked. "Very bad. And I have no idea what I should do."

"What happened? I was going to call her tomorrow because she's been vague every time we talked. And she's always too tired or out of it to chat. And it doesn't sound like her."

For the next twenty minutes, I filled my friends with everything from the moment we came home after we left the hospital to when Addison cut me and everyone else out.

"She hasn't stepped in the nursery once. She never holds him, never kisses him, or even looks at him."

Dahlia's hands flew to her mouth. "Geez, I had no idea it was that bad. I thought she just required some time to get used to her new role. I'm so sorry, Tuck. What can we do?"

I traced my eyebrow with a finger. "If only I knew. I booked her a day at the spa tomorrow and an appointment with her doctor next week. Now I'm afraid each time she goes out, she may not come back. That she'll abandon us." I coughed, doing my best to clear my clogged throat. "She wants nothing to do with everything. With either of us. I'm not complaining, but I barely sleep, and I can't think straight. It's just too much. What am I supposed to do? Force her to be a mother when she clearly doesn't wanna be? Or let her be and cross my fingers, hoping she'll grow out of it? That it's just a phase?"

"Man, you should have called us sooner. We're not doctors or shrinks, but we could've given you a hand. Don't shut us out when it gets too tough," Nick said.

"Thank you, guys. But you already have your hands full with two businesses and Jack. You don't need my shit piled on top of it."

I sighed and kissed Jamieson's head as he squirmed against me. He opened his eyes, stared at me, and a new wave of warmth filled my chest. Releasing him from the wrap, I held him over my forearm so he could face my friends.

"Oh, he's getting cuter by the day," Dahlia said.

A genuine grin stretched my lips now.

"I know it's hard, but you're doing it right, Tuck. I can tell."

New tears blurred my vision on hearing her words.

"Thanks," I croaked. "It means a lot."

"Saturday morning, we'll be there. Let us help you out," Nick said.

I nodded. The thought of having support sounded great right now.

"Let me make a few phone calls. One of my employees told me once she had dealt with post-partum depression during her last pregnancy. I have no idea if this could be it, but I'll ask questions. Talk to my doctor. See what I can learn. With Addi's family history, we can't rule out the possibility." She relaxed her shoulders. "I'm sorry it's happening to you two. But I'm sure there's a reasonable explanation. Addi would never abandon you or push her own son away if everything was all right with her. This I know for sure. Can you hold the fort till Saturday?"

I bowed my head. "Yes. What else can I do, anyway?" I

breathed out. "Her doctor said something about being depressed too. I have no idea what to make of it."

"Gimme a day. And for what it's worth, Addi is lucky to have you, Tuck. You're a pillar in her life. I know it doesn't excuse or fix anything, but I wouldn't want anyone else caring for my best friend. I trust ya."

I swallowed hard.

"Thank you, Dah. I shouldn't say those words to my best friend's wife, but I love you. Your heart is pure and precious. Wilde is lucky to have you in her corner too."

I closed my eyes and pressed my lids with my thumb and forefinger, trying to dissipate the ache in my heart. Dahlia's words replayed, and I stared at her.

"Dah, what did you mean earlier when you said with her family history? I'm desperate for answers. If you know something I don't, please share. I'm at my wit's end."

"Listen, if she hasn't told you about her daddy, it's not my place to tell, but I'll say this. After her last breakup, Addi has been worried about her mental health. It has never happened before. But she was down, then she got pregnant, and it explained most of her symptoms, so she filed it under hormonal changes."

"I don't understand. What does that even mean? How bad is it?"

"Tuck, depression runs in her family."

I stopped breathing. "I had no idea. She never said anything. She's usually always so cheerful and bubbly."

"I know. Let's not jump to conclusions just yet. It might be something else. I'll make those phone calls tomorrow and keep you informed."

"Thanks."

We hung up, Jamieson now fussy in my arms. My heart broke into a million pieces at the thought that my wife was suffering, and I had no clue how bad it was.

———

After I bathed Jamieson and changed him into fluffy pjs, I searched the chest of drawers in his room for a pacifier. I couldn't find the one he usually had. It probably had fallen in the car earlier when we went to get Addison, and with the downpour outside, I had no intention of getting it right now. I was sure she bought a few when we went shopping days before his birth.

I grabbed a basket full of baby stuff from a shelf in his closet when I discovered a white box. On the lid was written in gold letters which I recognized as Addison's artsy handwriting: *Baby, I love you to the moon and back.*

Curious, I lifted the lid and found a book lying inside. With care, as if it could detonate at any moment, I placed it on top of the changing table.

Jamieson had fallen asleep in my arms, and I switched him to my left side as I flipped the pages quickly, my heart pounding in my chest. My breathing whistled. I felt dizzy and held myself up against the piece of furniture. Why didn't I know about the existence of this book before? How did Addison forget to mention it? With Jamieson now securely pressed against my chest, I stepped back and hit a hard surface, then slid my tall self down the wall until my ass hit the floor.

The title, made of cardboard square tied to the front page with safety pins, read: *How I Fell in Love with your Daddy.*

One by one, starting from the beginning, I turned the pages, my focus on all the words and objects my wife had attached to them.

I used my shoulder to wipe the tears rushing to my eyes. "Baby, mommy loves you so much. You have no idea."

I read the message she wrote on the inside cover.

Dear baby,

I've been making this as a storybook to gift you the day you are old enough to hear our story. It depicts every moment when I fell more and more in love with your daddy. It's full of keep-sakes, memories, little things that make our love story as incredible as it is today.

Tears ran freely down my cheeks now, and I pressed my son's sleeping body against my heart as I continued reading.

Each page had a handwritten note with an item attached next to it, the first one being the hotel keycard from the night of Nick and Dahlia's bachelor-bachelorette party in Nashville. The one I thought I threw away with my ripped shirt that night.

This is the hotel card from the weekend your daddy and I met. He looked so handsome, dressed in one of those suits he wore all the time, with a glint in his eyes every time our gazes met. From the time I first laid eyes on him, I couldn't look elsewhere. He was all I could see. Back then, he thought he'd lost his keycard and invited himself into my room. When we came back to this hotel, it was late, and I had forgotten I had put it in my purse. But now I know this was the best thing I ever did. Because that night cemented something between us.

This is one of the buttons of the shirt your father tore when he climbed that fence after I made us late for the night events. He was upset and annoyed by me, I could tell, but even then, I was mesmerized by him. And when he wore that groom T-shirt, the one I designed, way too small from him, my heart became beyond excited that he would trust me. That he would follow my lead. And at that moment, I fell for him for the first time. Then later in the night, he sang to me (see lyrics of our song on the next page), and I knew my heart was in trouble. He'd stolen a big chunk of it. Because even if we were just supposed to pretend to be in love, the chemistry between us couldn't be faked. To everyone else, it was, but I knew better. That kiss was as real as it could get. And I fell for him a second time.

This is the speech I wrote for Dahlia at her bachelorette party. My head was all over the place, and I forgot to write it. Your daddy, even though he barely knew me, read me like an open book. He figured me out when I had the hardest time doing so myself. He came to my room, sat with me, and didn't leave until I was done with my speech and was happy about it. He believed in me for the first time. And to this day, it still means a lot to me. And my heart. Your daddy is a special kind of man. And when he loves, he loves hard. And he's my favorite person in this world. Along with you.

I kept reading, my lips pressing against the top of our baby boy's head.

This is the menu of Cosmos. One day, I was feeling off. I was so tired all the time and had no idea I was pregnant. Your daddy flew in for a few hours, just to take me out on a date to this amazing restaurant and cheer me up. We traversed the city on scooters afterward, and up to now, it's still one of the best nights of my life. And I fell for him a little more with every passing hour we spent together. I never told anyone, but when he walked away that night, I felt sad. Our relationship made no sense, and we didn't tell anyone, but our friendship was everything to me. It still is. Falling in love with your best friend is something quite amazing.

Those are my plane tickets from the time I surprised your father in Chicago. I landed there with only a suitcase and no plans except to see him and ended up spending the weekend with him at his place. We chatted for hours, and he opened his heart to me for the first time. He brought me to his special place on the rooftop of his building. When I returned home, I cried for hours, missing him from the moment we separated at the airport. Back then, I wished my heart wouldn't feel so much when it came to Tucker Philips because I was scared of love. Of being heartbroken. But I couldn't help it. I fell in love with your daddy all over again. Even though it made no sense to me.

This is the invite to Dahlia and Nick's wedding, where your daddy was not only the best man (I was the maid of honor), but also my plus-one. In all honesty, I would've been so crestfallen if he had invited any other woman to go with him that day. I was an emotional mess. I was pregnant and had no clue. Those hormones are quite something, I'm telling ya. Your daddy worried about me. He cared for me. Held me when I cried and brushed my hair when I slept in his lap. It was also the weekend when he told me he loved me for the first time. I told him he was crazy because I didn't want to acknowledge my growing feelings toward him. And yes, I was falling for him a lot more than I should have.

This is the bus ticket that drove me out of Green Mountain the same weekend. When I broke your daddy's heart for the first time. Because I ran away (I'm telling you the truth because you deserve it). I thought I wasn't pregnant and decided to put some distance between us to assess our growing feelings. I felt it would do us good. That weekend, your daddy opened his heart to me, selflessly and completely. I already knew I loved him, but I tried to avoid taking spur-of-the-moment decisions to avert another broken heart. If there's one thing I regret doing in my life, it is not listening to my heart sooner. I remember being so miserable without him. You were the sign I prayed for. The one that would lead me back to him and prove we belonged together.

This is the first picture I have of you. It's a sono-gram from the day I learned I was really preg-nant with you. The day my life took a turn for the better. I should've been freaked out, but I wasn't. The only things I feared was your daddy's reaction. Not that I ever believed he'd be mad or anything. But I worried I would be too late and that he would've forgotten all about me. But after a few days, I went to him, and we reunited. And from the moment he learned about you, he's been nothing but loving and supportive. He never left our sides. We moved in together and learned to be a couple. We solidified our relationship, getting ready to welcome you. You're lucky; I hope you realize it. Your daddy is the greatest man I know. He's fearless, resilient, strong, and generous. And I fell in love with him all over again when he carried me in the rain, refusing to be separated from me ever again.

At this point, I couldn't see through my tears, my vision blurry and my shoulders heaving. "See, Jamieson, you've got yourself an incredible mama. I know things are hard right now for all of us, but hang on with me for just a little longer. She'll come back to you. She'll come back to us. I believe it. Because this woman, she's unable to not love with all her heart. In the meantime, let's stick together, okay? And help her get through this. I'm sorry for everything. But I'm here and not going anywhere. It's you and me against the world. And I'll fight for you forever."

I buried my face in his mass of dark baby hair, relishing the scent of his honey and lemon shampoo, reminding me of the one his mother used.

With my little boy in my arms, I spent a few hours on the floor of the nursery, my legs bent and my heart heavy. Until my lids weighed too much and it pained me to keep them open. After I laid him in his crib, I went to my room, undressed, and slipped under the covers, wrapping my arms around my wife's waist, craving her warmth and the beating of her heart.

"I love you, Wilde. Never forget it. When you are ready, I'll be here. I waited for you once, and I'll wait for you all over again. Because what we have can't be explained. It's stronger than love. It's a bond from the core. It's fireworks. Get better, okay? Jamieson and I, we need you. We always will. Fight for us too."

I sealed my lids to prevent a fresh batch of tears from drenching my face and dozed off in no time, hoping Addison and I would meet in our dreams. And we could be happy there, at least for the time being.

38

ADDISON

D ahlia knocked on my bedroom door after arriving less than ten minutes ago. I didn't know Nick and she were flying here. Tucker hadn't said anything. Was it meant to be a surprise? I didn't feel good enough to dress up and be social, so I had shut myself in our room, avoiding our guests when I spotted them in the entryway.

"Hey girlfriend, can I come in?" she asked.

"Sure." I smoothed the fabric of my shirt to flatten the wrinkles and adjusted the covers around me. I shut my eyes, probably looking so out of it right now.

Two days ago, I spent a few hours at the spa, at my husband's request. I left after the massage, not in the mood to be around people any longer.

Yesterday, I barely got out of bed, too tired to stand up or eat food. Tucker ordered in dinner, and I slept next to him on the couch after I gulped a few bites of orange-glazed chicken and rice, which used to be my favorite. Not anymore. It just tasted blah nowadays.

He had kissed me when we finally made it to bed, and

for a moment, my body recognized him, and I lost myself in the comfort he brought me. He whispered to me how much he loved me. It had been weeks since we had gotten any sort of intimacy, and for once, his touch didn't repulse me. It actually felt good to be in his arms.

Dahlia sat on the bed beside me, her legs stretched forward, and her back pressed against the headboard. She intertwined her fingers through mine. "How is it going?" she asked.

I shrugged. "Okay."

She draped an arm around my shoulder and pulled me to her. "No need to pretend. It's me. You've seen me at my worst."

My breath hitched in my lungs. My head spun.

"I'm numb, Dah. I'm not even sure I love Tucker anymore." My heart hurt so bad as I said it out loud. "He's been nothing but incredible, but it just feels wrong being with him, you know. Like he says nice things to me and I can't even return them. And when I do, it's like I've rehearsed it, and it doesn't sound genuine."

"What about Jamieson?"

I scratched my temple. "Same with the baby."

"Your son."

"Yeah, yeah."

"Do you recall Jeff after he returned from war? You were away in college by then, but you visited, and we talked almost every night."

"It seems like a lifetime ago."

"Yep, it does. Do you remember how he was back then? How he had changed?"

I nodded.

"He was lost. And sad. And couldn't figure out how to get better. He had become an agitated and angry version of himself. War had fucked with his mind. He saw images in his head, images that he couldn't get rid of. And he never told me what they were about, but I had a pretty good idea. Anyway, for a while, I lost him. It got so bad I refused to let him join me on that second world tour."

She paused, and I was well aware she didn't like revisiting those painful memories of her past.

"I remember."

"Anyway, back then, he didn't confide in me. Yelled at Carter. Pushed all of us away, his pain overtaking every aspect of his life, destroying every good thing he had going for him. And that's when our lives turned chaotic. He fucked up. I did too. Because we couldn't find a way to communicate, to be there for each other. We were kids, for god's sake. I was nineteen. I made bad choices. All I'm saying is that he needed help, and for the longest time, he battled against the idea. Until he decided he wanted to get better. To feel better. To regain the control of his own life, of his own mind. Until he decided fighting for himself, and for us, was worth more than his ego."

Mixed emotions rose inside me. Dahlia's story got to me. I had been a witness to Jeff's life turning hell. And all the hurt he caused around him due to something he had no control over.

"What if nobody can help me, Dah? I miss my old self. Everyday. But she vanished. I can't find her. But it's just a few bad days, right? It will get better."

"I'm no doctor, and I don't pretend to be one, but Tucker and I, we talked. I won't hide the truth from you. He's desperate, Addi. He's not doing so great either. He's sad and tired and so worried about you. And before you get mad, he never asked me to come over to talk to ya. He didn't even tell me you were struggling. He tried to deal with all of it on his own. But it's too much. You guys have a newborn to care for. And I did my research. Talked to people. Do you know anything about postpartum depression?"

I shrugged. "Not really."

"It's more common than we think. It affects women after they give birth. And there are people trained to help you with whatever issues you're dealing with. They can advise you, give you cues and tips on how to overcome the bumps on your road. To heal and get better. We're not in the fifties when it was a shame to be honest about mental health struggle. Society has come a long way since then. It's valued now to be honest, to admit when we're down. There's a center an hour's drive from here. Came highly recommended."

I forced the next words out. "Do you think it's because of him? Of his genetics?"

"Your daddy?"

"Yes. I have no memories of him at his lowest point. But I've heard the stories."

"I don't know. Whatever it is, we won't let anything bad happen to you. You're not alone, girlfriend. We'll help you to figure out whatever is afflicting your mind."

"Dah, I'm not crazy."

"Nobody said you were. And you're not. But you and I, we've never shied from the truth either. And you gotta get help, Addi. I think it really could be postpartum depression. Or something else. I won't speculate. In any case, you won't heal magically without outside support and medical care. And it's not your fault. Nothing to do with you. Just bad luck. Some chemical imbalance in your brain or stuff like that. Perhaps genes are to blame. Perhaps they're not."

Dahlia putting my feelings to words brought hot tears to my eyes. Maybe I wasn't going nuts after all. Maybe there existed some explanation for how I felt inside. Could it be something that could be cured? Using the back of my hand, I wiped my teary cheeks, the void in me not feeling so bottomless anymore.

"I'm not crazy, I swear. Do you think they can fix me? Find out why I'm so detached from everything? And so tired all the time?"

Dahlia wrapped both arms around my heaving shoulders, combing my hair away from my face. "Yes. Many women go through this. You're not alone. And I'm here. Tuck is here. We love you so much, and all we wish is for you is to get better."

"It's easy for all of you to say. None of you pushed an almost ten-pound baby out of their vagina a month ago."

"No, I didn't. You're right. But I'm a mother too. And I know how overwhelming it can be at the time. And how sleeping two-hour shifts is hard on your mood and your sanity. But Tuck said you voiced not loving Jamieson. And that's the part that worries me the most, to be honest. Sleep-deprived, normal. Anxiety to do everything right, normal. Mood swings due to shifting hormone levels, normal. Not liking your baby, not normal. Preferring to plan happy-hours with coworkers than feeding your newborn, not normal. Do you see the difference? And I'm not saying the words so you feel ashamed. I'm saying it so you realize something is wrong and you gotta address it."

I let out a sarcastic laugh. "When you put it this way, I sound like a monster."

"I promise you're not."

"You really think they can help me?"

She nodded. "Try this facility. You can enter their one-month program. See how it goes. Just step away for a moment, assess the situation, and see if their therapy and methods are helping you. And if you feel more like yourself afterward."

"Did Tucker put you up to it? Because he's upset about being a full-time parent?"

"Nah. He's just concerned. He loves you. Nick and I called the other night, and he cracked when we started asking questions. He feared it was something he did. Something he said. Or that he didn't do enough."

"I really am a bad person. I…we…"

"Just focus on yourself for now. I'll help him out, okay? Nick and I will be there for your men. As much as possible. And for you too. You'll see; it'll improve. Give it time. Don't push yourself too hard. The brain is a complex structure, and too many hormones and lack of sleep would do that to you. Now breathe, and let me know if you'd like me to drive you when you're ready."

"What will Tucker say?"

"He's already packed a bag for you. I helped him over the phone when you were at the spa. You know, he cried the entire time. Said he'd miss you so much and all he prayed was for you to come back to him."

"He *what*? He cried?"

"Don't be mad at him. It was my idea. The facility. If you agree to go, great. If you don't, we'll find another way to get you help. You have my word. When did I ever let you down?"

"I think I should go…"

"I agree."

I said nothing, lost in my thoughts for a long time. Mental breakdown or postpartum depression, could this be it? Or would they just force me to swallow a bunch of colorful pills supposed to make me believe unicorns were walking on rainbows?

"I'm not getting drugged, Dah."

She smiled and pushed back to look at me. "You think I'm not aware, girlfriend? This place offers meditation and holistic approaches. Pills don't fix everything. They told me they try to avoid them as much as possible. Their therapies are based on more natural ways. It seems like a good fit. They have a garden with beautiful flowerbeds. A stream with a wooden bridge in the backyard. It looks peaceful."

Going away for a month? Would I survive in a place with a bunch of strangers, when even going to the grocery store right now seemed too much most of the time?

"What do you say?" my friend asked, and I snapped back to the present.

"Will he wait for me? Tuck, I mean."

"Addi, he'd wait for you till the end of time. That's how much he loves ya."

"But I've been awful to him."

"He cares about you. And wants what's best for you."

"Can I see him before we go?"

"Sure. He's in his home office. Nick went for a walk with the kids, so you two have time to talk. I'll come to get you in a little while. Take your time. Listen to what he has to say. And don't be hard on him. The guy can barely hold it together as it is. And don't be hard on yourself. Recognizing you need help is the first step to healing."

Dahlia helped me change and fixed my hair. Fidgeting with my hands, I reached my husband's office down the hall.

"Hey," I said, knocking on the ajar door. "Can we talk?"

"Sweetheart—"

He rose to his feet, and I noticed the despair and sadness etching his eyes. How had I never seen it before now? How had I been so out of it that I missed the love of my life hurting? Standing a few meters away in front of me, he waited, his head hanging low, his hands stuffed in his pockets. He looked vulnerable right now. And weary.

"Well, I've decided to accept Dah's offer to get help." I couldn't breathe properly, the lump in my throat so big I believed I would choke on it. "Go away for some time. You've been right all along. I'm not myself. And I might require some professional help to find my way back."

I averted my eyes, heartbroken at the sight of the tears pooling in his.

"I recognize something is wrong with me, and I might have said things I didn't mean. That could be hurtful toward you. And the baby."

Tucker stepped forward, decreasing the distance between our bodies.

"Wilde, I love you so much. All I want is for you to be happy again. To go back to your crazy ways. So you're present when you're with us, mentally and physically." We stared into each other's eyes, our souls having their own conversation as we stood there, charged particles of air spiraling around us, witnesses to our despair.

"I'm not breaking up with you. It's temporary. A month. To fix whatever is not okay with me."

He huffed a trembling breath. "Why would you think I would break up with you? I'd never do that." His voice shook, and tears prickled my eyes.

Going away from the man I loved sounded like I was deserting him. Like his mother. The idea twisted my stomach. "Because you've been abandoned before. And I hate the idea you'd feel like I'm doing it too. I swear I'm not."

"Wilde, you're nothing like my mother. You're my best friend. And the love of my life. Not only that, but you're the mother of my child. I know your heart. And you'd never leave us on purpose or due to selfishness."

I stared at him, my words dissolving before they could form on my tongue.

As if he sensed the battle in my head, Tucker added, "Can I hug you?"

I nodded. At first, his arms around me felt stiff and foreign, but soon, I warmed to them and nestled my body in his loving embrace. Sobs I'd been holding in shook me, rocking my core. Weeks of pain and distress poured out all at once.

"I'm so sorry. I'm not okay. I don't feel okay. And I have no idea who I am anymore. Where I belong. Or what's going on with my life. I know I've hurt you. And that you and the baby don't deserve my mood swings and absence. But I can't do otherwise. It's like being around you burns me. Like I'm lost in space and have no idea how to come back home. Almost like watching my own life through a glass-mirror and having no way to connect with people on the other side."

Tucker cupped my cheeks. "Don't chastise yourself, sweetheart. I know you. I know your heart. I'll wait for you. As long as it takes. Because I love you and this will never change."

"I'm not leaving you, okay?" I repeated. Insecurity grew in me at the idea he could fall in love with someone else during my absence. I had to convince myself more than him. "Don't forget about me, please. Don't lose faith in me. Or I'll never find the courage to heal if I have to do all this by myself. Or if I have to come back to an empty house."

We both cried, his inner strength pouring onto me and keeping me safe. Protecting me from myself and the rest of the world.

"I'm so proud of you for agreeing to do this. For recognizing you need help. I'm sorry I can't be the one giving it to you. I tried. I really did. But I'm not equipped to do more."

"Don't ever blame yourself. Right now, I'm not sure I deserve you. I'm the one who's sorry. For putting you through hell. It was never my intention. You waited for me. From the first day, you've been my hero. Where would I be without your unconditional love and support?"

"Sweetheart, I'll be here when you come back. When you're ready to come home. I love you. So much. Never question it."

My husband kissed me, and for the second time since I gave birth, I let myself melt against him and abandoned my whole being to the love outpouring from him.

"Can I tell you about my daddy?" I said.

"You can tell me anything. I'll never judge you."

I cleared my throat. "A few times in the last year, I've tried to open up about it. But I was so afraid this could be it. I didn't want you to think I was damaged. Or that I could be damaged. My father... Well, depression runs in his family-tree. When I was eight, my parents separated because he wouldn't get help for the longest time. He refused to acknowledge he had problems and that they impacted his life and his family. My parents never had another child because my father worried he'd pass the gene to us. To Phoenix and me. And up until last year, it never occurred to me I could carry it. After my breakup, before we met, I was down. And it took me a while to get my vibe back. You're the one who snapped me out of my funk. Who painted colors back into my world."

I paused, clearing the fog taking over my brain.

"I'm sorry I didn't tell you before. I really wanted to. Now I'll get better. You don't deserve just a part of me, but all of me. I'm not sure if I want it to be depression or not. All I know is that I don't want to suffer anymore. And I don't want you and the baby to suffer either."

Tucker pulled me into his arms once again. "Whatever

it is, we'll fight this. I'm not going away, and I'll lend you all the strength you need."

"Thank you. For being you."

We stood still for a long while, connecting for the first time in almost a month.

"Do you want me to drive you?" he asked.

I shook my head. "Dah will take me. It will be too hard if you're there. To see the pain in your eyes. The hurt I've caused our family. To walk away." I stepped away from his embrace. "I'll get better."

In front of my son's nursery, I stopped and scanned the room, my heart heavy and bruised in my chest. With tentative steps, I walked in. It had been weeks since I entered the room. The last time was before his birth. My heart closed in on itself. Painfully. More tears cascaded down my cheeks. Holding against my chest a stuffed-elephant I picked up from the crib, I let the tears flow. "I'm sorry, baby."

He wasn't here, but I could feel his energy all around me and somehow, I preferred him not hearing my words.

"I'll try to be a better mother. To love you the way you deserve. You won't see me for some time. I'm going away. But I'll be back. Wait for me. And take care of your daddy. I'm sorry I'm not a mama to you. It was never supposed to be this way. I was so excited to hold you in my arms the first time, and I have no idea where it went wrong. But things won't change unless I accept help. All I want is for you to be proud of me. And to be able to rock you to sleep or feed you without having a meltdown. None of this has anything to do with ya. It's all on me. My brain is... I don't really know myself, but it's making me this way. I wanna love you so much, and you have no idea how painful this is." My tears drowned my last words. I kissed my fingers and grazed the comforter. "Can I keep this one?" I asked nobody, clutching the animal tighter than required. "It's my promise to come back to you."

With a giant boulder pressing against my ribcage, I exited the room, closing the door behind me. From the corner of my eye, I noticed Tucker watching me from our bedroom doorway, looking dejected. He offered me a tiny smile when our eyes locked and a nod. Dahlia came back at the exact moment, and they exchanged a few words. My husband left with my suitcase as my best friend joined me.

"Come on, Addi. It's time. Let's do this. For what it's worth, I'm proud of ya. And Tucker is too. Jamieson would be if he could talk. It's a great example you're setting up for him, even if he can't tell you right now."

A loud cry tumbled out of my mouth. A cry of pain. And helplessness. "Will he even remember me?" I asked through my tears.

My friend's arms circled my shoulders. "You're his mama, Addi. He spent nine months in your womb. He would recognize you, your voice, your body, your scent anywhere, anytime. Would you like to kiss him goodbye?"

I shook my head. "No. I can't. It's too hard being around him. I'm a terrible person."

"No. You're stronger than you think. And that's what matters."

I nodded and followed her outside.

I caught sight of my baby tucked in Nick's arms, Jack standing tall beside them. I waved in their direction, and the toddler ran my way, his little arms fastening around my thigh.

"Addidi, where you going?"

I caressed his short dark hair. A lone tear traced the length of my cheek.

"I'll be back soon," was all I could muster to reply.

We broke apart, and he watched me.

Nick stepped forward, but I shook my head. He nodded his agreement and grabbed Jack's hand, leading him to the house.

Tucker kissed me before helping me into the car. "Be brave, sweetheart. We'll come to get you when you feel okay. When you want to come home."

He closed the door, and I pressed my palm against the window. He replicated the gesture, our stares unflinching.

The sad bent of his lips shattered my heart.

"I love you," he mouthed.

I nodded, breaking the contact.

For the first time in a month, a streak of confidence woke up in me at the thought of getting my life back. And to regain control over myself.

I would put in the work. Because my family was my universe. And I wouldn't let them down.

39

TUCKER

This was the day. The one when my wife would come back home. To us. When we visited her last weekend, she looked stronger. She spent over an hour with Jamieson nestled in her arms, whispering in his ear while he watched her with adoration. Like he was seeing her for the first time. And in a way, he was.

I shed a few tears and snapped too many pictures, knowing one day Addison would like to have them. We had lunch together, by the stream, and she told me about her therapy and her friends. Dahlia visited her two weeks ago. As promised, she stood by her friend's side. And even joined her for a therapy session when Addison said she couldn't have me there because it'd hurt her too much to face me after everything we went through and she wasn't ready. I'd never force her to do anything unless it came from her. I respected her decision, even if it hurt. But if it meant she'd get better, I'd forget about my pride.

I watched my reflection in the mirror of our bedroom for the tenth time. Yeah, it would do. Dark jeans, a white V-neck T-shirt. "How do I look?" I asked Jamieson, who sat in a baby chair at my feet. He nibbled on his thumb and made a funny noise. "Yes, you're right. We should go and get Mama." I lifted him up in my arms and kissed his cheek. He wore Addison's *A Little Wild* onesie, the late spring heat slightly high to dress him in any more clothes. And it fit him perfectly, too adorable for his own good.

The one-hour drive seemed to last forever. Nick and Dahlia called to wish me luck and asked me to keep them updated. They also made me promise to call them if I required their help. In the last month, they'd flown over two consecutive weekends to gimme a hand. Thanks to them, I had packed full nights of sleep and felt much better than I did a month ago.

My heels dug in the ground when I reached the back-yard of the facility. The sight of Addison stole my breath away.

As usual, my woman looked beautiful, but more serene. More put together.

Before I left last weekend when I visited, she even kissed me of her own volition, sending my heart into a frenzied dance.

Addison ran in our direction when we exited the car, wearing a flowery sundress, half her hair tied in a braid. She halted a foot in front of us, making no movement to take Jamieson from my arms. Instead, she kissed his fore-head, which to me equaled progress. A big fucking step forward in her healing process. Turned out Dahlia was right. She suffered from postpartum depression after all. Since the time she'd been here, she found relief in daily meditation—something she had stopped practicing after giving birth. Small self-care actions peppered her days, along with a special well-balanced diet and individual and group therapy, and yoga.

One night, Addison called me and opened up a little

more about her father's struggle with depression. How it affected her growing up. How she learned to accept the genes that could have triggered her breakdown, even if there were no certainties.

Standing in front of me, the tilt of her lips drew me in. I scanned the length of her, burning this more joyful image of her to my memory.

Color had returned to her cheeks. And sparks to her eyes.

Right now, I had real hopes we'd be okay.

Eating the space between us, my hand closed around her waist in a protective and possessive gesture, my lips descending on hers, itching to taste her essence. "I've missed you like crazy, sweetheart."

Her hand rested over my thrumming heart. "I've missed you too. And I'm sorry. For everything."

I shook my head. "Wasn't your fault. Don't apologize. I'm just glad you're doing better. That's all I've ever prayed for."

"I will. You gotta be patient with me, but I'll get there. Life isn't as dark anymore. Light is coming back. A tad more each day."

I kissed her again, unable to resist, and she let me. "That's fantastic. I love the sound of it. Ready to go home?"

She bobbed her head. "Oh yes."

She went to hug and thank everyone as I spoke with her doctor and a nurse who offered me some pointers and an envelope containing brochures and the special treatment plan she had to follow. We had an appointment scheduled every week with them for another month so they could measure the progress and help us find our rhythm when left on our own in our daily lives.

The road ahead of us was still bumpy, but I trusted that we'd make it to the other end.

The following month went by smoothly. Addison still didn't feel comfortable caring for Jamieson by herself, but she now put him to bed, sang him songs, and held him for longer periods of time each day.

Sometimes I found her crying in bed or calling herself a failure, but with a lot of love and patience, no obstacle seemed impossible to overcome. If we'd made it this far, I was confident we could tackle everything life put on our journey.

We also spent more time outside, at the park, having picnics and walking around with the stroller, the sun and fresh air doing great for her mood.

We celebrated Jamieson turning four months with cupcakes Addison baked and a low-key lunch, just the three of us. Our son slept almost the entire time, but this milestone was a huge deal for my wife and me. Even more considering we celebrated it together.

I scratched the side of my skull and swiveled to face my wife after I put the dishes away. "I was thinking," I said, "if you'd like to join me in the shower. We don't have to do anything. I just missed being with you this way. The intimacy. It's not even about sex, but the connection."

I stayed still, praying she'd say yes, that we could move forward a little more as a couple too.

She fidgeted with her fingers, avoiding my gaze.

"What's the matter?" I asked, holding her hands in mine.

"My stomach. It's still flappy. And wrinkly. I'm not sure you wanna see me like that. It's not pretty anymore. Nothing like it used to be."

I tipped her chin up with a finger, forcing her eyes to meet mine. "No. Don't go there. Don't avoid me. I'm in love with _you_. All of you. Sure, I enjoy your body, but I'm more impressed that it created life than the aftermath of such a miracle. In my eyes, you're always beautiful and will forever be."

"You won't find me disgusting? Or not good enough?"

"Never." I linked our hands. "Come on, let me show you how beautiful you are."

40

ADDISON

Tucker led me to the en-suite in our bedroom. The hammering of my heart could probably be heard miles around. Up to this day, I had succeeded in covering my body around my husband. But I was aware this day would come when he would request more. That we'd resume our intimacy. And the thought of it got me so anxious I always pushed it far away. With my hand firmly in his, he glanced at me over his shoulder, and the smile that he shone on me sent sparks of confidence in me. Confidence I could let go with him. That he meant every word he spoke earlier. That I was safe with him.

We entered the bathroom, and I flicked the light switch off, plunging the room into semi-darkness, only a soft glow coming from the bedroom window illuminating the room.

My husband turned it back on and rested both hands on my hips. "No. I wanna see you. No more hiding."

His voice sounded so soft, so comforting, how could I resist him? Tucker Philips always had that pull on me. A magnetism I couldn't escape.

"Okay," I whispered, my gaze on my feet.

"Can I?" he asked, gripping the hem of my shirt with a delicate gesture.

I closed my eyes and swallowed my uneasiness.

Deciding to let go of my fears, I nodded.

In a slow motion, he peeled the shirt over my head. I battled with myself to avoid covering my stomach, my eyes still shut. Shivers traversed me when his fingertips grazed my arms.

I risked a look at him, and it stole my breath away. His face gushed with love. And I believed his words. That I could do this. With him.

Bending forward, his eyes on mine, Tucker kissed the length of my neck, the valley of my breasts, the soft skin of my belly. His fingers hooked onto my shorts, and kneeling before me, he slid them down my legs. When his thumbs glided to the elastic waistband of my panties, he looked up at me, asking for my permission to remove them.

I nodded, missing the way we used to love each other in the past and the adoration he always showered me with.

His mouth pressed against my inner legs, and he kissed me there, his tongue warm against my center when he laved the seam with gentle strokes.

Chills of pleasure I hadn't felt in so long moved up and down my spine.

My hips rocked forward, chasing the building pleasure only my husband could provide.

Carefully, he stood, his lips molding to mine. "I love you, Wilde. And I always will."

He unclasped my bra, and it pooled on the floor. His palms kneaded my breasts, his mouth never detaching from mine.

With every movement of his tongue, I felt more confident about myself. Like we could still be us. Even after everything we went through.

Hand in hand, we entered the shower, and Tucker took his time washing my hair and every inch of me with the upmost care.

"Can I touch you?" he asked in my ear.

I nibbled on my lower lip and said, "Yes."

"You tell me if it's too much."

I nodded, meeting his eyes.

Feelings I had forgotten about developed in my core. Goosebumps blossomed all over my arms when Tucker's digit descended between my thighs, and he circled my clit in slow motions. I gasped, unable to keep all the sensations swirling in me inside.

"Jesus, I've missed this," he said, his voice husky with unmistakable need.

Coating his fingers with my arousal, he pushed one digit inside. A cry left my mouth, and I trembled at the contact.

My fingernails dug into his biceps, holding him in place and making sure he wouldn't remove his hand.

"You like it?" he murmured.

He positioned himself behind me, his erection pressing against my lower back, his fingers increasing their pace, and his other arm fastened around my waist. I relished the sturdiness of him against me.

Pleasure built in my core, little fireworks igniting the deepest parts of me. Flames that were dead rekindling.

Tucker's thumb pressed against my bundle of sensitive nerves and I came, my head tilting back and resting in the crook of his shoulder. His mouth found mine, and we kissed like we hadn't kissed in such a long time. My toes curled and my body electrified, another orgasm washing over me, his fingers relentlessly gliding in and out of me.

His tongue danced with mine. We fused together, unable to break apart. I didn't need air to feel alive anymore, my husband the only source of oxygen I required.

He groaned into my mouth, and I deepened the kiss, not wanting to break apart from him, scared I would crumble if I did. Tucker was not only my rock. But also my better half. The pillar I could always count on.

"Fuck, sweetheart." His words drowned in my mouth.

His teeth toyed with my lip, and I moaned.

He grabbed a handful of my ass cheeks, and my fist curled around his manhood.

I worked him in slow thrusts when he stopped me with his hand. "Not today, sweetheart. Let's go slow, okay? I don't want us to skip steps or do things you're not ready for."

I pursed my lips to argue, but he kissed me, making me forget about everything as he spun my world in the best possible way. And reminded me why I had to battle with my demons to be worthy of his love again.

Because this, what we shared, was the fuel of my life. And I wouldn't trade this for anything else. Flickers of the darkness that had been surrounding me for months parted away. And burying my face into my husband's chest, I had the certitude we'd be okay. That I would get better and we would find our peace.

———

We exited the shower, and Jamieson's cries reached our ears through the baby monitor in our bedroom.

Tucker kissed the side of my face and dried himself up. "Take your time. I'll get him."

I stopped him with a hand on his forearm.

"Let me," I said.

He frowned. "Are you sure?"

I bowed my head before meeting his eyes. "I am. Please. I can do this."

He tucked my hair behind my ear. "I know you can."

I started dressing up when I spun to face him. "Why don't you take a nap? I'm sure you could use the rest. We'll be all right, Jamieson and I. If something's wrong or if I can't deal with it, I'll come to get you. I promise."

Tucker studied me. Like he was searching for answers in the words I didn't speak out loud. "Fine. I'll take you up on your offer. Thanks."

He linked our fingers, and they brushed together until I walked too far away from him.

A new spur of excitement woke up in my heart. I could do this. If I could let Tucker see the vulnerable side of me, my body that I had to learn to love again, I could take care of my son without panic rising in me.

"Hey you," I said, picking up the fussy baby. "I'm here now. You'll be fine. You and I, we'll be okay." After I changed his diaper, I went to make him a bottle in the kitchen.

Sitting in the rocking chair by the giant window of the nursery, the sunlight casting the shadows away, I fed my baby on my own for the very first time. Basking in the late spring glow, I caressed his cheek with a finger.

His little fingers fastened their grip over the bottle, and his blue eyes fixated on me.

"I'm sorry I've been away for so long. But I'm here now, and I won't leave ever again. I might not be back to being myself again, but I'll get there. I'm aware I'm asking a lot from you, and it wasn't my intention to lose myself after I gave birth. It happened. And it makes me so sad, thinking I failed you. From this day on, I never want you to feel like you can't count on me. Gimme some more time, okay? I'll prove to you I can do this."

His tiny hand let go of the bottle and wrapped around my finger. He tightened his squeeze, and a single tear leaked from my eyes.

"Jamieson, I love you. And I always will." My lips lingered on his forehead. He babbled, pushing the nipple of the bottle out of his mouth. "You agree with me?" I asked. He blinked and returned to his milk.

We floated in our tiny bubble a little longer until my baby fell asleep in my arms.

Strong emotions rushed through me.

They suffocated me, and I placed a hand over my thundering heart.

I can do this. I can do this. I repeated in my head. Those incapacitating thoughts didn't appear as much as they used to, but sometimes they took me by surprise and I froze, not knowing how to react.

I breathed in. One. Two. Three. And breathed out. Three. Two. One.

That's when my eyes caught a glimpse of him, standing in the doorway, an adorable sleepy expression painted on his face. And some of my panic died at the sight.

"Are you okay?" Tucker asked, hurrying to my side, not missing the alarm painting my face. "Hey, you're doing good. It's okay. Just breathe." He lifted the baby from my arms and placed him in his crib before returning to my side. "Wilde, you did it. You spent," he checked the time on his watch, "an hour alone with him. On your own. It's a big step."

He kneeled beside me.

"An hour?" I asked, my words now mixing with tears.

He bobbed his head. "Yes. It's huge."

My entire body quivered, and I had no clue how to stop the tremors. Tucker pulled me to my feet, and after he closed the curtains, he held me in his arms.

"Do you wanna talk about it?"

I shook my head. "Not now." I cocked my head to look at our son. "I did it," I muttered, mostly for my own sake.

My husband never let go of me. His lips caught mine. And once again, I released my fears as I invited his strength to rub on me a little more.

We exited the nursery, and a hint of a smile grazed my lips.

Yes, I did it.

41

TUCKER

J amieson had just turned five months when one morning, I sat my wife down after we had breakfast. She had our baby propped on her leg, kissing his nape, the sound of his laughter warming my heart. And the sight of them together, fulfilling my wildest dreams. Again, I immortalized the moment with my phone. Our family was fragile but strong, and we were determined to grow and heal together. This was the price-less promise linking us all together.

"How are you doing? For real?" I couldn't conceal the worry in my gaze. We had that same exact conversation almost every week.

My wife extended her arm to reach for my hand. "I'm getting there. I was thinking of spacing my therapy sessions."

"You are?"

"I talked to my therapist, and he agreed. If it gets too overwhelming, I'll return to a weekly schedule. What do you think?"

"If you're confident about it, I'll support your decision.

Try it. We'll see how it goes. But I agree you're doing much better." I leaned in to drop a kiss on her forehead. "I'm proud of you. Always am." I studied her. "Wilde, you know that secret project I've been keeping from you?" She nodded. "I'm ready to show you. But for that, we have to go on a road trip. The three of us. If you feel you're strong enough to go."

Her back firmed. "Oh, sounds exciting. What is it? I wanna go."

"Do you trust me?"

"Always."

I kissed her lips and laced our fingers together. "Jamieson already agreed to it. We just have to convince you now."

We exchanged grins, and my fingers entangled in her hair as I leaned forward to claim her mouth when she rose to her feet. My arms locked around her, holding her close to me, Jamieson resting between us.

"Sweetheart, I've missed you so much. I've missed us."

She pressed her hand against my chest, just over my throbbing heart. "Thanks for believing in me. Even when I didn't believe in myself. It means the world to me. And for the record, I love it when you call me *sweetheart*."

"Sweetheart, I've always known. My heart belongs to you. Forever. I'm just happy you found your way back."

"Can we go today? I'm really excited about doing something together, the three of us. Like families do."

I nodded, my forehead pressed against hers.

"But first, let's put Jamieson to bed because I really want to make my husband feel good right now. I've been dying to thank him the proper way."

I tilted my head back. "You sure?"

Her fingers glided under my shirt and grazed my abdomen. Shivers traveled along my spine. "Yes."

I took the baby from her arms. "Then you won't have to tell me twice. This little guy is due for a nap, anyway. Meet me in the bedroom in five."

I turned around, the sound of her snicker doing nasty things to me. Things I hadn't let myself feel in such a long time.

When I entered the bedroom, Addison stood in the middle of the bed, wearing nothing else but a new set of lacy lingerie I'd never seen before, looking like the temptress she had always been. My temptress.

"Jesus, Wilde." I removed my clothes as fast as I could and stood before her, my dick hard as a flagpole, drooling at the sight before me, viewing every delicious curve of hers. "We should take our time."

She shook her head. "I'm not made of porcelain. And it's been so long. I'm missing the connection we share when we love each other. Don't go slow or gentle. Just love me like you used to."

"In that case, spread those legs. I have months to make up for, and I'm starving. Wanna play with me?"

"Always, *Tuuuck*." Need laced her voice, and it almost shattered me, my restraints already weak.

"God, don't say it like that, or I'll come before we even get started."

"Then don't make me wait, big guy. I'm soaking wet right now."

I plunged forward, and taking my sweet time, I savored every inch of her flesh.

When my tongue connected with the apex of her thighs, Addison wriggled underneath me, her muffled cries my undoing. My fingers joined my mouth, cherishing the woman I love.

"Oh, Tuck. I love you."

Those words. I could never live my life fully without hearing them from her.

She pivoted on the mattress and positioned herself over me, reaching for my cock. It'd been forever since he got playtime of his own, and I almost came just from her attention. When her lips circled the tip, I jerked my head back, the sensations too intense. Heat swirled in my balls. My spine tingled with an upcoming release. "Be careful, sweetheart. The guy—" She sucked me into her mouth, and I could barely hold it together. "He hasn't had a lot of attention in a long while. I have no idea how long I can last if you're being your vixen self."

A loud laugh bubbled out of Addison while her tongue licked me in long, moist strokes. "I'll go gentle on you," she said. "How did we survive so long without this?"

Lifting her hips to switch position, I plunged forward and flicked her clit with my tongue, pushing my fingers back into her tight channel and gliding them back and forth.

We both lost ourselves in our desire.

Every whimper from Addison induced a growl from me. Her pleasure wet the lower half of my face as I devoured her, making up for all the months I couldn't.

She rolled her hips over my mouth, purring around my dick, never releasing her grip around it, the jerky movements of her hands almost impossible to resist any longer.

Increasing the tempo of my digits, Addison came on my tongue and begged me to bury myself in her. Pounding inside her, her body locked around mine, we pleased each other until neither of us could draw a full breath in.

Her folded legs fell on either side of her, and I changed the angle to be able to increase the connection of our bodies.

Her hand molded to my nape, and she pulled me to her, kissing me without restraints.

"I love you," I murmured against her lips.

"Then fuck me," she said with a sharp intake of air.

"No. I wanna love you."

I kissed her back. Intertwining our fingers, I brought our linked hands over her head.

We moved together. No more walls existed between us. Flipping her on her knees, I entered her from behind and cupped her ass as I rammed into her with everything I possessed. Her eyelids, half-masted by the pleasure coursing in her, broke me, only to send a new surge of want through me.

The sound of our mixed breathings and flesh hitting flesh filled my ears.

Leaning forward, I peppered kisses along her spine, shaping my upper body to the delicious curve of her back.

Moving out, I turned her until we faced each other, and with my body upright, Addison enveloped herself around me. I held her head while I slid back where I belonged, and we kissed some more.

We moved together, unable to break apart even after we came.

"Now I'm ready for that road trip," Addison whispered against my shoulder as we lay together, entangled in sheets after the second time.

"Pack a bag for four nights. We're not coming back here this weekend. We'll spend at least two nights there. If you like it."

She frowned with a smile and detached her body from mine. "On it."

I jumped to my feet, my heart beating fast in my chest at the idea of showing her the project I'd been working on for months.

"I'll take care of the baby stuff. Meet me downstairs when you're done."

I kissed her reddened lips and slid back into my clothes.

————

We arrived in Nashville in the evening after we stopped multiple times to feed Jamieson or change dirty diapers. The sun hung low in the sky, and the warm breeze swept our faces as we exited the car.

With our son strapped to my chest in the baby wrap and my wife's hand nestled in mine, we walked down the sidewalk.

My heart felt lighter in my chest. The scene right now fit the images I'd painted in my head multiple times.

Just before we entered a door, I spun to face her. "Listen, it's a two-part project. When I started it, we weren't a couple yet. But somehow, along the way, and with everything that happened in our lives, this just made so much more sense than it did back then. Because it fits who we are and what we're aiming for. Love, a low-stress lifestyle, nature, and family time. You'll tell me what you think, but I believe this could be it."

Excitement bubbled inside me at a vertiginous speed. Never before had I made plans this big for people other than myself. And I really wished Addison would get on board with everything.

"Even though it started as my project, it's ours now. And truthfully, it was always meant to be ours. If something bothers you, you tell me. You don't agree and want to forget all about it? No worries. It has a great resale value. I already checked. But I'd appreciate it if you would at least give it a thought before saying no."

My wife watched me with a smile that made me feel virtuous in her eyes.

"Ready?"

She sucked in a breath and nodded.

We entered the space Nick and his guys had been renovating for months. They finished shortly after Jamieson's birth, but I had to wait a long time to show the one person whose opinion mattered the most. The weekend Dahlia visited Addison at the center, Nick, the kids, and I had driven here to finish the final touches. Beside me, my wife gasped, her eyes perusing the space around her. High industrial ceilings, plank floors, stainless steel countertops, black-iron chandeliers, and a wooden stage with a *Wild and Country* sign behind it.

"What is it?" she asked, now facing me.

"Our own bar. Or event venture, I should say. *Wild and Country*. A bit wild, a bit country. It's you and me."

"How? I'm speechless. It's amazing. You did all this on your own?"

I shook my head. "Had lots of help. Nick has been taking care of all the remodeling and improvements. Dahlia helped with the decor since she worked with Nick on some of his projects, and Riley, you know, her ex-manager? Well, he loved the idea so much that when we asked for his expertise for the stage and sound system, he invested in it. So now it's our big project, but it also involves your friends. Carter agreed to play on opening night and to do his next album launch party here too. His way of supporting you. Or us, I guess." Addison watched me with rounded eyes. "Oh, and that's not all. Follow me."

I held her hand, leading her to the third floor.

"This," I said, motioning her through the open space, "is your own event business. One day, when you're ready. The rooftop is yours too, where you'll be able to throw baby showers, bachelorette parties, or weddings. Or anything you'd like. Sky is the limit." We crossed a set of barnwood doors. "And this is your office. Your own Little Wild headquarters. There's a crib, a playroom, a highchair, and everything else if you decide to work here with Jamieson. My official office is downstairs, but I've added an extra desk here on the days we wanna work together. Or have dirty office sex."

She blinked, mute.

"Wilde, are you okay?"

"Tuck...I'm more than fine. I'm impressed. I'm over the moon right now. It's all I've ever dreamed of. Right here, you've made my wildest wishes come true. You did that for me?"

"I did it for you. And me. For us. The rules haven't changed, though. You'll start working again when you're ready. When you can deal with the hours and hectic schedules, and not a day before. I won't let you."

"Are we moving here?"

I cradled her face. "That's the plan. If you're on board. I fell in love with a girl when I visited this city over a year ago, and it seemed fit to continue our story here. I know how much you love this city too, so it wasn't a hard choice to make."

Addison rested both palms on my chest. "Jamieson, you knew about all this?" she asked him. He smiled, drool covering his chin, and she kissed his chubby cheek. "Thank you. Both of you."

"Ready for part two?"

"Oh, this wasn't part two?"

I shook my head. "We can take the car, or we can walk for fifteen minutes. What do you prefer?"

"Let's go for a walk. It's a beautiful day outside."

Hand in hand, we made it to a giant tree-lined street

with craftsmen-houses. We halted in front of number twenty-two.

"Is it—?" Addison asked, watching the powder-blue property.

"Our new home. If we do this."

Her eyes yearned to explore inside, and I nodded with a chuckle. "Go ahead. Go wild, sweetheart. Nick's team has been working on it too, and he said he can change anything you don't approve of."

I heard a loud cheer seconds after she walked in, and the grin on my face just grew bigger.

My wife rushed back outside, watching me with a heartwarming expression on her face. "How did you know?" she asked.

I shrugged. "I'm pretty good at reading you by now. And Dahlia. She still had the journal you two did that summer where you sketched your dream house with pictures from magazines. We used it as an inspiration."

"Are we spending the night here?"

"That's the idea. If you like it."

"You're kidding, right? I love it. When can we move in?"

"Whenever you're ready."

"Can I go back inside? Take a look around?"

"It's all yours. As I said, go wild."

In a sweet gesture that melted my heart, Addison released Jamieson from the wrap around my torso and pulled him into her arms. He wiggled his arms and legs, ecstatic to be freed and in his mama's embrace.

"Jamieson, this is your new home. Our new home. I'm sure we'll be very happy here. Wanna show me around? Daddy said you've already visited the place before, and I'd like you to gimme a tour."

Our son flapped his arms again in a happy dance, and my wife kissed his small button nose.

Right now, everything in my life made sense again. And nothing we went through was in vain.

"Tucker, there's a swing set in the backyard. Come and see," Addison yelled from inside the home as if I hadn't put it there myself.

Even my heart smiled.

We watched the stars from the back deck after we were done with dinner. My wife sat on my lap, her arms around my neck. "Think we will be okay?" she asked after a moment.

"I'm confident. We're already halfway there."

She kissed me, slowly and seductively, moaning against my mouth when my tongue slipped between her lips and stroked hers.

My hands skimmed the skin of her back after I bunched her sundress over her hips. My palms kneaded her soft breasts as they moved to her front, and I toyed with her diamond-hard nipples between my fingers.

"Oh Tuck, we never did it outside. Think the neighbors will complain?"

"Sweetheart, I got the house with the biggest lot and tallest trees so we would have all the privacy we deserve. One day, we'll build a treehouse and have a pool. This is our piece of heaven. Only ours. And I'm allowed to fuck my wife anywhere I see fit."

She peeled the dress over her head, offering me the perfect view of her body. The one that created life. And that kept her safe while she lost herself for a moment. I bent over to suck one of her nipples as her fingers dug into my scalp to prevent me from moving away as she purred her pleasure.

"Tucker, I love you. And I promise here and now to

show you every day of my life. I've been a mess for so long, but you always stayed by my side and believed in me."

She whimpered as I cherished her other breast.

"Get better. That's all I'm asking for. And let me in. Even when it's tough."

She bobbed her head.

I checked the time on my phone. Three minutes past midnight.

"Happy birthday, Wilde."

"You remembered?"

"I recall everything. About you. With you. We have plans tomorrow night—well, tonight, I guess. But right now, let me love you the way I long to and give you your first present. It begins with *cli* and ends with *max*."

Addison released my pulsing erection and positioned herself over me as I pushed her panties to the side. She welcomed all of me into her warmth, rolling her lips over me while her lips tasted mine. With passion.

"Tuck, I can't wait for this new life of ours to start. Everything is perfect. I don't wanna change anything. You're way too good for me."

"Wilde, you freed me. You freed my soul. I'll forever be grateful you entered my life." I got to my feet and with her long legs wound around my waist, I discarded all my clothes. Laying her back on the outdoor couch, I loved my wife with everything I had. And a whole lot more. Right there on the deck under the stars.

EPILOGUE
ADDISON

A year later

"Okay, what's the big surprise?" I asked as Tucker guided me, his strong hands acting as blindfolds. "Where's Jamie? I don't hear him. Are you sure he's fine?"

My husband moved around me, and without removing his hands from my eyes, kissed me. He sucked on my lower lip, and I melted against his hard chest, the one keeping me safe every night.

"Wilde, stop worrying. Jamieson is fine. Enjoy your birthday. I'm taking care of everything."

I nodded as he stepped back.

"We're here. Don't open your eyes until I tell you."

Why was he being so mysterious? Earlier, Dahlia had come home and helped me choose a dress for tonight. Two months ago, she'd expanded her business and now had a satellite store in Nashville, the headquarters still in Green Mountain. We saw each other every few weeks when she came to town.

It took me eight months last year to feel confident and strong enough to resume work. And thanks to Tucker, I was now my own boss. Like I'd always dreamed.

And it fulfilled me.

Tucker quit his job before we moved to Tennessee. The bar was a success, and he never looked back. He said he had never been so happy. Gone were the pressed suits and silk ties. My husband now worked in jeans and plaid shirts most of the time and had never looked so hot. The Southern lifestyle suited him. A lot.

Our lives were blooming. In the best ways.

My heart pummeled in my chest when I heard hushed voices around me.

Tucker trailed kisses down my neck, and I shivered. He linked our hands together and said, "Open your eyes, sweetheart."

A high-pitched cry escaped my lips when my eyes traveled around the backyard.

"Tuck, what is it?" My jaw slackened. My hand cupped my chest.

All around us were dozens of white rose bouquets, round wooden tables with white centerpieces, and garden chairs in pastel colors. The late afternoon sky was painted in pink and orange stripes.

Warmth filled me. I tried to take it all in, wanting to immerse myself in the beauty around me.

"I'm not sure I understand," I said, my voice shaky with emotions.

My friends, my family, and everyone I cared about stood near a small stage.

"Tuck?"

I turned around, and he locked his arms around me. "Addison Samantha Wilde, we eloped to Vegas two years ago, but we never had a wedding reception. In front of everyone we loved, I wanted to make this moment the one you deserve." He dropped to one knee, and I gasped. "We exchanged wedding bands when we got married, but I never actually put a ring on you." A small black velvet box appeared in his hands, and he flipped it open. "I've been in love with you since the minute our eyes met for the first time. Our journey has been wild and crazy, but I wouldn't change a thing, except for letting you walk away that day. Would you do me the honor of marrying me all over again?"

"Ohmygod, yes. Yes, yes, yes," I said, bobbing my head nonstop, a river flowing down my face.

"Is that a yes I hear?"

"It's a million times yes. I love you." The teal Montana sapphire mounted on a platinum band fit perfectly on my ring finger. "It's magnificent." I fanned myself with my hand, trying to prevent the tears from ruining my makeup.

On his feet again and with his hand around my nape, Tucker brought our lips together. Fuzzy feelings danced in my belly. My heart swelled, bigger than it'd ever been before.

We exchanged vows in front of a pastor, and everyone cheered as we kissed some more.

Carter and Dahlia stepped onto the small makeshift stage, sitting on wooden chairs, a single microphone in front of them. They looked just like the kids who sang for their friends and families in her backyard all those years ago.

"Addison. Tucker. This song is for you," Dahlia said with a wink. They played some of their most famous Carter Hills Band songs. It'd been years since they'd been on a stage together. And now here they were. For me. More tears shone in my eyes. This day would forever be imprinted on my memory.

They finished, and my husband let go of my hand. He climbed on the stage and grabbed a guitar someone handed him. Sitting next to Dahlia and Carter, they sang "A Girl Like You," the song Tucker sang to me in that karaoke bar the weekend we met. After the first chorus, my husband jumped to his feet, ripped open his dress shirt, exposing the too-stretched and tiny pink groom T-shirt he wore that same night, and resumed the song, now on his own.

My eyes stayed glued to him.

How could I look anywhere else?

How could I want to be with anybody else?

I had no idea he played the guitar. He never hinted about it.

The grin on my face was probably three sizes too big, and I wasn't even sure my feet touched the ground anymore.

Carter and Dahlia joined in for the last chorus.

My friends and family all cheered and applauded, but I stood there, frozen, my heart bouncing in my chest, my breaths short and shallow, and my insides about to turn into fireworks.

"I love you, Wilde," Tucker shouted into the mike before joining me. I blinked, unable to speak, my words dissolving on my tongue. Nothing I said out loud would be enough to express how I felt.

Nearing me, he circled my waist, and I sank my head into his chest, listening to the beating of his heart.

"You play the guitar?" I asked once I landed back on planet Earth.

"Got private lessons. Back in Green Mountain. After you left. A good friend of yours is quite talented." He kissed the tip of my nose. "Wilde, I just played on a stage with the Carter Hills Band. How crazy is that?"

I shook my head, unable to stop grinning.

"You were great up there. And so sexy. That T-shirt, it really suits you. Big guy, you might have just become my new favorite country star. Don't tell Cart and Dah I said that."

He silenced me with a bruising kiss.

We all sat for dinner, eating in the twilight, the food delicious, and the laughter and chatter of all our friends around the table precious.

My mama, whom I tried to see more often since I moved back to Tennessee, brought Jamieson over, and nestled between us, we danced as my friends sang their greatest hits under the moonlight.

I needed nothing more in life.

My heart was full.

And I was blissfully happy.

I was still wild and crazy, but I had found my perfect match. Someone to follow me in all my over-the-top ideas. And always there to catch me when I fell or to propel me forward when I required a push in the right direction. We had each other's backs always, for better or for worse.

"I can't believe you did this," I said to Tucker, enjoying his warmth all around me, as he held me tight to his chest with one arm and held Jamieson with the other. "This is so romantic."

"If you didn't know by now, I'm gone for you. You once said love, soulmates, and weddings matter to you. They matter to me too. When it's with you."

"Then let's get out of here for a while because I gotta test that theory."

After putting Jamieson in his crib, we retreated to our bedroom, undressing each other as if our lives depended on it.

"You're so beautiful, sweetheart," Tucker said in a

husky voice as he bent forward and circled a stiff nipple with his tongue. "Do we have to go back there afterward?" he panted, pointing in the direction of our backyard.

I nodded. "You invited all those people. You just can't throw them out now. It's not even ten o'clock yet."

He drew in a breath. "You're right. But let's love each other first because I couldn't bear to see you in that dress for another minute and not do anything about it. Now spread your legs, woman. I need my fix."

I fell with a soft thud on our mattress, Tucker fucking me with his tongue before I could even comprehend what was happening.

"Oh God," I moaned. "Best birthday ever." I fisted the sheets around me as my hips shot off the bed, rivers of heat flowing inside me, as pleasure built deep in my core. My body went rigid, and a thousand volts rushed inside me, making me beg for more. I came in a series of seizures. Tucker rose to his feet, and I climbed his body, monkey-style. His thick erection pushed inside me, and with his fingers digging into my ass cheeks, I rolled my hips over his.

"Sweetheart, I'm not done with you. I have a lot more to give you." His mouth feasted on mine, and we kissed until my lips swelled, my toes curled, and I had a hard time breathing on my own.

Moving me up and down, he speared into me in luscious strokes. I came undone all over him, and the satisfied expression on his face brightened the entire room.

"Happy birthday, Wilde."

Once the waves of bliss lessened, my husband laid me down on our bed.

Kneeling between my legs, he flipped me on my front, placing a pillow underneath my stomach, and positioned himself so he could slide back inside me, my body humming at the sensation of his fullness. With a hand flat on my lower back and one kneading my breast, he rammed into me until all I could say was his name and all I could see were stars.

I turned over, and my husband pounded into me, lust in his eyes.

He stared at me with adoration. And that smile. The same one he sent across to me the night we first met. The one I never saw aimed at anyone else.

We came together, entangled, never breaking apart, breathing the same air, intoxicated on our love. His heart pounded strongly against mine. With one hand, he held my face and kissed me. His mouth ventured lower, sucking and teasing my skin with his tongue. "Happy birthday, sweetheart. Ready for your cake?"

I nodded, unable to speak, still overwhelmed by the after-orgasm bliss running through my bloodstream, my body not responding to orders anymore.

"Mamamamama" followed by a cry startled us both, breaking the enticing slumber in which we were drowning. Jamieson was awake, telling us he wanted to go back to the party. Like us, he loved people, music, and gatherings.

We dressed, and I fixed my hair and makeup before joining our guests in the backyard. Dahlia came to me minutes later, a big, round chocolate cake in her hands, friends and family in tow. They crooned the birthday song, my baby snuggled in my arms, and my husband pulled me to his side, keeping me close and safe against him. Like he always did.

His warm breath tickled the shell of my ear as he whispered, "Make a wish." I squeezed his hand, closed my eyes, and prayed I'd be as happy as I was tonight for the rest of my life.

———

Four years later

"You sure you're ready for this?" I asked my husband as I smoothed his jersey, my fingers lingering on his ab muscles for longer than required. "This is a big job. You can't lose patience or throw a fit. You gotta be a role model. This is serious shit."

He cracked a smile and devoured my mouth. I lost myself in him when he deepened the kiss, his strong arms locked around me.

"All the events in my life have brought me to this moment, sweetheart. As long as I know you'll be rooting for me—for us—from the sideline, I can move mountains if that's what you want. Don't worry about me."

Something, or rather someone, caught our eyes on the kitchen floor.

"You should worry about him, though," Tucker teased. "He's trying to fit his right shoe on his left foot. Again."

I slapped his hard chest and stepped back, squatting. "Honey, try the shoe on your other foot. Yeah. This one." I paused. "Better?" My baby jumped to his feet and looped his little arms around my neck.

"Love ya, Mama."

"Oh, I love you too. Now get your brothers. You don't want to be late on your first day."

Tucker helped me up to my feet, looking picture-perfect with our ten-month-old baby girl cradled in his arms.

"Oli, Spence, Jamie, we're leaving," I said as Tucker went to buckle Nelly in her car seat.

My little men stomped down the stairs looking fierce

and happy in their matching black jerseys, the ones I designed for the occasion.

"You're beautiful, Mama," Jamieson said as he walked past me. My sweet boy, always making sure I was well. Like he could sense things had been rocky back in the day. He adjusted his baseball cap over his tousled curly brown locks. He was his daddy's spitting image, except for his eyes that were like mine. Vibrant blue.

His brothers joined us.

"I love you guys. Now hurry up," I said as I locked the door behind us. "Daddy says he's fine, but you know what fine means." I wrinkled my face, and my sons and I shared a laugh.

"Yeah, we know," Jamieson said with a loud huff. "Are we going to Aunty Dahlia's this weekend?"

"Yes. We're leaving tomorrow morning. I have a big surprise planned for Daddy's birthday, but don't tell him." His small fingers snaked around mine. "Now let's go. I can't wait to see you in action."

Tucker never really had birthday parties growing up, something I learned before Jamieson turned one. Every year now, I planned something special for him. Last year, we spent a weekend in Chicago. This year we were going to Green Mountain. I had rented one of Carter's cabins and had a caterer coming over, a bouncing house for the kids, and a whiskey degustation for the adults.

With my hands clutched in front of me, Nelly in a baby wrap, I paced along the field and looked at my guys kicking the ball, or at least trying to. They were all focused, doing their best to remember everything their coach taught them.

The twins saw butterflies, and their attention shifted to the flying insects.

"Oliver. Spencer. The game is here," the coach said, pointing to the soccer field. At three years old—I got preg-

nant a month after my birthday slash wedding reception—
they weren't interested in playing ball. But the coach
insisted on teaching them the game early. I didn't disagree
because the four of them in matching jerseys were a sight
warming my insides.

The coach ran after my boys, holding their hands in
his, showing them where they should be positioned on the
field.

Our gazes locked, and he mouthed, "What should
I do?"

I tilted my head back, unable to stop laughing at his
expression.

"Not funny," he mouthed.

I pinched my lips together, my forefinger and thumb
almost pressing together, then blew him a kiss.

He grinned, and my pulse picked up like it always did
every time we were together. Even after all these years. We
had found our rhythm in life. And moving to Nashville had
been the best thing we could have done. We were blissfully
happy. The kids were thriving. We had family and friends
around, and above everything else, we had each other.
Good days, bad days, we were it. A mix of chemistry, fireworks, and love, as Tucker once said. And I couldn't agree
more.

The man I loved winked at me, and I knew the
promises this simple gesture bore. And in that instant, I
loved the coach something fierce.

———

Want more? Carter Hills and Riley Burns
are back in *The Love Song For Two* series.
Last Hope is Riley and Devon's story.

Read ***Last Hope*** now

———

Thank you for reading Tucker and Addison's
emotional and beautiful love story.

*If you like this book, please talk about it and post a review. This is
the best way to help me find new readers who would love it too and
keep written amazing and touching love stories.*

———

The *Love Song For Two* series follows Riley Burns, Aisha
Jones, and Sam Stevens's journey toward love
and a happily-ever-after.
<u>Keep reading for an excerpt and bonus content.</u>

Read ***Last Hope*** now

emmanuellesnow.com/last-hope

———

FREE bonus chapter
Want even more? Your bonus chapter awaits here
emmanuellesnow.com/bonus-content

THANK YOU
DID YOU ENJOY THIS BOOK?

Thank you so much for reading Tucker and Addison's story. If you enjoyed reading this book, please help spread the word about it. **Each review**—as brief as it might be—is **invaluable** in **helping me** pursue my career as a full-time writer.

Please, for other readers' sake, avoid spoilers in your reviews.

I'm really lucky to count you as a reader, and I truly appreciate your support.

Emmanuelle

ACKNOWLEDGMENTS

Wow, who would have thought *Wild and Country* (now titled *Breathless*) would be my biggest book so far? Not me, I swear. I hadn't planned to write Tucker and Addison's story, but I got to know them better in *Second Tear* and couldn't miss the opportunity to present them to you.

And yes, what a wild ride these two put me through. I love their energy, their loyalty, and mostly their hearts. They are two people we would all love to have in our friend circle. They are passionate and strong-headed. I wrote the first draft of this book on a whim before I even finished *Second Tear*. Both Addison and Tucker were living in my head, and they wouldn't let me finish the other book first. Yeah, they can be loud. And pushy. But in the best of ways.

Tucker and Addison's tale isn't your typical love story, but it was one that had to be told. If you've ever suffered from postpartum depression, remember you're not alone. Just please don't isolate yourself. There are people who can help you through this. My heart is with you.

I wrote this book in two countries, six provinces and as many states, a dozen cities, living at home, at other people's houses, and hotels, trying to put the final touches to it.

I have many people to be thankful for.

First, my husband and children. I love you. I think those words sum it all up. I'm so happy each time you get excited about my newest literary project.

Shalini, one more project we can proudly say, "It's a wrap." And Tucker, wow, he was a love-at-first-sight main character, right? What's not to love about him? Thank you for all your hard work and for being there for me as a friend along the way. I'm happy we're doing this together around the moon. Always.

Mom and Dad, thank you for having us over when we had no home and when all our plans changed overnight. This was really generous, and I truly appreciate it. Mom, thank you for reading my postpartum depression chapters and confirming I was right on track with Addi's struggles.

Jo and Catherine, thank you for having us over when, once again, we had no place to stay after we decided to drive across the country with our kids and all our belongings, with no real plan. I know they're six of us and it can be wild, but you showed us what true friendship is all about.

Jacynthe, Virginie, thank you for always encouraging me and making me a better person.

To my readers, thank you from the bottom of my heart. Seeing my books in your hands, and reading your positive comments and encouragements are always the greatest joys an author can experience. So thank you! Truly.

To my ARC team, you guys rock. I'm always excited to put a new book out there because I can't wait to hear your feedback. Many of you have become friends over the last few releases, and I'm happy to be able to share these stories with you. Thank you for your love and support!

To the bloggers, Bookstagrammers, BookTokers, and Youtubers, who love and share my work, I'm super thankful for all of it. None of this would be as great if it weren't for you. You make me proud to be the author that I am when I see you loving and sharing my work.

To all y'all, cheers!

ABOUT THE AUTHOR

Smart, Sexy, and Sassy Love Stories

USA Today and International Bestselling author Emmanuelle Snow is a contemporary author of mature YA and New Adult love stories, who gives life to strong characters who'll fight with all they have to reach their life goals and find their own happiness.

Emmanuelle is in love with love. Especially complicated, deep, and passionate feelings that make a relationship extraordinary and complex all at the same time.

In her spare time, when she's not writing or reading, she likes to go on road trips—with her four kids and her own soulmate—watch movies, paint, or do some DIY, always with a cup of green tea in her hand and listening to country music.

She splits her time between beautiful Canada and the small US towns she adores.

Find all of Emmanuelle's books here:
emmanuellesnow.com/books

———

Want to connect with Emmanuelle online?

ALSO BY THE AUTHOR

CARTER HILLS BAND UNIVERSE

(suggested reading order)

Carter Hills Band series

False Promises

HEART SONG DUET

BlindSided

ForeverMore

Whiskey Melody series

Sweet Agony

SECOND TEAR DUET

Cruel Destiny

Beautiful Salvation

BREATHLESS DUET

Wild Encounter

Brittle Scars

Upon A Star series

Last Hope

Midnight Sparks

Love Song For Two series

LONESOME STAR DUET

Fallen Legend

Rising Star

Read them all

emmanuellesnow.com/books

Available on author's bookshop

emmanuellesnowshop.com

LAST HOPE

RILEY

Our eyes met. Something passed between us. Attraction. Recognition. Yearning. Maybe a mix of all three. And much more. I brought the tumbler to my lips, relishing the burning sensation of whiskey as it slid down my throat.

A gear shifted inside me.

And my heart did one of its moves. The one where it got all bothered and excited.

I fastened my grip around the glass in my hand.

The woman pushed her long, curled blonde hair over one shoulder, giving me a perfect view of her lickable, slim neck. *Lickable?* Was that even a word? I pushed the thought away. I was a man on a mission.

The vampiric side of me, the one I didn't know existed until now, emerged in full strength.

I blinked.

The temptation to bite the soft flesh of her neck multiplied by the second.

The woman smiled, and all my restraints broke loose. They caught fire and burned to ashes in the dark night.

I gave her a subtle nod as I continued staring, hoping for a slight hint of encouragement from her.

Her red-painted lips pursed as she mouthed a "Hey" my way.

Smoothing my moist hand over the dark fabric of my trousers, I made a beeline for her, my steps light and focused, not allowing the sea of people to break our eye contact. The air around us heated up. We were outdoors, but it felt as if someone had cranked the thermostat up. Slowly, I raked my fingers through my brown hair, gelled for tonight, doing my best to not mess it up. No one in the business needed to know how unruly my heart was behaving. Or the tremble that had started in my fingers. The flickers of excitement that burned in my core.

A server passed me. I discarded my tumbler before grabbing two champagne flutes from his tray.

In two long strides, I reached the woman in the red lace dress. Her smile spread to her eyes when I offered her the bubbly alcohol.

"To a great night and even greater company," I said as we clinked our glasses. "I'm Riley." I held out my hand for her to shake. Our palms met, and her warmth sent tingles of electricity through me, lighting me up and heating my insides like no woman had ever done before. I felt I'd combust from her touch alone.

"I'm Devon."

I lifted our joined hands to my lips and kissed her.

Her soft chuckle resonated through me. "I can already tell you're a gentleman."

"My mama taught me well. So, what brings you here, Devon? I've never seen you at one of these country music parties before."

"Oh, you go to these a lot? This is my first time. It's

quite intimidating. A friend of mine invited me, but she's running late."

I followed her gaze across the rooftop bar. Country music stars counted for more than half of the patrons here, and all together they had won enough awards to fill an entire room. Woven through them were music producers, managers, movie stars, and their dates. Yeah, I guess the crowd could be quite impressive from an outsider's point of view.

My man, Carter Hills, waved at me when my eyes drifted to him. I raised my glass in his direction. Carter was not only my biggest protégé but also one of my best friends. Over the years, we rose to the top of this industry together, our friendship growing stronger with each album. We had each other's backs. Always.

"All these people, they aren't as intimidating as they look once you get to know them. Most of them are pretty great actually. Down to earth. And genuinely nice. Don't let their success make you nervous. Looking great is part of their job description. But there's much more to them. Well, to some of them at least."

The woman snickered and clutched my elbow, balancing her weight on her four-inch nude stilettos.

"You seem like the kind of man who knows a lot about the country music scene, am I right?"

I took another sip of my drink and shrugged, my eyes trained on her face, enjoying the tilt of her red lips. "You could say that. I've been around these folks my entire life, but an active part of their world for almost a decade."

Devon's gray-blue eyes flared. "You're a country singer? Ohmygod, I'm sorry if I didn't recognize you." A flush crept along her neck and cheeks. The same neck I was still dying to feast on.

"No. I'm not. Believe me, you don't want to hear me sing. It may burst your eardrums. No kidding."

She grinned at me. And my heart swelled in my chest. "Who are you then? What's your superpower?"

"I'm a manager." I pointed to Carter, now deep in a conversation with Rita L. Sterling, a music producer. "I manage this fellow's career, amongst others."

Devon moved closer and lowered her voice to a whisper as if she feared someone would hear her. Not a chance with the chatter and music surrounding us. "Is that Carter Hills? I'm sorry. I'm not a groupie, I swear, but I thought I recognized him earlier when I walked in."

"Yeah, that's him. I can introduce you later."

Devon shook her head, the color on her cheeks now darker. "No, you don't have to. I'm nobody here. I'm not part of this world. This night is surreal, I—"

A waitress bumped into my side and dropped an entire tray of glasses filled with red wine all over me.

I blinked as my clothes absorbed every drop.

"Oh, shit. I'm so sorry. It's my first night here. I'm so, so sorry. I messed up. What can I do?" she asked, her eyes tearing as she righted the now-empty wine glasses on the splattered tray. "I ruined your shirt, sir. This is so unprofessional. I'll get fired over this. Wait here, I'll be right back, I'll get my purse. Dry-cleaning is on me."

I circled her wrist before she ran away and leveled my eyes with hers. "Stop. Breathe. It's just a shirt. I own a dozen more just like it. You won't get fired because nobody will say anything to your boss. I might even have been the one bumping into you. I should've stood on the side of the deck. See, I'm standing in the way." The waitress raised her watery eyes, studying me as if there was a *but* about to come out of my lips. There wasn't. "What's your name?"

"Daphne."

"Well, Daphne, breathe in. Breathe out. It'll help to calm your nerves."

She filled her lungs with a deep inhale.

"Yeah, like this." Her shoulders dropped. "See? Much better. Listen, now you go back there," I pointed to the bar, "fill this tray up, smile, and get on with your night. Don't let this little incident affect you. You're doing a great job."

She blinked and swallowed hard, a quiver of a smile trembling over her lips.

"How can you tell? You don't even know me, sir."

"It doesn't matter; I'd recognize a hard worker anywhere. I have a flair for finding good people. It's my superpower." I fished a card from the pocket of my now damp jacket. "If waitressing doesn't work out or you're ever looking out for a job, gimme a call. I might be able to put in a good word for you. Don't worry. The sun always comes out after the storm."

"Wow—Thank you. I—This—That's the nicest thing someone has ever said to me." She clutched my business card, pressed it against her chest as if I'd just promised her the world, and offered me a shy smile before walking away, her chin up and back straight. Warmth filled me. Daphne would be okay. She just needed a pep talk. And I happened to be good at those too. Perhaps I had more than just one superpower after all.

Devon leaned closer, her eyes filled with a stunned expression. The scent of her tipped my senses; she smelled like spring and rain. Fresh and flowery. I burned the fragrance to my memory. Even my heart seemed to enjoy it as it expanded in my chest and drummed faster.

"Wow. That. Was. Amazing. Most people would have screamed at the poor girl or threatened to get her fired. You boosted her self-confidence instead. That's very noble of you. You are a good man, Riley."

I looked down and pinched the fabric of my stained shirt to unglue it from my chest. "Thank you. It was just a clumsy mishap. Now, would you excuse me for a minute? I need to freshen up." I grimaced as she grinned at me, the gleam in her eyes captivating me.

Devon's smile widened, and she nodded. "Go ahead. I can't wait to see how you manage to come back still dressed in these clothes. This should be interesting." She motioned to my soaked self, her nose scrunched up.

I smiled. Like a fool. There was no way I could hold it back. Falling under this woman's charm felt like breathing. Easy. Natural. And imperative. "Wait and see. I may surprise you. I always find ways to turn impossible situations around."

Devon chuckled. "I'm sure you do. While you are in there cleaning up, I'll order us more drinks. Whiskey?"

"On the rocks," I said, holding back a grin. Did Devon notice what I was drinking earlier? If so, it made her even more attractive. I dreaded walking away from her, not ready to escape the magnetism that had settled between us. "I'll be quick."

We eye-fucked each other for a few seconds, my pulse spiking at the way her eyes brightened her face.

Full lashes, high cheekbones, straight nose, heart-shaped lips.

This woman had captured my heart the moment I saw her on this rooftop. It made no sense, but I refused to over-think it.

Our encounter was the highlight of my night. Of my day or even my week.

With a sigh, I broke eye contact.

In a hurry to get back to her, I weaved through the bar crowd, my jacket now open, my soaked shirt sticking to my abs, and the front of my trousers molded to my thighs.

Nothing about being wet and dressed up felt good. And I was pretty sure even my socks were damp. I frowned at my conundrum and wondered how I'd be able to go through the night wearing clothes drenched in red wine. It wasn't as if I had a change of clothes in my car or something. And no way could I go back home to change, even though I lived only ten miles away. I had no intention of letting Devon out of my sight tonight.

In the men's room, I removed my once-white shirt, tsked at it, and threw it in the nearest trash can. A complete loss. I couldn't save it even if my life depended on it. After dabbing my trousers with paper towels, I turned the undershirt around and tucked it into my pants. I used more paper towels to soak up the excess wine from my jacket and put it back on. The look wasn't perfect, but in the dark bar, nobody would look too closely to notice.

I eyed myself in the mirror one last time, fixed my hair and the lapel of my jacket, and with determination in each step, made my way back into the night, looking for the woman in the red dress.

———

Read Riley and Devon's story,
Last Hope, now

emmanuellesnow.com/last-hope

Author's bookstore at emmanuellesnowshop.com

"Once again Emmanuelle Snow has created such amazing work. I went through an emotional journey with this story, I had happy tears, sad tears and laughter. It was just so heartfelt and pure. I couldn't put the book down." **(Goodreads)**

*"I always love it when an author is able to make me feel all kinds of emotions. And with 'Hope and Country', Emmanuelle definitely managed that. This read was romantic, fun, sad, heartbreaking and wonderful." (**Goodreads)**

emmanuellesnow.com/last-hope

FALLEN LEGEND

SAM

Fisting my hands at my sides, I paced the room, a ball of lightning bouncing around my chest. This was a nightmare. A disaster about to happen. How had I not seen this one coming? How could I have been so blind?

My nails dug trenches in my palms, drawing pinpricks of blood, but I would keep my composure.

The lump in my larynx rubbed against the chaffed walls of my throat.

I reeled in some of my wrath and tried another approach. My voice a ragged whisper. But calmer this time.

Putting my pride to rest. And urging my sanity to stay in the game.

"Lisa, you can't be serious. Listen, there must be something *I* can do. Can we talk about it first? And what about the kids? How am I going to explain it to them? We'll get help. You can't just leave like this."

No emotions, rather not the ones I wished to see, crossed her hardened features. No I'm-having-second-thoughts. Or you-might-be-right-we'll-get-help.

My wife had turned into a stony version of herself.

Hoping the pain would numb the one ripping my chest in two, I tugged the roots of my hair. How could I have been so clueless about the woman I'd been married to for the last four years?

She pushed another shirt into her bag, ignoring my words.

Maybe I could reach out to the mother inside her.

"Lisa, your leaving will fuck them up for the rest of their lives. Abandoning your own children, really? That's not what motherhood is all about." I halted and turned around to face the woman, who I thought I knew so well, zipping up her royal-blue suitcase. The one that had traveled around the world with us for years. Yeah, what a joke.

She raised her gaze finally, and I saw determination pass through her eyes this time. She wasn't doubting her decision to walk away from us. Her family. I studied her for a minute, wishing I could see tears glistening somewhere in them. Or regret marring her features. But there were none.

She was done.

When did my wife harbor a rock in place of her heart?

"Is it about the miscarriages?" I asked, praying she'd say yes and that I could call her doctor and set up an appointment to discuss her psychological distress. "I know how difficult it's been on you. But it's been hard on me too. We can get through this. Together. We're a good team. We love each other."

Lisa sighed and shook her head, her eyes still showing no sign of hurt. Or sadness. Or anything. "That's the thing, Sam. I don't love you. I did. Once. But both miscarriages were eye-opening. I need to find myself. I'm twenty-eight. For the last six years, I've followed you around the globe. I liked that. For the last four, I've played wife and mommy. And I enjoyed it. At some point. But being a parent is your thing. We had babies because you wanted to be a daddy. I never asked to be a mother. In all honesty, I thought it'd grow on me." She shrugged. "But it didn't. I crave fresh air. To be free to do whatever I want. Whenever I want it. And being a parent isn't just what I hoped it'd be. I'm sorry, but I'm over it."

I blinked. What? Was she serious right now? *She's over it?*

I was having one of those crippling nightmares that felt too much like reality. This was it. No woman in her right mind would say such horrible things about her own children. About her family.

Her flesh.

Her blood.

My Adam's apple bobbed, and bile rose in my throat. Tinted with disgust. And disdain.

My wife was delusional.

Who should I call to get her some help?

Could her state of mind be ruled a mental breakdown? Did she require psychiatric professionals? Or a vacation? She looked sane.

Lisa smiled at me as if quitting on us was just a daily occurrence and not something about to wreck our entire world.

My shoulders fell, and so did my heart. I inched closer when she moved to her feet.

"Can we talk about this? Please. You owe me that. We've been through so much together. Did you forget everything?" I asked, forcing my voice to sound even, trying my best to keep my anger under wraps.

She offered me another twist of her lips. She looked diabolical. Who was this woman? Where did my wife go?

"I owe you nothing, Sammy. The ride has been fun,

but I'm not playing this family game anymore. I'm out. Oh, and I'll send you the divorce papers in a week or two."

My eyes sprang wider.

What the actual fuck.

"Divorce papers? Don't you think it's a little early to talk about a divorce? We haven't even fought about anything serious in the past, and now you're talking about dissolving our marriage. Tell me you're kidding. Where are the cameras? The crew? Is it for a celebrity prank TV show?"

My wife—or soon-to-be ex-wife if she had her way— huffed. As if anything I said sounded childish. Asking her to stay seemed to scrape on her nerves.

"C'mon, Sammy. I'm moving to the other side of the world. I won't return. Ever. Come to terms with it. Nothing you do or say will change anything." She sighed again and shook her head, looking desperate. "I. Am. Not. Coming. Back. Ever. This"—she gesticulated with her finger to the space around her—"is over. You and I, we're done." A car honked outside. "Now move, my cab is wait- ing." She pushed past me, rolling her suitcase behind her.

I stood there, frozen. Nothing of this made sense. The dream had lasted long enough. I could wake up now. *Please make this nightmare go away.*

My heart stuttered, and I snapped back to the present when the sound of little feet neared our bedroom.

I spun on my heels and watched Lisa as she stood in the doorway, a mask of annoyance painting her frigid face.

My heart froze. Ice frosted the blood inside my veins. I held my breath.

Mikaella, our four-year-old, ran our way in her one- piece unicorn white PJs, her wild, curly light-brown hair looking like a bird's nest, a fluffy baby-pink blanket hanging from her tiny hand.

She stopped before Lisa, her round golden eyes traveling from her mama to the suitcase beside her. "Going on a trip, Mama?" Sparks shone in our daughter's eyes, and she lifted a finger. "I love going on the plane. Nneeeaowww," she said, her hand imitating the aircraft. "The ladies always gimme chocolate. Justine *lovvvves* chocolate too. She always eats mine. Can I bring Miss Froggy with me? She's never been on a plane. She wanna come. You said she could come next time. You promised."

Lisa looked at our daughter, her gaze empty and back held taut. I prayed to see an emotion crossing her flat gaze. None made an appearance.

Mikaella tugged at her hand. "Mama, can I pack by myself? I'm a big girl. Can I bring my purple dress? And my ballet shoes? Can Boa raccoon come too? And Holly? She always misses me when I'm gone. She hates being a doll. She wants to be a real baby. Or a lady. And drink tea."

Lisa finally said something. My ears scorched the moment the words left her mouth. "Mama is going on a trip by herself, Mika. To Thailand. You can't come, I wanna be alone."

Tears pooled in our baby's eyes. She tugged at her mother's hand once again. "But I wanna come. Justine wants to come too. She'll be sad if you leave without her. Mama, we'll be good, good girls. And be silent if your head hurts."

Lisa ruffled her hair. "Sorry. You're not coming. I gotta go. Be nice to your daddy. And take care of Justine. Can you be a big girl, Mika?" Our daughter nodded, a wide smile now brightening her sweet face. Lisa ignored her and stalked away when the cab honked a second time. My heart sank deeper in my chest at the sight of my wife padding away from our baby girl.

She turned to face me once at the top of the staircase. "Bye, Sammy. Have a good life." She removed her wedding ring and placed it on the banister.

My heart tumbled down my chest until it hit the hardwood floor. Smashed and bleeding.

I stood there, acid filling my throat and dissolving the words I wanted to speak.

Mikaella's sobs brought me back to her. "She didn't kiss me goodbye. Mama. Mama. Come back. I'll be a good girl."

I rushed to my daughter and lifted her in my arms, both of us needing each other's love and affection now more than ever.

I brushed her hair with my fingers, dried her tears, and hugged her closer so my heart could soothe hers. Because I had no clue how to heal her pain with words.

I followed Lisa down the stairs. My eyes zoomed in on the front door. My head pounded, and my chest cavity filled with piling rocks as the sound of the revving engine outside faded away. What just happened?

Two hours ago, everything was fine. Or I thought it was. We bathed the girls, read stories in bed… Where did it go wrong?

My stomach heaved. Lisa left. She fucking left.

"Shhh, sweet pea. It'll be okay. We'll be okay. I'm here."

In that instant, I didn't even believe my own words.

I fished my phone from my back pocket to call my wife. We needed to talk. Before she left for good. Before she regretted any of it. Before it was too late to fix that rift keeping us apart.

Beep. Beep. Beep.

The last thread of hope holding me together burned to ashes.

Chills lined my back.

Lisa had disconnected her number.

Reality hit me. It wasn't a prank or a spur-of-the-moment decision. It was premeditated.

How long had she been planning her escape?

How long ago had she decided the girls and I were inconveniences in her life?

Oxygen could barely make the journey from my lungs to my brain anymore.

My wife had vanished in the night without giving me any kind of explanation. Or a way to reach her.

I buried my face in the crook of Mikaella's neck, hiding my numbing emotions from her.

My head spun. A weight I'd never carried before grew in my chest, crushing my organs. How would I ever be able to tell my baby girls their mama had ditched them for a reason I still didn't get?

The last fragment of my heart broke free as my baby's sobs doubled, now heart-wrecking, coming from some place deep down her little body, her sadness drenching my shirt. "I want Mama. I love the plane. She didn't kiss me. I want a hug. From her."

My eyes glazed over.

My little girl tilted her head back and stared at me, her lower lip trembling and her face a map of confusion and sorrow.

She cupped my cheeks with her hands and blinked.

"Daddy, why are you crying? Do you miss Mama too? Did she forget to kiss you goodnight?" She wrapped her baby arms around my neck and fastened her hug around me. "Don't cry, Daddy. I'm here. I love you. Don't cry, okay?"

I pulled my daughter against my heart. "I love you too,

sweet pea. I'm not going away. Ever. You hear me, Mika? I'll never leave you. I promise."

We held onto each other until she relaxed in my embrace, and sleep claimed her.

I tucked my daughter in, doing my best to avoid waking Justine, my two-year-old, sleeping in the adjacent bed. In one corner of their bedroom, sitting in a rocking chair, I watched my children fast asleep, their steady breathing a bandage around my hemorrhaging heart.

With a slow look around, I took in the pastel-pink walls, the glittery matching unicorn bedspreads, the dolls sitting around a small wooden white table with tiny porcelain teacups in front of them, the net with over twenty stuffed-animals hanging across the ceiling, the fairy lights casting a golden glow wrapped around the princess-inspired headboards.

Would we ever be okay again?

My eyes landed on the family picture framed on the wall we took last Christmas.

Our smiles looked so genuine.

I studied Lisa. Was she faking being happy the entire time?

I slouched forward, my face landing in my hands, my shoulders heaving as sobs rocked my body.

The fresh wound ripping my chest in two widened. How did I go from having a picture-perfect family at dinner time to being a single dad mere hours later?

How did I not see my world crumbling? There must have been signs leading to this moment. How did I miss all of them? How could have I been so blind?

That's the thing, Sam. I don't love you. I did. Once.

My life was built on a lie. It was a fucking illusion.

Lisa faded into the night like she never existed.

That was when the truth hit me. Like a ton of bricks

weighing on my fractured heart. I was on my own. And had no one to connect to on this journey.

My daughters had become motherless.

Not because their mama died, but because she chose to leave them behind.

Not because she was incapacitated, but because she couldn't love them the way they deserved to be loved.

My hands cupped my thundering organ. Every cell in me hurt as the truth of my new reality, our new realities crashed on me and settled in my soul.

My girls' lives would never be the same.

My life would never be the same.

Tonight, I'd lost not only the mother of my children, but also the woman I loved. The one I'd been sharing the last few years of my life with. The one I traveled the world with, went through great moments of joy and hardships with. The one I promised forever to. The one who said in front of our dearest friends and family I was her only true love.

I perused the bedroom for the final time, my eyes locking on my babies fast asleep.

They had no idea that by the morning, nothing would ever be the same.

That the light of a new day would carry a truckload of sorrow in its wake.

How would I ever be able to do this on my own? Be a single dad.

How would I ever be able to explain the harsh truth to my girls without shattering their hearts in the process?

Closing my eyes, I let darkness descend upon me because right now, I had no clue how to do this by myself and survive the heartbreak at the same time.

Read Sam Steven's story,
Fallen Legend, now

emmanuellesnow.com/fallen-legend

Author's bookstore at emmanuellesnowshop.com

"Emmanuelle Snow doesn't just tell a story, she creates an entire world." **(ReadaholicDeb)**

"Emmanuelle Snow has done it again! This powerful, heartwarming, slow-burn love story will break your heart on page one and slowly piece it back together. **(Goodreads)**

Fallen Legend is book one in the
Lonesome Heart duet.

emmanuellesnow.com/fallen-legend

Manufactured by Amazon.ca
Bolton, ON

34426265R00358